S0-AIP-994

GUILTY
AS
CHARGED

**Center Point
Large Print**

**This Large Print Book carries the
Seal of Approval of N.A.V.H.**

ॐ श्री गणेशाय नमः

GUILTY AS CHARGED

A MYSTERY WRITERS OF AMERICA ANTHOLOGY

SCOTT TUROW

EDITOR

CENTER POINT PUBLISHING
THORNDIKE, MAINE • USA

COMPASS PRESS
AUSTRALIA • NEW ZEALAND

This Center Point Large Print edition
is published in the year 2001 by arrangement with
Pocket Books, a division of Simon & Schuster.

This Compass Press edition is published in the year 2001 by
Bolinda Publishing Pty, Ltd., Tullamarine, Victoria, Australia
by arrangement with Penguin UK.

Copyright © 1996 by the Mystery Writers of America.

Copyright Notices: Introduction copyright © 1996 by Scott Turow • "Dogs and Fleas" copyright © 1996 by John Lutz • "Lou Monahan, County Prosecutor" copyright © 1996 by Andrew Klavan • "Real Life" copyright © 1996 by Sarah Shankman • "Knives at Midnight" copyright © 1996 by Marcia Muller • "Justice" copyright © 1996 by Stuart M. Kaminsky • "Cruel and Unusual" copyright © 1996 by Carolyn Wheat • "The Grip" copyright © 1996 by Jay Brandon • "Beat Routine" copyright © 1996 by Stan Washburn • "Last Licks" copyright © 1996 by Valerie Frankel • "Turning the Witness" copyright © 1996 by Jeremiah Healy • "That Day at Eagle's Point" copyright © 1996 by Ed Gorman • "Celebrity and Justice for All" copyright © 1996 by John Jakes • "For the Good of the Firm" copyright © 1996 by Maynard F. Thomson • "Dead Drunk" copyright © 1996 by Lia Matera • "The Court of Celestial Appeals" copyright © 1996 by Susan Dunlap • "Boobytrap" copyright © 1996 by Bill Pronzini

All rights reserved.

The moral right of the authors has been asserted.

The text of this Large Print edition is unabridged. In other aspects, this book may vary from the original edition. Printed in Thailand. Set in 16-point Times New Roman by Bill Coskrey.

US ISBN 1-58547-047-3 • BC ISBN 1-74030-214-1

Library of Congress Cataloging-in-Publication Data

Guilty as charged : a Mystery Writers of America anthology / edited by Scott Turow.
    p. (large print) cm.
    ISBN 1-58547-047-3 (lib. bdg. : alk. paper)
    1. Legal stories, American. 2. Large type books. I. Mystery Writers of America. II. Turow, Scott.

PS648.L3 G85 2001
813'.087208355--dc21

                                                                        00-031464

Australian Cataloguing in Publication Data

Guilty as charged / edited by Scott Turow.
ISBN 1740302141 (hbk.)
1. Large print books.
2. Detective and mystery stories, American.
3. Short stories, American.
I. Turow, Scott.
II. Title.
813

GUILTY
AS
CHARGED

Contents

Introduction

In my last four years as an assistant United States attorney, I was a supervisor of the new recruits to our office. As part of this job, I would occasionally go to court as an observer, watching trials I knew next to nothing about, appearing there only in order to assure myself that my younger colleagues knew how to structure a direct examination, to put a leading question on cross, to address a judge with appropriate deference.

But sitting with the elderly court buffs on the back benches, I frequently lost track of time. I discovered that even the most routine trial—for stealing treasury checks or passing small quantities of dope—could be spellbinding. The witnesses and their inquisitors would struggle with the elusiveness of the truth, whether it was obscured by shady recollections or the suspect motivations of guilty-pleading collaborators, or the simple parallax of different viewpoints on the same event. Even then, the substance of the testimony given was often gripping, this news of how evil somehow happened in the midst of the everyday.

I had gone to law school after a protracted spell in university settings, where the somewhat academic novels I was writing had not met the taste of any publishers in the known universe. Still searching years later for themes that would give me some hope of getting a novel in print, I decided to write about what I was seeing in court. Here, I thought, was truly a universal drama. The whole notion of trial by jury meant that the issues explored had to be ones

9

that citizens, without specialized training, could grasp. What motivated a criminal trial were not fine points of the law but moral imperatives: Had the accused been proven to have done something so heinous that he deserved to be censured and severed from the rest of society? The chief judge in our district used to say that jury instructions—the court's guidance to the jury on the applicable law—were a waste of time. "You might as well lock them in back there and just tell them, 'Do the right thing.' That's what they do anyway."

My recognition of the power of legal themes became the inspiration for *Presumed Innocent*, which I worked on for eight years on weekends and evenings and on my morning commuter train. After publication of the book, I was accused of inventing something called "the legal thriller." The substance of the charges was that I had devised an amazing novelty and thereby unleashed upon bookstore shelves and airport paperback racks the present flood of novels, most written by attorneys, about courtrooms and cases and legal settings. I am not guilty. Stories set to legal themes have been with us virtually forever. Think of Plato's description of the trial of Socrates or *The Merchant of Venice*. With its neat categories and iron rules, the law often fails to admit conflicting moral claims, or the slipperiness of the truth, ambiguities that literature can both acknowledge and dramatize. Some of the best work of Melville and Dickens is about the law. In this century, James Gould Cozzens wrote two majestic and generally forgotten novels about the law, *By Love Possessed* and *The Just and the Unjust*. And even in my childhood, two wonderful trial novels—*Anatomy of a Murder* and *To Kill a Mocking-*

bird—were gigantic popular successes. There are many other examples.

To my mind, the legal stories being written today differ from their predecessors only in one significant regard, and that is in the extent to which they dwell on legal detail. The longtime theory of storytellers—Hollywood screenwriters were the worst offenders—was that a popular audience would find the rigmarole of the law tiresome. But, generally speaking, the legal thriller is a chockablock with intricate renderings of the mechanics of the courtroom, lawyers' stratagems, and the rationales of judges' decisions. As I set out to write *Presumed Innocent*, my certain audience went no further than myself, my wife, and my erstwhile agent. Given that, I decided to please myself, and, therefore, I was determined not to write trial scenes like the ones I saw on the *Perry Mason* TV show, so jarringly inaccurate that the scenarist might as well have skipped the dialogue and let the players scrape their nails across a blackboard. In my book, the questions asked, objections offered, and rulings made were, to the best of my ability, accurate, typical, and in conformance with the rules of evidence. When the novel was published, most readers seemed, rather than bored by this precision, enthralled by it. Again and again, readers have told me that the trial was their favorite part of *Presumed Innocent* (although I have always assumed that there were certain other passages that many readers also enjoyed, albeit more privately).

It is the audience that craves that land of detail, and which has gobbled up legal thrillers like confectionery items, that bears more scrutiny than do the authors. The epochal event of my high school years was the assassination of JFK; for my daughter, it will be the trial of O. J. Simpson. Law and lawyers dominate this society as never before.

The reasons for this rise of the law in America strike me as complex. For one thing, the 1960s brought to an end a certain informal invulnerability to the reproaches of the law that various figures of authority used to enjoy. These days, everybody gets sued: doctors, lawyers, priests, school districts, employers. Americans have cheerfully accepted the law's equation of money for injured parts and feelings, and as a result we're all conscious of the many defensive steps now undertaken by most institutions. No swimming in the high school pool for anyone but students. You know, the lawyers say so.

But even beyond the ubiquitousness of legal issues in daily life, I suspect that Americans have grown intensely curious about the law because it has also become, to a degree it never was before, the forge for the shaping of national values. As the United States has changed in this part of the century, as it has become more self-consciously pluralistic, as the authority of other institutions—churches, schools, and local communities—has tended to fade, as media and marketing have blurred regional identities and turned us, more essentially, into a single nation, Americans have looked to the courts to provide answers to questions that would have never been posed there before: the propriety of abortion, of surrogate motherhood, of unwelcome sexual advances, of discrimination on the basis of sexual preference. Fifty years ago, all of these issues would have been regarded as religious or moral questions that had no business being mentioned in a courtroom, let alone decided there.

It is, in turn, this new American consciousness of law that accounts for books like the one you hold in your hands. From its rise in the eighteenth century to the present, the novel has always performed an educational function, and there can be no question that law-related novels and stones have gained much attention simply because they respond to public curiosity about an institution that has interfered in all, our lives with increasing frequency, to the occasional, if not perpetual, exasperation of us all. It is doubtful that this collection would even have been published a decade ago. Instead, I would be just one more buff in the back of the courtroom, sitting there spellbound.

—Scott Turow

Dogs and Fleas

John Lutz

"He's out there," Doris said to Mead Blasingame, "and he looks ready to talk deal."

She was referring to high-powered criminal defense attorney Horton Lang, whose present notorious client was the unofficial chieftain of crime in Bayville, Willie Stark.

But if Lang was a successful defense attorney, Mead Blasingame was just as successful—if not as rich—in the role of Bayville's most effective prosecutor. Willie Stark wouldn't be the first upper-echelon criminal to be convicted because of Blasingame's expertise with the law, and with juries. A short but erect and handsome man still in his forties, with black hair and blue, painfully earnest eyes, he might have been cast as Sir Lancelot had he been an actor instead of a lawyer. Sometimes, in fact, Blasingame thought of himself as a knight in the service of justice.

He sat at his wide oak desk and looked at his assistant, Doris Jones. She was more to him than a paralegal; he considered her invaluable in research and jury selection, and from time to time she provided an audience for his dramatic Theater of the Law.

Mounted on the wall behind Doris was the framed homily that Blasingame's mother had continually quoted to him in his youth: "Those who lie down with dogs will rise up with fleas." Blasingame had heard her say it so often that it had stuck. He believed it, and it was the reason he was a prosecutor.

From the beginning of his law career, he'd refused to act as a defense attorney. He knew he couldn't detach himself emotionally from the human scum he might have to defend in court. He feared that if he did mount an effective legal defense and got someone he believed actually guilty acquitted, he'd be responsible for that person. And some of the guilt, some of the evil, would rub off on him like soot. He'd be more like his client than before the acquittal, and he'd be a *de facto* accomplice in future misdeeds. It was a prospect he couldn't think about with dispassion.

"Mr. Blasingame? Mead?"

Doris was looking down at him, a pretty blond woman with a heart-shaped face, creamy complexion, and clear gray eyes; beauty masking such a wicked intelligence.

"Sorry, Doris. Mind wandered. Tell Lang to come in. He can talk deal all he wants, but the cards have already been dealt, and we have the aces."

She smiled as she went out. A moment later, she ushered Horton Lang into the office, then left the two of them alone.

Blasingame stood up, smiled, and shook hands with Lang, then motioned for him to sit down in the comfortable black leather chair angled to face the desk. After Lang had sat, Blasingame sat back down, made obligatory small talk, then waited patiently for his visitor to get to the point.

Lang was a sixty-eight-year-old man with expensive gray suits, gray hair and eyes, and expressive bushy gray eyebrows that sometimes writhed like caterpillars. The skin stretched tautly over his long, hawkish face which had a gray tint to it. Looking at all that gray, the much younger Blasingame wondered when age would finally begin to slow Lang's clever mind, play tricks with his recall. If it

16

occurred during the Willie Stark case, Blasingame would take full advance of it.

Stark deserved the death penalty twenty times over. He was the kind of man Blasingame hated, the kind who'd dealt his own warped idea of justice through the barrel of a gun. This time, he hadn't used a gun, though, and someone had seen him.

"Mr. Stark has permitted me to begin the process of plea bargaining," Lang said.

Blasingame raised his eyebrows. " 'Permitted' you?"

"Yes," Lang said seriously. "He wants to plead not guilty because he isn't guilty. But he knows the weight of the evidence, misleading as it is, is against him. What would you say to a reduced charge of unintentional manslaughter?"

"I'd say no. We have a witness who saw your client behind the wheel of the car that struck and killed George Blake, then deliberately backed over him to make sure he was dead. Stark had the motive—"

"Which was?" Lang softly interrupted.

"Blake saw him shoot two women to death in cold blood, prostitutes who worked for him indirectly and wanted out of their agreement. He made examples of those women. First with a gun, then he mutilated them with a knife in case any of their coworkers might be mulling over the same liberating ideas." Blasingame felt himself getting angry. Always a mistake. He lowered his voice. "Your client, Willie Stark, is an animal."

"Your witness, Laurie Stone, is herself a prostitute," Lang pointed out. "The jury won't believe a woman like that, and you know it."

Blasingame stood up behind his desk. "We'll have to find

17

that out in court."

Lang sighed, smiled, and stood up, buttoning his double-breasted suit coat across his narrow body. "You should bend sometimes, Mead. You've lost a few because you refused to bend. You're going to lose this one."

"We both know better, Horton."

Lang's smile turned vaguely sad, as if he couldn't understand Blasingame's hopeless position but could easily cope with it. Then he nodded and walked from the office.

A few minutes later, Doris knocked, then stuck her head in. "Deal?" she asked.

"No deal. Our witness is going to put Lang's client on the road to his execution, and Lang knows it. He has nothing to deal."

Doris grinned. "Such a pit bull you are."

Blasingame knew she was right. Knew *he* was right.

He wished he could concentrate entirely on Willie Stark, but that wasn't the nature of his job. Crime begat crime begat crime. Bayville needed Blasingame.

"Willie Stark isn't our only case," he said, as if Doris had maintained that it was. "Bring me the file on Martin Vinton."

Vinton had been the girls' volleyball coach at the junior high school Blasingame's own twelve-year-old daughter, Judith, attended. He'd been accused of molesting more than a dozen students. Photographs and videotapes of him with some of the girls had been found in a search of his house. The evidence against him was overwhelming.

Blasingame was almost as eager to convict Vinton as he was to nail Stark for murder. The infuriating part was that while Vinton was in jail awaiting trial, Stark was walking

18

around free on bond. Stark had better legal counsel. And he'd drawn the lenient Judge Rudy Moss. Judges these days!

Blasingame sometimes daydreamed about when he'd become a judge.

He was eating lunch in Ollie's Café near the courthouse when a short, heavyset man with close-cropped gray hair and pink-rimmed blue eyes sat down across from him. He had on a wrinkled brown suit, checked shirt, and red tie, and he smelled like cheap deodorant or cologne.

He smiled with yellow teeth that tilted inward at an odd angle, as if long ago he'd been struck hard in the mouth. "I'm Benny Natch, Mr. Blasingame."

Blasingame was sure they'd never met. He liked to dine alone, and he resented this intrusion. "We don't know each other, Mr. Natch. If you want to make an appointment to see me in my office—"

"That wouldn't work for what I have in mind," Natch said. He blatantly helped himself to one of Blasingame's French fries. Blasingame sat very still and began to worry.

When Natch had finished chewing and swallowing the French fry, he said, "I'm here as a sort of emissary from Mr. Vinton."

"The child molester," Blasingame said.

"Allegedly." Natch consumed another French fry. "The point is, Mr. Blasingame, that one of the young girls allegedly involved with Natch, and who allegedly posed quite willingly for photographs and videotaping, is your daughter Judith."

A cold, deep fury took root at Blasingame's core. A

19

vacuum that somehow fed a fire. It was all he could do to restrain himself from reaching across the table and strangling Natch. "No one is alleging that," he said in an icy voice that surprised even him with its calmness.

"I am," Natch said. "But it doesn't have to go any further, Mr. Blasingame."

"I don't believe you," Blasingame said.

Natch smiled. It was ugly. "That's why I brought one of the photographs," he said. And he laid the photo on the table next to Blasingame's iced tea.

Blasingame stared at it in disbelief, then snatched it up before anyone else might see it.

"Keep that one," Natch said cheerily. "It's only one of lots of prints. Then there's the video she stars in."

Blasingame actually edged close enough to grab Natch, but he didn't. His fingers twitched.

Natch flashed his nasty smile. "You'd like to kill me, I know."

"I would," Blasingame admitted. He lowered his hands beneath the table, out of sight.

"That's understandable; you're blaming the messenger. But we've both got your daughter's interest at heart here. If Mr. Vinton is acquitted, all prints and tapes of Judith will be destroyed."

"I should take your word for that?"

"You've got no choice. But think about it; why would Mr. Vinton double-cross you? Even if he did continue to have something on you, if he used it, he'd be risking prison. The child pornography case against him could be reopened. There could be as many counts against Mr. Vinton as there are girls he's involved in his . . . er, activities."

20

Blasingame had to admit it made sense. "Blackmail,' he said with distaste.

"More like reasonable accommodation. Is it a deal?"

The two men stared at each other.

"Let's put it this way," Natch said, "since I've probably got more experience at this sort of thing than you. You cooperate, and we never have to talk or even see each other again. If Mr. Vinton walks away a free man, everything involving your daughter gets destroyed. But if he gets convicted, there'll be more videocassettes and photographs of her floating around, not just Bayville but the whole country, than you can imagine. And don't consider raiding Mr. Vinton's premises to confiscate those photos and tapes. They're in the possession of his attorney."

"You?" Blasingame asked.

"Me. Who, if it comes down to it, will certainly deny this conversation ever took place."

"Are you working in concert with Vinton's defense attorney?"

"No. Only you, I, and Vinton will know about this agreement and how it relates to whatever develops during the trial."

He nodded pleasantly to Blasingame, then stood up.

"Those are terrifically good French fries," he remarked, and walked away.

Blasingame agonized over the conversation with Natch for almost a week. The Vinton case was fast approaching on the docket; he'd have to make up his mind soon.

Judith, his blond, petite only child, acted as if nothing were wrong, yet Blasingame had seen the photograph. He could sense when people were telling the truth, and he believed Natch. Judith's normal behavior didn't fool Blasingame. He'd seen multiple murderers behave like saints, and he'd sent them to hell.

He said nothing to Judith; he knew he couldn't be positive Vinton and Natch would actually destroy all the tapes and photos of her if Vinton walked away free. Yet, even if they didn't, Judith might still put everything behind her and live an untroubled and fulfilling life despite her youthful mistake. Blasingame also knew that once the pornographic material was spread across the country, she would be marked for life.

At night, he would lie motionless in bed, listening to his sleeping wife, Ann, breathing deeply and evenly beside him. He'd chosen not to burden her with what Natch had told him. What had happened to Judith was something that for all concerned needed to be buried deep and kept secret. So they could pretend it hadn't happened.

On Friday, he visited the motel where the police were guarding Laurie Stone, the eyewitness in the Willie Stark case.

She was an attractive woman with red hair and an edged hardness that was already beginning to penetrate her youth like protruding bones. Blasingame realized with alarm that she was twenty-one, not even ten years older than Judith.

She paced back and forth on the worn blue carpet. Though it was just past noon, the drapes were closed and the lights were on in the tiny room.

"I'm scared, and I feel cooped up, Mr. Blasingame," she said. "You don't realize what it's like, hiding like this, staying in one spot when you know somebody like Willie Stark is moving around out there, him and his killers, looking for you. I don't know if I can hold out another month till the trial."

"Stark doesn't know where you are," Blasingame assured her. "Or how to find you. And the police are on the alert if he would happen to locate you. You're well protected."

She shook her head and brushed back a strand of red hair. "You don't know Willie Stark. Really vicious people like him, they think of ways to get things done. And he's desperate."

"You're the only one who can convict him, Laurie. We need you so we can arrange his appointment with the executioner and put him away until he keeps it. He won't be able to hurt anyone then. You're not going to let us down, are you?"

"You don't understand. People like you just don't understand people like Willie Stark!" She made a face as if she might begin to cry, and her hands began to tremble. "I'll try not to let you down, Mr. Blasingame, but you gotta protect me!"

"You have my promise," Blasingame told her. Then he surprised himself by adding, "For whatever it's worth."

As he left the motel, he checked and made sure the police guards were still at their posts.

Horton Lang sat again in the black leather chair before Blasingame's desk. This time, Blasingame had sent for him— and asked him to bring his client.

Standing with his back against the wall, Willie Stark looked the part of the regional king of crime. The dark side

23

of royalty. He was forty-five, tall, broad, dark, with a prognathous jaw that would always need a shave. His chalk-stripe blue suit looked expensive and fit perfectly. Blasingame had heard somewhere that Stark had his suits tailored so a gun in a shoulder holster wouldn't spoil their lines.

"I want to talk to Mr. Stark alone," Blasingame said.

Lang looked surprised. "I'm not sure—"

"Why not?" Stark interrupted. "Leave us alone for a few minutes, Horton, okay?"

Lang didn't say it was okay, but he left the office.

Stark sat down in the black leather chair and stared at Blasingame with eyes that would have made a shark's seem warm. But there was a glint of curiosity in them that wouldn't be seen in a shark's.

"Yours isn't the only case I'm trying," Blasingame said.

"I'm not surprised," Stark said. "You're a busy and ambitious prosecutor, maybe even with a shining political future."

"And you might have a very limited future."

"Might," Stark agreed. He settled back in the chair and waited.

"I'm also prosecuting a man named Vinton," Blasingame said, "a child molester."

"Those guys should be hung by their—"

"We agree on that," Blasingame said. "An attorney named Natch talked to me about some photographs and videotapes of my daughter. They're Vinton's, but they're in Natch's possession."

Stark looked interested. "Your daughter, huh? Why would you tell me this, counselor?"

Blasingame said nothing.

"They trying to blackmail you?" Stark asked softly.

Blasingame swiveled in his chair and stared out the window. "I have a dilemma. My daughter would be ruined if Vinton were convicted and that pornographic material was widely circulated. But if he *isn't* convicted, he'll be free to molest more children."

"He definitely should go to prison," Stark said. He sounded sincere. "I've played the game hard, but I never harmed a kid. They should be out of bounds."

"Including my kid?" Blasingame asked.

Stark shrugged. "Sure. But you've gotta put Vinton inside the walls. I'm afraid your daughter got the short straw, counselor. Bad luck."

"I talked to the eyewitness who can send you to the executioner," Blasingame said. "She's scared."

"I'm not surprised, the kind of lies she's been telling."

"So scared she might not testify if she gets just a little more scared."

"It's your job to reassure her, isn't it?" Stark said.

Blasingame nodded. "I wouldn't want her harmed, even if she did get too frightened and refused to testify. Do you understand that?"

Leather creaked as Stark leaned farther back in the chair. He looked at the ceiling, then at Blasingame.

"If she refused to talk once, she'd refuse again," Blasingame said. "Especially if no one bothered her."

Stark continued to stare at him, then nodded. "True enough."

"We agree that Martin Vinton should be in prison," Blasingame said.

He began to straighten papers on his desk. The only

sound was the soft, intermittent whirring of Doris's printer in the outer office. Then even that ceased.

The silence began to take on weight.

"That it, counselor?" Stark asked, after almost a minute had passed.

Blasingame didn't look up from the papers.

"That's it," he said."

Two days later, Blasingame caught it on the ten o'clock TV news. Benjamin Natch, an attorney in Pineburg, a small town fifty miles south of Bayville, had been found stabbed to death in his office. He'd apparently been tortured. His safe and combination-lock fireproof file cabinets had been opened, but authorities couldn't say what, if anything, had been removed.

Blasingame used the remote to turn off the television, then glanced over at his wife, Ann, talking on the phone at the other end of the room. He wondered how Natch had been tortured, and he shivered. Something truly frightening stirred at the core of his mind.

Then Judith walked past in the hallway. She glanced in and smiled and waved to him. Her smile was the warmth and fight of his life; he knew she was the only person he loved unconditionally. Maybe he'd done the right thing, the only thing possible, after all.

He told Ann he had some work to do at the office, then went out to his car and drove to the motel to confess to Laurie Stone that he honestly couldn't guarantee her total safety if she testified against Willie Stark. If she chose not to testify and Stark went free, he, Blasingame, would understand and personally see to it that she had money to

26

start a new life in another city.

That was all she needed to hear, something to tilt her one way or the other.

By the next morning, she was gone.

Everything dropped into place like destiny. A furious and incredulous Martin Vinton was convicted of child molestation, contributing to the delinquency of a minor, and trafficking in child pornography. The judge complied with the jury's recommendation and sentenced him to thirty years in the state penitentiary.

And three weeks later, Willie Stark left the courtroom a free man. Blasingame had mounted a competent defense, but without his key witness a conviction was impossible. He was glad to see that Stark avoided his eyes as he left the courtroom to be congratulated by admirers.

So Stark was free, but Vinton was in prison. Win one, lose one. Maybe that was the most you could expect in today's complicated world, even if you were Sir Lancelot jousting with the forces of darkness.

It had worked and continued to work. The next week, Blasingame and Ann pulled Judith out of the junior high school and enrolled her in a private girls' school in the next state. She was resistant at first, but within a month she wrote that she was making good grades and was happy. When six months had passed, she'd become cocaptain of the field hockey team and was running for class president.

Also at the end of that six months, Blasingame learned from a police contact that Laurie Stone had been found dead from an overdose of barbiturates in her apartment in Chicago.

Blasingame felt a thrust of pity, and perhaps guilt. But there was no reason to think Laurie Stone hadn't committed suicide. The pressure on her must have been unbearable. The powers she'd ascribed to Willie Stark bordered on the supernatural, and her fear probably never left her. So the woman's short and tragic life had ended in suicide, like so many others who'd chosen the wrong path. She was doomed from the night she'd witnessed the murders. Her death had nothing to do with Blasingame.

The next morning, he read in the *Bayville Register* that Martin Vinton had been strangled to death with a length of electrical cord in prison. An investigation was proceeding, but prison officials had few leads.

Blasingame knew how prison investigations were carried out. Child molesters were at the bottom of the pecking order in prisons. No one mourned Vinton's passing, and no one would talk. The identity of the inmate who'd killed him would never be discovered.

Blasingame felt a weight rise from his chest when he read about Vinton's death. Judith was completely safe now, from Vinton's wicked knowledge of her, from Vinton himself if a lenient parole board had moved to set him free before his full term was served.

So that was the end of the problem. It had played itself out and was finally over.

Blasingame didn't like to admit it, but it was possible that crime paid.

It was early the next spring, and Blasingame was in the middle of prosecuting two men who'd been passing through Bayville and shot to death a family of five, including infant twins, when Doris entered his office wearing an odd expression and told him Willie Stark was in the anteroom and wanted to see him.

Blasingame smiled with a confidence he didn't feel and told her to send Stark in.

Stark had put on about twenty pounds and had a deep, even tan, as if he'd just returned from the tropics. He looked healthy and prosperous in his expensive beige suit and white shirt, yellow silk tie. He wore two diamond rings on each hand, one of them a pinky ring. Gold cufflinks flashed as he sat down and rested his huge hands on the chair arms. Something about his attitude bothered Blasingame. Then he realized what it was. Stark was acting almost as if this were *his* office.

"Counselor," Stark said, still smiling, "I've got a favor to ask of you concerning a case you're working on. I know you won't mind."

Blasingame fought off a wave of nausea. He knew he would mind, and he knew it wouldn't be the last favor he'd do for Stark. A shadowy part of his mind he seldom visited had long feared this day. He was trapped. He had no choice.

"Does the favor have to do with a murdered family?" he asked.

"Bingo," Stark said.

Looking into the future, Blasingame saw only a darkness that horrified him.

He reached for the gun in the second drawer, then brought it up and rested it in front of him on the desk.

Stark had recognized something in Blasingame's eyes and stopped smiling. "Don't act in haste and repent at leisure, counselor," he said in a soft, level voice. His smile returned, but it was forced and cold.

Blasingame raised the gun to eye level and sighted along its barrel. He knew the basic truth of maxims, but Stark's was far too late.

"There's no way you can do this, counselor. It isn't in you. It's not the way you were raised."

Beyond Stark's tan features and stiff smile, Blasingame could see his mother's framed, wise words mounted on the wall.

He began to itch all over.

Lou Monahan, County Prosecutor

ANDREW KLAVAN

The things you remember; the things you regret. Funny, Monahan thought—they were such little things. That last week of summer vacation. Rick Ellerbee's bash. It was more than twenty years ago now. It was the last week before they all went off to college. The evening had grown cool by the water after the leaden heat of the day, and he had smelled the edge of September, and he had smelled the sea. The Sound was a silver ridge out beyond the white mansion, and the lawn, beryl in the dusk, swept down from under the house's foundations and swelled beneath his feet and swept away again. Liveried waiters angled among the clusters of teenagers. A jazz quartet in white tuxedos neutered the latest hits beneath the yellow-striped tent. "Jive Talkin'." "Love Will Keep Us Together." Whatever—it was just a white pudding of noise in there. All the same, the couples danced to it. And the girls were so pretty, their necks and arms so fresh in their sleeveless dresses.

For Monahan, to whom Ellerbee had always been kind, the setting was the element, the music the heartbeat, the girls the very soul of sophistication, wealth, and grace. Ellerbee himself seemed their presiding genius: his smooth, animated features gracious and manly and without arrogance; the figure he cut both slender and solid—and casual, too, in tan chinos and an open-necked shirt; the way he gestured to the circle of smiles around him as if he were con-

31

juring the whole occasion out of thin air only to enhance the comfort and sweetness of their lives. To Monahan, he sparkled, it all sparkled, and he stood watching them—Ellerbee, all his classmates—a little apart, drink in hand, knowing full well that, after today, they would become strangers to him. In a week, Ellerbee would be starting at Princeton, and after that, almost surely, would go on to Harvard Law. Monahan would cram and labor his way through the state school in Westchester and get his law degree at NYU, if he was lucky, if he was very lucky and worked very hard. They would meet during vacations. They would chat on the street and part. There would never be this friendship again, this intimacy, not for him. Not that Monahan was bitter about it—he had never expected more, not even this much—but he couldn't help feeling wistful that last evening. They were charming—his high school friends—and they were charmed; and he knew he was there to say good-bye.

His drink finished, the glass spirited away, Monahan moved across the lawn to the tent, his hands in the pockets of his green suit, his tie stirring in the first breeze off the Sound. He reached the edge of the tent and stepped within the shade of the canvas, stepped up onto the wooden floor. He surveyed the dancers absently, casually tapping his foot to the quartet's thumpingly bland "Behind Closed Doors."

And he saw a girl. Leaning against the far tent pole. Resting her cheek against it dreamily.

She could not possibly have been as beautiful as he remembered her twenty years on. Her skin could not have been so white beneath such thoroughly raven hair. Her figure, lightly pressed against the support, outlined, in her floral dress, against the beryl lawn and the azure sky, so graceful and enchanting—women looked like that in memory, in movies, not in real life. All the same, even then, Monahan was made breathless by the sight of her.

And then she raised her eyes to him, saw him watching her. And she smiled at him across the dance floor.

The smile lanced his rib cage; it made his head swim. Only half-aware, he began to approach her. He wove slowly through the couples dancing around him. The music, in his woozy state, seemed to shatter into glistering bursts and dabs in the summer air. There was nothing but that music as he moved, and the pulse in his head, and her heartbreaking beauty. Monahan was amazed. He could not believe the sudden possibilities. Everything, he knew, was about to become wonderful.

She straightened from the pole to await him. He neared the edge of the floor. A couple moved between them, cutting her from his a view for a moment—just for a moment. Then they passed.

The girl was gone.

Monahan blinked. The pole stood alone. He moved out of the tent and looked over the lawn. There was no sign of her, no sign at all. Monahan was too prosy a fellow to believe that she had vanished—but he didn't go hunting for her, either; he was too unassuming for that. No, he figured he had simply made a mistake. She had not been smiling at him. She'd been smiling at someone else, someone behind him probably. That made more sense; the whole world made a lot more sense that way. He would have made a fool of himself if he'd reached her, if he'd spoken. She would have looked at him blankly. "Excuse me," she would have said, and walked away. He'd been spared that, at least. He should have felt grateful.

Instead, for twenty years, he remembered her, he regretted losing her. There were days—there were nights—when he imagined entire lifetimes with her. Which was funny. Well, it was pretty stupid, really. It wasn't like down-to-earth Lou Monahan at all.

Yet there it was. That memory, that moment. From time to time, out of nowhere after years, it turned up again and melted him, wrung him. The things you remember, the things you regret.

They were there to haunt him in force the night the rock star got his throat cut.

Monahan had never even heard of the guy. What did he know about rock stars nowadays? They were just monstrous images on T-shirts to him—those shirts on the sad little punks he sent to juvenile hall. But this one, Thrust—yes, that was his name—he must've had a fairly sizable following. Because when Monahan pulled the department Chevy into the dead man's driveway, reporters converged on him like black flies.

The prosecutor had never seen so many of them. Not on any case he'd ever caught. As he shut off the car, he had a glimpse through the window of their straining faces. He saw Rorke from the local weekly, and Helen Martin from the county's lone ten-thousand-watt sundowner. But these two, usually the only two to show up anywhere, were quickly jostled out of sight by the swarming others. Flashes went off, spotlights; camera lenses jutted at him; outstretched hands held microphones that chittered against the pane. And the mikes had big-time logos on them, city call letters, and the networks', too. Monahan even noticed a few glamorous newswomen out there, women he recognized but couldn't name. How the hell had they gotten up here so fast?

As he pushed his door open, he tried to look bored and beleaguered because—well, because that's the way prosecutors always looked on TV shows. But as the cameras started flashing and the shouted questions deafened him and the microphones and minicams were pushed into his face, Monahan felt himself going sweaty and muslin-headed. He had never been through anything remotely like this before. He had no idea, finally, what he said to them. He spoke thickly, his tongue swollen, his brain stuporous. All he could think about was how wrinkled his brown jacket was—and how brown it was!—and how he had to hold it closed to cover the coffee stain on his shirt pocket. Then it was over. Investigator Corvo drew him out of the throng—like being hauled out of quicksand—and the deputies pushed the reporters back. And then Monahan, still trying to button his jacket, was climbing beside Corvo up the front path through a spotlit rock garden dotted with bonsai trees.

"Wow, huh?" said Corvo.

"Jesus," said Monahan. "Who was this guy?"

They approached the long, low front of the ranch house. Corvo was a small man, short, thin, with a round, squinched face and a dogged gait. Monahan had to take long strides to keep up with him.

"It's not the guy," Corvo said, "it's the young lady that did him. Old Thrust was sticking Ginny Reingold. Only it looks like she stuck him, right?"

Corvo spoke the woman's name with such weight that Monahan thought he must know it, but there was nothing there. "Who the hell is Ginny Reingold?"

Corvo snorted. "Who the hell is Ginny Reingold? You know your wife?"

"Yeah," said Monahan. "I know my wife."

"You know the magazines she reads? You know the face on the cover? That's Ginny Reingold."

Monahan slowed down, trying to form an image. Corvo kept walking. "Which magazine?" said Monahan.

"All of them" said Corvo. He reached the door and looked back at him, gestured at the press in the driveway below. "You better get used to that shit down there," he said to the prosecutor. "You're about to become a star."

The body lay half off the bed, and the head lay half off the body. The blood had spilled over the singer's face and drenched his long black hair and stained the tan shag under him red. A sheet, also stained, still covered him to his thighs, and the man's pale, hairy nakedness, and his gaping mouth and his staring eyes and his blood and the metallic smell of his blood and the sour smell of his urine made the murder scene—for all the cameras and glamorous news babes outside—as dingy and miserable and sordid as every other Monahan had seen.

"Is everyone done with him?"

"Yeah," said Corvo, "but we thought you'd want a look."

"Thrust? That was his name? Thrust?"

"That's what he called himself. He was lead singer for Fatwa. Fatwa." Corvo shook his head.

Monahan snorted. "Fatwa and Thrust."

"Born Jerry Finkelstein," said Corvo, and laughed.

Monahan looked around the bedroom casually. "So what about her?"

Corvo told him what they had while Monahan studied the place. It was a large room, all shag below, a wall of mirrors facing a wall of windows open on the September night, a wall of shelves and stereo equipment connecting them. A crime scene man was dusting the CD player for prints. Monahan took it all in, and Corvo went on detailing the evidence against the suspect: the bloodstains, the possible skin traces, the maid who'd sometimes heard them fighting. Monahan took this in, too. He was the most successful prosecutor in three counties, and he was known for his unspectacular, sturdy, determined mastery of every case.

So he took it all in. But a part of his mind was elsewhere. Still thinking about those reporters outside. Excited about them now. His first astonishment had passed, and he could feel the chill of excitement in his chest, the wind of it across his nerve endings. *Assistant District Attorney Lou Monahan told reporters at the scene that he would act quickly to secure an indictment . . . he thought.*

Strangely enough, it was just then—not later—that the memory came to him. Rick Ellerbee's end-of-summer bash. The dancers under the tent. The girl, against the tent pole, smiling at him. Standing beside the shabby corpse, he felt a ridiculous surge of yearning and love.

"Why the hell would she do it?" he said sharply, snapping out of it. "The legendary Ginny Reingold."

"Old Thrust," said Corvo, showing a fig. "Boom-boom—tsk-tsk—you know? Hell hath no fury like a woman punched."

Monahan raised his eyebrows. "She said that?"

"Not her. She's not talking till her lawyer gets up from the city. You're gonna be in some very fancy company on this one, my friend."

Monahan lifted his chin, ready for it.

"She's bringing in Richard Ellerbee," said Corvo. "Run for your life."

Wendy Monahan kept saying the same thing. "You were on the eleven o'clock news!"

Monahan kept eating. Wendy kept putting food in front of him. Cold roast beef, string beans, rolls. A dish of coleslaw now. "The eleven o'clock news!" She kept saying the same thing. "I tell you, the phone would *not* stop ringing. I thought Sandy was just going to fall over dead." Usually, if he came home at this hour, Monahan had to forage for himself, scour the back reaches of the refrigerator. Now Wendy fetched him another beer, poured it into his glass for him. He wondered if Rick Ellerbee's wife treated him like this all the time.

"So?" She plunked down in the seat next to him. Peered at him, her chin on her fists, as if he had tales to tell of a Polar expedition. "Did you see her? What does she look like?"

" 'What does she look like?' " Monahan sat like Old King Cole, his fists on the table before him, his fork in one, his beer in the other. "She's on every magazine in the house— I can't go to the bathroom without seeing her . . ."

"I mean in real life."

"In real life? In real life, she has a black eye."

Wendy reeled back with a full-volume gasp. "You mean he hit her?" Monahan nodded. "The creep! Well, then he

38

deserved it."

"On television, he deserved it," said Monahan, digging into the slaw. "In court, they tend to consider it an over-reaction."

Wendy's blue eyes grew bright, and she leaned in toward him again, making him feel strange: warm; good. "But the court's going to be *on* television," she said. "'They have cameras now."

He hadn't actually thought of that. Uncertainly, he said, "Nah. Up here?"

"For this?" said Wendy. "Are you kidding? The trial'll be on every day. You'll be like a show."

He tried to laugh it off. *"Lou Monahan, County Prosecutor,"* he said. But it bounced around inside him. Cameras at the trial every day, like a show.

"I'd watch it," said Wendy. And she stood up, slipped around the edge of the table, and sat on her husband's lap.

Monahan remembered now about Ellerbee's wife. She was some muck-a-muck's daughter—some rich guy's. Monahan had seen a picture of the two of them at some kind of charity function. The wife was very beautiful and posh with wavy black hair.

Wendy nestled against him. She moved her hands gently over the back of his neck, and he put his hands on her bottom. She was a little pudgy now—she hadn't lost all the weight she'd gained before their second son was born—but she still had a cute round girlish face under the short hair she kept blond. She'd look okay standing beside him, he thought. A good wife for a man-of-the-people type. Viewers would see he had a solid family life . . .

She leaned forward and put her lips to his ear. "I married

a star," she whispered.

Monahan had a stray thought: maybe the girl at Rick Ellerbee's party would see him on television . . . "You're a goof," he said aloud, and he nuzzled his wife's neck and kissed her.

Prosecutor Lou Monahan today came face to face with the man who was once his friend but has now become his ruthless opponent in the trial of the century, Monahan thought as he ambled down the courthouse hallway to meet with Ginny Reingold and her lawyer. He was careful to amble, casual, his hands in his pockets, his expression thoughtful, distant. In truth, he hadn't been this nervous since the Sunday school nativity play when his trembling lips had turned *myrrh* into a six syllable word.

So far, though, things were going pretty well this morning. His performance before the press on the courthouse steps, for instance, had been a big improvement over yesterday's. This time, he'd been prepared for them. Wendy had chosen his clothes, so he felt confident and well dressed. He'd rehearsed his statement as he drove to work, and practiced pointing his finger as he spoke and narrowing his eyes forcefully. He'd talked briefly and clearly as the mob of them congealed around him like pork fat. Then he'd turned and marched away from their shouted questions as if he had more important things to do. He hadn't had time to review the film clips yet, but some of the deputies who'd seen them on the ten o'clock report had teased him— "Looking good, Lou!"—so he guessed it had gone okay.

Now, though . . . Now came the meeting he dreaded. His first confrontation with Ellerbee. And even though they would meet in the interview room with no one to see the moment but Corvo and the deputy and the defendant, those cameras, those reporters—they stayed in Monahan's head; he could see the film of himself in his head, he could hear the newsman's narration there. *Prosecutor Lou Monahan strode to the interview room door and nodded grimly to the deputy . . .*

Monahan strode to the interview room door and nodded grimly to the deputy. He had to get this just right, he thought. From the very first, the first greeting. Friendly but not eager; poised; a handshake; a manly nod of recognition. Nothing that suggested how he had revered Ellerbee in youth, how Ellerbee had gone on to become everything Monahan knew he could never be. Film of his inferiority at eleven.

"Jesus," Monahan whispered under his breath as the deputy pushed open the door.

Corvo was already in the room, standing before the table. The deputy, Ellen Brown, was against the wall. Ginny Reingold, the skin over her high cheekbone purple and broken, sat with her hands clasped on the table and stared forward blankly. She was long-haired, long-, silky-, chestnut-haired, wide-eyed, shapely but frail. The "neo-waif look," his wife had told him. Whatever it was, every time Monahan set eyes on her, he felt himself stirred as by some primitive instinct to rise to her defense.

Which was pretty unhelpful under the circumstances. Because there, seated beside her, was her defender in fact.

Jesus, he looks great! Monahan thought. *What a great suit!*

Ellerbee had thickened over these twenty years; he was

41

not the winsome Boy King of the Suburbs he had been. But he was still trim, clearly muscular. His width only gave his figure power and maturity. There was none of Monahan's paunch, nor his widows peak. And where Monahan felt his own features had spread and blurred with time, Ellerbee's dauntless profile seemed to have solidified, sharpened, the soft lines straighter, the boy's face a man's.

On top of which, it really was a great suit. Sleek and black. Pinstripes so faint, so suggestive, they almost disdained to be there at all.

"Mr. Ellerbee," said Corvo. "Louis Monahan, the ADA on the case."

Monahan shot his hand out a little too quickly. But he hit the correct expression perfectly: a tight half-smile, a narrowed eye, knowing, amused. *So we meet again, old friend.*

Ellerbee stood. He pumped Monahan's hand. His brilliant eyes seemed to drink the prosecutor down in one smooth swallow. "Mr. Monahan," he said. Then he sat again. Then he said, "My client would like to make a statement."

Everyone started moving around Monahan. Ellerbee tamed to his client. Ginny Reingold straightened, drew breath. Corvo nodded to Deputy Brown, who stepped to the door and spoke to the deputy outside. Only Monahan himself remained motionless. Frozen. Staring. Gaping at Ellerbee.

He . . . didn't recognize me, he thought. It was his only thought for the moment, the only thought of which he was aware, a neon billboard of a thought, all other thoughts fading in its blaze. *Didn't. Recognize. Me? Me?* Monahan kept standing, kept staring. *But . . . we were in school together. We ran . . . we ran track together. Track. At school.*

42

Together. I beat him—I beat him in the fifty-yard dash. And he doesn't recognize . . .

"Uh . . . Lou?" said Corvo.

"Miss Reingold, this session is now being videotaped," said Monahan smoothly, pulling out the chair across from her, sitting, facing her. "So I'll inform you of your rights again for the record, and then you can begin." *Didn't . . . ? Me? Lou?* he thought. *The fifty-yard dash? I hit the line a yard ahead of you. A yard at least, Freddy Markham was there he saw it . . .*

"Last night," said Ginny Reingold. She cleared her throat. "Last night, before Jerry died, before he was killed . . ."

That's why you only ran the three hundred after that, thought Monahan sullenly, shaking his head at the Formica tabletop. He was suddenly very depressed.

"We had a fight," Ginny Reingold went on softly. She had the voice of a boy's fantasy, half flute, half whisper. Monahan, drawing his gut up with a breath, forced himself to listen to her. "It wasn't anything big. I just made some joke, you know, about his hair, he needed a haircut, teasing him, you know, but . . . well, his last album didn't do so well, and he's been kind of down about it, you know. And, anyway, he started yelling, and it got out of hand, and he—he hit me. In the face. And see, he never—I told him he could never hit me in the face. I *told* him, you know. I said I'd leave him. But he was just wild. He was crazy. And I got scared, you know. So I ran out. Outside. I got in the car, the tan one, the Mercedes. And I locked all the doors, you know, but . . . I didn't have the key, see. It was in my purse. And Jerry came out, and he was pounding on the windows, screaming. I kept hoping someone would hear, you know,

43

call the police, I even leaned on the horn, but . . . well, there's really only woods around us, and, anyway, I guess people are kind of used to it. Anyway, after a while, he said, you know, that he was going in to get the key. And then he said he was going to come back out and teach me a lesson. And then he—he laughed this kind of maniacal laughter, you know, and . . . he went back inside." Ginny Reingold gulped back tears, glanced at her attorney, her big eyes appealing. Ellerbee reached out and put his strong hand over her thin, white fingers. Monahan watched them touch. *I beat him, you know,* he told Ginny Reingold in his mind. *A solid yard. Reddy Markham saw it. He had to be all noble and sportsmanlike about it. It killed him.* Ginny Reingold swallowed again and went on. "I didn't know what to do. I was afraid to try and run. I just stayed there. But Jerry didn't come back. I was out there over an hour, you know, and then . . . well, it started to get really cold. I didn't have my jacket or anything. So, finally, you know, I got out. And I went around the back. I wanted to . . . peek in at the window, the bedroom window, I was hoping maybe Jerry had gone to sleep. Like, passed out. He'd had a lot of vodka and, and some dope, too, so I thought . . ." She touched the corner of her eye with a fingernail, as if to keep a tear there neatly contained. "So, like, anyway, I kind of crept around to the back, and . . . there was a man. A big . . . I don't know . . . a big fat guy, white guy with, like, real short hair. He was climbing out of the window . . ."

Monahan's mouth opened, but he didn't speak. Suddenly, the heaviness in his belly began to lighten. *Hey,* he thought.

"He was wearing . . . kind of one of those checkered hunting jackets, you know," Ginny Reingold said. "He

44

didn't even see me, he didn't look at me, he just climbed out of the window and . . . started running. He just ran off into the woods in back. And I ran to the window and looked in, and . . . and there was Jerry . . ."

Now she shuddered, covered her mouth, with her hands, and her tears spilled over. They coursed over her bruised cheek, and her silken hair covered the other side of her face as she leaned toward her attorney. Ellerbee squeezed her shoulder, and she pressed her forehead against his lapel. Investigator Corvo clenched his fist at his side. Ginny Reingold looked like a beaten child.

But Monahan wasn't looking at Ginny Reingold now. By now, his mood had transformed entirely, and he was looking at Richard Ellerbee. Running his gaze over the bold, thin nose, the forthright brow, the whole expert etching of his countenance. Looking at him as one lawyer to another, one savvy courtroom practitioner to another. Excitement, like cold water boiling, was rising up through his chest, into his throat. And he was thinking. *Hey. Hey, what do you know? What do you know, counselor? Her story is crap. Craparoni. And you know it's crap, Mr. Counselor Ellerbee. And the jury will sure as hell know it, too.* He almost let himself laugh out loud. *And I'm going to beat you* he thought in surprise. *I'm going to beat you blind. On TV. On TV every ding-dong day For everyone to see every day For her to see. At your lousy party. I beat you once. At the fifty-yard dash. You arrogant son of a bitch. And I'm going to beat you now. Again. For everyone to see.*

Monahan shoved into his office, riding his confidence. This time, Corvo had to hurry to keep up with him.

45

"You better find an all-girl jury, boy," Corvo was saying, " 'cause there's not a man in the world who'd vote to convict her. Even I wouldn't vote to convict her, and I know she's guilty."

Monahan's desk was covered with pink message slips. Newspapers and TV stations and radio stations had been calling him. People from the Sonny Charleston talk show were calling him. Sonny wanted to have him on.

"They'll convict her," he said. "She's lying. They'll convict her."

He cleared a space at the corner of the desk. He had brought one of the portable JVCs in from the squad room. He hoisted it onto the desk and switched it on. It was almost time for the twelve o'clock report.

"That Ellerbee, he's something, huh," said Corvo. "Nice suit."

"Yeah," said Monahan. "It's a great suit." The picture on the set came up fast. A woman was holding up a box of detergent. She looked a little like Monahan's wife—round-faced, blond—only thinner, prettier, in a crisp, pretty yellow blouse. If Wendy could make herself look a little bit more like that, she'd be perfect, Monahan thought.

"He's actually a really nice guy," Corvo went on, as if he'd met a movie star who'd given him the time of day. "I was talking to him on the way out. He was asking me about the fishing up here. You know, he says he thinks he went to school with you."

"Oh yeah?" said Monahan. "I didn't recognize him."

"What do you think he makes? Like a million a year or something?"

The news came on then. Music like Morse code played

46

on violins. An exciting swoop toward the anchorwoman's desk, the keen beam of her gaze at the camera. And behind her, a glamour shot of Ginny Reingold over the image of a broken guitar.

The anchorwoman's lead was quick, sharp. Revelations today that Thrust had repeatedly battered his supermodel lover. Then they were into the tape, and there was Monahan, pushing up the courthouse steps as the reporters closed around him like the sea.

"Hey—looking good," said Corvo.

But Monahan briefly shook his head. He knew he did not look good. He did not even look like he looked. In real life, he had a candid, intelligent face, more handsome than not. On TV, his features seemed thick and coarse, his hair thin and unkempt. His attempts to speak forcefully, jabbing the air with his finger, seemed ludicrous, stagey and stiff. From a competent, honest, small-county prosecutor, the cameras had somehow transformed him into a bullying, beady-eyed thug of a bureaucrat.

But his new energy, his new confidence, did not falter. He was not experienced in this, that's all. The cameras, the press. It had caught him off-guard. Now, though, now that he knew he could win, he had a plan.

Ellerbee came on. "This case has been mishandled from the start," he said. He spoke quietly but precisely, addressing the reporter, and thus the audience, as a colleague, an equal. "The town police were on the scene before the county sheriff's department, and they wandered all over the property. Contaminated the evidence completely. Obliterated any trace of an intruder. No attempt to find another suspect has been made. And there's been no attempt to trace the ownership of the murder weapon."

"Yeah, those townies," Corvo said.

Monahan didn't hear him. *He's slick;* he was thinking. Ellerbee's approach to the camera was practiced, slick. He included the audience in his thoughts as if they were all lawyers trying the case together. Monahan nodded, thinking, *But this is my county, counselor, my track. And the jury will come from here.*

This was his plan. Monahan was going to change. Now, right away, before the reporters had time to notice. He was going to become a local boy. He'd lived here long enough; he knew just how to do it. *Well, that Mr. Ellerbee, he sure is one fine city lawyer,* he was going to tell the reporters. *I guess a small-county prosecutor doesn't have much chance against him in court,* he would say, *so I'll just have to tell folks the truth and hope they'll listen.* Monahan, staring at the TV, smiled without knowing it. It would work. He knew it would work. Even the fact that they had gone to school together would play right into it, sharpen the clash of personalities. Every day, the people would see it. Small-county David against big-city Goliath. The cameras would be on them. In courtroom, every day. Just like a show. And he would amble back and forth before the witness stand, one hand in his pants pocket, the other scratching at his head, his shirt rumpled, his tie undone. The Honest Bumpkin, Shrewder Than He Looked, Justice on His Side—that would be him—Alone Against All the Power of the Rich and Famous. The jury would love it. And he would win. On TV. The whole country—maybe even the whole world— would be watching it. *Lou Monahan, County Prosecutor.*

"What're *you* thinking?" said Corvo with a laugh. "With

that look on your face—what're you thinking about?"

"I'm thinking about a blouse I'm gonna buy for my wife," said Monahan. "Yellow." And he picked up the phone to call the Sonny Charleston show.

Lou Monahan, County Prosecutor, looked at the murder scene in the fading light, Monahan thought. He looked at the murder scene in the fading light. He was standing in back of the ranch house, out of sight of the deputy guarding the front. He was standing in the grass with his hands in his pockets. A cool breeze full of dusk and autumn traveled up the gentle slope of the hill from the woods below.

He had wanted to come and inspect the place again, get a sense of it. Supply himself with ammunition against Ellerbee's charges that the scene had been contaminated. Well, *now,* he would tell Sonny Charleston, that *Mr. Ellerbee has some real fancy ideas, but I had a look-see at the place myself, and, well, if there was any sign of an intruder . . .* He smiled as he turned to look down at the trees below him. He was going on the TV program tomorrow. The Lou Monahan show would begin its run tomorrow. Everything, he knew, was about to become wonderful.

The leaves in the forest rustled faintly. He could smell them beginning to die. And suddenly, his soul was in the past, and he was full of yearning. Walking across the dance floor to where she stood. The girl so achingly near and youth so achingly near again that he nearly groaned aloud in his desire to touch them both.

He had been wrong, he thought. Wrong all this time. She *had* been smiling at him. Beckoning him. He should have searched for her, found her, spoken to her. Everything would have been different. He would have been . . . something. Something else. He didn't know what. Some gleaming thing he could now only hanker for blindly.

Monahan began to walk toward the woods, down the slope of the lawn. He thought he was still examining the scene, but really he was just walking, feeling himself walk, as he had walked twenty years ago beneath the tent. He was wandering toward the woods and the source of the wind, and toward that smell of summer's end that he remembered. He was approaching the forest shadows and their sense of mystery as if he hoped to wander there right through the veil and into the un-happened thing.

But he slowed, stopped, right at the tree line. Gazed into the deeper darkness wryly, because he knew it was only the darkness after all. There was no going back, of course not. There were no alternative histories. Everything had to be as it was. His time had not been then. But his time was coming now.

He drew his gaze back to the front rank of trees and was about to turn away. But then he noticed something.

Lou Monahan, County Prosecutor, stepped forward, his eyes narrowing. He looked down at a young maple growing at the forest's edge, its lower branches. On one of them, there was a small puff of color trembling in the air. Red and black among the leaves that were still green. He leaned closer to it, and he knew exactly what it was. It was a trace of fabric, a few threads. Pulled from one of those checkered hunting jackets. Like the jacket Ginny Reingold said had been worn by the murderous intruder.

Something in Monahan greeted the sight without surprise, as if he had known all along it would be there. Just as he had known, somehow, that the girl at the edge of the dance floor would be gone by the time he reached her. This made sense to him, too. That Ginny Renigold was innocent. That she would not go to trial. That there would be no trial. Some drug-crazed drifter would be busted for the murder and would confess. The model would leave the county, and Ellerbee would leave, and the cameras would leave. *Lou Monahan, County Prosecutor* would be canceled before it even premiered. It did not surprise him at all. The world made much more sense to him that way. It always had.

And yet . . . thought Monahan dreamily. *And yet . . .*

He reached out and pinched the little scrap of cloth between his thumb and finger. He tugged it, and it came free from the snag of the branch on which it hung. He held it up, a little above his eyes, as if to examine it in the darkling. The breeze blew up to him from its mysterious source in the woods. And he opened his fingers.

And the little scrap of cloth blew away.

Real Life

SARAH SHANKMAN

If there were a space more deadly than Room 1517, 100 Centre Street, New York, New York, Clare Meacham didn't want to know about it.

She'd been sitting in the dreadful room for two hours, and her bones were overdone linguine. Her neck could barely support her curly head. The room had sucked off what energy she'd packed in with her—which had been precious little, God knows, on this steamy rotten morning. A month into the heat wave of the century, Manhattan had all the appeal of an overripe dinosaur carcass.

Besides which, since David dumped her, Clare had been mightily depressed and hadn't been sleeping worth a damn. She yawned now, and Room 1517 seemed to open its jaws in answer around her. The giant municipal maw filled with long rows of dark blue cushioned armchairs. Cream-colored walls, splotched as an adolescent's complexion. Cheap particle-board wainscoting. White acoustic ceiling tile mushed whispers into a slow steady hiss. On the floor, patched beige linoleum squares cheated at hopscotch.

Dust motes floated in the refrigerated air, recycled, no doubt, thought Clare, through the dead dinosaur's respiratory system. Yes, the very air itself was dank and dangerously gelatinous. Teeming, one felt, with tuberculosis, cholera, hantavirus, Ebola. (Good. Maybe she'd contract one of those and die a spectacular lingering death, and then David would be sorry.) God knows, the fluorescent lighting, which cast a greenish pallor over the room's captives, gave them the look of disease.

The two hundred and seventy-five prospective jurors slumped and lumped in the blue armchairs.

Oh, God, could it be borne, their faces asked, that this was only the first, the number one, the maidenhead of their ten endless days of jury duty? Ten, that is, if an actual trial didn't glue them even longer into some angry crouch of deliberation.

Clare shifted in her seat, careful not to upset the notebook computer perched on her lap. Thirty-nine, a tall, languorously attractive brunette despite the dark circles of despair beneath her eyes, Clare wore brown woven leather loafers, a short khaki skirt, a red-and-white striped shirt, and gold hoop earrings. Her long, dark, curly hair was pulled back off her face with a tortoise barrette. She was as presentable as she could bring herself to be under the circumstances.

The circumstances being (a) a broken heart and (b) the fact that this little trip down the lane of civic responsibility was most certainly going to cost her her livelihood. Her inevitable financial ruin and bankruptcy proceedings could later be traced back to this precise and fetid A.M. Not only was she not in the mood, but Clare could not, goddammit, *afford* to be on jury duty.

Try telling that to Norman O. Goodman, New York county clerk of court. Or any of his stiff-necked minions. Did they care? Ho ho. *That* was a good one.

The freshly blondined woman in the appalling gold-braided fuchsia suit behind the desk in Room 105 or 106 or whatever it was downstairs, where Clare had gone two

53

weeks earlier to beg for just one more reprieve from her civic responsibility, had said, "Forget it, Ms. Meacham. No more excuses, no more deferments. We, the puffed-up, jealous, self-righteous, civilly employed we, hereby sentence you to jury duty. Or else."

That had been the peroxided bitch's final word. On the exact same day that Arnie, Clare's producer, had called her in and said, "The ratings go up, Clare. Or else."

It was the O.J. trial that had set in motion the avalanche of the viewer share of *Real Life*, the soap opera on which Clare was head writer.

"Court TV is a fucking vampire," Arnie had said. "We've got to jazz *Real Life* way up, Clare. Pick up the pace. Add some sizzle. Give those sofa tuberettes some blood and guts along with their romance. *Real Life*'s gotta be more like real life. Grittier. Sexier. Meaner. Hotter."

Then his terrible last words: "The whole story line has to be in overdrive in the next three weeks—even if you have to write ninety-six hours a day."

That had been two weeks ago, and Clare, bleak and blue, hadn't written a word. Now, with one week left to save her ass, here she was locked in Room 1517. Squashed cheek-by-jowl with almost three hundred of her fellow Gothamites of every race, nationality, and socioeconomic category.

Earlier this morning, in the long line behind the security check, the sticky crowd had made nervous jokes about knives and guns and bombs, all the while sussing one another out with the quick once-over that is second nature to every New Yorker assessing caste, class, tailoring, and degree of homicidal impulse in a millisecond. Then, after they'd received their guides to restaurants in neighboring Chinatown and Little Italy and had watched the video on the ins and outs of jury duty, they'd filed into Room 1517 and the sea of dark blue chairs.

But inevitably, the stew of strangers had settled into the reality of their task.

It was theirs to wait.

And wait.

And wait.

They'd looked around, then, okay, damn it, with a collective sigh they'd opened their briefcases, backpacks, purses, and bags and unearthed newspapers, magazines, books they'd been meaning to read, find-a-word puzzles, needlework, the paperwork that had long been shoved aside. They'd clamped on Walkmen. Clare spotted two other people, both Wall Street types, bent over laptop computers. A young Hispanic woman in the last row, next to the windows, fiddled with the antenna of a tiny television. Here and there, a couple of people talked quietly. And fully a third of the room lurched and listed and snored and snuffled through mid-morning naps.

Clare stared accusingly at her computer's blank screen. Her brain was frozen. It was totally quiet in there. Except for a constant interior refrain. *Nobody loves you. Never will again.* That was the main melody.

Then, winding in around it, a wading glissando: *Why is it my job to turn the tide of thirty-odd years of sappy story lines about soggy romance, all slow as molasses? Why do I have to make the shift from slow-rising yeast to Pop Tarts? Horse and buggy to the Concorde? Whalebone corsets to Madonna and her jet-nose tits?*

55

Because they said so, that's why. Because they paid her the big bucks to swallow what she might have once fancied herself possessed of, zip her lip, and deliver whatever crap they demanded. On time and in the flavor of the moment. No matter what her personal problems. Who gave a shit about them?

The cursor on the small green screen before her blinked. *Write, Clare. Suck it up. Get your ass in gear. Take a deep breath. Push some oxygen in and out. Get the old gray matter moving.*

Could she do that? Maybe.

It wasn't as if she didn't know these characters. These silly people, most of whom she'd inherited from her predecessor, who had, incidentally, hanged herself in the bathroom of her East Hampton beach house one fine morning two summers earlier. Just down the lane from Martha Stewart's house. Her death had made the six o'clock local news. Clare wondered, would *her* suicide play as well?

But she digressed. Well, Christ, who wouldn't? What the hell else was there to do with Dirk and Carol and Josh and Trish and Richard and Paula, the three main couples of *Real Life*? They were such stupid people with such stupid problems. *Slow* stupid problems. Problems that moved at the pace of a banana slug (or a soap) and were about as fascinating.

No, actually, a banana slug was a hell of a lot more interesting than the ailing marriage of Trish, played by a busty brunette with the voice of a mosquito, and Josh, the simpering nephew of Arnie the producer, who couldn't act his way out of a damp Kleenex.

Clare couldn't even *think* about Richard and Paula, her

whiny preppie couple.

So she'd have to start with Carol and Dirk—C for Clare and D for David, get it? Ms. Clare Meacham Herself and her erstwhile lover, Dr. David Teller. Yes, Carol and Dirk were loosely based on her own pathetic life.

"Excuse me."

Clare jumped. It was the woman to her left. An attractive middle-aged black woman in a navy business suit, good pumps, substantial gold jewelry. "Do you have change for a dollar? I need to call my office."

Clare checked her wallet, handed the woman three quarters and two dimes "I'll have to owe you a nickel."

The woman's smile was warm. "Nope, I owe you." And she headed off to the phone room.

She'd be a while. Clare had already checked it out: three machines vending poisonous substances, a water fountain, and more of those damned blue chairs in which to wait for the four phones. Four phones for nearly three hundred New Yorkers, and no cellulars allowed? You might as well have cut off their oxygen.

Clare stared back at the blank screen. Okay. Dirk and Carol, step up, please, front and center. In *Real Life*, they'd weathered many problems, such as the time when Dirk, who was a plastic surgeon, had been called away to Wisconsin for two months to reconstruct the faces of an entire family of protected witnesses (as had David) and had strayed with a Scandinavian scrub nurse (which Clare had suspected). Then there'd been Carol's automobile accident and the coma and the long while after she'd come out of it when she thought Dirk was an extraterrestrial.

Now, lagging about six weeks behind Clare's real life,

Dirk had just leaned over a table in an Italian restaurant and told Carol he was calling off their engagement. Because, well, he was marrying someone else. Carol had burst into tears and bolted out of the restaurant. (As had Clare.)

"What are you writing?"

Again, Clare started. This time, her interrogator was to her left, a very short man sitting two chairs over. About her age, late thirties, he was nicely turned out in fine fawn-colored trousers, a T-shirt in chocolate, a handsome blue, brown, and beige jacket. Armani probably. His dark, clean profile reminded her of David.

David. Clare's stomach flip-flopped.

Meanwhile, the gorgeous little babe was waiting.

What was she writing?

Nothing. Not a word. She was simply staring at her screen. Listening to the computer's tiny hum, much quieter than the terror gnawing at her intestines. The hideous, bright yellow fear that she couldn't do it. Couldn't, couldn't, couldn't revamp *Real Life*. They'd fire her ass, she'd be a bag lady, within a year. Reeking of urine. Scratching at herself. Begging for alms, from real people, with real jobs, like she used to be. And then, for sure, no one would ever love her again. She'd die all alone, her grave in a potter's field dug by inmates from Riker's Island.

"A script," she finally said.

"A screenplay?" The dapper little man slipped one chair closer.

"No." She shook her head.

What did this guy want? This was New York, for Christ's sake, where strangers might ask you where you bought your shoes—and how much you paid for them. But your

58

business? They stayed out of it.

He smiled brightly and extended a hand. "I'm Vinnie. I'm in the restaurant business, but I'm starting to write screenplays on the side. I figure, hey, everybody else is."

"I write for a soap."

Usually, when she said that, eyebrows rose. Wasn't she prostituting herself? Why didn't she write novels? Publish arty stories in little magazines? She'd done both. She wasn't cut out for the life of the starving artist.

But Vinnie said, "Cool." Then he said, "Could I borrow a quarter till after lunch? I don't have any change, and I need to make a phone call."

What did she look like, a bank? "I think I gave all my change to somebody else a few minutes ago," she said. But then she dug in her purse and came up with a shiny new quarter that had been hiding in a corner.

But before Vinnie could make his call, an officer of the court sauntered from behind the tall wide desk at the front of the room and began calling names from the summons slips he pulled at random from a bingolike contraption. They were to answer to their names, then follow him to a courtroom where *they* would be judged on their worthiness to judge another.

Juan Reyes. Kashonda Smallwood. Gillian Holch. Duncan McKenzie III. Ellen Bradley. Yolanda Ramirez. Estelle Krim. Angela Wong. Jacqi Albano. Rita Sitnick. Vincent Gallo.

"That's me." Vinnie waved at the clerk.

Clare Meacham.

Clare groaned and raised a hand. She *couldn't* get stuck on a jury. Not now. Please, God.

59

The woman Clare had given change to reentered the room just as the last of the forty names was being called. *Wilma Paris.* "Oh, Lord," she cried. "Wouldn't you know? And my boss just said he's going to kill me if I don't get my butt back to the office."

Behind the judge, huge letters spelled out "IN OD WE TRUST."

Vinnie pointed at the words, whispered to Clare, "Kind of makes you wonder, doesn't it?" They were two of the twelve seated in the juror's box, the remainder of their panel of forty spread across the spectators' seats.

Frowsy-haired Judge Rabinowitz frowned over her horn rims at Vinnie. Their instructions had been to listen up, no eating, no sleeping, no talking. The judge had just finished introducing the prosecution, the defense, and the defendant, and outlining the bare bones of the case.

The defendant—a big handsome black lad, about twenty—was charged with attempting to hold up a Korean grocer. He'd purportedly used a gun; the plaintiff, a short but muscular man, had answered with a whirling baseball bat.

This was the stuff of real life, thought Clare. *This* was material. How would it work? Dirk follows Carol out of the restaurant. She runs into the Korean store. They're caught smack in the middle of the holdup. Carol grabs up a tray of hot sweet-and-sour pork from the steam table, heaves it at the robber . . .

The judge had chosen to conduct the voir dire herself, questioning the twelve citizens in the box: *Do any of you know me, the defendant, the plaintiff, either of the prosecu-*

60

tion or the defense attorneys, or any of the witnesses I've just named?

How?

Do you know the area, Broadway between Bleecker and Third, where the incident took place?

What is your knowledge of that site?

Are you related to any law enforcement officers, and, if so, how?

What is the nature of your employment?

What magazines do you subscribe to?

Have you ever been the victim of a street crime?

Have you ever been the victim of a crime involving a gun?

Wilma Paris, the advertising account exec to whom Clare had given change, had a brother who was a cop, and she said it was her belief that cops lied as much as anybody else.

Vinnie Gallo said he himself, as a customer, had been held up at gun point in a Korean store. By a kid. With a gun. (Clare wasn't sure she believed him.)

Clare declared that she herself didn't know anyone in the courtroom. She lived in the Village and had walked by the crime scene many times but wasn't certain if she'd ever stopped in. She was not related to any police officers, nor did she know any personally. She was the head writer on *Real Life*. She subscribed to the *New Yorker, New York, Saveur, Soap Digest,* and *Conde Nast Traveler.* She had lived in Manhattan eighteen years and had never been the victim of any crime whatsoever.

(Unless you counted having her heart run over and squashed flat by one Dr. David Teller, who was not a defendant here today.)

At the end of the questioning, Clare was excused, with no explanation, along with Vinnie and Wilma. Thank you. Good-bye.

Back in Room 1517, the chairs where Clare, Vinnie, and Wilma were sitting had been taken. Clare scanned the room. There was an empty bloc of seats back toward the windows, near the young Hispanic woman watching TV. She headed for them. She *had* to get to work.

But Vinnie and Wilma were close on her heels.

"I can't believe they didn't take you," said Vinnie. "Me, that's one thing, but you? You're perfect, except for that part about living in Manhattan for years and never even having your purse snatched. That made you sound like a liar."

Wilma leaned across him, interrupting. "*I* want to ask you about *Real Life*. My mom is a *huge* fan. She'll be so excited when I tell her I met you. You really make up all those stories?"

"I'm afraid so." Clare grimaced. *When I can. When I don't have writer's block. When I'm not scared to death. Depressed. Sleep-deprived. On jury duty.*

"She's writing right here." Vinnie pointed at the computer in Clare's hand.

"I don't know how you do it," said Wilma. "I'm an account exec. Not a creative bone in my body."

"Mine, either," said Clare.

"Come on." Vinnie laughed. "You're just being modest."

"No, I'm not." And then it just spilled out, the whole nine yards of her pathetic tale. How she was upset about her personal life and hadn't been sleeping well. How she had only a week left to revamp *Real Life*, to make it hotter than O.J., bigger than real life. How she didn't have a clue.

"You can do it," said Vinnie. "I know you can."

"I don't think so." Clare shook her head.

Just then, an officer stood, from behind the long desk. "Lunch break," he announced. "Be back at two-thirty. Did anyone not get a list of restaurants in Chinatown and Little Italy?"

The whole room stampeded for the door.

Except Julia, the young Hispanic woman in the row behind them, who was plugged into the earphones of her little TV. "Jesus!" she screamed. "I can't believe it! Shoot the fucker!"

Mid-flight, people stopped and stared.

"Shoot him! Don't let him get away with that!"

The officer started toward her.

"*Kill* the son of a bitch!" Julia shouted.

"Miss?" The clerk tapped her arm. "You're going to have to quiet down. And you can't use that kind of language in here."

"What?" Julia jumped and jerked out her earphones. "Was I loud? I'm sorry. But I get so excited at my program. That Dirk! He's such a . . ." She caught herself. ". . . bad person. I can't believe Carol lets him get away with that . . . stuff!"

"Oh, Christ!" Clare slapped a hand to her mouth. "She's talking about *Real Life*."

Vinnie grabbed both Clare and Wilma, then leaned over Julia. "Miss? You wanna go to lunch with us? My treat."

Vinnie took them to a restaurant where he was obviously

known, Luigi's on Mulberry Street. Restaurants were the only thing that remained Italian about Little Italy. The old families had long since moved to Staten Island, and the real estate was being swallowed up by the Chinese. But that didn't stop the tourists, especially the once who imagined gangland hits over every plate of meatballs and spaghetti.

The food at Luigi's, old-fashioned red-sauce Italian, was good enough to please the most demanding mobster. Vinnie had ordered a giant antipasto platter for the table. "Have some more coppa," he urged, pouring the Chianti. "And peppers. These mushrooms Luigi said he smuggled in from Italy last week. Finish them up. Then we'll get down to work."

"Work?" asked Julia, her eyes big as she looked up from her plate. It was clear this meal was a special treat for her. She was very impressed by Luigi's. Not to mention Vinnie.

"Sure," said Vinnie. "We're going to write Clare's story. *Real Life* is getting itself fixed right here. Right now. At this table."

Clare almost choked. Just as the food and the wine and the company were beginning to make her feel a little human, Vinnie had to bring *that* up.

"You think we can't?" Vinnie reared back in his chair. " 'Cause we ain't professional writers? I'm telling you, we can, and we will. We are the people. The people who *know* about real life. We are your friggin' audience you don't ever give no respect."

Clare raised her glass. "Hear, hear."

"I don't like the idea of using the stickup in the Korean store," said Julia, sipping her coffee.

64

"Why not?" Wilma asked.

"The stickup is real," insisted Clare.

"It'd be more real if somebody got killed. In my neighborhood, every time there's a stickup, somebody gets killed."

"So who do you pick to die?" Vinnie signaled for more grappa. "You got the black kid. You got the Korean. You got Carol and Dirk."

"Carol," said Julia.

Clare put down her glass. "Why Carol?"

" 'Cause she's a wimp," Julia said. "Take today's show. Dirk tells her he's marrying another woman, what does she do? She just leaves the table. Carol makes me sick."

"Oh, really?" said Clare, a little defensive. "What do you want her to do? Kill him, like you were saying back upstairs?" Clare pointed a thumb in the direction of 100 Centre Street and the courthouse. At least she thought it was in that direction. She was getting pretty loaded.

"Yeah," said Julia. "Kill him."

"How? When? Where?" asked Wilma.

"How? Pick up a knife from the table and stab the sucker. When? As soon as he said he was dumping her for another chick. Where? In the gut."

Clare thought about that. How would that have gone down, the two of them in Bar Pitti having dinner when David had made his announcement. He had ordered the veal. There was a sharp knife at his place. It certainly would have been possible. Of course, she'd be in Riker's now. Or wherever it was they locked up female murderers. The Tombs, maybe, right next door to 100 Centre.

"If she'd killed him in the restaurant," said Wilma, "then

65

they wouldn't be in the Korean store together."

"Screw the Korean store," said Julia.

Clare said, "Look, folks, we can't go back to the scene in the restaurant and do it differently. It aired today, remember? Then there are three more weeks of shows already in the can. That's where we have to pick up."

"Okay, so what happened after Carol ran out of the restaurant?" asked Julia.

Clare could tell from Julia's tone that she was thinking, *I bet not much.*

And she was right. "But it's not my fault," Clare insisted. "This was before they wanted the show to pick up speed. To be more like real life."

"Let's hear it," said Wilma.

"Dirk's ex-wife, Molly, who has always hoped that Dirk would come back to her, is shattered when she hears that Dirk is marrying yet *another* woman. She flips out and has to be institutionalized. She ends up in the hospital where David does most of his cosmetic surgery, and she rages in while he's in the middle of doing somebody's face. The patient, who is Richard of Richard and Paula, has been in a terrible skiing accident and ended up with no nose."

"Now, *that's* interesting," said Vinnie.

"Who's David?" asked Wilma. "You said David was performing the surgery."

Clare blushed. "I meant Dirk. David's my real ex-boyfriend. The real plastic surgeon."

"And did David dump you like Dirk dumped Carol?" Wilma asked.

Clare nodded.

"Then forget what I said," said Julia. "Let's get him back

in that Korean store and shoot that sucker full of holes."

"I like the Korean store, too," said Vinnie, knocking back the last of his grappa. "But now it's two-fifteen, and we've got to scoot back over to Centre Street."

Back in Room 1517, the four of them clustered in a corner. They were picking up speed. Dirk lay dead in the grocery store, and they were arguing over whether or not the Korean grocer or Carol subdued the shooter, when the court officer stepped from behind the desk and called their names once more and they had to file into another courtroom.

This time, the defendant, as Judge O'Banion explained, was a twenty-two-year-old man who, when his girlfriend jilted him, had thrown her in front of a subway train which cut her to ribbons.

The four cowriters stared at one another. *Dirk,* mouthed Julia. *It's even better. It's perfect.*

They couldn't wait to get out of that courtroom and back to *Real Life.*

Vinnie had said that he thought the jiltee was justified. Wilma had said that her eighty-six-year-old mother was once dragged by a train and she just couldn't listen to the testimony. Julia's he was that she had gone to high school with the victim. Clare said that she was obsessed with this case, had followed every smidgen of news about it, and thought the defendant should be strung up. They were all excused.

"Okay," said Vinnie, back in Room 1517, "I take it that you like running David, I mean Dirk, over with a subway train?"

"I love it," said Wilma. "Carol pushes him, and the train

67

runs over his gorgeous face."

"Oh, yeah," said Julia.

"Absolutely," said Clare. "It's perfect. It's poetic justice."

"And does Clare, I mean Carol, get caught?" asked Vinnie.

"No way," said Julia. "She doesn't do it herself. Somebody else does it."

"Somebody she paid?" asked Vinnie.

"Probably," said Wilma.

"How much?" asked Vinnie. Then he reached in a pocket of his lovely fawn slacks and pulled out the quarter Clare had loaned him for the phone earlier that morning. He flipped it a couple of times and gave her a wink.

"Not in real life." Clare laughed. "Not nearly enough."

But it was.

Shortly after that conversation, the prospective jurors of Room 1517 were dismissed for the day. Clare, energized for the first time in weeks, went straight home and wrote like a crazy person. As the four of them had plotted, Dirk died, his pretty face mangled beyond recognition, and Carol got away with it. Then Dirk's long-lost twin brother, Dylan, a pediatrician, comes to New York, and the two of them fall madly in love. But then a child in his care dies mysteriously, and an autopsy discovers that the child's heart is missing. It turns out that Dylan, whose only child drowned ten years ago, has snapped. He's become a kind of Frankenstein, and there's a terrible trial . . .

Involved in the narrative, Clare had lost track of time. Even though she hadn't slept in weeks, she was alive with energy. It was almost eleven when her phone rang.

"Turn on the TV," said a familiar voice. One she'd heard recently but couldn't quite place. "The news."

"Who is this?"

"Vinnie."

"What . . . ?"

"Just turn on the TV, okay?"

Clare did as he said, and there was blond Chuck Scarborough looking deadly serious as he reported a horrible accident that evening at the 79th Street station of the IRT. "The victim, Dr. David Teller a prominent plastic surgeon, was waiting for a train about 8 P.M. this evening when he seemed to fall onto the tracks and was dragged by the head and killed. There were no immediate witnesses to the accident. No one noticed him standing at the far end of the platform. At this point, there's no indication of foul play . . ."

"Vinnie!" Clare shrieked. "You killed him."

"What makes you say that?"

"I didn't mean for you to really kill him! He was a son of a bitch, but I didn't mean . . . we can't be judge and jury . . ."

"What makes you think you had anything to do with this little incident? How do you know Dr. Teller wasn't just an accident waiting to happen?"

"What an you talking about?"

"Let's just pretend . . ." And then Vinnie chuckled softly. "You know, pretend, like we were writing a story, that Dr. Teller had really pissed off some important people by giving new faces to some reprehensible characters in the feds' witness protection program. Like on *Real Life*, but in real life, too."

"Oh, my God," Clare breathed."

"And let's say that these very important people wanted to

69

deliver a very strong message to Dr. Teller. Well, more than a message. They wanted to make damned sure that he cease and desist these practices. Immediately. And permanently."

"Oh, Vinnie," said Clare. She could feel something rising in her chest. Something like relief. Could that be? Something like joy? Delight? Something that tasted like sweet revenge?

"And let's say that a friend of these very important people was asked to take care of this Dr. Teller who was causing them so much grief. And this friend had set out to do that very thing when he, by a piece of great coincidence, ran into the former girlfriend of said Dr. Teller in a jury room. And she was having a problem with *Real Life*. And so he and some other people helped her with her problem."

"With *Real Life*?"

"Yeah," said Vinnie. "And this guy, he liked their story so much he rolled it over into little r, little l real life."

The feeling in Clare's chest bubbled over into laughter And once she started, she couldn't stop.

"Good night, Clare," said Vinnie. She could hear his grin. "Sweet dreams. And good luck with *Real Life*. If I was you, I'd use this, babe. Use *this* material. We *like* this poetic justice business out in the real world."

Clare did. She used it all. And when *Real Life* became number one in its time slot, and the Emmies and the money started pouring in, Arnie , Clare's producer, raised a glass of champagne to her. "How sweet," he said, "real life is."

Knives at Midnight

A Sharon McCone Story

MARCIA MULLER

My eyes were burning, and I felt not unlike a creature that spends a great deal of its life underground. I marked the beat-up copy of last year's *Standard California Codes* that I'd scrounged up at a used bookstore on Adams Avenue, then shut it. When I stood up, my limbs felt as if I were emerging from, the creature's burrow. I stretched, smiling.

Well, McCone, I told myself, *at last one of your peculiarities is going to pay off.*

For years, I'd taken what many considered a strange pleasure in browsing through the tissue-thin pages of both the civil and penal codes. I had learned many obscure facts. For instance: it is illegal to trap birds in a public cemetery; anyone advertising merchandise that is made in whole or in part by prisoners must insert the words "convict-made" in the ad copy; stealing a dog worth $400 or less is petty theft, while stealing a dog worth more than $400 is grand theft. Now I could add another esoteric statute to my store of knowledge, only this one promised a big payoff.

Somebody who thought himself above the law was about to go down—and I was the one who would topple him.

Two nights earlier, I'd flown into San Diego's Lindbergh Field from my home base in San Francisco. Flown in on a perilous approach that always makes me, holder of both a single- and a multi-engine rating, wish I didn't know quite so much about pilot error. On top of a perfectly natural edginess, I was aggravated with myself for giving in to my older brother John's plea. The case he wanted me to take on for some friends sounded like one where every lead comes to a dead end; besides, I was afraid that in my former hometown I'd become embroiled in some family crisis. The McCone clan attracts catastrophe the way normal people attract stray kittens.

John was waiting for me at the curb in his old red International Scout. When he saw me, he jumped out and enveloped me in a bear hug that made me drop both my purse and my briefcase. My travel bag swung around and whacked him on his back; he released me, grunting.

"You're looking good," he said, stepping back.

"So're you." John's a big guy—six-foot-four—and sometimes he bulks up from the beer he's so fond of. But now he was slimmed down to muscle and sported a new closely trimmed beard. Only his blond hair resisted taming.

He grabbed my bag, tossed it into the Scout, and motioned for me to climb aboard. I held my ground. "Before we go anyplace—you didn't tell Pa I was coming down, did you?"

"No."

"Ma and Melvin? Charlene and Ricky?"

"None of them."

"Good. Did you make me a motel reservation and reserve a rental car?"

"No."

"I asked you—"

"You're staying at my place."

72

"John! Don't you remember—"

"Yeah, yeah. Don't involve the people you care about in something that could get dangerous. I heard all that before."

"And it *did* get dangerous."

"Not very. Anyway, you're staying with me. Get in."

John can be as stubborn as I when he makes up his mind. I opted for the path of least resistance. "Okay, I'll stay tonight—only. But what am I supposed to drive while I'm here?"

"I'll loan you the Scout."

I frowned. It hadn't aged well since I last borrowed it.

He added, "I could go along, help you out."

"John!"

He started the engine and edged into the flow of traffic. "You know, I've missed you." Reaching over and ruffling my hair, he ginned broadly. "McCone and McCone—the detecting duo. Together again."

I heaved a martyred sigh and buckled my seat belt.

The happy tone of our reunion dissipated when we walked into the living room of John's little stucco house in nearby Lemon Grove. His old friends, Bryce and Mari Winslip, sat on the sofa in front of the corner fireplace; their hollow eyes reflected weariness and pain and—when they saw me—a kind of hope that I immediately feared was misplaced. While John made the introductions and fetched wine for me and freshened the Winslips' drinks, I studied them.

Both were a fair number of years older than my brother, perhaps in their early sixties. John had told me on the phone that Bryce Winslip was the painting contractor who had employed him during his apprenticeship; several years ago,

73

he'd retired and they'd moved north to Oregon. Bryce and Mari were white-haired and had the bronzed, tough-skinned look of people who spent a lot of time outdoors. I could tell that customarily they were clear-eyed, mentally acute, and vigorous. But not tonight.

Tonight the Winslips were gaunt-faced and red-eyed; they moved in faltering sequences that betrayed their age. Tonight they were drinking straight whiskey, and every word seemed an effort. Small wonder: they were hurting badly because their only child, Troy, was violently dead.

Yesterday morning, twenty-five-year-old Troy Winslip's body had been found by the Tijuana, Mexico, authorities in a parking lot near the bullring at the edge of the border town. He had been stabbed seventeen times. Cause of death: exsanguination. Estimated time of death: midnight. There were no witnesses, no suspects, no known reason for the victim to have been in that place. Although Troy was a San Diego resident and a student at San Diego State, the SDPD could do no more than urge the Tijuana authorities to pursue an investigation and report their findings. The TPD, which would have been overworked even if it wasn't notoriously corrupt, wasn't about to devote time to the murder of a *gringo* who shouldn't have been down there in the middle of the night anyway. For all practical purposes, case closed.

So John had called me, and I'd opened my own case file.

When we were seated, I said to the Winslips, "Tell me about Troy. What sort of person was he?"

They exchanged glances. Mari cleared her throat. "He was a good boy . . . man. He'd settled down and was attending college."

"Studying what?"

"Communications. Radio and TV."

"You say he'd 'settled down.' What does that mean?"

Again the exchanged glances. Bryce said, "After high school, he had some problems that needed to be worked through—one of the reasons we moved north. But he's been fine for at least five years now."

"Could you be more specific about these problems?"

"Well, Troy was using drugs."

"Marijuana? Cocaine?"

"Both. When we moved to Oregon, we put him into a good treatment facility. He made excellent progress. After he was released, he went to school at Eugene, but three years ago he decided to come back to San Diego."

"A mistake," Mari said.

"He was a grown man; we couldn't stop him," her husband responded defensively. "Besides, he was doing well, making good grades. There was no way we could have predicted that . . . this would happen."

Mari shrugged.

I asked, "Where was Troy living?"

"He shared a house on Point Loma with another student."

"I'll need the address and the roommate's name. What else can you tell me about Troy?"

Bryce said, "Well, he is . . . was athletic. He liked to sail and play tennis." He looked at his wife.

"He was very articulate," she added. "He had a beautiful voice and would have done well in radio or television."

"Do you know any of his friends here?"

". . . No. I'm not even sure of the roommate's name."

"What about women? Was he going with anyone?

75

Engaged?"

Head shakes.

"Anything else?"

Silence.

"Well," Bryce said after a moment, "he was a very private person. He didn't share many of the details of his life with us, and we respected that."

I was willing to bet that the parents hadn't shared many details of their life with Troy, either. The Winslips struck me as one of those couples who have formed a closed circle that admits no one, not even their own offspring. The shared glances, their body language, the way they consulted nonverbally before answering my questions—all that pointed to a self-sufficient system. I doubted they'd known their son very well at all, and probably hadn't even realized they were shutting him out.

Bryce Winslip leaned forward, obviously awaiting some response on my part to what he and Mari had told me.

I said, "I have to be frank with you. Finding out what happened to Troy doesn't look promising. But I'll give it a try. John explained about my fee?"

They nodded.

"You'll need to sign one of my standard contracts, as well as a release giving me permission to enter Troy's home and go through his personal effects." I took the forms from my briefcase and began filling them in.

After they'd put their signatures on the forms and Bryce had written me a check as a retainer, the Winslips left for their hotel. John fetched me another glass of wine and a beer for himself and sat in the place Mari had vacated, propping his feet on the raised hearth.

"So," he said, "how're we going to go about this?"

"You mean how am *I* going to go about this. First *I* will check with the SDPD for details on the case. Do you remember Gary Viner?"

"That dumb-looking friend of Joey's from high school?"

All of our brother Joey's friends had been dumb-looking. "Sandy-haired guy, one of the auto shop crowd."

"Oh, yeah. He used to work on Joey's car in front of the house and ogle you when he thought you weren't looking "

I grinned. "That's the one. He used to ogle me during cheerleading, too. When I was down here on that kidnapping case a couple of years ago, he told me I had the prettiest bikini pants of anybody on the squad."

John scowled indignantly, like a proper big brother. "So what's this underwear freak got to do with the Winslip case?"

"Gary's on Homicide with the SDPD now. It's always best to check in with the local authorities when you're working a case on their turf, so I'll stop by his office in the morning, see what he's got from the TJ police."

"Well, just don't wear a short skirt. What should I do while you're seeing him?"

"Nothing. Afterward, *I* will visit Troy's house, talk with the roommate, try to get a list of his friends and find out more about him. Plus go to State and see what I can dig up there."

"What about me?"

"You will tend to Mr. Paint." Mr. Paint was the contracting business he operated out of his home shop and office.

John's lower lip pushed out sulkily.

I said, "How about dinner? I'm starving."

He brightened some. "Mexican?"

"Sure."

"I'll drive."

"Okay."

"You'll pay."

"John!"

"Consider it a finder's fee."

Gary Viner hadn't changed since I'd seen him a couple of years earlier, but he was very different from the high school kid I remembered. Gaining weight and filling out had made him more attractive; he'd stopped hiding his keen intelligence and learned to tone down his ogling to subtly speculative looks that actually flattered me. Unfortunately, he had no more information on the Winslip murder than what John had already told me.

"Is it okay if I look into this for the parents?" I asked him.

"Feel free. It's not our case, anyway. You go down there"—he motioned in the general direction of Baja California—"you might want to check in with the TJ authorities."

"I won't be going down unless I come up with something damned good up here."

"Well, good luck, and keep me posted." As I started out of his cubicle, Gary added, "Hey, McCone—the last time I saw you, you never did answer my question."

"Which is?"

"Can you still turn a cartwheel?"

I grinned at him. "You bet I can. And my bikini pants are still the prettiest ever."

It made me feel good to see a tough homicide cop blush.

My first surprise of the day was Troy Winslip's house. It was enormous, sprawling over a double lot that commanded an impressive view of San Diego Bay and Coronado Island. Stucco and brick and half-timbers, with a terraced yard landscaped in brilliantly flowering ice plant, it must have been at least six thousand square feet, give or take a few.

A rich roommate? Many rich roommates? Whatever, it sure didn't resemble the ramshackle brown-shingled house that I'd shared with what had seemed a cast of thousands when I was at UC Berkeley.

I rang the bell several times and got no response, so I decided to canvass the neighbors. No one was home at the houses to either side, but across the street I got lucky. The stoop-shouldered man who came to the door was around seventy and proved to like the sound of his own voice.

"Winslip? Sure, I know him. Nice young fellow. He's owned the place for about a year now."

"You're sure he owns it?"

"Yes. I knew the former owners. Gene and Alice Farr— nice people, too, but that big house was too much for them, so they sold and bought one of those condos. They told me Winslip paid cash."

Cash? Such a place would go for many hundreds of thousands. "What about his roommate? Do you also know him?"

The old man leered at me. "Roommate? Is that what you call them these days? Well, he's a she. The ladies come and go over there, but none're very permanent. This last one,

I'd say she's been there eight, nine weeks."

"Do you know her name?"

He shook his head. "She's a good-looking one, though— long red hair, kind of willowy."

"And do you know what either she or Mr. Winslip do for a living?"

"Not her, no. And if he does anything, he's never talked about it. I suspect he inherited his money. He's home a lot, when he's not sailing his boat."

"Where does he keep his boat?"

"Glorietta Bay Marina, over on Coronado." The man frowned now, wrinkles around his eyes deepening. "What's this about, anyway?"

"Troy Winslip's been murdered, and I'm investigating it."

"What?"

"You didn't read about it in the paper?"

"I don't bother with the paper. Don't watch TV, either. With my arthritis, I'm miserable enough; I don't need other humans' misery heaped on top of that."

"You're a wise man," I told him, and hurried back to where I'd left the Scout.

Glorietta Bay Marina sits at the top of the Silver Strand, catty-corner from the Victorian towers of the Hotel Del Coronado. It took me more than half an hour to get there from Point Loma, and when I drove into the parking lot, I spotted John leaning against his motorcycle. He waved and started toward me.

I pulled into a space and jumped out of the Scout. "What the *hell* are you doing here?"

"Nice way to greet somebody who's helping you out. While you were futzing around at the police department and Troy's place, I went over to State. Talked with his adviser. She says he dropped out after one semester."

"So how did that lead you here?"

"The adviser sails, and she sees him here off and on. He owns a boat, the *Windsong*."

"And I suppose you've already checked it out."

"No, but I did talk with the marina manager. He says he'll let us go aboard if you show him your credentials and the release from Bryce and Mari."

"Good work," I said grudgingly. "You know," I added as we started walking toward the manager's office, "it's odd that Troy would berth the boat here."

"Why?"

"He lived on Point Loma, not far from the Shelter Island yacht basin. Why would he want to drive all the way around the bay and across the Coronado Bridge when he could have berthed her within walking distance of his house?"

"No slips available over there? No, that can't be; I've heard the marinas're going hungry in this economy."

"Interesting, huh? And wait till you hear what else—" I stopped in my tracks and glared at him. "Dammit, you've done it again!"

"Done what? I didn't do anything! What did I do?"

"You know *exactly* what you've done."

John's smile was smug.

I sighed. "All right, other half of the 'detecting duo'— lead me to the manager."

My unwanted assistant and I walked along the outer pier toward the *Windsong*'s slip. The only sounds were the cries of seabirds and the rush of traffic on the strand. Our footsteps echoed on the aluminum walkways and set them to bucking on a slight swell. No one was around this Wednesday morning except for a pair of artists sketching near the office; the boats were buttoned up tightly, their sails furled in sea-blue covers. Troy Winslip's yawl was a big one, some thirty feet. I crossed the plank and stepped aboard; John followed.

"Wonder where he got his money," he said. "Bryce and Mari're well off, but not wealthy."

"I imagine he had his ways." I tried the companionway door and found it locked.

"What now?" my brother asked. "Standing around on deck isn't going to tell us anything."

"No." I felt through my bag and came up with my set of lock picks.

John's eyes widened. "Aren't those illegal?"

"Not strictly." I selected one with a serpentine tip and began probing the lock. "It's a misdemeanor to possess lock picks with intent to feloniously break and enter. However, since I intend to break and enter with permission from the deceased owner's next of kin, we're in kind of a gray area here."

John looked nervously over his shoulder. "I don't think cops recognize gray areas."

"For God's sake, do you see any cops?" I selected a more straight-tipped pick and resumed probing.

"Where'd you get those?" John asked.

"An informant of mine made them for me; he even etched my initials on the finger holds. Wiley 'the Pick' Pulaski. He's currently doing four-to-six for burglary."

"My little sister, consorting with known criminals."

"Well, Wiley wasn't exactly known when I was consorting with him. Good informants can't keep a high profile, you know." I turned the lock with a quick flick of my wrist. It yielded, and I removed the pick and opened the door. "After you, big brother."

The companionway opened into the main cabin—a compactly arranged space with a galley along the right bulkhead and a seating area along the left. I began a systematic search of the lockers but came up with nothing interesting. When I turned, I found John sitting at the navigator's station, studying the instruments.

"Big help you are," I told him. "Get up; you're blocking the door to the rear cabin."

He stood, and I squeezed around him and went inside. The rear cabin had none of the teak-and-brass accouterments of the main; in fact, it was mostly unfinished. The portholes were masked with heavy fabric, and the distinctive trapped odor of marijuana was enough to give me a contact high. I hadn't experienced its like since the dope-saturated seventies in Berkeley.

John, who cultivated a small crop in his backyard, smelled it, too. "So that's what pays the mortgage!"

"Uh-huh." My eyes were becoming accustomed to the gloom, but not fast enough. "You see a flashlight anyplace?"

He went away and came back with one. I flicked it on and shined it around. The cabin was tidy, the smell merely a residue of the marijuana that had been stored there, but crumbled bits of grass littered the floor. I handed John the flashlight, pulled an envelope from my bag, and scraped some of the waste matter into it. Then I moved forward, scrutinizing every surface. Toward the rear under the sharp cant of the bulkhead, I found a dusting of white powder. After I tasted it, I scraped it into a second envelope.

"Coke, too?" John asked.

"You got it."

"Mari and Bryce aren't going to like this. They thought he'd kicked his habit."

"He wasn't just feeding a habit here, John. Or dealing on a small scale. He was distributing, bringing it in on this boat in a major way."

"Yeah." He fell silent, staring grimly at the littered floor. "So what're you going to do—call the cops?"

"They'll have to know eventually, but not yet. The dealing in itself isn't important anymore; its bearing on Troy's murder is."

Back on Point Loma, I waited just out of sight of Troy Winslip's house in the Scout. John had wanted to come along and help me stake the place out, so in order to otherwise occupy him, I'd sent him off on what I considered a time-consuming errand. The afternoon waned. Behind me, the sky's blue deepened and the lowering sun grew brighter gold in contrast. Tall palms bordering the Winslip property cast long easterly shadows. At around six, a white Dodge van rounded the corner and pulled into Troy's driveway. A young woman—red-haired, willowy, clad in jeans and a black-and-white African print cape—jumped out and hurried into the house. By the time I got to the front door, she was already returning, arms full of clothing on hangers. She started when she saw me.

I had my identification and the release from Troy's parents ready. As I explained what I was after, the woman barely glanced at them. "All I want is my things," she said. "After I get them out of here, I don't care what the hell you do."

I followed her, picking up a purple silk tunic that had slipped from its hanger. "Please come inside. We'll talk. You lived with Troy; don't you care why he was killed?"

She laughed bitterly, tossed the armload of clothing into the back of the van, and took the tunic from my outstretched hand. "I care. But I also care about myself. I don't want to be around here any longer than necessary."

"You feel you're in danger?"

"I'd be a fool if I didn't." She pushed around me and hurried up the walk. "Those people don't mess around, you know."

I followed her. "What people?"

She rushed through the door, skidding on the polished marble of the foyer. A few suitcases and cartons were lined up at the foot of a curving staircase. "You want to talk?" the woman said. "We'll talk, but you'll have to help me with this stuff."

I nodded, picked up the nearest box, and followed her back to the van. "I know that Troy was dealing."

"Dealing?" She snorted. "He was supplying half the county. He and Daniel were taking the boat down to Baja three, four nights a week."

"Who's Daniel?"

"Daniel Pope, Troy's partner." She took the box from my hands, shoved it into the back of the van, and started up the walk. "Where can I find him?"

"His legit business is a surf shop on Coronado—

Danny P's."

"And the people who don't mess around—who are they?"

We were back in the foyer now. She thrust two suitcases at me. "Oh, no, you're not getting me involved in *that*."

"Look—what's your name?"

"I don't have to tell you." She hefted the last carton, took a final look around, and tossed her hair defiantly. "I'm out of here."

Once again, we were off at a trot toward the van. "You may be out of here," I said, "but you're still afraid. Let me help you."

She stowed the carton, took the suitcases from me, and shook her head. "Nobody can help me. It's only a matter of time. I know too much."

"Then share it—"

"No!" She slammed the van's side door, slipped quickly into the driver's seat, and locked the door behind her. For a moment, she sat with her head bowed, her hands on the wheel; then she relented and rolled down the window a few turns. "Why don't you go talk to Daniel? If he's not at the surf shop, he'll be at home; he's the only Pope on C Street in Coronado. Ask him . . ." She hesitated, looking around as if someone could hear her. "Ask him about Renny D."

"Ronny D?"

"No, Renny, with an e. It's short for Reynaldo." Quickly, she cranked up the window and started the van. I stepped back in time to keep from getting my toes squashed.

The woman had left the front door of the house open and the keys in the lock. For a moment, I considered searching the place, then concluded it was more important to talk to

Daniel Pope. I went back up the walk, closed the door, turned the dead bolt, and pocketed the keys for future use.

Daniel Pope wasn't at his surf shop, and he wasn't at his home on C Street. But John was waiting two houses down, perched on his cycle in the shade of a jacaranda tree.

I raised my eyes to the heavens and whispered to the Lord, "Please, not again!"

The Lord, who in recent years had been refusing to listen to my pleas, faded to eradicate my brother's presence.

I parked the Scout behind the cycle. John sauntered back and leaned on the open window beside me. "Daniel Pope owns a half interest in the *Windsong*," he said out of the corner of his mouth, eyes casing the house like an experienced thief.

I'd assigned him to check into the yawl's registry, but I hadn't expected him to come up with anything this quickly.

John went on, "He and Troy bought the boat two years ago for ninety thousand dollars cash from the yacht broker at Glorietta Bay. They took her out three or four times a week for about eight hours a stretch. In between, they partied. Men would come and go, carrying luggage. Some of the more conservative—read that 'bigoted'—slip holders complained that they were throwing 'fag parties.' "

"But we know they were holding sides meetings."

"Right."

"Where'd you get all that?"

"The yacht broker. I pretended I was interested in buying the *Windsong*. He's probably got the commission spent already. Shit, I feel really guilty about it."

A blue Mercedes was approaching. It went past us,

slowed, and turned into the driveway of the white Italianate house we'd been watching. I unbuckled my seat belt and said, "Ease your guilt by telling yourself that if you ever do buy a boat, you'll use that broker."

He ignored me, straightening and watching the car pull into an attached garage. "Daniel Pope?"

"Probably."

"So now what do we do?"

Thoughtfully, I looked him over. My brother is a former bar brawler and can be intimidating to those who don't know him for the pussycat he is. And at the moment, he was in exceptionally good shape. "We," I said, "are going in there and talk with Pope about somebody called Renny D."

Daniel Pope was suffering from a bad case of nerves. His bony, angular body twitched, and a severe tic marred his ruggedly handsome features. When we'd first come to the door, he'd tried to shut it in our faces; now that he was reasonably assured that we weren't going to kill him, he wanted a drink. John and I sat on the edge of a leather sofa in a living room filled with sophisticated sound equipment while he poured three fingers of single-malt Scotch. Then I began questioning him.

"Who's Renny D?"

"Where'd you get that name?"

"Who is he?"

"I don't have to talk about—"

"Look, Pope, we know all about the *Windsong* and your trips to Baja. And about the dealers who come to the yawl in between. The rear cabin is littered with grass and coke; I can have the police there in—"

"Jesus! I thought you were working for Troy's parents."

"I am, but Troy's dead, and they're more interested in finding out who killed him than in covering up your illegal activities."

"Oh, Jesus." He took a big drink of whiskey.

I repeated, "Who's Renny D?"

Silence.

"I'm not going to ask again." I moved my hand toward a phone on the table beside me. John grinned evilly at Pope.

"Don't! Don't do that! Christ, I'll . . . Renny Dominguez is the other big distributor around here. He didn't want Troy and me cutting into his territory."

"And?"

"That's it."

"No, its not." I moved my hand again. John did a fair imitation of a villain's leer. Maybe, I thought, he should have taken up acting.

"Okay, all right, it's not. I'll tell you, just leave the phone alone. At first, Troy and I tried to work something out with Renny D. Split the territory, cooperate, you know. He wasn't having any of that. Things've been getting pretty intense over the last few months: there was a fire at my store; somebody shot at Troy in front of his house; we both had phone threats."

"And then?"

"All of a sudden, Renny D decides he wants to make nice with us. So we meet with him at this bar where he hangs out in National City, and he proposes we work together, kick the business into really high gear. But now it's Troy who isn't having any of that."

"Why not?"

"Because Troy's convinced himself that Renny D is small-time and kind of stupid. He thinks we should kick *our* business into high gear and take over Renny's turf. I took him aside, tried to tell him that what he saw as small-time stupidity was only a matter of different styles. I mean, just because Renny D doesn't wear Reeboks or computerize his customer list doesn't mean he's an idiot. I tried to tell Troy that those people were dangerous, that you at least had to try to humor them. But did Troy listen? No way. He went back to the table and made Renny look bad in front of his *compadres,* and that's bad shit, man."

"So then what happened?"

More threats. Another drive-by. And that only made Troy more convinced that Renny and his pals were stupid, because they couldn't pick him off at twenty feet. Well, this kind of stuff goes on until it's getting ridiculous, and finally Renny issues a challenge: the two of them'll meet down in TJ near the bullring and settle it one-on-one, like honorable men."

"And Troy fell for that?"

"Sure. Like I said, he'd convinced himself Renny D was stupid, so he had me set it up with Renny's number two man, Jimmy. It was supposed to be just the four of us, and only Renny and Troy would fight."

"You didn't try to talk him out of it?"

"All the way down there, I did. But Troy—stubborn should've been his middle name."

"And what happened when you got there?"

"It was just the four of us, like Jimmy said. But what he didn't say was that he and Renny would have knives. The two of them moved damn fast, and before I knew what was happening, they'd stabbed Troy."

"What did you do?"

Pope looked away. Went to get himself another three fingers of Scotch.

"What did you do, Daniel?"

"I froze. And then I ran. Left Troy's damned car there, ran off, and spent half the night wandering, the other half hiding behind an auto body shop near the port of entry. The next morning, I walked back over the border like any innocent tourist."

"And now you think Renny and his friends'll come after you."

"I was a witness, it's only a matter of time."

That was what Troy's girlfriend had said, too. "Are you willing to tell your story to the police?"

Silence.

"Daniel?"

He ran his tongue over dry lips. After a moment, he said, "Shit, what've I got to lose? Look at me." He held out a shaky hand. "I'm a wreck, and it's all Troy's fault. He had fair warning of what was gonna go down. When I think of the way he ignored it, I want to kill him all over again."

"What fair warning?"

"Some message Renny D left on his answering machine. Troy thought it was funny. He said it was so melodramatic, it proved Renny was brain-damaged."

"Did he tell you what the message was?"

Daniel Pope shook his head. "He was gonna play it for me when we got back from TJ. He said you had to hear it to believe it."

The message was in a weird Spanish-accented falsetto, accompanied by cackling laughter: "Knives at midnight, Winslip. Knives at midnight."

I popped the tape from Troy's answering machine and turned to John. "Why the hell would he go down to TJ after hearing that? Did he think Renny D was joking?"

"Maybe. Or maybe he took along his own knife, but Renny and Jimmy were quicker. Remember, he thought they were stupid." He shook his head. "Troy was a dumb middle-class kid who got in over his head and let his own high opinion of himself warp his judgment. But he still sure as hell didn't deserve to die in a parking lot of seventeen stab wounds."

"No, he didn't." I turned the tape over in my hands. "Why do you suppose Renny D left the message? You'd think he'd have wanted the element of surprise on his side."

John shrugged. "To throw Troy off balance, make him nervous? Some twisted code of drug dealers' honor? Who knows?"

"This tape isn't the best of evidence, you know. There's no proof that it was Renny D who called."

"Isn't there?" He motioned at another machine that looked like a small video display terminal.

"What's that?"

"A little piece of new technology that allows you to see what number an incoming call was dialed from. It has a memory, keeps a record." He pressed a button, and a listing of numbers, dates, and times appeared. After scrolling through it, he pointed to one with a 295 prefix. "That matches the time and date stamp on the answering machine tape."

I lifted the receiver and dialed the number. A machine picked up on the third ring: "This is Renny D. Speak."

I hung up. "Now we've got proof."

"So do we go see Gary Viner?"

"Not just yet. First I think we'd better report to Mari and Bryce, ask them if they really want all of this to come out."

"I talked with them earlier; they were going to make the funeral arrangements and then have dinner with relatives. Maybe we shouldn't intrude."

"Probably not. Besides, there's something I want to do first."

"What?"

"Get a good look at this Renny D."

An old friend named Luis Abrego frequented the Tradewinds tavern in National City, halfway between San Diego and the border. The first time I'd gone there two years before, John had insisted on accompanying me for protection; tonight he insisted again. I didn't protest, since I knew he and Luis were fond of each other.

Fortunately, business was slow when we got there; only half a dozen Hispanic patrons stopped talking and stared when they saw two Anglos walk in. Luis hunched in his usual place at the end of the bar, nursing a beer and watching a basketball game on the fuzzy TV screen. When I spoke his name, he whirled, jumped off his stool, and took both my hands in his. His dark eyes danced with pleasure.

"*Amiga*," he said, "it's been much too long."

"Yes, it has, *amigo*."

Luis released me and shook John's hand. He was looking well. His mustache swooped bandit-fashion, and his hair hung free and shiny to his shoulders. From the nearly black shade of his skin, I could tell he'd been working steadily on construction sites these days. Late at night, however, Luis plied a very different and increasingly dangerous trade; "helping my people get where they need to go," was how he described those activities.

We sat down in a booth, and I explained about Renny D and Troy Winslip's murder. Luis nodded gravely. "The young man was a fool to underestimate Dominguez," he said. "I don't know him personally, but I've seen him and I hear he's one evil *hombre*."

"Do you know where he hangs out down here?"

"A bar two blocks over, called the Gato Gordo. You're not planning on going up against him, *amiga?*"

"No, nothing like that. I just want to get a look at him. Obviously, I can't go there alone. Will you take me?"

Luis frowned down into his beer. "Why do you feel you have to do this?"

"I like to know who I'm up against. Besides, this is going to be a difficult case to prove; maybe seeing Renny D in the flesh will inspire me to keep at it."

He looked up at my face, studied it for a moment, then nodded. "Okay, I'll do it. But he"—he pointed at John—"waits for us here."

John said, "No way."

"Yes," Luis told him firmly. "Here you're okay; every-body knows you're my friend. But there, a big Anglo, like you, we'd be asking for trouble. On the other hand, me and the *chiquita* here, we'll make a damn handsome couple."

94

. . .

Reynaldo Dominguez was tall and thin, with razor-sharp features that spoke of *indio* blood. There were tattoos of serpents on his arms and knife scars on his face, and part of one index finger was missing. He sat at a corner table in the Gato Gordo bar, surrounded by admirers. He leaned back indolently in his chair and laughed and joked and told stories. When Luis and I sat down nearby with our drinks, he glanced contemptuously at us; then he focused on Luis's face and evidently saw something there that warned him off. There was not a lot that Luis Abrego hadn't come up against in his life, and there was nothing and no one he feared. Renny D, I decided, was a good judge of character.

Luis leaned toward me, taking my hand as a lover would and speaking softly. "He is telling them how he single-handedly destroyed the Anglo opposition. He is laughing about the look on Winslip's face when he died, and at the way the other man ran. He is bragging about the cleverness of meeting them in TJ, where he has bribed the authorities and will never be charged with a crime." He paused, listened some more. "He is telling them how he will enjoy stalking and destroying the other man and Winslip's woman—bit by bit, before he finally puts the knife in."

I started to turn to look at Dominguez.

"Don't." Luis tightened his grip on my hand.

I looked anyway. My eyes met Renny D's. His were black, flat, emotionless—devoid of humanity. He stared at me, thin lip curling.

Luis's fingernails bit into my flesh. "Okay, you've had your look at him. Drink up, and we'll go."

I could feel those soulless eyes on my back. I tried to

finish my drink, but hatred for the creature behind me welled up and threatened to make me choke. Troy Winslip had in many respects been a useless person, but he'd also been young and naive and hadn't deserved to die. Nor did Daniel Pope or Troy's woman deserve to live, and perhaps die, in terror.

Luis said softly, "Now he is bragging again. He is telling them he is above the law. No one can touch him, he says. Renny D is invincible."

"Maybe not."

"Let's go now, *amiga.*

As we stood, I looked at Dominguez once more. This time, when our eyes met a shadow passed over his. What was that about? I wondered. Not suspicion. Not fear. What?

Of course—Renny D was puzzled. Puzzled because I didn't shy away from his stare. Puzzled and somewhat uneasy.

Well, good.

I said to Luis, "We'll see who's invincible."

I'd expected the Winslips to pose an obstacle to bringing Renny D to justice, but they proved to be made of very strong stuff. The important thing, they said, was not to cover up their son's misdeeds but to ensure that a vicious murderer didn't go free to repeat his crime. So, with their blessing, I took my evidence downtown to Gary Viner.

And Gary told me what I'd been fearing all along: "We don't have a case."

"Gary, there's the tape. Dominguez as good as told Winslip he was going to stab him. There's the record of where the call originated. There's the eyewitness testimony of Daniel Pope—"

"There's the fact that the actual crime occurred on Mexican soil. And that Dominguez has the police down there in his hip pocket. No case, McCone."

"So what're you going to do—sit back and wait till he kills Pope and Winslip's woman, or somebody else?"

"We'll keep an eye on Dominguez. That's all I can promise you. Otherwise, my hands're tied."

"Maybe *your* hands are tied."

"What's that supposed to mean? What're you going to do? Don't give me any trouble, McCone—please."

"Don't worry. I'm going to go off and think about this, that's all. When I do give you something, I guarantee it won't be trouble."

When I'm upset or need to concentrate, I often head for water, so I drove north to Torrey Pines State Beach and walked by the surf for an hour. Something was nagging at the back of my mind, but I couldn't bring it forward. Something I'd read or heard somewhere. Something . . .

Knives at midnight, Winslip. Knives at midnight.

Renny D's high-pitched, cackling voice on the answering machine tape kept playing and replaying for me.

After a while, I decided to do some research and drove to Adams Avenue to find a used book shop with a large legal section.

Crimes against the person: homicide. Express and implied malice . . . burden of proving mitigation—no.

Second degree . . . penalty for person previously convicted—no.

Manslaughter committed during operation of a vessel—certainly not.

Death of victim within three years and a day—forget it.

What the hell was I combing the penal code for, anyway? Mayhem? Hardly. Kidnapping? No, Troy went willingly, even eagerly. Conspiracy? Maybe. No, the situation's too vague. Nothing there for me.

Knives at midnight, Winslip. Knives at midnight.

Can't get it out of my head. Keep trying to connect it with something. Melodramatic words, as Troy told Pope. A little old-fashioned, as if Dominguez was challenging him to a—

That's it! Duels. Duels and challenges. Penal code, 225.

Defined: Combat with deadly weapons, fought between two or more persons, by previous agreement . . .

Punishment when death ensues: state prison for two, three, or four years.

Not much, but better than nothing.

I remember reading this now, one time when I was browsing through statutes that had been on the books for a long time. It's as enforceable today as it was then in 1872. Especially section 231; that's the part I really like.

Gotcha, Renny D.

"I'll read it to you again," I said to Gary Viner. He was leaning toward me across his desk, trying to absorb the impact of the dry, formal text from 1872.

" 'Dueling beyond State. Every person who leaves this State with intent to evade any provisions of this chapter, and to commit any act out of the State as is prohibited by this chapter, and who does any act, although out of this State, which would be punishable by such provisions if committed within this State, is punishable in the same manner as he would have been *in case such act had been committed within this State.'*

"And there you have it." I closed the heavy tome with an emphatic thump.

Gary nodded. "And there we have it."

I began ticking off items on my fingers. "A taped challenge to a duel at knife point. A probable voiceprint match with the suspect. A record of where the call was made from. An eyewitness who, in order to save his own sorry hide, will swear that it actually *was* a duel. And, finally, a death that resulted from it. Renny D goes away for two, three, or four years in state prison."

"It's not much time. I'm not sure the DA'll think it's worth the trouble of prosecuting him."

"I remember the DA from high school. He'll be happy with anything that'll get a slimeball off the streets for a while. Besides, maybe we'll get lucky and somebody'll challenge Renny D to a duel in prison."

Gary nodded thoughtfully. "I remember our DA from high school, too. Successfully prosecuting a high-profile case like this would provide the kind of limelight he likes— and it's an election year."

By the time my return flight to San Francisco left on Saturday, the DA had embraced the 1872 statute on duels and challenges with a missionarylike zeal and planned to take the Winslip case to the grand jury. Daniel Pope would be on hand to give convincing testimony about traveling to Tijuana primed for hand-to-hand combat with Dominguez and his cohort. Renny D was as yet unsuspecting but would

99

soon be behind bars.

And at a Friday-night dinner party, the other half of the "detecting duo" had regaled the San Diego branch of the McCone family with his highly colored version of our exploits.

I accepted a cup of coffee from the flight attendant and settled back in the seat with my beat-up copy of *Standard California Codes*. I had a more current one on the shelf in my office, but somehow I couldn't bring myself to part with this one. Besides, I needed something to read on the hour-and-a-half flight.

Disguised Firearms or Other Deadly Weapons. Interesting.

Lipstick Case Knife. Oh, them deadly dames, as they used to say.

Shobi-zue: a staff, crutch, stick, rod, or pole with a knife enclosed. Well, if I ever break a leg . . .

Writing Pen Knife. That's a good one. Proves the pen can be mightier than the sword.

But wait now, here's one that's *really* fascinating . . .

Justice

STUART M. KAMINSKY

A woman had been brutally murdered. She was the Baroness Anastasia Volodov-Kronof.

The baroness was a woman of great wealth and social power who threw an annual celebration with wine, wild fowl, and an assortment of cakes in the park near the New Hermitage. All were invited. The tradition had begun eight years ago when her husband died. The celebration on the anniversary of the baron's death was considered to be either a sign of respect for a loyal officer of Tsar Nicholas or a sign of relief that the widow was finally free of an abusive martinet. She had married the baron when she was a girl of fourteen and he an officer of thirty years.

Her death did not sit well with the populace of St. Petersburg in 1862. She was a benefactor, an emulator of the aristocracy of France which had repeatedly rejected her. Her husband was an official hero of the state. Though she lived like a grand dame of western Europe, holding salons for young artists, she, in quite general but sincere terms, espoused the causes of justice, freedom for all, and an eventual abolition of some of the more unjust practices of the aristocracy.

It was said that Tsar Alexander himself invited the baroness to all palace parties and looked upon her with favor.

Accused of her violent murder was a young man she had taken under her broad wing, into her ample bosom, and

101

under the silk sheets of her French bed.

The thin young man of twenty-five was one of the new breed, the ones with long hair, mustaches, black coats, and words of nonsense uttered about the rights of serfs. He was the grandson of a Decembrist, one of the officers who had staged a revolt against Tsar Nicholas. His grandfather, Peotor Marlovov, had returned to St. Petersburg from Siberia five years earlier under pardon from the tsar.

The thin young man, flanked by two soldiers and a strange-looking little man, paused in front of the Bronze Horseman inspired by a poem of Pushkin and commissioned by Catherine the Great in 1768. At the base of the statue is the inscription: "To Peter the First, Catherine the Second, 1782."

The young man, whose name was Vladimir but who called himself Louis, looked up at the idealized Peter, wearing a laurel crown and flowing robe, astride a rearing bronze horse, and shook his head.

The quartet was standing in Senate Square directly across the Neva River. Almost forty years earlier, Louis's grandfather, a young army officer, and three thousand rebel soldiers joined by a significant portion of the educated and the elite of St. Petersburg, had crossed the pontoon bridge to the Square and challenged the new emperor Nicholas, claiming that his brother Konstantin was the rightful heir and ignoring the fact that Konstantin had no desire to rule and welcomed the crowning of his brother.

But the confusion led to the revolt of the three thousand, many of whom were veterans of the Napoleonic Wars, who came demanding reforms. It was no mere rabble. Their leaders, inspired by the American and French revolutions, demanded a republic, an end to the monarchy. It was a revolt of the heart and the heat of democracy. It was also a revolt badly planned by its five leaders. They failed to capture Nicholas and gave him plenty of time to summon loyal troops while the Decembrists continued to shout their demands and talk to designated nobles who had been volunteered by the tsar. The rebels fought, repelled a cavalry charge, and were then cut down by cannon fire. The honor of ordering the cannon fire had gone to the husband of the widow Baroness Anastasia Volodov-Kronof.

The five leaders of the revolt—Pavel Pestel, Petr Kahhovsky, Kondraty Ryleev, Sevei Muravev-Apostol, and Michail Bestuzhev-Riumin—were all hanged. Hundreds of others, including Louis's grandfather, had been exiled to hard labor in Siberia.

For the remaining thirty years of his reign, Russia was ruled by Nicholas with iron hoof, cannon, rifle, and little tolerance for dissent. And no place felt the heel of the boot more heavily than St. Petersburg, the home of the tsars.

But, in 1856, with the death of Nicholas, the few Decembrist survivors were allowed to return. Louis had grown up in a cabin in the Siberian town of Irkutsk, where his father and mother had died. Only Louis's grandfather, who before the failed revolt had led a famous charge against a Napoleonic attack, had survived, bent, cynical, but not broken.

Alexander II would have been happy to maintain his father's reign of terror, but the issue of freeing the serfs lingered in heated debate. How much land would free serfs get, if any? From where would this land come? Could Russia survive with a confused mass of noble landowners and freed serfs who had no idea of how to survive without a centuries old structure? The solution was to create the *mir* or village compound to which the former serfs were bound. This in turn led to collective farms and turned some of them into simple *kolkhoznik,* collective farmers who were not better off than their fathers had been. Now, instead of working for a possibly benevolent noble, they worked for *kulaks,* farmers who had worked their way up, buying land, bribing, being smarter than their fellow former serfs, working hard and being lucky.

But there were other reforms that worked a bit better. Before the reign of Alexander II, stupid, corrupt clerks administered the law. Cases could drag on for years. Papers piled up with reports unread. Judges would usually make their decisions based on whatever part of the pile of papers they chose to read. Laws were vague and uncertain. Bribes to judges were the rule. There were few lawyers, only middlemen who identified those to be bribed and passed on the negotiated amount.

In 1856, this began to change. Courts with real judges and trials by juries were instituted. Lawyers began to appear ready to argue for precedent, mercy, and the law, but justice was far from served. Jury members—storekeepers, *kulaks*—could attack defendants for their political beliefs. Judges could bestow mercy on the clearly guilty simply because the accused came from a good family. In short, a defendant, regardless of the evidence, had no idea what his or her fate might be and for what reasons.

Working within this system was the slightly grotesque little man who stood next to Louis Dandorov. The two were a remarkable contrast. Louis, in spite of or because of his youth in Siberia, stood tall, thin, erect, and handsomely confident, with his hair cut stylishly long in the French manner. If any look dominated his face, it was superiority.

He had built a career as a poet patronized by the wealthy widow of whose murder he was accused, the Baroness Anastasia, whose husband had been given the honor of ordering the first cannon fire at the Decembrists. The irony had not escaped the young man.

The little man at his side was another matter altogether. He had great difficulty keeping up with the long-striding prisoner and the brightly uniformed guards.

His name was Porfiry Petrovich, well dressed, about forty, fat and clean-shaven. His hair was short, and he had a large, round head which was unusually bulbous in the back. His soft, round, snub-nosed face was yellowish in color as if he had seldom ventured out into the daylight. He wore a perpetual knowing smile as if he kept a secret which he might someday share with you. There was something decidedly feminine about the little man, except for his eyes below white lashes, moist eyes that were quite serious. He was a prosecuting court lawyer, an investigator who did his best to resolve cases before they reached the court. He definitely did not make a good impression on judges or juries. if by chance it was actually necessary, as it seemed to be today, he appeared with his fellow lawyer Fredkin, who looked like a weary ancient saint, a man whose presence almost demanded respect. One problem was that Fredkin was a fool. It was Porfiry Petrovich's good fortune that Fredkin was well aware of his deficiencies, was bewildered by the madness of trials, and gladly deferred to Porfiry Petrovich's advice.

Another problem was that Fredkin was home ill.

"If we were to walk a bit slower," said Porfiry Petrovich, trying to keep up, "I would not breathe so heavily, and we could talk."

It was summer, warm, the trees were blocking a view of the Admiralty facade.

Louis preened his mustache, shrugged slightly, and glanced down at the ridiculous little man. He and the two armed guards slowed just a bit.

"Thank you," said Porfiry Petrovich, producing a large handkerchief and mopping his brow. "May we sit briefly?"

Louis sighed with annoyance and looked at the two guards, one of whom looked at the little lawyer and nodded Louis strode to a concrete balustrade and sat. The lawyer sat at his side. The soldiers stood.

One of the soldiers said, "Ten minutes. No more. We'll be in trouble if we don't deliver him for trial on time."

Meaning the wooden benches were packed to see the man who had murdered the popular Baroness Volodov-Kronof.

"You have not confessed to the murder," said Porfiry Petrovich, turning his large eyes on the handsome young poet. "You have refused to talk to a lawyer. You refuse to admit your guilt. You refuse to proclaim your innocence. You should be easy to convict and hang. Judge Valorov, at his own request, has been assigned to this case. He was a personal friend of the baroness. He holds a long-standing grudge against the Decembrists and their survivors. He has no fondness for European dilettantes."

"Is that what you take me for?" asked the young man with a sigh.

"It is what the judge and jury will take you for," said Por-

106

firy Petrovich. "And, I must confess, it is what you appear to be."

"You have read my poetry?" asked the young man, crossing his legs.

"Some. The thin book published by the baroness."

"And?" asked the young man.

"You are more interested in the review of your work by a lawyer than in possibly saving your life?"

"Your assessment of my work?" the young man repeated.

"Self-indulgent. Mediocre. Unoriginal. Insincere," said Pod" Petrovich. "But what do I know? I'm a lawyer, not a critic of poetry."

"Went to the theater," the young man said, looking toward the river. "The play was about the Russian fool Filatka. Laughed a lot. They had a vaudeville show as well, full of amusing verse lampooning lawyers, so outspoken that I wondered how it got past the censor. Civil servants are such swine . . . you won't catch clods like them going to the theater, not even if they're given free tickets."

"Gogol, *The Diary of a Madman*," said Porfiry Petrovich, "but you left out merchants and newspapermen who criticize everything."

The young man looked at the little man beside him with a new respect. "You do read?"

"Fluently," said Porfiry Petrovich. "And I help send people to prison and occasionally help them if they are innocent. Are you innocent of this murder, Vladimir Dandorov?"

"I am innocent of the murder," the young man said with little interest. "And I prefer to be called Louis."

"More French," said Porfiry Petrovich.

"Five more minutes," said one of the guards.

A warm wind blew down the corridor of buildings.

"I must tell you that you will be a terrible defendant," said the little man. "Arrogant. Superior. Unafraid."

"And innocent," Dandorov said.

"That is of little importance," said Porfiry Petrovich.

"They mean to kill me," said Dandorov with a shrug. "There is little I can do."

The little man stood and began to pace slowly in front of the young man, who appeared slightly amused.

"I have asked for a continuance of the trial." Porfiry Petrovich said. "The murder happened only two days ago, and you have refused to speak to a policeman or a lawyer."

"Your request for a continuance has been denied," said Dandorov, "as we can plainly see from the fact that I am soon to face a jury and judge who will convict me in rather short order."

Porfiry Petrovich wished they were in his curtained office with the big desk. A little intimidation and time to break down the suspect were his strengths, not hurried talks in the square with third-rate poets who were decidedly unlikable."

"Facts," said the little lawyer. "On the morning of July 3, three days ago, there was a scream in the apartment of the baroness. It was heard by a maid who came running into the lady's chamber, where you stood nude over her equally naked body on the bed. In your hand was a knife covered in blood."

"Rather damning evidence," admitted Dandorov.

"But you did not commit the murder?"

"I did not. I was in the washroom undressing and bathing.

108

I had to pay frequent dues in the form of sex with the baroness in return for her patronage. A duty for which I should be given a round of standing applause and admiration. The baroness, as you know, was well past sixty, with a tendency toward too much make up, though she was certainly presentable. When I came out of the washroom I saw her on the bed, a knife at her side. I realized she must have been murdered when I was bathing. I picked up the knife for possible protection from the killer. And then the maid came in."

"If she was dead," said Porfiry Petrovich, "how could she have let out the scream that brought the maid rushing in?"

The sigh this time was enormous.

"It is was not she who screamed," said Dandorov. "It was me. I screamed when I saw the body. Now you may add cowardice to the other traits of which you will accuse me."

"How long were you in the washroom?" asked Porfiry Petrovich.

"Ten minutes, perhaps more, as long as I could prolong it and put off my duty to my patroness," said Dandorov.

"Is there any other way in or out of the bedroom besides through the door the maid entered when she heard the scream?"

"A door to the balcony," said the young man. "Three flights up. Another door to the corridor leading to the rear of the apartment, the kitchen."

"How many servants were present when the murder occurred?" asked Porfiry Petrovich.

"Surely you must know that?"

"Humor me."

"Just the maid," he said.

"Could she have killed the baroness, gone out, in the parlor, and rushed back in when she heard your scream?"

Dandorov began to laugh. "I can see her now," he said, "brought before the judge and jury, a frightened, skinny little dolt, half the size of the cow I bedded. The idea is ridiculous."

"Do you know who else has apartments in the building where your . . . patroness was murdered?"

Again Dandorov shrugged. "Five others. Each floor was a complete suite. I met none of the other tenants other than to exchange nods. I didn't wish to. Anastasia did not wish me to."

"Odd," said Porfiry Petrovich, rubbing his forehead. "I would have thought that since she had paid for you, she would want to show you off to everyone."

"We had readings in her parlor. Her friends attended."

"But none of her neighbors?"

Louis shrugged again. "Who knows? They were all much the same. Eating what they could get, drinking what they could reach. Applauding graciously to my garbage poetry rendered palatable only by my intentionally haughty and defiant readings, which I kept mercifully brief for which those assembled were properly grateful."

"So," said Porfiry Petrovich, "who murdered the baroness?"

"Who knows?" said Louis. "I am going to be hanged for it."

"Have you not noted one thing particularly odd about what is taking place in this trial?"

"Injustice," said Dandorov.

"That is not the least bit odd," said Porfiry Petrovich. "I

have come to a conclusion about you, Vladimir Dandorov. Would you like to hear it?"

"Not particularly."

"Indulge me," Porfiry Petrovich said, now wiping his sweating face with a wrinkled handkerchief. "You have sufficient good sense to know that you have limited intelligence. You also have a mirror to show you that you have good looks. You present a dignity and superiority you believe you have earned by your loyalty to the baroness. You expect that you will be convicted whatever you do, and you choose to die with dignity. It is the one thing about you I respect."

"I certainly live for your respect," said Dandorov sarcastically.

"We must go," said one of the guards.

"I may yet save your life in spite of you," said Porfiry Petrovich.

Dandorov now stood, towering over the little man. The guards flanked the young man and began to lead him off in the direction of the court. Porfiry Petrovich did not join them. He did not move. He reached into his pocket for a list he had written the day before. He had spoken to four of the five people on his list and learned much. He was about to speak to the last person on the list, and he was well aware that the discussion might end his career and send him back to his family's carpet business.

The little lawyer took five minutes to get to the court and was drenched in sweat when he arrived. His white suit was now patched in dark, uneven spots.

The clerk, a tall young man, frowned at Porfiry Petrovich's request to see the judge a few minutes prior to an

111

important case, but Porfiry Petrovich Pleaded the importance of his visit and promised that it was urgent and would take only minutes.

The tall young man disappeared through a door and returned within a minute to usher Porfiry Petrovich into the large office. The tall man left, closing the door behind him. The judge's chamber was a large office, much larger than Porfiry Petrovich's office across the river.

Judge Valorov, tall, robust, an imposing man in his sixties with his trademarked pure white flowing hair, stood at a mirror in the massive office adjusting his robe. Judge Valorov was reported to be a personal friend of the tsar himself, a friend who had been largely responsible for the court reforms Tsar Alexander had ordered.

Satisfied, Valorov turned to face the perspiring little lawyer across the large room dominated by a massive desk.

"I have seen you before," Valorov said in a deep voice, moving to the chair behind his desk.

"I am an investigating lawyer in the prosecutor's office," said Porfiry Petrovich.

"Ah," said Valorov. "I see. You are trying the case?"

"Yes," said Porfiry Petrovich.

"Please, sit," said Valorov. "You look very . . ."

"Tired, frightened, and a bit confused," said the pale little man as he took a seat in a large, dark wooden chair across from the judge.

"What confuses you? What frightens you? Your case is simple, clear. You call the maid. She testifies. Dandorov testifies. The jury finds him guilty, and I sentence him to death. He murdered a much beloved member of the city of St. Petersburg. The tsar himself has a great interest in the case."

"I have four additional witnesses," said Porfiry Petrovich, pulling out his now moist list. "Two have refused to appear. The others will be in court. I am awaiting the delivery of papers of appearance for the two who have refused to appear. Which means I will need a bit more time."

Valorov turned in his chair and looked out his windows at the three-story yellow Menshikov Palace directly across the river from the Senate. The modest palace had been built by Aleksandr Menshikov, who began as a stable boy and became the best friend of Peter the Great and eventually the second most powerful man in all of Russia. The building was constructed in 1710, the first stone palace in a city of cathedrals and palaces.

"Do you know why I like that view?" Valorov said actually pointing to the window.

"It is a historic and beautiful landmark," said Porfiry Petrovich.

"I was a stable boy like Menshikov," said Valorov. "Did you know that?"

"Yes, I know that, and your service to the tsar. Your accomplishments and history are well known."

Valorov adjusted his robe and turned to Porfiry Petrovich, folding his large hands on his massive desk.

"One of my services to the tsar is to make the judicial system function honestly and with dispatch. You understand this? It is your job to facilitate this. We are far from achieving what they have in England or even France and America. It is not the system at fault. It is the people we must rely upon to dispense justice, the jurors inclined to make decisions based on whether they like or dislike the face or politics of the defendant rather than on the evidence.

Do you understand where I am taking you with this?"

"I think so," said Porfiry Petrovich uncomfortably. "You would like me to withdraw my request to call the four witnesses."

Valorov nodded and said, "Unless you can convince me in the few minutes left before the scheduled trial why I should do this?"

"Because," said Porfiry Petrovich, "I believe Vladimir Dandorov is innocent of the murder of the Baroness Volodov-Kronof."

The judge shook his head and let out a low rush of air. "Go on," he said.

"I have interviewed four of the five other tenants in the apartment building where the Baroness lived," said Porfiry Petrovich. "They all confirm, with various degrees of reluctance, that the baroness had a relationship, a very long-standing relationship, with the fifth tenant of the building."

The judge looked at the strange figure across the desk and waited. "They have all identified the same man, the fifth tenant, you, Judge Valorov."

Valorov looked up at the ceiling and turned his eyes fully on the little man before him.

"You know you are quite mad," he said.

"I might never have questioned the other tenants, never learned you lived in the apartment, but for one thing," said Porfiry Petrovich, who was now sweating profusely.

"Which was?" asked Valorov.

"You requested to preside over this case," said Porfiry Petrovich. "You are an important man. This is, by all appearances, an open-and-closed case. Why bother?"

"Because, as you have discovered, the baroness was my

114

friend, and I want to ensure that justice is done."

"I examined the rooms of the baroness and found that by going out of the corridor outside her room, one could get to the kitchen and through another door that leads to a stairway that passes each of the apartments in the building."

"I am well aware of that," said Valorov.

"What you are not aware of," said Porfiry Petrovich, moving in his chair to free his pants slightly from between his legs, "is that after the other tenants told me about your friendship with the baroness, I examined your apartment while you were in court yesterday. I did so by obtaining the proper papers of suspicion without mentioning your name. Do you know what I found?"

Valorov was silent, hands still folded before him.

"A key to the kitchen door to the apartment of the baroness and a pair of very fine Japanese silk pajamas which had been recently washed but were clearly stained with blood."

"I cut myself," said Valorov.

"May I see the cut?" asked Porfiry Petrovich. "It must be substantial."

"No, you may not. It is on my left thigh, and I have no intention of taking off my trousers to humor you."

"The four tenants will testify that you and the baroness had a relationship and that you were jealous of her protégés, particularly of Vladimir Dandorov."

"Nonsense," said Valorov. "You are very creative but totally wrong."

"Then we must believe that Dandorov undressed as did the baroness, that they had a fight, and that Dandorov went naked to the kitchen to get a knife and kill her. She was his golden goose. Why would he kill her?"

"Why would I kill her?" asked Valorov.

"My guess is that you intended to marry her," he said. "She had a substantial fortune. After years of working on that project, she told you that she planned to marry Dandorov. You lost your temper and killed her."

Valorov shook his head again and said, "I loved her."

"For what it is worth," said Porfiry Petrovich, "I think I believe you."

"You do not have sufficient evidence to convince the jury," said Valorov.

"It is my understanding that it is for the jury to decide. That is the system you have helped to develop. I present the four witnesses, the key, the stained silk pajamas, evidence of your jealousy and long-standing relationship to the baroness and your request to try the case."

"You'll never convince them."

"I? No, I know what I look like, how I appear, but I have a colleague who is most convincing."

"Who, Petrovich?" Valorov said, suddenly standing. "You are supposed to prosecute the accused, not save them."

"I thought our duty was to see justice done," the little man said.

"It is," said Valorov.

"You asked me who my convincing colleague would be. It is you, Judge Valorov," said Porfiry Petrovich. "It is also your duty to see justice done."

Valorov shook his large head, his serious craggy face twisting into a pained smile.

"You are a good judge," Porfiry Petrovich said. "Your

work is valuable. Dandorov is a parasite who took advantage of a vain woman."

"A vain, tender, and handsome old woman," Valorov amended.

Porfiry Petrovich shook his head to acknowledge that he had been corrected. "However, the fact remains . . ." the little man began.

". . . that Dandorov is innocent of murder," the judge said. "Then," said the judge, "we are on the same side."

"It would appear so," said Porfiry Petrovich, wiping the back of his bulbous neck with an already quite moist handkerchief.

"I have the power to drag you out of here and accuse you of treason, of falsifying evidence and witnesses because of your Decembrist sympathies," said Valorov, meeting the lawyer's eyes.

It was Porfiry Petrovich who turned away. "That is my fear," he said.

"Or," the judge went on, "I can try to find a way out of this. There are reasons I am a judge."

"That, I confess, is my hope."

"I did have a key to the servant's entrance to the apartment of the baroness," said Valorov with a deep sigh as he looked up at a painting of the tsar on the wall. The man in military uniform on the wall glared out with confidence and superiority. "We did not think it proper for my position to be in an open relationship with a woman of questionable actions and morals. This was her decision, not my own. On the night of her death, I went up to her apartment thinking that since it was Tuesday, all but one servant, the parlor maid, would be out. It was common practice. I wanted to try to talk her out of her increasingly serious and laughable relationship with Dandorov. I was in my pajamas, silk pajamas as you have noted, a gift from her. I think she liked the idea of having an important judge as a lover. When I arrived in her room, she was undressed. I heard water running in the bath and a male voice humming. She told me to hurry up and leave, shooed me out like a servant. I tried to argue. She would have none of it, wanted me out before Dandorov came into the room and found me. I left, stopping by impulse in the kitchen to pick up a knife. I returned to her room, determined to kill Dandorov. He was still not out of the bath. Anastasia saw the knife and knew my intent. She stepped in front of me. I tried to push her gently away. We grappled for the knife. And then . . ."

"She was dead," said Porfiry Petrovich. Again the judge nodded.

"The door to the bath began to open. I dropped the knife and ran."

"And here we sit," said Porfiry Petrovich.

There was a knock at the door. At first, both men ignored it. And then there was another knock, a more insistent knock, and a woman's voice saying, "Judge Valorov. The court is full. The defendant is being held in the chamber. The jury grows restless."

"Coming," said Valorov, rising slowly.

Porfiry Petrovich also rose and waited while the judge walked to the door, where he turned to face the lawyer, who reminded him rather of a slightly bloated fish. "Justice will be done," said Valorov.

Porfiry Petrovich said nothing. The door closed, and the lawyer slumped back in his chair, trying to control his trembling. His career, perhaps his very life was at stake, and he had been unable to keep from speaking.

And now it was worse. Valorov seemed an honest, honorable man. They could both suffer and Dandorov walk free if . . . and it was an enormous if, if the judge confessed or found a way out.

Porfiry Petrovich arrived late at the chamber where the trial was being held. The police officer at the door recognized him and let him push past a crowd of angry people, mostly women, who pressed forward in the hope of sneaking into the already crowded courtroom.

The judge was seated, and the court full of people struck Porfiry Petrovich in two ways. First, they were unusually quiet, probably having been given fair warning by the judge. Second, the stench of the room was almost unbearable. A dominant smell was tobacco, but there was more than the tincture of cheap alcohol and partly digested food. However, the most powerful smell of all was that of human bodies forced into a space intended for fewer than half of those in the room.

Porfiry Petrovich worked his way forward to the small table where Dandorov sat alone, back straight, hands folded, looking not only at the crowd behind him but at the jury on his right with open contempt.

A portrait of the tsar hung over the head of the judge, who sat behind a table only slightly elevated on a platform. For no reason that anyone had explained to Porfiry Petrovich, the jury consisted of seven men, all of whom looked at Dandorov with, at best, hostility. A few of the jurors were talking to each other. There was no rail between the jury and the court, just a row of wooden chairs for them to sit on.

"There is a table for the prosecution," Dandorov said, nodding to an identical table closer to the jury.

"I prefer to sit here if you do not object," said Porfiry Petrovich, pulling out his notes and looking around the room to see if his two witnesses were present. They were. The other tenants of the apartment building where the baroness was murdered sat apart at a witness table. They were all far better dressed than the jury and infinitely better dressed than the spectators.

"I do object," said Dandorov.

Porfiry Petrovich gathered his notes and moved to the other table.

The bailiff, a former sergeant in the tsar's guard, stepped out in dark suit and overstarched collar.

"The court of the First District of St. Petersburg, by order of Tsar Alexander II and in accordance with the law passed down to us by Peter the Great who founded this city, this court, and this nation, will now sit in judgment of Vladimir Dandorov."

Dandorov immediately rose and in the heat of the small courtroom said, "I demand to be called by the name I have chosen, Louis, Louis Dandorov."

The bailiff, having no precedent for such a request, turned to the judge, who said, "Your request will be granted, but all documents will bear both the name Louis and that of Vladimir."

Dandorov had already alienated the court by insisting on being referred to by a non-Russian name. A rustle of disapproval crackled through the court.

"Is the city of St. Petersburg prepared to present a case?" asked the judge.

"Well . . . yes," said Porfiry Petrovich. "Though I do not normally try cases before. . . ."

"Representing the accused?" asked the judge.

"I need no representation," said Dandorov. "I have committed no crime."

The crackling of the crowd and jury rose, and the judge roared over them that they would remain quiet or face armed expulsion. The crowd grew quiet. A fat man on the jury, his face red, his hair white, rose and demanded of Dandorov, "How do you earn a living?"

"Off of foolish old women," the young man said.

Clear anger on the part of the jury. The crowd did its best to remain quiet.

Porfiry Petrovich was almost overcome by the stench.

"Your views on the land reforms," said another jury member, so thin that he looked tubercular.

"A fraud," said Dandorov. "You give serfs land, and they beg to continue to work for landowners. You insist that they work their own land and sell their own goods, and they destroy the economy."

"And what of the sins of the church?" Another juror stood screaming and looking at the crowd for approval.

"What," said Dandorov, "does any of this have to do with whether or not I murdered Anastasia?"

"It speaks to the kind of person you are," said the judge. His voice almost broke, but Porfiry Petrovich was certain he was the only one who had noticed.

"I'll answer no more such questions," said Dandorov, looking directly at the jury. "I'll answer only questions about the crime."

"Treason is a crime," said the fat juror.

"But not one of which I stand accused," said Dandorov. Porfiry Petrovich stood and waved meekly toward the judge, who acknowledged him. The court was now dead silent, looking at the grotesque creature at the prosecutor's table.

"Louis Dandorov," he said, "did you murder the Baroness Anastasia Volodov-Kronof?"

"No," said Dandorov.

"But you were having a dirty affair with a woman old enough to be your mother. Hell, your grandmother," shouted someone in the courtroom.

"That is not why I am on trial," said Dandorov.

"What was your relationship to the dead woman?" asked Porfiry Petrovich, looking at the judge, who was deep in thought.

"She was my patroness," said Dandorov. "I, in turn, allowed her to show me off, and I shared her bed from time to time. I got by far the better of the bargain."

The jury was irate.

"Bloodsucker!" shouted one juror.

"Liar!" shouted another.

The judges gavel, a gift from his cousin a genuine French gavel, came down hard on the table. The court went silent as Valorov rose. He had something to say. They wished to listen.

"There are facts about this case which have not yet been brought to light," said Valorov, steadying himself with his huge hands on the top of the table. "This man. . . ."

". . . is guilty," finished Dandorov.

The court went mad. Armed soldiers filed in, ordering the audience to sit and be quiet. One young soldier in full neat uniform leveled his rifle at the fat juror, who sat back, mouth open, stunned.

"You said earlier you were innocent," Porfiry Petrovich said.

"There is no way this court will hear me or find me innocent," said Dandorov. "I will be humiliated, demeaned, and then found guilty and hanged. Better to end it now and go with some dignity. She is dead. It is she who was the greater parasite, though she never treated me anything but decently. I see no reason for her lifestyle and indiscretions to be printed in cheap newspapers and on the tongues of oafs like all of you."

Had the soldiers not been there, Porfiry Petrovich was certain the crowd, led by the jury, would have rushed the confessed killer and torn him apart.

"The only thing that would save me at this point would be if the tsar himself or the judge were to confess to the crime," said Dandorov.

"It is not the privilege of the accused in this court to tell it what should and should not be said and how it should proceed," said Valorov, his voice booming off the walls.

In the row behind Porfiry Petrovich, someone belched ripe fish.

"The prosecution will present its case," said Valorov, looking at Porfiry Petrovich. "Regardless of who is harmed, what is brought to light. There will be justice, and you, Louis Dandorov, will not be given the release of martyrdom. That must be earned."

The meaning of this was clear to only two people in the room. The rest sat baffled.

"Make your case, prosecutor," said the judge, sitting.

"Present your evidence, call your witnesses, and put in the witness chair any of whatever rank or station."

There were several problems. First, Porfiry Petrovich was a weak figure, a near caricature who could circle his quarry, wear him down, confuse him. He spoke quietly and perspired easily, as he did now. For these reasons, Porfiry Petrovich had seldom had cause to appear before a court or even a judge. If Fredkin could miraculously appear . . . but it was not to be.

The lawyer looked at the jury, which was still under rifle and bayonet, and then at the judge and Dandorov, who were looking at each other. And then it seemed to Porfiry Petrovich that recognition appeared in the eyes of the young man. Judge Valorov went pale.

"You," said the young man. "Now I recognize you. She told me of you. And now you mean to kill me to protect yourself."

Everyone in the court, with the exception of the judge and Porfiry Petrovich, thought that the defendant had gone mad.

"Justice will be done," the judge said. "I promise you."

Dandorov began to laugh, and before he could be stopped, he kicked the small table before him out of the way, took several quick steps toward the judge's table, and leaped at the larger, older man.

A shot spat out, followed by another and a mass of people running, crushing toward the exit. Three soldiers were trampled; one later died as a result. Spectators scattered. A confused jury ignored the young man with the rifle and fought one another to get through the door behind them.

Only Porfiry Petrovich and Valorov sat silently.

An officer with golden epaulets and a tall black hat strode forward now in charge, holding his sheathed sword at his side in case the dead Dandorov should rise and again attack the judge.

The officer inspected the body draped over the judges table and announced, "He is dead."

Valorov nodded.

"Are you harmed?" asked the officer.

Valorov shook his head no and looked at Porfiry Petrovich, who put his notes away.

The courtroom was clear except for the soldiers. Those unhurt were tending to those who had fallen under the panic.

The lawyer approached the bench, and the officer enlisted the aid of two privates to remove the bloody body of Vladimir Dandorov. It was at this point that Porfiry Petrovich noted that one of the bullets had passed through Dandorov's open right eye. The other one was closed. He seemed to be winking.

When they were alone, lawyer and judge looked at each other.

"I will submit my confession to the tsar and resign," said Valorov.

"What will that accomplish?" asked Porfiry Petrovich, feeling more than slight nausea.

"Justice," said Valorov.

"A blow to what little we have that passes for democracy," said Porfiry Petrovich.

"You think I should continue to sit in judgment of others after what has happened here?" asked Valorov. "After what I have done?"

"No. The pressures of your duties and the events of today have taken a great toll on a respected judge," said Porfiry Petrovich. "The judge might wish to resign, to retire to engage in an area of special law or something that interests him."

Valorov looked at the empty jury seats.

"I collect insects," Valorov said, looking now far beyond the walls of the courtroom. "Anastasia thought it a disgusting hobby."

"Sounds fascinating to me," Porfiry Petrovich said, hoping he was not about to be invited to view the collection.

"I'll think about it," said Valorov, holding out his huge, rough hand. He engulfed the little lawyer's soft white hand, and, though he barely squeezed, Porfiry Petrovich felt both their pain.

Cruel and Unusual

CAROLYN WHEAT

New York City, November 1994

It was a typical Ambrose Jeffers file: thick as the Manhattan telephone directory, every page neatly aligned, color tabs for the sixteen exhibits at the end. Avery Nyquist had thumbed through hundreds of case files in her seven years as an associate with the prestigious firm; read thousands upon thousands of legal documents, digested millions of words designed to throw a cloak of legalistic obfuscation over the simplest fact.

Never had she read, or even imagined reading, the words of Petitioner's Exhibit A. They lay before her, their coal-hard reality sending a chill through her. It was as though a black widow spider had walked across the pristine surface of Avery's designer desk: ". . . there to be taken to a place determined by law, to be subject to execution by means of the electric chair, until he shall be pronounced dead by a duly authorized coroner of the State of Wyoming."

A death warrant. She was looking at a death warrant. A piece of paper, duly signed, stamped, and filed with the county clerk, a piece of legal paper just like all the thousands of papers she'd read in her legal lifetime. But because of this paper, a boy would die.

She had been asked to do many things since her first day at the most prestigious law firm on Wall Street. Work from eight in the morning until midnight, then show up bright and eager for more at seven the next morning; argue a major securities fraud appeal before the Court of Appeals in Albany, then dash to a top-secret merger negotiation on Maiden Lane that evening, and be fully prepared for both, facts, figures, and legal precedents at her polished fingertips; visit a hapless junior arbitrageur at the Metropolitan Correctional Center, then go to an elaborate sushi lunch with Japanese bankers and know just the right things to say to both.

But this was too much.

Avery stared at the file for a few more minutes, considering her options with the same cool detachment she brought to her clients' affairs. Could she afford to say no? And if she could, how should she do it?

At last, sighing, she ran a hand through her shoulder-length blond hair, pushing it back from her forehead in a gesture her colleagues would have identified at once as signifying Decision Mode. She pushed herself back from the polished desk and hefted the file. Heavy. Too heavy.

She marshalled her arguments as she strode down the hall toward her mentor's office. Harrison Jeffers III had always supported her at the firm, had always recommended her for the tough assignments other partners doubted she was ready for; he had run interference for her on those few occasions where her suggestions fell on deaf ears. Surely he would see how absurd it was to waste her valuable time and talent on a case more suited to a Chambers Street criminal lawyer.

It took all of thirty seconds for Avery to see that her optimism was unfounded. The deep wrinkle between Hal's eyebrows became a canyon as he listened to her carefully

128

worded reluctance to handle the case.

"Avery," he began, in the near-condescending tone he'd used when she first arrived at the firm a bright-eyed, eager law graduate. "I wouldn't have assigned you the case without good reason."

His ice-blue eyes looked into hers. She was supposed to lower her lashes, defer to his masculine authority, agree that of course he was right and she'd been a fool to question his wisdom.

But that was not how she'd earned the respect of one of the sharpest minds on Wall Street.

She kept her eyes locked with his. "I am probably the best securities fraud litigator in this country," she said. "I know more about the Securities and Exchange Commission's rules than people who've spent twenty years at the SEC. I know Blue Sky law better than the people who deal in speculative stocks. I have the complexities of civil RICO at my fingertips." She paused to let her words and her air of confidence sink in. Then she went for the jugular of her argument.

"So what am I doing representing a berserk teenager who killed his family with a shotgun? In Wyoming, no less?" She softened the challenge with a smile and a shake of her head. She could afford a touch of femininity so long as she didn't let it detract from her edge.

"You're fulfilling this firm's commitment to pro bono litigation. Hal leaned back in his custom leather swivel chair, puffed on his pipe, and waited for her comeback. He was, as usual, enjoying the verbal tennis match.

So was she. Leaning back in the client chair, which was three inches closer to the ground than Hal's she copied his

129

pose of leisured ease. They had all the time in the world, and she was his equal. Those were the messages her body sent across his uncluttered ebony desk.

She crossed expensively stockinged legs. "I know what pro bono means. It's the legal equivalent of Mobil Oil sponsoring a public television program on the environment. It's the WASP version of Yom Kippur: one days atonement for a year of sins. I understand all that. What I don't understand is why this case isn't being handled by a two-year associate hungry for litigation instead of one with a desk already piled with matters that should have been conferenced yesterday."

"For one thing, you've already been to the Supreme Court," Hal said. He took the predictable three puffs on his pipe before continuing. "I want someone who can go before the Court and *argue,* not sweat bullets because he's finally made the big time. Someone who won't be awed by just being there. Someone who—"

Avery raised a weary hand. "All right," she conceded. "Understood. You want experience. So why not let me supervise one of the younger associates from here, then fly down to D.C. on the day of argument? That way, you'll get the benefit of my experience, and I'll still have time for my important cases."

Hal raised an eloquent eyebrow. "A young man is about to be electrocuted by the State of Wyoming, and that's not an important case?"

"You know what I mean," she retorted. "Important to the firm."

"Important to your career," he countered, but his tolerant smile took the sting out of the words.

130

"That's always been the same thing," Avery argued. She abandoned her pose of leisured ease and leaned forward in her chair. "What's good for the firm is good for my career, and vice versa. That's the way it should be. And that's why this is different: it doesn't matter to the firm, and it could even damage my career by taking me away from cases I should be prioritizing."

She didn't bother to add what they both knew, that it could damage her career if she didn't win in court. And the odds of winning a death penalty case in the present political climate were very low indeed.

Hal sighed. He laid his now-cold pipe on the marble ashtray that flanked his left arm. "I had hoped never to hear you use language like that, Avery," he said, more in sorrow than anger. "There is no such word as *prioritize*."

Avery grinned. This was the Hal she'd always loved to do battle with—the nitpicker, the elitist, the world-weary cynic. Surely descending into a discussion of syntax meant she'd won her point. Her shoulder muscles relaxed in anticipation of victory; she considered asking her mentor if he wanted to share a late lunch at Fraunces Tavern.

"The thing is, my dear," Hal said, his tone one of patient finality, "I made a promise to a friend. A very old friend. I said I would send my best lawyer on this case. And that, I'm afraid—or, rather, I am not afraid, I am in fact pardonably proud to say—is you."

Cody, Wyoming, June 1987

Mr. Farkas was a practical man. He kept saying so, over and over, in a louder and louder voice, as if no one else in

131

the jury room could come close to him in the matter of practicality.

Mr. Dundee didn't care how practical Mr. Farkas was. He was tired of being bullied, and his weariness showed in the droop of his eyelids and the cutting edge of his tongue. "Give it a rest, Farkas. We all know where you stand. Give someone else a chance to talk, will you?"

Farkas grunted. "If they say something worth listening to," he grumbled.

" 'Something worth listening to,' " the little teacher with the pageboy hairdo echoed. "I suppose that means something you agree with."

"I'm tired of hearing a bunch of crap about how that kid isn't responsible for what he did," Farkas retorted.

The teacher's favorite technique was to repeat what others said and put little quotation marks around it, give it an ironic twist that mocked the speaker. " 'A bunch of crap,' " she repeated, her tone speculative. "I don't think I've ever heard that particular phrase before. I'm not at all certain you can actually have a bunch of—"

"I wouldn't mind going home sometime in the next decade," the tall, thin man with the goatee interjected.

Mrs. Barstow couldn't remember all their names. Twelve jurors meant eleven names she had to hold in her mind all at once. Mr. Farkas she had no trouble remembering, he was a florid man with a big mouth who reminded her of that actor who always seemed to play generals in 1950s movies. She couldn't remember the actor's name anymore, but Mr. Farkas looked and sounded just like him, all bluster and noise.

Mr. Dundee was black. Well, not black exactly, more like

coffee with cream. He worked for the post office, and Mrs. Barstow could just see him doing it, could picture him standing behind the counter making little jokes while he waited on people. He was the kind who'd show up during the Christmas rush with a fuzzy Santa Claus hat. The kind who when you asked for a special stamp, he'd open the drawer and look for it, not just snap that they were out of those and couldn't she see there were people waiting behind her.

No wonder Mr. Dundee thought Tyler Baines was innocent. He was the kind of man who thought the best of people.

The others she tended to think of by looks or occupation. There was the schoolteacher and the man with the goatee and the pregnant girl and the two young men with Mexican names; she could never remember which was Hernandez and which was Lopez. One worked in a garage, but she couldn't remember for the life of her what the other one did. There was the bottle blond—although Mrs. Barstow had to admit they made hair dye a lot more natural now than they had in her day; you couldn't really tell except that this girl didn't have the complexion that went with real blond hair.

The last three jurors were closer to her own age. One was a widow, the other two, in that strange coincidence that happened on juries, had both worked for Montgomery Ward. They lunched together every day exchanging stories about people they had known in common. Mrs. Barstow thought one looked familiar from her own shopping days, but she hadn't said anything. The other one looked like somebody she wouldn't have wanted to return something to.

133

The widow was speaking her mind. ". . . have to remember what that doctor said about Tyler's ability to control his impulses. The boy is just not like other people. We can't forget that."

Farkas snorted and was about to put his two cents in when one of the Mexicans jumped in. "Man, I don't know about them doctors," he said with a shake of his head. "I don't want to sound like I'm ignorant or nothing, but I can't accept that some kid blows his father and sisters away with a shotgun, and we gotta let him go on amount of what some doctor says."

"But if he didn't know what he was doing," the nice Montgomery Ward lady said, "then he shouldn't be found guilty."

There were too many people talking. Too many egos vying for attention. Mrs. Barstow leaned back on the hard chair and closed her eyes, trying to recapture her sense of herself. She tended to lose herself when there were too many voices in the room.

The sour-faced Montgomery Ward's clerk nudged her. "You have to try to stay awake, dear," she said in a tone that put Mrs. Barstow's teeth on edge. "I know it isn't easy at your age, but you owe it to the rest of us to make an effort."

Mrs. Barstow, at seventy-five, was the oldest member of the jury. She sensed the defense attorney hadn't wanted her, but she was the second alternate, and he was probably out of preemptory challenges. She remembered preemptory challenges from Court TV; she was proud of all the things she'd learned from that program. She'd always thought she'd like to be a court buff when she got old, and now she could do it without leaving her couch. She liked watching trials, liked hearing from the lawyers about why they were doing what they were doing. Some lawyers were slick and smart, and she felt they weren't to be trusted, although she would certainly want them in her corner if she were ever in trouble. Others were just like regular people, only they talked faster. They were never at a loss for words, lawyers; that was what she admired most about them. They never stood in front of store clerks, groping for the name of the thing they wanted, the thing they knew perfectly well what it was, could draw a picture of, except that they couldn't remember what you called it.

She opened her eyes. She would have liked to tell Miss Monkey Ward to keep her comments to herself, that she hadn't been asleep and wasn't going to fall asleep and didn't need any officious reminders from prune-faced old bats like her. But although she remembered the word "officious" when she was thinking to herself, there was always the danger that what she wanted to say wouldn't be what she actually said when the time came.

Washington, D.C., December 1994

"If you can give me one good reason—one, count them, one—why we need some Wall Street yuppette on this case, I'll—" Max Jarvis sawed the air like an old-time actor as he paced the tiny office on Wisconsin Avenue. The walls were lined with towers of cartons whose weight lay heavy on the bottom box, which bent under its load. The desks were littered with legal papers, cardboard coffee cups with logos of Greek diners on the side, computer printouts listing cases spewed out by the legal research program in the corner. On

135

the wall behind Max's desk, a hand-lettered sign read "Cruel and Unusual, Attorneys at Law."

"Cool down, Maxwell," a lazy Southern voice drawled. "I got a favor comin' from a friend up north, and this is what he's givin' me for Christmas. A nice shiny WASP who can argue our case without the old farts on the bench goin', 'Here come those crazy death penalty fanatics' the minute she opens her mouth. Someone who can help us lift Tyler Baines from the mire of all the other boys scheduled to die this year. Someone who can get us a little ink and won't look half bad on Court TV. A new face, Max, that's what she is. And a new face is what we need on this one."

Max Jarvis fixed his partner and friend with the look that had earned respect on the streets of Bensonhurst and said, "And what's wrong with our faces? You make a good appearance on the tube, Ren. Those wide blue eyes, that John-Boy Walton accent. The six o'clock news bunnies eat it up like shoo-fly pie."

Renshaw Craley leaned forward, his large bony hands clasped in an attitude of prayer. "We agreed once upon a time, old buddy, that we would do whatever it took to save our clients from the chair. *Whatever* it took. And if it takes us using a Wall Street designer suit with real pearls and a head of hair that cost more than our monthly salaries combined, then so be it. So be it, for Tyler's sake." Ren's horsey face was dead serious, his blue eyes bored into Max's as he repeated, "For Tyler's sake, Max."

Max took in a lungful of dusty air and whooshed it out. "Okay, I get the point, Ren. Tyler Baines is gonna fry if we don't pull a rabbit out of our hats. And you think our hats are empty and we need a new face. Well, I think we've won our share of cases—big cases, newspaper cases, not just penny-ante shit—and I know we've got more knowledge and experience with the death penalty than anyone else in this country, so—"

"A slight exaggeration, Maximilian," Ren interrupted. "The ACLU has a few good lawyers working on Death Row, the NAACP Inc. Fund are no slouches, and even Amnesty International—"

"All right." Max lifted an exasperated hand. "Jeez. Let me finish my point, okay? Which is that no Wall Street hot shot, male or female, white, black, or green, can come in here and do anything like the job on this case that we can do. So what the fuck do we need her for? And don't give me that me suddenly need a pretty face instead of good lawyering."

Ren Craley spun around in his swivel chair, pointed to a picture on the wall. It was an ordinary family picnic—at first glance. When you looked closer, you saw that two of the boys were Asian, one girl had tiny crutches under her arms, and the beaming blond parents couldn't possibly have given birth to all the children of various colors and ages that surrounded them at the picnic table.

"The Baineses were mighty special people," he said, his Southern accent deepening as he spoke. "Folks thought highly of them, even the ones who didn't think it was right for them to adopt outside their own kind. Face it, partner, Lonnie and Dora Baines were nigh onto saints in West Hamburg, Wyoming. And Tyler blew them away. Just picked up his foster daddy's shotgun and sprayed shot all over that little house with the picket fence. Got two of his sisters as well, one nine and one twelve. And the mother maimed for life. Add to that the fact that people out west don't hold much with the insanity defense, and you've got Tyler practically sitting in the electric chair even as we speak. He's dead, Maxeleh, dead meat. Unless we can pull that rabbit from our hats. And, yes, I'm counting on a fresh face, a female face. To get people thinking that a nice looking young woman wouldn't take a case like Tyler's if she didn't think the boy was seriously screwed up."

"Like using a woman on a rape case," Max said. He'd slowed his pacing and said the words as though thinking out loud. "Yeah, it could work. It's sexist bullshit of the worst kind, but it could work."

"So you're with me, finally? You'll help show our new associate the ropes?" When Max didn't answer at once, Ren repeated his earlier plea. "For Tyler."

Max nodded. "For Tyler."

Cody, Wyoming, June 1987

The man with the goatee was the foreman. Mrs. Barstow knew Mr. Farkas thought he should be the foreman and was bitterly disappointed when the others chose the bearded man instead. She herself had voted for Mr. Dundee, who after all was trusted to run an entire post office.

"Perhaps we should take another vote," the goateed man said, trying vainly to infuse a little enthusiasm into his voice.

"What for?" Farkas demanded. "It will just come out the same way it did last time and the time before that and the time before that. Six for conviction, six for acquittal."

"They were such a wonderful family," the pregnant girl

138

whispered. "I saw them on television once. A real inspiration, that's what they were."

This was true, but it didn't stop Mr. Farkas from giving the girl a hard glare. "That kind of talk isn't helping one bit," he blustered. "Who cares what kind of family they were? Lonnie Baines and those two little girls are dead, and that no-account Indian kid of his did it, and that's all she wrote."

Both Mexicans and Mr. Dundee opened their mouths to protest, and Mrs. Barstow couldn't blame them one bit. Whatever Tyler Baines had or hadn't done, it had nothing to do with his being an Indian.

Or did it? The schoolteacher began to talk about fetal alcohol syndrome and how it was more prevalent among children of Native American ancestry. Mr. Farkas's red face wasn't the only one to scowl at her terminology, here in Wyoming, most people still said Indian, even if they said it with a hint of defiance, as if daring those Eastern liberals to make something out of it.

"I don't give a good goddamn how much rot-gut whiskey that little brat's momma drank when he was in the womb," Mr. Farkas exploded at last. "He killed Lonnie Baines and those children in cold blood, for God's sake."

"I don't see how this discussion is furthered," the widow said in a shaking voice, "by taking the name of the Lord in vain."

"Oh, Christ," Mr. Farkas muttered, wiping his brow with a limp handkerchief. "Haven't we got more important things to talk about?"

Mrs. Barstow could see that the widow had every intention of telling Mr. Farkas that in her view there was precious little that was more important than respecting the Lord.

139

"Mommy was afraid Tyler would get the gun, like he did before." That was what Melissa, the ten-year-old, had said. Melissa was born without a foot, but you'd never know it to watch her walk. They could do such wonderful things these days, Mrs. Barstow thought, but then she thought about Tyler and how nobody could do anything for him, and she decided maybe things hadn't changed all that much.

What could it have been like, Mrs. Barstow wondered, to be a little ten-year-old with only one foot and a brother who might find the shotgun and blow the whole family to bits?

Why did a family with a son that hard to handle keep a gun anyway?

The answer to that one was easy; it came to Mrs. Barstow unbidden. "This is Wyoming; we need our guns." That was what her late husband had said every time she begged him to get rid of the gun that stood for thirty years behind the kitchen door, in the little hallway they called the mudroom. He needed a gun, he said, in case a coyote came prowling around the garden, or in case a cougar attacked their dog, or in case—well, just in case.

In case mad killers came out of the mountains and tied them both up and slit their throats with her carving knife. Like that farm family in Indiana that funny little writer wrote the book about.

Thinking about the funny little writer brought back images of Junior: blond and elfin, not at all like her or her husband. Some people joked that Junior had been left by elves, with his wispy golden hair and pointed ears and heart-shaped face.

"Tyler found my money and stole it," the Vietnamese boy named Peter had said. "I hid it, but he always found it."

140

Mrs. Barstow could sympathize with that. Hadn't her big cousin Annie always found things she hid? Annie came to the ranch in the summer, she was two years older and shared Mrs. Barstow's room. She seemed to think that gave her the right to take anything she fancied, so Mrs. Barstow took her most precious things and hid them in places she didn't think Annie would look, but Annie always did. She always did, and she always found them, and she always broke or ruined them.

Ma said it was okay because Annie was their guest and you had to be nice to guests, but Mrs. Barstow never thought it was right, and when she became a mother she knew she would never let anyone steal from Junior no matter what. Guest or no guest, her child would come first.

Did Dora Baines feel the same way? She and Lonnie had two children of their own, two blood-children in addition to the adopted family. Did they make a distinction between their own children and the little guests?

She couldn't blame them if they had, especially when it came to Tyler. It was one thing if your own blood-child turned out bad, but when you had a bad one and he wasn't really yours, you couldn't be blamed for wishing he'd never come into your life.

A fragment of testimony came back to her. Just a little wisp of a phrase; for a moment, she couldn't even remember who'd said it: ". . . considering bringing a suit to compel the agency to resume custody due to a failure to disclose a material fact."

Long words. Legal words. Thank goodness for Court TV; Mrs. Barstow knew that *compel* meant to make somebody do something, and that *failure to disclose* meant that someone had kept something a secret. *A material fact* meant that it was a big secret, an important omission—like the agency not telling the Baineses their adopted boy might have been born with fetal alcohol syndrome.

Had the Baineses been trying to send Tyler back to the orphanage?

It didn't sound as if the orphanage wanted him back.

Washington, D.C., February, 1995

"The first trial ended in a hung jury in 1987, Your Honor," Avery explained. "One of the jurors was taken ill during deliberations, and the alternates had already been discharged. On retrial in 1988, the State of Wyoming managed to convince twelve jurors that Tyler Baines was legally sane within the meaning of Wyoming law despite a documented history of fetal alcohol syndrome."

Ren Craley leaned over the makeshift judges bench and stepped out of character. "I'd watch that hint of sarcasm if I were you, Avery," he said. "You know, that part about the state managing to convince twelve jurors. That kind of stuff's been known to piss off the Supremes."

Max Jarvis nodded; he looked about to add something, but Avery glared at him and he shut up. It was bad enough to be lectured by a backwoods lawyer who'd probably read cases by kerosene lamp, but she didn't have to take backseat lawyering by two guys instead of one.

Still, it made a lot of sense to moot-court the argument as often as possible before the big day. Ren and Max sat at a long table, shooting questions at her while she tried to stick to the argument she'd prepared while at the same time

142

answering their concerns. It was the only way to prepare for appellate argument: pretend you were before the court, and field as many questions as your colleagues could come up with.

"Here's a Sandra Day O'Connor question," Max said with a wicked grin. "Counselor, how do you respond to the state's argument that your client received all the due process of law he's entitled to because the jury was permitted to consider the fetal alcohol syndrome in the second trial?"

"Your Honor is correct that the jurors were told they could take into account the medical history of Tyler Baines," Avery replied, trying for the same deferential tone she intended to use on the real Supreme Court, "but the defense contends that the judge's charge effectively undermined the impact of the medical testimony by not directing the jurors to consider fetal alcohol syndrome a form of insanity under Wyoming law."

"Oh, so this case isn't about the fetal alcohol syndrome as such," Ren Craley drawled. "Instead, it's about the precise wording of the judge's charge. Is that your contention, counselor?"

Avery shot the tall Southerner a sour glance. "Is that supposed to be Rehnquist or Scalia?" she asked.

"Take your pick," Ren replied. "They're both going to stick it to you."

Cody, Wyoming, June 1987

"We couldn't have a normal life," Dora Baines had said, sobbing. She wiped away her tears with a hand that had only three fingers; her adopted boy had blown the others

143

away with the shotgun. "Tyler was getting too big for me to discipline. He got mad at Sarah and broke her arm; she's only five years old."

Five years old and blind, Mrs. Barstow recalled. A Romanian orphan who'd been left to the in a miserable institution. *They wanted him dead,* Mrs. Barstow thought to herself. *They needed him dead It was the only hope they had for a normal life.*

Her eyes filled with tears. A normal life; that was what she and her husband had had after Junior died. A normal life, a life that wasn't spent caring for a child who demanded every minute of your time and gave nothing in return because he had nothing to give. A child they labeled autistic, a child who would never hold a job or get married or even laugh at a joke.

The gun was hidden where Tyler wouldn't find it.

But Tyler found everything; there was no hiding place he couldn't ferret out. The gun wasn't loaded. At least, Peter, the Vietnamese boy, had sworn it wasn't supposed to be loaded. What good an unloaded shotgun would be against marauders from the mountains Mrs. Barstow couldn't say, but Peter had insisted the shells were kept in another, quite separate hiding place. A hiding place little Melissa had testified Tyler knew about, because he'd found the money she'd been saving for a new Barbie. He'd stolen it only a week before the night of the gun.

The gun was supposed to be unloaded; the shells were supposed to be hidden.

But when Tyler Baines ran for the gun, grabbed it, and pointed it at his adoptive family, it had been loaded and deadly.

Why? Mrs. Barstow let the question nag at her while the others argued diminished capacity. Why had the gun been left where the family must have known Tyler could find it? Why had the shells been hidden in a place he'd only recently raided?

Why had a jar of sparkling water been left on the picnic table where Junior could pick it up and drink from it?

She thrust her fist into her mouth to stop the involuntary cry. The sour-faced Montgomery Ward's clerk gave her a suspicious look.

Mrs. Barstow leaned back against the hard chair and murmured something about feeling faint. Mr. Dundee stood up and walked over to the water cooler, where he filled a little paper cup and brought it back to her. She took it gratefully and sipped, the water felt good going down, even if it did have a hard time getting past the lump in her throat.

They had set him up. The family had set Tyler Baines up.

That was not a phrase she'd learned on Court TV, but it was a good one anyway.

Mr. and Mrs. Baines had wanted Tyler to go for the gun. They had come to the end of their rope. Everyone knew Tyler's temper, everyone had said it was only a matter of time before he killed someone out there on the ranch.

No one would have blamed Mr. Baines if he'd been forced to kill his son, if he'd defended himself and his family from the boy he couldn't control.

Tyler's gun wasn't supposed to be loaded. He would brandish a weapon and scream at his parents, his father would shoot him in self-defense, then sob as the gun in the boy's hand proved to be empty. It would all be a horrible mistake.

Washington, D.C., April 1995

"She did a good job, Max," Ren Craley said. "You can't blame her for what the Supremes did."

"Yeah, I suppose," Max agreed. At least, his words agreed. His face said something else. "She didn't have her heart in it, though. If one of us had argued Tyler's case, we'd have shown some passion, for God's sake."

"Do you really think that would have impressed anybody, Maxie?" Ren countered. His blue eyes were sad. "Hell, boy, we feel passion for all the poor fuckers about to die in the chair or the chamber or whatever, and what the hell good does our passion do any of them?"

"Nine-zip," Max said, tossing the *Washington Post* onto the battered desktop. "Not one dissent. Not even Ginsburg, and you know she hates the death penalty. Nine-fucking-zero and our little yuppette is back on Wall Street making the world safe for hostile takeovers, and it doesn't matter to her one bit that an Indian kid with the IQ of a turnip is about to—"

Ren held up a large, bony hand. "Peace, Maxeleh. What's done is done. I have here in my hand a case about a girl in Tennessee who met up with the wrong guy, and the two of them knocked off a Seven-Eleven. Boyfriend held the gun, but she drove the getaway car, and now she's looking at the chair. He's already been fried; you think we got a chance of getting her life without parole instead?"

Max Jarvis's answer held a world of cynicism. "We might if you don't get any of your fancy Wall Street friends to help us out."

Cody, Wyoming, June 1987

"It was a terrible mistake," Mrs. Barstow had told the deputy when he came to the house the day Junior died. She'd told nothing more or less than the truth, but he'd misunderstood her and kept on misunderstanding her no matter how hard she tried to tell them: it was a terrible mistake.

"Of course it was, dear, now don't you worry about a thing. Junior's in a better place now, dear, it was all for the best."

She had grown to hate being called "dear"—it was what people called you when what they really meant was "shut up."

They thought she meant it was a terrible mistake that Junior drank the Drano thinking it was soda water. This was before they made it blue so children could see it wasn't water, the liquid in the jar had been clear and bubbly, and it ate Junior's entire gullet right out, and he died a horrible, writhing death.

But that wasn't the mistake she was talking about. She meant it was a mistake for her late husband to think that getting rid of Junior would return their lives to normal.

The Baineses had made the same mistake. Life without Tyler was supposed to be normal, but here they were coming into court at Tyler's trial, every one of them lying about the truth, every one of them mourning a husband and father and two little girls who wouldn't have died if they hadn't been so set on becoming normal again.

You couldn't go back to normal once your life was changed by someone like Junior or Tyler, she knew that now.

New York City, April 1995

Avery Nyquist folded her expensively manicured hands on the cool surface of the ebony desk. She gazed with expectant calm into Harrison Jeffers III's appraising eyes. She pretended indifference to what her mentor at Ambrose, Jeffers was about to say, but inwardly she swelled with pardonable pride.

"I'm pleased to be able to offer you a partnership in this firm," Hal said in his rich voice. "The partners met last night, and I want you to know the vote in your favor was unanimous. No dissenting votes. Everyone here knows what you've accomplished in the last seven years, and we're eager to welcome you to partnership rank."

Partnership. The Holy Grail of Ivy League law graduates turned Wall Street associates. Seven years of working one-hundred-hour weeks, of playing tennis at one A.M. with someone who worked the same gruesome hours at Simpson, Thatcher, of dashing to JFK to meet a client between flights from London to Hong Kong, of choosing clothes, jewelry, hairstyle with one end in view-does it look like it belongs on an Ambrose, Jeffers partner? And now the Holy Grail was hers.

She smiled at the man across the desk from her, the man who had helped make it possible. Helped, not waved a magic wand for her. She'd earned it, but earning wasn't everything in the cutthroat world she worked in. There were, she knew, equally hardworking lawyers at the firm who were in the offices of other partners being told they weren't quite partner material.

As she opened her mouth to thank Hal, her eye caught the headline in the mornings *Law Journal*. "High Court Refuses to Overturn Death Penalty in Case of Wyoming Youth," it read. The subhead went on: "Unanimous Court Leaves Issue of Fetal Alcohol Syndrome Defense to Lower Courts; Baines to Die Tomorrow."

Tomorrow? Wasn't there one more stay, one more appeal? She'd have to call Ren, find out what he and Max intended to do now. The Supreme Court had affirmed, but surely another habeas to the District Court, or perhaps a motion for rehearing before the Wyoming Supreme Court . . .

"Avery, are you listening to me?" Hal's tone held an edge underneath its bantering surface, he wasn't used to being tuned out by those lower in the pecking order.

"Sorry," she murmured. "I just didn't know I'd lost that case." She gestured at the neatly folded *Law Journal* on his desk.

"Which case?" Hal asked, then followed her eyes to the newspaper. "Oh, that," he said, shaking his head. "I should have mentioned it. You can go ahead and say 'I told you so,' " he invited. "You said it was a dead loser. Maybe I should have listened to you and sent somebody else to Washington."

When she got home, Avery promised herself, she'd call Ren Craley to commiserate with him about the demon, to bitch about the fact that it wasn't even a-real opinion, just a quickie affirmation that would give the State of Wyoming a green hot to go ahead and snuff out Tyler Baines's young, meaningless life.

She had a sudden, vivid recollection of the gleam in Ren's

149

deep blue eyes as he talked law, force-feeding her with every nuance of the Supreme Court's vagaries on the subject of the death penalty.

He cared.

That was the difference between Ren Craley and the across the ebony desk, the man who'd taught her everything she knew about surviving on Wall Street. That was the difference between Ren Craley and all the men she'd ever dated, ever done business with.

Ren cared.

That was the difference between Ren and her, she realized with a suddenness that wiped away the triumph of making partner. He cared.

She didn't. Not really. Not about this man who'd treated her like a precocious child whose achievements reflected well on him, not about the SEC hearing she'd attended earlier that afternoon or about the IRS consultation she was going to have in the morning. She didn't give a good goddamn about any of them.

She didn't even care about making partner. Once upon a time, it had meant everything to her, but now that it was here, all she could think about was that big, stupid boy being strapped into the electric chair. Could he understand what was happening to him and why? He had picked up a gun in rage; could he know that stone-sober people doing their jobs were going to take his life because there was a piece of paper that said they should?"

"Avery?" Hal's voice came to her from far away, sounding concerned. "Are you feeling all right?"

She shook her head. No, she wasn't all right. She didn't know why, exactly, but she was far from all right. She got up from the deep leather chair and made her way, with increasingly swift steps, to the ladies' room. She headed into the nearest cubicle, sat down on the commode, and burst into noisy tears.

Cody, Wyoming, June 1987

Mrs. Barstow tuned in to the heated argument still going on in the smoke-filled room. Only two jurors smoked, and they'd voted to separate for smoke breaks, but this was Wyoming, and you didn't tell men they couldn't light up when and where they wanted to out here in the West. Oh, maybe in California, but that wasn't the real West.

Mrs. Barstow didn't mind the smoke; her late husband had puffed himself to death, and the smell was a familiar reminder of the days when she'd shared a life with another person. Funny how the smell of something that caused death made her feel alive.

She had to tell them. She had to make them see.

"It all went so wrong," she said, shaking her head. "So terribly wrong."

"It went wrong from the day those do-gooders took that kid into their house," Mr. Farkas said.

"No," Mrs. Barstow replied. "That's not what I mean. The gun was in the wrong place."

"Yes, dear," the nice Montgomery Ward clerk said in her saccharine tone. "If they'd hidden the gun better, Lonnie Baines and the two little girls would be alive today. But that doesn't help us decide about the insanity plea, now, does it, dear?"

Why couldn't they understand, she wondered, as she

stared at first one face and then another. They all looked at her with varying degrees of concern on their faces, concern that said they had no comprehension of her words. They knew she was upset about something, and that upset them, but they had no clue what she was talking about.

"It was just like Junior," she said, certain that would explain everything. As the words left, she reached a trembling hand to her mouth as if to recall them; she had never before spoken of Junior to strangers.

She wasn't sure she could do it now. But then she thought about that boy, that hulking dark-eyed boy with his straight Indian hair and expressionless face and dim brain, the boy who was going to be sent back if anyone would take him, only nobody would. The boy who had reached for a gun his parents had made certain would be where he could find it. She had to go on, for his sake.

She tried. She said the words over several times, in several different ways, trying to make the others understand about the gun and about the Baineses' terrible need to rid themselves of the boy they'd tried unsuccessfully to tame.

The words wouldn't come the way she'd planned. She got mixed up, too, calling Tyler Baines "Junior" and trying to explain about the bubbling water that had eaten him up from the inside and how wrong her late husband had been—as wrong as Lonnie Baines.

She began to cry. It had been so long since she'd even thought about Junior, so much longer since she'd said his name, the name that brought back the reality of him.

"This is too much," the little schoolteacher had said. "This is really too much for the poor old thing."

"Yes," Mr. Dundee agreed. "We've got to tell the judge

we're deadlocked. It's cruel and unusual punishment to keep us here when we're never going to come to a verdict."

"No!" Mrs. Barstow wailed. "Let me finish. You have to let me explain." Her breath was coming in little pants; she felt weak and strange. Why couldn't they shut up and listen? Why wasn't there enough air in this little room? Why did juries need twelve people, twelve mouths, twenty-four eyes, too many voices and legs and arms?

Too many.

Dizziness swept over her; the words she needed to say about Tyler Baines crawled into a corner of her brain and fell asleep. She let her head fall to one side and was horrified to realize that spittle dripped down her cheek.

What was happening to her?

"My God, she's having a stroke!" the little schoolteacher cried. "Somebody call the guard. We have to get her to a doctor."

Mr. Farkas ran from the room. The others bustled and exclaimed and reached for her as though their touch could restore her. The nice Montgomery Ward's clerk took out a handkerchief and wiped her chin as gently as you would a baby's.

She opened her mouth to tell them, to make them see what she'd seen, but all that came out were garbled sounds that reminded her, horribly, of Junior.

"Don't worry, dear," the nice Montgomery Ward's clerk said, patting her hand. "It's almost over. We'll get you out of here, dear, don't you worry."

"Cruel and unusual punishment," Mr. Dundee repeated, shaking his head.

"If it please the court," counsel for the petitioner began, "the execution of Rosalee Jenkins Pruitt is contrary to the Sixth Amendment to the Constitution of the United States of America because—"

"Too wordy," Max Jarvis cut in, stabbing the air with a stubby finger. "We need to stay polite, but cut that down to the bare minimum."

Avery Nyquist ran her fingers through her hair and turned exasperated eyes on her new partners. "Is he always this nitpicky?" she asked Ren Craley.

The tall, bony lawyer smiled, showing huge horse teeth. "Yeah, he's a real pain in the behind, but you'll get used to him, Ave."

I'll get used to him, Avery thought. *And I'll get used to working twenty hours a day trying to keep people alive, and I'll get used to shopping at Penney's instead of Saks, and using a drugstore rinse on my hair instead of consulting a master colorist, and I'll get used to working in an office the size of a telephone booth instead of one with a view of New York Harbor. And I'll get used to a steady diet of Supreme Court arguments and last-minute stays and visits to Death Rows all across the country.*

I'll get used to caring.

But will I ever get used to the idea that a piece of paper, stamped in triplicate, can take a man's life as surely as a loaded shotgun?

No, she wouldn't.

She hoped she never would.

The Grip

Jay Brandon

Medieval lawyers invented a very reliable method for pre-serving the records of land boundaries in living memories. They would round up a batch of neighborhood children and take them out to the site where the land was being sold. The children were marched around the property in question, and at each turning or corner of the land, a lawyer (or more likely a good sturdy bailiff) would select one of the children and beat the stuffings out of him, preferably leaving him scarred for life. This had a wonderfully focusing effect on the child's memory. Even after he got to be an old man, he'd be able to point out to interested surveyors the exact spot where he'd been beaten.

This story from property law reminds me of my grandfa-ther, who raised me. He was a kindly man, at least to me, and as far back as I remember, he was already the oldest man I'd ever seen. After my mother died from complica-tions following my birth (grief was said to be one of the complications, embarrassment another), her father brought me up. Grandfather always took a lively interest in me, and he was a physically affectionate man, often patting my head or resting a hand on my shoulder. The only times I can remember him hurting me were those few occasions when a full-lipped, thin-cheeked man with black, curly hair came to see us. The first time I remember seeing the black-haired man was when I was perhaps four years old. Grandfather and I were walking on the lawn when the man suddenly appeared. He was dressed in what I now know to be the moddest of fab clothes—striped bellbottoms and a polka-dot shirt with a white collar tall enough to brush the bottoms of his bushy sideburns—but at the time, I thought he was a clown. The redness of his cheeks solidified this impression.

My grandfather's hand was on my shoulder, and when he saw the dark man, his grip tightened as if from a convulsion. Throughout the brief interview, his grip did not let up. It was so painful I wanted to cry out, but I didn't like to disturb the conversation of the grown-ups. My grandfather had pushed me half behind him, but I stared at the face of the black-haired man as I gritted my teeth to keep from groaning. It was an affable face with bright eyes and a long nose, but it gradually darkened until he turned and stomped away. Only then did the pain in my shoulder subside. Watching the man's retreat, I rubbed my shoulder.

We lived in Olmos Park, a tiny city surrounded by San Antonio, Texas. My grandfather's brick house was large, the grounds extensive, but I never felt isolated, or as if I were raised in a lonely, echoing mansion. I ran through the house, I ran out its doors, to friends' nearby houses. This was at a time when children were given the freedom of their neighborhoods. Nor was our house inaccessible. The mailman came to our front door, and so could anyone else. I sometimes looked up suddenly from my play, thinking the black-haired man's shadow had fallen across me again, but when I looked around, I couldn't see him.

The next time we did see the man with black, curly hair, it was by appointment. I was only present for the first few minutes, after which my grandfather asked me to leave. It

156

was a relief to do so, because from the moment the dark-haired man walked into the room, my grandfather was pinching my shoulder quite painfully.

"Do whatever you like," my grandfather meanwhile, was saying to the man. "You can't hurt me, and if you try to hurt the boy, I'll put a stop to you."

It was odd that he spoke of putting an end to my hurt, because as he said it, he was hurting me himself. The black-haired man seemed solicitous by comparison. He looked directly at me as he said, "I would never do that."

He knelt to my level, and I opened my mouth to reply but only grimaced instead, because with a final pinch my grandfather sent me out of the room. I looked back a last time. The black-haired man's curls were gone that time; he was wearing his hair very close-cropped, which went with the combat fatigues and boots he was wearing. Whether he was actually serving in the military I have no idea, though he certainly had a soldier-of-fortune air about him.

He was an adventurer, no doubt. I didn't know what was passing between him and my grandfather, but the black-haired man sightings were so rare that I always remembered all the details of his visits. That time, when I was perhaps six or seven, I understood little except that the grown-ups were arguing, but I remembered what my grandfather had said to him. Years later, I realized that the black-haired must have known the circumstances of my birth and was trying to blackmail my grandfather with the information. He didn't know what a hard target he'd chosen.

There were a few other meetings, not many, with the black-haired man before I was grown, and each time my grandfather was present and sent tendrils of pain through

157

my shoulder. I didn't blame my grandfather for this; I knew him to be my protector. I always associated the strong-fingered pinches with the black-haired man. Like those medieval children, I remembered well the spot where I'd suffered pain. My spot was wherever the black-haired man was.

My grandfather tried hard to spare me the effects of his wealth while remaining the strongest influence in my life, and he succeeded at both. I didn't go into my grandfather's profession—land grabbing—but I did develop a strong interest in the ways he used his holdings, an interest that led me into property law. I was in my last year of law school when Grandfather died.

We tend to forget that inheritance can pass both up and down. My grandfather had seemed capable of outliving me, and if he had, and I had left neither will nor wife nor child, my small estate would have passed into the higher branches of the family tree, perhaps to my grandfather. Grandfather himself had taken no chances on letting his money wander untended after he was gone; his will went on for pages and pages. I was worth a paragraph or so. That made me the principal individual beneficiary, but my grandfather believed charity should make only a small beginning at home. He left me a trust to see my education finished, and a nice chunk of money to set me up in professional life, and another trust to my children—if any, if ever—but the vast bulk of his estate went to various charities, as I had known it would. His name can still be seen on a few plaques around the city. I did not hold his generosity to others at my expense against him. My grandfather believed, as I've come to agree, that there is no greater stumbling block to character than early fortune. (I hold this principle so firmly that I plan, as soon as I have children of my own, to do my very best to steal their trust funds from them.)

One of the last times I saw the black-haired man was immediately after the reading of my grandfather's will, an event at which the black-haired man had been neither present nor mentioned. Nonetheless, he seemed generally familiar with the will's pronouncements. I flinched when I saw him, but he came up to me, greeted me by name, and shook my hand, congratulating me in a very friendly way on my inheritance. Now that I think of it, perhaps he didn't know so well the terms of the will and assumed that because I was the main individual beneficiary, I had come into most of the money. At any rate, he was very friendly and seemed as bright-eyed as ever, though there were gray ham scattered among his black. He promised we would meet again soon. I was in a strange way glad to see him. The black-haired man had always fascinated me, with his air of travel and adventure; I'd always wanted to learn more about his connection to my grandfather. I felt nothing to fear from him myself, since any attempt to blackmail me would be a dismal failure. First, I didn't have the money to pay. Second, I wouldn't have; the rumors of my scandalous birth, the few that faintly persisted, gave me the only intrigue I possessed.

Nonetheless, I didn't prolong the conversation with the black-haired man, because it was a relief to see him turn away. My shoulder throbbed all the time he was talking to me, as if I felt the grip of a dead hand.

During the following year, I had much more to think about

than the man with black, curly hair. I finished law school and took a job with a largeish firm that was happy to have me because they suspected I had contacts among the old money in town. I took up the practice of property law. My upbringing had instilled in me more firmly than most the idea that all our lives are shaped by property—by money, to put it more vulgarly—or the lack thereof. Nothing in my practice discouraged this idea. Clients came to me because they wanted to loosen what we trust and estate lawyers call the grip of the dead hand—to shake off the encumbrances of instructions that had come with inherited property. Others, older, more experienced, having lived long enough to grow enmities, came to me to establish such a grip, to dictate the courses their money would take long after their demises. I was sympathetic to both kinds, being very familiar with the grip of a dead hand.

I wasn't obsessed with work. Well, maybe I was for a while, but then I met a girl, decided after some contemplation that I was in love with her, and then actually did fall in love with her, which was such a different experience from intellectual devotion that it startled me right into engagement. Her family, who had some no-longer-young money of their own, were familiar with my name—it was the same as my grandfathers, perhaps my best legacy from the old man—and, like so many others, they assumed I had come into most of my grandfather's money. Jennie, who knew my true situation, let her parents think what made them happy.

The wedding date we set was not far off. I am a traditionalist, and that last week before the wedding, I went around in a traditional love-struck daze. I broke things, I mislaid keys, I talked to people for long minutes without later remembering the conversations. One afternoon, I even tried to joust with a speeding car.

This was 1990. The economic boom that had crested and died in other Texas cities had bypassed San Antonio altogether. Though it had almost three-fourths of a million people, San Antonio retained a small-town feeling. I was always running into people, mere acquaintances, who knew my marital plans and other details of my life. Even people who don't know each other in San Antonio appear to; a stranger would think we're all friends from the way we greet each other on the streets. It was lucky for me that I lived in such a friendly city. In other places I've been, bystanders would only have watched interestedly as I stepped off the curb and was broken down into my component parts, but in San Antonio the stranger beside me grabbed my arm and pulled me back. The car hurtled out of sight as I pumped the stranger's hand and explained what a favor he'd done me, because I was getting married Saturday. He refused a reward but accepted my invitation to the reception.

Jennie and her mother left me out of all the wedding preparations, which was a sensible and terrible thing to do, because it left me at very loose ends for most of the week. Once her father had me to his club for a rollicking hour of anecdotes about the futures market, and old friends called to invite me out for drinks, but no evening was so diverting as the one on which I opened my door to find the man with black, curly hair smiling at me

"Well. Hello," I said, putting my hand on my shoulder and then having to lower the hand to shake his.

161

"This is a surprise," he said, which was going to be my next line and so threw me silent. It didn't take much, that week, to make me lose the thread of a conversation.

"That is what you were going to say, isn't it?" he asked heartily. I nodded. "But why should it be?" he went on. "I read the paper, I know what's happening in San Antonio. You're probably thinking that we never see each other, but then there's very seldom an occasion as happy as this one, is there?"

I nodded again. It was nice of him to carry on both sides of the conversation, lessening the strain on both of us.

"I've seen the bride-to-be." He twisted his head so that he was staring at me with one merry blue eye, which winked. "You're a lucky boy."

"Thank you," I said formally, before I remembered my manners. "Won't you come in?"

"I was hoping you'd come out with me instead. You can't be a host the week before your wedding, you have to let me buy you a drink."

While I was trying to think of a believable excuse, my careless tongue was accepting his invitation. He stepped inside and closed the door while I went off to find a jacket. I had a nice apartment, five rooms in a half-renovated block of downtown, and my guest surveyed the living room appreciatively. When I came back, he was fingering some trinket of my grandfather's as if he recognized it.

"Ready?" He smiled.

I suggested we go down to the Riverwalk, just below my windows, but he dismissed that idea with a single word, "Tourists," and said he knew some places of his own.

The second thing I saw when we got down to the sidewalk was my car parked at the curb. The first was the monster between me and the car. He was a carelessly bred dog larger than an average-sized Doberman, and with a head the size of a Great Dane's, enormous; a brown patch on his forehead was the size of my fist. He was a black, somewhat ungainly-looking animal, but frightening. I was glad to see that his leash was tied to a lamppost, and I hoped it was secure. I wondered how we could get around him to the car, but my crazy companion walked right up to the beast.

"What are you doing? Don't untie him!"

But the black-haired man already had the leash in his hand and was scratching the dog's ears.

"Somebody probably had him tied up for a reason," I said nervously.

"Because I didn't want to bring him up to your apartment," the dark man said, and grinned again. "Can we take your car?"

That wasn't my idea of a good idea, but as they both stood there patiently, I felt compelled to acquiesce. "Yours?" I asked about the dog, stalling.

"I'm keeping him for a friend. He's really very gentle."

In, truth, the dog looked very mild and lazy. "What's his name?" I asked.

My friend smiled. "Chester."

That settled it. It was hard to fear a dog named Chester. I unlocked the car doors, and Chester climbed slowly into the backseat. "He really prefers to ride in the front, but this will do fine," the black-haired man informed me, "as long as he doesn't get carsick." I kept glancing over my shoulder as I drove, but Chester just lay on the seat, completely relaxed.

The black-haired man did know some places of his own, places I'd never heard of at all. He directed me northward to a club that looked like a shack from the street but was surprisingly pleasant inside, well but discreetly lighted, with a high grade of fake leather in the padded booths and more plants than I've been able to keep alive in my apartment. Chester came in with us. For my upholstery's sake, I was glad, but I expected his presence in the club to provoke discussion. He lay docilely at the black-haired maws feet, like the statue of a dog, or perhaps of a small horse.

The bartender, who looked as if he served as bouncer as well, walked toward us, frowning. "Chester," the black-haired man said in a low, sharp voice. Chester seemed to become only a trifle more alert, but he turned his head toward the approaching bartender.

"The dog's gotta go," was the first thing the bartender said. He was a beefy man, his stomach preceding him, with hands as big as Chester's head.

"Oh, I'm terribly sorry," the black-haired man said. "Would you just do me the favor of taking him outside? He'll stay wherever you leave him."

The bartender-bouncer glared as if he were being challenged, but my companion just turned to me and asked what I'd have. I kept an eye on the bartender. He reached aggressively for Chester's collar, stooping to get at it. And Chester—yawned. It seemed mere coincidence that the yawn opened Chester's enormous jaws around the bartender's hand. Chester held that pose, not biting the hand, just engulfing it. I had been wrong about the size of the bartender's hand. It was a dainty little thing.

The bartender grunted, straightened, and the dog wasn't

164

mentioned again. I waited until the bartender had returned to his post before laughing. The black-haired man patted Chester's head affectionately. "Dogs have been good friends to me," he said, with such earnestness that the simple statement opened vistas of a life lived mostly alone.

"To your marriage," he said when the drinks came. "May it be as long and as happy as Queen Victoria's reign. Drink it all down at once," he advised me, "so the toast will come true,"

So I did, and managed not to cough. My host beamed at me. I soon began beaming myself. My companion had been all over the world and knew a great many toasts. Most of them required the same ritual. I soon realized that downing the drinks at one gulp was a duty I owed to Jennie, to ensure our happy union. I was very conscientious.

"Are you married?" I asked.

"Once," he said with a distant smile, "for a few blissful weeks," an answer that deterred further questioning on the subject.

"I had worked for him, briefly," he said later in response to a different question, about how he had known my grand-father.

"In the house?" I asked. "Or for one of his companies?"

He gave me a quick, sharp look, as if I had pried, then smiled his open, engaging smile. "There at the house. He had me wrong, you know. All I ever wanted from him was another job—one I was well qualified for. Or his backing on one project or another I brought him good, solid ideas, I had the experience. The oil fields in Venezuela, ranching in Australia. I have a sheep ranch near Brisbane now, a big operation."

I had my doubts about that. His clothes fit him well, but they hadn't been, bought this year, or last. One cuff was turned under to hide fraying. But there's no shame in failure. I couldn't deny what he was implying about my grandfather's hardness.

"Yet you kept coming back here," I said.

"This was my home. This was where I wanted to have my life." Another sad-eyed smile.

I was enjoying the black-haired man's company, but perhaps I have inherited something of my grandfather's suspicious nature, too. I couldn't help questioning him again. "If they were good projects, why didn't you take them to someone other than Grandfather?"

He smiled at my naïveté. "I guess you don't know the influence your grandfather had in this town. This was when you were just a boy, things were much fighter in San Antonio, all the money knew each other. Once your grandfather's opposition to something—or someone—was known, it was doomed."

I had a twinge of empathy that felt like guilt Grandfather had taken me in when he needn't have. That decision had given me my life. But his enmity, just as randomly fallen, had given the black-haired man an entirely different life, one used up in forced travels and failed "projects." His life could as easily have been mine, mine his.

"It's a shame we haven't had more evenings like this," I said some time later.

"I'm glad to hear you say so."

We were in yet another bar my friend knew. This one, if I hadn't been in such a cheerful frame of mind, I would have described as a low place. It was in a small old stone building south of downtown, off one of those narrow ways that seem to deposit the unwary tourist in Mexico. The room was narrow and darkened, its occupants absorbed in their own concerns. The place was such that no one had bothered about, or even seemed to notice, Chester. The black-haired man and I sat on kitchen chairs at a scarred table drinking beer chasers after shots of something from a bottle with a worm in it, the worm's thin body moving in the currents of the liquor like a languid dancer on a distant stage.

"That grandfather of yours," my companion went on. "Well, he was only being protective. But it must have been a strange life for you."

"I wouldn't know, since it's the only one I've had."

We talked about other things after that, ocean voyages and Montana, sheep ranching, European marriage customs. We talked almost exclusively of things I had never seen or done, and they sounded wonderful. I began genuinely to regret that I hadn't gotten to know the black-haired man better when I was younger. That was a lapse we vowed to correct.

After one more toast to my bride, my companion asked, "What's the matter? That one go down the wrong way?"

"I just need a little air, I think. Will you—?"

I stumbled outside while he stayed to pay the check. A lamppost at the curb stayed my progress, and I clung to it, taking deep breaths. If I'd been more alert, I would have been concerned about where I was, for the street was narrow and dark, pocked with doorways out of which any number of hard-eyed men could emerge in an instant. But the god of drunks protected me while I breathed deeply.

167

The world had settled down a little by the time my companion rejoined me. "Beautiful night," he observed, and looked more closely at me. "Time to go home?"

I nodded. I was only a trifle unsteady as I bent to unlock the passenger door of the car for him. When I straightened, he had stepped back to the sidewalk.

"I think I'll just stay here for a while," he said. "Would you do me a favor, though? Keep Chester tonight? I'm staying at a hotel, and they really—"

I looked at the dog, who looked at me. Why not? He'd been so quiet, I had forgotten he was along. If he'd be no more trouble than that at my apartment, I could certainly tolerate his company for one night.

"He's housebroken?" I inquired first.

"Oh, yes," said the black-haired man. "He's very well trained."

I shrugged and held the door wider. At a word from my companion, Chester climbed elaborately into the front passenger seat, and I shut the door behind him.

My host followed me around the car and caught my shoulder after I'd opened my own door. I winced slightly, turning the wince into a smile for the benefit of the black-haired man, who looked rather perturbed by my expression. "It's been fun," he said. "I'll call tomorrow to get Chester."

"And be sure to be at the wedding Saturday," I reminded him.

He nodded. "I'm very happy for you," he said, smiling. I smiled back and climbed inside the car. I was sure I needed my seat belt but took some time with it, tangling the lap belts and shoulder straps in great loops around the front seat.

"Are you sure you can drive?" the black-haired man

asked. I nodded, and he closed my door and stepped away.

Before starting the car, I turned back to look at him and saw that he was calling. I opened the window a crack to hear him.

"Chester!" he said sharply. So it wasn't me he was calling. Last words of admonition to his pet, I thought. The dog's head came around ponderously until it was at my shoulder. He blinked at the man outside.

"Chester" the black-haired man said again, and then: "Kill!"

Beside me, the dog suffered an abrupt personality change. He snarled, his lips pulled back from his huge teeth, and his head was coming toward me before I even had time to turn in that direction. I felt his breath, though. Instinctively, I threw up my right forearm as my left hand groped frantically for the handle of the door. Chester's teeth closed on my elbow, and we both howled. When he opened his jaws to try for a better grip, I jerked free for an instant. But then I made the mistake of trying to push him away, which took my hand away from the door handle, so I was still trapped with the dog.

Chester was a big dog, but he was smaller than a grown man; he had more room to maneuver than I did. I couldn't escape him in the confines of the front seat. He lunged at me, pinning me under his paws, and his mouth opened to enormous size. The awful teeth came toward my throat.

I kicked, but it was an awkward, twisted kick that only made Chester miss his first lunge, and not by much. His teeth grazed my car. I screamed. He growled in response.

I pushed him again, got my hand on the door handle, and finally pulled it, my heart opening with relief until nothing happened. The door didn't move. I remained trapped. I turned my head and saw the black-haired man leaning against the door, holding it closed. He had the most amazing look of awful expectancy on his face, so that I thought I could have talked him out of his purpose if I'd had a moment—if he could have heard me. But I didn't have a moment.

Chester's teeth weren't his only weapons. His paws were as big as my hands, and carried claws. He planted one on my leg, and when he scrambled for position, the fabric ripped, and I felt blood trickle down my thigh. Again his jaws closed on my arm, and blood spurted there as well.

The twin springs of blood energized me. I thrust upward, banging the dog's head against the ceiling. When he released me, I pushed backward and fell back over the seat. I managed to reach the door handle on the opposite side of the car from the door the black-haired man was holding closed, pulled, and fell out onto the sidewalk.

There was no salvation in that. My back was on the ground, my feet still entangled in the car. Chester turned his huge neck, growling horribly, gathered his paws beneath him, and sprang.

And the seat belt I'd looped loosely around his neck when he first got in the car pulled tight, choking him and stopping his lunge. He turned, snarling, and when he had slack, he managed to jerk his head free. But by that time, I'd rolled completely out of the car and slammed the door in his face.

My danger wasn't over. I leaped, suddenly strong as Chester himself, onto the roof of my car and over it. The black-haired man was moving slowly, looking dazed himself. Otherwise, I might not have reached him in time. He

170

was just opening the door when I came over its top, butted him with my head, and closed the door again as I fell down past it. I scrambled to my feet, found my car keys still in my pocket, and locked the door, which in my wonderful Volvo locked all four doors.

When I turned back to the black-haired man, I heard the click of a knife. He held it at his chest, the blade displayed before his face.

"Go ahead," I said, standing straight and ready. He didn't move. "You don't have the nerve, do you?" I said. "You'd rather use a dog, or a car."

That was a stab in the dark—I hadn't seen the driver of the car that had almost hit me earlier in the week—but I thought I saw it register on his face.

The street was unnaturally quiet. It was the kind of block where people resolutely refused to be witnesses to trouble. The black-haired man and I stared at each other until growling mixed with whining drew my attention back to the interior of my car. Chester was possessed. Spittle flew as he bit and snapped at the glass, then at the steering wheel, the seat, and everything else within his reach. He still seemed capable of coming right through the glass and metal of the door to get at me. The mild dog of earlier in the evening was completely gone, devoured by this monster.

The black-haired man came up beside me, looking contemplatively at Chester. I turned to face him so that I was between him and the door handle.

"He won't be happy until he's obeyed the command," the black-haired man said musingly.

I grabbed his arm, pulling him away from the car, remembering too late the knife. My hand closed on it, cutting my palm and all my fingers, but I was so full of adrenaline that I snatched it away from him. His resistance was only slight. What I'd said of him was true, he hadn't the nerve. But, of course, the same was true of me. He made an empty-handed gesture at me, and I simply threw the knife as far down the street as I could. We heard it clatter in the darkness.

I looked at him for a long moment, fear and fury and pity so mingled I felt like throwing up.

"What a wasted life," I finally said.

His head came up with a measure of pride that erased some of the sudden aging he'd done in the last few minutes. "Not many men get that close to such a fortune so young," he said, eyes flashing.

I was breathing deeply, and I realized my fists were clenched, still ready for attack. The black-haired man, though, seemed entirely stripped of purpose. He looked at me strangely, not with anger, not smiling as he done throughout the evening. His closed mouth made his jaw line firmer. I saw how handsome he must have been years ago when he'd worked in my grandfather's house.

"I'm going straight to the police," I said tightly.

The threat didn't seem to concern him. "They'll find it hard to believe," he said, looking into the car.

"I just want them to have the report. Besides," I added, "after Saturday, it won't matter, will it?"

He nodded sadly at the logic of that. My subconscious mind must have been working furiously as I'd fended off Chester's attack, and I'd emerged from the car understanding everything. Why the black-haired man hadn't tried to blackmail me, and what his only possible motive could have been for trying to kill me. I had been his only conduit to my grandfather's money, and my impending wedding hadn't given him much time. I watched him resign himself to having lost his last chance at fortune, something that must have been a lifelong quest with him. I almost felt sorry for him. But when he reached toward me, I pulled back. He had only been reaching to squeeze my arm with his own twisted version of affection, but when he saw my reaction, he smiled and turned away. I never saw him again.

It was my grandfather who had saved my life. Much as I'd grown to like the black-haired man during the course of the evening, I was uncomfortable every moment I was with him. That had made me take precautions like surreptitiously putting the seat belt around the dog's neck. I had felt the grip of my grandfather's dead hand, its message written in the nerves of my shoulder. This man means you harm. I still felt that pain every time I saw the black-haired man. In the end, that was of more significance—to either of us, apparently—than the fact that the black-haired man was my father.

Beat Routine

Stan Washburn

Betty and I liked working together. Our appearance disarmed people: black woman cop, very spruce and correct; white man cop, a little casual.

Betty's beat ran along one side of the university. My beat was adjacent to hers, and so it was natural for us to team up for odds and ends of beat routine. Each beat has its own problems, and beat routine is all the little odds and ends that the officer has to take care of between priority calls. Most of the time you can handle this solo, but sometimes you want to work with a partner.

Betty wasn't the obvious choice for a beat full of students because she was quite conservative. She wasn't uptight, exactly, but she equated dignity and responsibility with cleanliness and self-control, which as a campus concept is a nonstarter.

Betty met me at our beat boundary one long spring evening and said, "Toby, let's walk," by which she meant that we should do foot patrol on the main commercial street that leads up to the university. We parked in the middle of the area so that we could get back to our cars quickly if there were some priority call, and ambled up the street.

Some of the merchants didn't want cops in their establishments, but unless that preference had been made clear, Betty would go in each door, say hello, and pick up on any news or problems. There were loiterers blocking the sidewalk, and we moved them along. We spoke to a merchant

174

who was having trouble with panhandlers. We laid a ticket on a car parked by a fire plug and called for a tow.

We found three teenage girls in from the suburbs, standing outside a convenience store holding five-dollar bills and asking the over-twenty-one people going in to buy them beer. We ID'd them and told them we'd be calling their parents later in the evening.

"Oh, God," said one, rolling her eyes. "My mom's gonna totally freak out."

"Totally," said the second. "My dad said if it happened again, I'd be grounded for a *week*."

"*Please* don't call," said the prettiest girl to me, turning her back a little to Betty. She pouted. "We're, not supposed to be here." She laid one finger on my arm and stuck out her bust a little. "We'll get in *so* much trouble."

"Spare me," I said.

"You should be ashamed of yourselves," said Betty, looking severely at the prettiest girl.

When they had stomped off, I said, "Things like that make me feel so pompous. Did you ever try to get someone to buy you beer?"

"No," said Betty. "Did you?"

"No," I said. "I wanted to. But I was too embarrassed to try."

"I didn't even dare to want to," said Betty. "I grew up in a neighborhood where everybody knew everybody. Any kid messed around, people made sure the parents knew all about it. Some friends and I got some cigarettes once after school and went traipsing around smoking them—and when I got home, my momma didn't even have to tell me someone had called. Just the set of her shoulders told me all

I needed to know. If someone had told her I was trying to buy beer—well, I don't even want to think about it."

"Well, one of that bunch may get grounded for a week," I said. "That's something."

"It isn't much," said Betty.

We stopped a bicyclist, sort of a scraggly radical, who was riding against the traffic, threading his way in and out between the hurrying cars. Scraggly radicals put Betty off. She'd never known any personally. Her radical friends in college had thought of themselves as social revolutionaries with responsibilities. Betty understood them. Whites who acted out by not washing offended her sense of thrift: they had what so many people she knew couldn't have, and they were wasting it. In her eyes, it was like tearing up money.

Betty got the bicyclist's ID and began writing out a citation. He started giving her a rap about Thoreau—or it may have been Trotsky—anyway, it was about the state versus the individual. She listened for a while, and then she said, "I try to keep my beat safe. Besides, it's discourteous to ride against the traffic."

"*What?*" he said. He was synthesizing the great themes of civilization, and she was talking about courtesy.

"It's worth thinking about," she said, writing.

"You mean you're really going to give me a ticket for nothing?" he said.

"It's not for nothing," she said. "It's for riding the wrong way on a one-way street. You could have caused a serious accident. Sign here."

"Is this really the best thing you can find to do with your time?" he said.

"It is at the moment," she said. "But since you're so solicitous about my time, why don't you just go ahead and sign that ticket, and then I can go look for something more important?"

Now, I was never a scraggly radical myself, but I knew several, and some of them really were trying to live principled lives, according to their lights. They weren't what you'd call amusing people, and they tended to confuse their convenience with their principles—jaywalking as a revolutionary act, for example—but they were often less offensive than frat boys and sorority girls, who are usually cleaner but just as willful, far less thoughtful, and no funnier. I pressed this view on Betty on more than one occasion. She didn't buy it.

When we had made a circuit of the strip, Betty had another matter—kids growing marijuana in one of the housing co-ops. We drove over and parked our patrol cars in plain view across the street and stood on the opposite sidewalk.

"I don't want to bust anyone," Betty said. "They're dinky plants. They're growing it for personal use and not for sale. But it's a felony, and we need to show the flag a little." She meant both that dumb kids should have fair warning because any cop who saw the plants could bust them, and some would—and also that people shouldn't commit crimes, because the law should be respected.

"See there," she said, "and there." She was quite right. There were several fine young marijuana plants growing in pots on window sills and fire escapes. "There are more around the side," she said. We moved along to where we could see up the driveway to the rear. We made notes, counting how many windows in from the corner each item of contraband was. Nobody paid us the least mind.

The center front window had two plants in it. As we crossed the street, a young woman was visible right behind them at her desk. She looked up for a moment and saw us coming. Our eyes were meeting right through the lacy interstices of the contraband foliage, but she didn't show any sign of having made the connection between marijuana and cops and trouble.

"She is *not* thinking," said Betty as we went in the main entrance. "These kids amaze me, they really do."

We found our way to the second floor and rapped on the door corresponding to the center front window. The young woman opened it. The plants were plainly visible beyond her. She was a little surprised to find us at her door, but not alarmed.

"Hi," she said.

"Hi," said Betty. "We were driving by and happened to notice the marijuana plants in the pots on your window sill there."

The young woman spun around, horrified. The magnitude of her folly came home to her in that terrible moment. I'd never seen the blood actually leave someone's face before. She tottered. It was sort of funny if you knew how it was going to turn out.

"I'm sure," said Betty quickly before the young woman could say anything, "I'm sure they're not yours, right?"

Her eyes met Betty's. She gulped.

Sometimes basically honest people act in a reflexively honest manner. It can be very inconvenient if you're just trying to do a little justice and be on your way. "They're *not* yours, right?" repeated Betty, anxious to head off any

178

foolishness.

The young woman shook her head several times.

"That's what I thought. Okay to come in?" Betty said, stepping past her into the room. "You seem like a law-abiding citizen, and the possession of marijuana plants is a serious criminal offense."

People had seen us come up the stairs, and by this time several other residents were gathered in the hall, pressed around the doorway. Addressing the young woman, I raised my voice slightly for their convenience.

"You should know that possession of a marijuana plant is a felony in this state. A felony is a crime punishable by imprisonment for a year or more in the state prison."

The poor kid looked as if she were going to have a heart attack. "But I tell you what," said Betty. "Since these aren't yours, and there's no way of establishing the owner, why don't you just take them down the hall to the bathroom and flush them down the toilet? That'll save me a lot of paper-work." She nodded her head at the plants and smiled encouragingly.

After a moment, the young woman recognized her cue. She took the plants and led Betty, me, and a small but growing clutch of residents down the hall to the bathroom. While she dismembered the plants and flushed them I said, fairly loud, "Yes, that's the way to take care of them." (FLOOSSSSSH!) "It'd really be trouble for the owner, if we caught him. Possession of a marijuana plant is a felony." (FLOOSSSSSH!) "A felony is a crime punishable by a year or more in state prison." (FLOOOSSSSH!)

Individuals were slipping away from the group in the hall and hastening off. Soon there was a distant but unmistakable sibilance coming from the bathroom directly over-head, and others more remote in the building. (FLOOOSSSSH! FLOOOSSSSH! FLOOOOSSSSH!) I wondered if the plumbing was going to be equal to so much simultaneous, urgent service.

The young lady's plants were gone. Betty thanked her for helping out.

"Let's go look for those other plants," she said to me, loud enough for anyone who cared to hear "I think the next one was over this way." (FLOOOSSSSH! FLOOOSSSSH!)

We ambled along the halls, followed by the silent party of residents. We found the next room. We knocked. Two women opened. One was placatory, the other silently hostile. But their plants were gone, and we moved on.

The little group of residents moved along with us, about a dozen in number. Sometimes they followed us; if we changed direction, they scurried along ahead. Sometimes someone would slip away. The occupants of the rooms we had checked came out and followed along. They didn't speak to us; they whispered a little among themselves, but mostly they were silent.

A young man opened the next door. He was blushing beet red and grinning absurdly. Involuntarily his eyes slipped from our faces straight to the window sill, which was bare. When he realized how he had given himself away, he lifted his eyebrows in droll helplessness. I liked him—none of this nonsense about injured innocence. We repeated our speeches. He listened wordlessly, nodding, still grinning and blushing, and wordlessly closed the door when we moved on.

We always came up empty. "It's a good thing," one or the

other of us said at each room, "because possession of marijuana plants is a felony in this state. A felony is a crime punishable by a year or more in state prison."

It all went very smoothly, until we had gone all the way around the building and come to the last room we had on our list.

The last room was at the front of the building. We'd seen one small plant in the window. Betty knocked. The door opened, but on a chain. Visible through the opening was a young man with moth-eaten facial hair, looking very alert. Behind him was a girl with the palest green eyes, looking anxious.

"Go away," said the young man, and closed the door again, firmly.

There was a little ripple among the residents in the hallway. Somebody snickered, and somebody else immediately shushed.

Two scraggly radicals in one day. It didn't seem fair.

Betty sighed and knocked again.

There was no answer. Without raising her voice, she said, "Please open the door."

The door opened abruptly, still on the chain. The scraggly young man peered around it.

"Go away," he said. "This is my room. I don't give you permission to enter. I don't want to talk to you."

"I don't want to talk to you, either, my friend," said Betty. "We saw . . ."

"Don't patronize me," said the scraggly young man. "I'm not your friend."

Betty's eyes met mine. Oh, dear. Things had been going so smoothly, and now the mood was being spoiled. The residents looked back and forth between us. It was time to be nonchalant. I leaned back against the opposite wall—which I would not otherwise have done, because my uniform was clean—and began to pick at a little snag on one of my fingernails. If I'd been choosing, I would have handled this citizen myself—these characters don't bother me so much, and if Betty had known what was coming up, she might well have said, "This one's yours." But it was her beat, and she was in charge unless she handed something over to me, and it was too late for that now.

She said, "We saw a marijuana plant in your window, and we want you to destroy it. As soon as it's destroyed, we're out of here."

"You can't come in unless you show me a search warrant," said the scraggly young man. Betty sighed.

"Let me explain," she said. "You're entirely right about the warrant. We can't come in without a warrant, or unless you give us permission. If you give us permission, then the plant gets destroyed, and that's all that happens. But if I have to go to the trouble of getting a warrant, then I'm going to use it, you dig? You cooperate with me, there won't be a problem. You don't help *me* out, I have no reason to help *you* out. If I have to get a warrant, then you go to jail. Have you ever been in jail? You won't like it."

He stared at her.

"I haven't got all day," said Betty. "If I have to go get a warrant this evening, then I want to get going. So you tell me right now how you want to handle this thing."

The pale-eyed girl came up behind him. The door closed, the chain scratched in its slot, the door opened. She stepped back, and in we came.

182

The plant sat on the window sill.

"Okay," said Betty to the scraggly young man, "let's do it."

"I'm not doing anything," he said, his mouth tight. "You can't prove that I have anything to do with that plant. It's a trick. If I pick it up, you'll arrest me for possession. Take it yourself. Go smoke it. That's what you cops do with all the stuff you steal. Put it in your own pockets." He gazed disgustedly at Betty. "*Him* . . ." and here he shrugged a shoulder at me. "*Him* I can understand. But *you,* one of the oppressed yourself, making common cause with your oppressor . . ."

"Oh, Toby's not so bad when you get to know him," said Betty. "He hardly oppresses anyone." I smiled amiably. Betty was smiling, too, but tightly. *Don't* tell Betty that she's an Aunt Tom. She doesn't like it.

"Funny!" he said. "Very funny! You got in here by a trick, an illegal trick! She . . ." He glanced at the pale-eyed girl. ". . . she doesn't live here. She can't give you permission to enter. So you have no right to be here. But since you're here, and since you claim to see something illegal, take it and get out."

The residents in the hall were grinning nervously. I couldn't tell whether they thought all this blather was thrilling or ridiculous. I was near the window, and I could see a few more people down below, looking up. The window was wide open. They could probably hear him pretty well.

"You're not listening," said Betty, her smile, such as it had been, pretty well faded. "I said you are going to flush that plant. Not Toby. Not me. You."

183

"No," he said.

The pale-eyed girl made a move toward the plant, but he held up a hand, and she stopped, anxious, watching his face.

"I won't," he said.

For a moment Betty seemed to be preparing another little tutorial on the laws of search and seizure, but he beat her to the punch.

"This entire intrusion is unconstitutional," he said. "You have no right to make me do anything. You can't prove that plant is mine, and you can't force me to destroy it."

Her jaw tightened. She said, "All right, Mister Constitutional Scholar . . ."

"I'm an adult. You call me 'sir.' "

"Mister Constitutional Scholar, we'll test that. I'll give you two options. I arrest you for possession of that plant, you fight it in court, and we see who was right. Or you can thank me for giving you a break, go flush it, and we all go our separate ways. You choose. Right now. You've wasted enough of my time. There's real police work to do out there, and you're keeping me from doing it. You've got one minute. If that plant isn't gone in one minute, you're busted." She noted her watch, and reflexively I glanced at mine.

He stared at Betty.

The pale-eyed girl stared at him.

The doorway was jammed with faces looking back and forth between them.

"All right," he said at last. He eyed her with loathing. "All right, I'll flush it. I'm a poor person, and I can't afford to have rights." He was advancing on her, working himself up into a tight fury, pointing and shaking his finger. A drop of sputum had formed on one stringy tendril of his mustache, and it trembled there, blinking like a crystal. "But I want you to know, and I want everyone within the sound of my voice to know, that this is not justice. This is blackmail, pure and simple. You have perpetrated an illegal, oppressive search of a private premises, and now you force me to choose between my rights as a citizen and my freedom."

He had come dancing right up to her, and he began shaking his finger in front of her face.

"Well, that's not my understanding of the situation," said Betty. "But if it's yours, and you're prepared to bet on it, you know what to do." She didn't change expression or move, except that her left hand was resting on the butt of her long baton, and now she gripped it a little more firmly, and pointed it around so that it was directed at his solar plexus. You can strike with the baton without drawing it first, just jamming it straight out from the belt ring. He didn't understand the mechanics of the situation, but he could see that Betty was in control. That little movement of her hand was enough to make him dance off again, out of arm's reach.

By this time, he had capered his way back to the window sill. He snatched up the pot and, fixing his eyes fiercely on the hallway so that he wouldn't have to look directly at Betty, he marched toward the door.

But Betty stepped right into the doorway and stopped him.

"Uh-uh," she said.

He stopped dead and froze, hunched over, holding the pot. His eyes were on her feet. He wouldn't look her in the face.

"I said, you thank me for giving you a break, and *then* you flush it."

185

His eyes rotated up to meet hers, incredulous. His jaw dropped. The sputum crystal glittered. His hands were trembling, and the delicate branches and long, feathery leaves quivered in the still air of the room. The pale-eyed girl took a step forward in alarm. Betty waited, motionless.

"You didn't make anyone else say that," he hissed.

"They didn't give me a lot of grief," said Betty. While he absorbed this, she said again, "I haven't got all day."

For a moment, they hung there, eyes fixed on each other Then he shot a glance at the door. There was just enough space on one side of her, and suddenly he dropped his head and went for it. She stepped squarely into it, braced, left foot forward, hand on her baton, ready to push him back or to strike.

"No," she said.

He stopped short.

They were a foot apart. She said, "You say to me, 'Thank you, officer, for giving me a break.' Then we'll go watch you flush it."

His face was purple. I thought he was going to burst. But he didn't. His eyes were focused on some far place, where, presumably, the People get their way.

Then he turned, moved deliberately back to the window, and placed the plant carefully on the sill, exactly where it had been before. He turned back to Betty and said, "Go fuck yourself."

Her expression didn't change at all. I couldn't tell if she was pleased or not. The watchers stood transfixed. The pale-eyed girl shifted her hand a little, as if to make a gesture of appeal, and then dropped it back to her side.

"I told you," Betty said, "I haven't got all day."

186

"Go fuck yourself." It was a little more aggressive. He was starting to work himself up again. A couple more go-rounds, and he'd be wild. I thought, We'll have a quick little tussle and off to jail.

"Think about it," said Betty.

"Fuck, fuck, fuck yourself!" he said, pretty loudly. I turned a little and shifted my weight so that when we all started moving he'd be jammed back into the corner where we could control him quickly without hurting him. Very soon, now.

The pale-eyed girl saw me move and saw what was about to happen. In three steps, she reached the window, straight-armed the pot right over the edge, turned square to Betty, and said, "Please don't arrest me."

I stepped to the window. There was a swirl of long hair and T-shirts down below, and the pot was gone. I caught Betty's eye and shook my head. She had been looking at the pale-eyed girl. Now she looked at the scraggly young man. She shook her head and said, "There must be more to you than meets the eye."

There wasn't a whisper in the room or in the hall. The watchers pressed silently back to let us by as we went out into the hall. Nobody followed us down the stairs. There were a dozen or so students standing around on the sidewalk where the pot had fallen. Somebody blew a raspberry as soon as we were past; somebody tittered, and somebody shushed. When we were halfway across the street, the voice of the scraggly young man burst out from the second-story window:

"The People, united, will never be defeated!"

He was leaning out, shaking his fist. Behind him were

several others. The pale-eyed girl was close beside him hand on his arm, eyes fixed on his face, anxious, resolute.

There were people in almost every window. Three or four of them took up the chant. "The People, united, will never be defeated! The People, united, will never be defeated!"

But it didn't build. After three or four repetitions, it began to sound self-conscious rather than righteous, and pretty quickly it died out. The scraggly young man slammed the window closed and turned away into the room. Faces disappeared all over. The people on the sidewalk began to drift back inside as we unlocked our cars.

"They don't say 'thank you' much, have you ever noticed that?" said Betty. "We're real nice, real responsible, saved those kids a peck of trouble, and all we get is the raspberry. Those kids are *not* thinking." She wasn't outraged, and she certainly wasn't surprised, but she noticed. She took the energy to have regrets. She said, "I'd write their mothers if I thought it'd do any good."

Dear Mrs._____,

I am very sorry to have to inform you that your son/daughter was thoughtless and rude during our recent marijuana raid in his/her housing co-op. He/she was in fact guilty of a felony, a crime punishable by a year or more in state prison. No doubt you will wish to speak to him/her about this matter, and decide what further steps may be appropriate.

As I said, I am sorry to have to mention this, but I was sure that you would want to know.

Sincerely,
Officer B. Moore

Last Licks

VALERIE FRANKEL

Judge Bloomfeld read her instructions to the fat, bald Spam of a man as he schlumped his way onto the witness stand. We were currently wading through the Victim Impact Statement portion of our program. The point was to give family members the opportunity to emote and tell the world just how profoundly I've ruined their lives. The witness was Mattie's husband. She always complained that he had the sexual snap of a soggy ham sandwich. His face was pink and shiny. His eyes were small and black—just slits on his round, honey-glazed face. I imagined him huffing and puffing on top of her, squealing when he came. Then rolling off her aerobicized thighs and saying, "I'd really love a cheddar omelet."

Mattie told me he always wanted breakfast food after sex. Morning, afternoon, or night. And he wanted it hot. Something that needed ketchup or syrup. If condiments weren't involved, he just wasn't interested. She'd described the scene to me: Porky in bed, naked, his dick having returned to its usual softness, blinking with confusion whenever she offered cereal in a bowl. Mattie would stand at the foot of the bed, tray in hand, feeling indignant and inadequate at the same time. She offered no satisfactory response to my question, "Why do you stay?" But I have a theory: after thirty years of marriage, Porky made her feel so useless that she started to believe him. If there was any fairness in the world, I'd be in the witness stand, impacting all over him.

189

But no. It just had to be the other way around. From what I saw and heard, not a single one of these husbands gave a rat's ass about his wife until she was transformed into a higher form of energy by yours truly. In fact, if one could believe what's printed in the newspapers, two of the husbands have already sold the rights of their stories to TV networks. It was plainly clear to me—as it should be to every spectator in this courtroom—that these so-called aggrieved spouses, all four of them, should be honoring me instead of sending me to jail. I made their wives happy. They could at least appreciate that effort.

I have a fool for a lawyer, as in "a defendant who chooses to represent himself has a . . ." My guilt was obvious. My methods mad. And my remorse absent. Of course, jail time was my repellent, if inevitable, future. I didn't see the point of surrendering my savings to a lawyer if I was going up the proverbial river anyway. I'd need that money for bribes when I got there. I pride myself on always thinking ahead.

Porky, meanwhile, was emoting. "Matilda always said she wanted to get out of the suburbs," he started. A few random titters from the press. I adored the press. Of course, they write the most scandalous things about me, as if they hadn't been offering me bribes/gifts of grapefruit juice the day before. I'd put out the word that I'd grant anyone an interview from my cell, as long as he or she brought fresh fruit juice. The Short Hills, New Jersey, detention center was a complete failure regarding fresh produce. Imagine being locked up for months, deprived of any kind of fresh fruit or vegetable. As if man could live on bologna and white bread alone.

Gail Peters was my favorite reporter. She worked for the

Star Ledger. She also created my *nom de crime*. In person, she calls me by my real name. This morning, as I walked into court, she asked me, "Hey, Reggie, getting in any good licks today?" Ah, ha, ha. We laughed. Yes, it's so fucking hilarious. Of course, I'll stop laughing, even ironically, when I'm shipped off to Newark. My life as a man will end the second I step through those prison doors. I'm sure the rapists and killers will have a field day with a piece of hairdressing, leg-waxing meat like me. On the outside, being a stylist is a great cover for a lady's man. What husband is going to be jealous of a fey open-shirted tresser at the Jalm salon? Only one caught on during my entire career as a Lothario. Now I'm quasi-enjoying my new career as a star: New Jersey's notorious "Cunny Killer." I might go down in the history of New Jersey for being the most depraved serial killer Essex County had ever seen. I supposed I should be happy that this socially liberal (though fiscally conservative) state does not entertain the death penalty.

Porky was pattering on: "My children have no mother." His two kids—a son and a daughter—have been out of college for years. The girl was an ungrateful little wretch who used her monthly stipend to support her newly fashionable heroin addiction in New York City. The son loved his mom and dad so much that he moved to Tokyo. He didn't even fly home for the funeral. Mattie was many things, but a good mother was not one of them. She knew it. She didn't love this about herself. But, she rationalized, why wipe noses when you can pay someone else to? From the witness stand, Porky continued, "The personal humiliation I've suffered has driven me to the brink of insanity." Mattie lived on the brink of insanity for years. If it wasn't for me, she would have died the same hollowed-out bulimic she was when I first met her. Then again, if it wasn't for me, Mattie would still be alive. Oh, well. You can only do so much to change a person's world for the better.

Porkpie was beginning to irritate me. He just stood up in the witness stand and damned me to hell. To think, I'd been welcomed to town like a hero just a year ago. Even before I'd stepped on Short Hills soil, I was already famous. The management at the Jalm salon, correctly assuming they'd create a stir in the hairdressing community, published my photo in the town newspaper with ad copy that read: "Maximus Coiffure's famed stylist, Reggie Juan Styvestant, has joined Jalm!" Big news in Short Hills. The ladies of the town flocked to our little boutique just to get a look at me. Modesty would be ridiculous: I'm a stunningly handsome man. Because of that ad, appointments at Jalm increased tenfold for my debut week. It seems the female population of the region was suddenly in desperate need of a new look. And I was just the man to create it.

Some vital stats: I'm thirty-two years old. I've got auburn hair and green almond-shaped eyes that have been described by admirers as "liquefying." My skin is naturally the color of self-tan, and I have long hands with well-shaped fingernails. I'm also tall—six-three with large feet. And you know what large feet mean: big shoes. Ha. I'm also known for my sense of humor. I have a flat stomach and long legs. I'm not describing myself to brag—these traits are facts. The facts help explain why the ladies of Short Hills were so drawn to me. Though I could have, I didn't sleep with all of them. I couldn't have seduced more than a hundred women and still manage to maintain my

192

body weight. I selected the women who needed me most: the depressed, groping, confused lovelies whom no one, especially not their husbands, paid much attention to. I picked women whose kids never called, never wrote. And the women I found beautiful.

Only an ogre would have set out to kill them. I never did that, but the killing did make sense to me. It felt right, as if I were performing a service not listed on the Jalm menu (the eternal manicure? the seaweed wrap to infinity? I must tell Gaff to use that concept). I made sure they died happy. After Stacy—my second "victim"—I came to understand that murder was one true way to make an effect on the world. It was certainly more meaningful than perming.

Mattie came into Jalm with a goal in mind: she wanted to be a redhead. At that point, she was a fake blonde. Her first words to me were, "I hear you're a god. That's good, because I'm looking for a miracle." I was instantly impressed by her voice: a deep, world-weary seepage of breath. Her body would have made any thirty-year-old envious. Mattie herself was fifty-five. On our third or fourth date, she told me she'd been on hormone replacement therapy for years and feared breast cancer. A bigger fear, she said, was that Porky would leave her for a woman her daughter's age. Personally, I was glad she was taking the hormones. Otherwise, she wouldn't have been interested in sex.

I examined her bleach job and took her into my personal coloring room. I washed her hair and started to explain how I'd change the color. She said, "I don't care how you do it, just make me look sexy. I'm not entirely sure that's possible, but I'll take whatever help I can get."

"You're already sexy," I said honestly, despite the telltale facelift scars behind her ears.

"You're not gay?" she asked.

I laughed. "I'm an undercover heterosexual." I had an erection, as I always did after washing a woman's hair. Something about a wet neck, I don't know. I performed this task about half a dozen times a day, so I was in a constant state of excitement at the salon. Baggy clothes would have defeated the effect—the women seemed to like what they saw. Mattie let herself glance at my jeans. She blushed furiously, hopped out of my chair, and left the salon, her hair a wet mass of straw on her head.

I thought that would be the last I ever saw of her. I almost told the boss at Jalm that I'd flirted a customer right out the door. But then I decided to let it go. He'd hired me to flirt. I couldn't help it if I did my job too well. The next day, Mattie came in again. She didn't have an appointment, so I gave her my lunch hour. As soon as I finished her wash and condition, she said, "You must think I'm a fool." I thought nothing of the kind. She was a woman clearly wrestling with her desires and her sense of what she, and her marriage, were worth.

I said, "Life is short. I, however, happen to be very long." This made her blush again, from her cleavage all the way up to her hairline. "I'm also very, very discreet," I added. It's true, I'm not much of a talker. I'm a thinker and a sexual communicator. My skills are those of a technician, but if aroused, I become a sculptor, an artist of form, fashion, and texture. Molding, shaping, and transforming one piece of matter—okay, hair, nails, skin—into a completely different form. I change ugly into beautiful, wretched into sublime.

It's a natural gift—and a power trip—to create miracles.

My mother always encouraged me to do so. She was a midwife on Long Island—has been for forty years—and she performed miracles daily. Some of my most erotic and secret memories were watching her give vaginal exams to her pregnant clients. I used to hide in a closet in her birthing room (really just a section of our living room with a cushioned stool, a rubber mat, and a cart with some medical supplies) and watch when she aided a woman in labor. Witnessing childbirth is both terrifying and exhilarating—it is an experience that dwarfs all others by comparison. The prosecutor's shrinks testified that my repeated exposure to childbirth as a boy skewed my perception of mundane daily living. That my life has been a constant struggle to up the stakes, in effect, to chase the constant high of witnessing a life being born. Ultimately, the only way I could get close to that kind of power was in causing death.

Blah, blah, blah. Those shrinks know nothing. True, I've always wanted to create miracles like dear old Ma. And I did. All the time. The first miracle I performed on Mattie was dyeing her hair. Within that fateful lunch hour, I'd colored, tinted, and cut her shaggy mess into a layered red flip. She looked incredible. She even said so herself before sobbing quietly in my private styling room. I was so moved by her reaction that I gathered her in my arms and kissed her shoulders and breasts. Then we made love. She leaned over the armrest, and I took her from behind. She watched everything in the mirror, and I watched her watch us. She didn't come. Apparently, she only had orgasms when alone with a vibrator. I said, "That's awful!" It was. Any husband worth his salt goes down on his wife. Not every man likes it, but the pleasure a woman gets from oral sex far out-weighs any discomfort he might feel. And I've found most women are happy to reciprocate.

The intercom in my styling room announced that my next appointment had arrived. Mattie straightened her clothes. I felt terrible. I told her that I would not rest until she'd had an orgasm. It was unacceptable for her not to take every pleasure I could give. She agreed to meet me later. She pulled into the Jalm parking lot behind the salon after everyone had gone home. I gave her the tongue lashing of her life in the backseat of her Infiniti Q30 that night. She came so hard I thought she might rip my ears off. From that point on, we became regular lovers.

My problem with this affair existed at the beginning. I didn't want her husband or any of her friends to find out. My tips depended on the idea that I was both interested in and available to any woman who came into Jalm. For the first month, Mattie held up her vow to keep our love private. And then she talked. Stacy Muldoon, Mattie's best friend and my Wednesday at 10:00 A.M. bikini wax, started dropping hints that she knew what was going on. I pretended to have no idea what Stacy was dancing around. Mattie swore she hadn't said a thing.

Meanwhile, Mattie was growing bolder and more confident with every orgasm I gave her. She wore louder clothes. Stood up for herself at the supermarket. Complained when she'd been short-changed at the gas station. I realize that to most people, this kind of progress might seem slight. But Mattie thought she had no value other than serving her piggish husband breakfast after he used her as a life-sized masturbation tool. She was blooming.

I, on the other hand, was fading. I did enjoy our sex. She reacted sublimely, and I liked the power trip that gave me. I trained Mattie to stay focused on the moment. To feel every tingle, tongue twist, stroke, and spasm. I got her to forget about her life, her car, her husband—everything but the probings of my lips and tongue, and the gentle blowing technique I used to tease her.

I heard a crash. It was Judge Bloomfeld banging her gavel. I looked up. Porkpie was screaming and flinging balled fists in my direction. Damn him for interrupting my fantasy with his pathetic fit of rage. I had a flagpole erection, and this ridiculous man was demanding I stand to face him. "Get up, you piece of human filth," he insisted as he tumbled out of the witness box. He wanted to fight. Right here. In court. How typical of cuckolds, needing to demonstrate their feeble masculinity in public. He spun toward me. "I'll rip that leer off your face, you disgusting pervert." I didn't quite know what to do. If I stood up, my erection would be obvious to all, and I'd prove myself to be the "disgusting pervert" Porkie, and no doubt every other person in that room, took me for. If being a lover of women made me a pervert, then I was guilty. I cringed as Porky rushed my table. Luckily, two large bailiffs caught him before he wrapped those chubby little fingers around my throat.

Judge Bloomfeld was still beating the hell out of her gavel. She called for order in the court—a cliché I found so comic that I laughed. My involuntary reaction seemed to ignite a wave of whispers from the spectators behind me. I turned around and watched the angry faces. They scowled as if I were laughing at the American justice system itself, the system they hoped would give me life in prison. I swept the room with my eyes, feeling very detached from the whole show. All those people—seated, standing in the rear, the TV cameras attempting to film everything from the outside windows—were there to get a glimpse of me and try to understand how I could have killed four women the way I did.

I knew the dead women were in a far happier place. That was a comfort, but I had some selfish reasons for killing them. Namely, money and freedom. Weren't those the same reasons people have been killing each other since the dawn of time? What was so hard to grasp? I asked Gail, my friend from the *Star Ledger*, to explain the public bafflement. She scribbled my not-so-rhetorical ponderance in her steno book and then said, "It's not the *why,* Reggie. It's the *how.*" No one in the history of the world had previously used my method to commit murder. Poison—for fools. Guns, knives, any blunt weapon—for brutes. I caused spontaneous natural death—leaving no clues, no marks, no indication at all that I'd done anything wrong. Months passed before there was even a thought that they'd been killed. I have to admit—as the newspapers have already noted—my so-called perverted modus operandi was ingenious. It continues to enthrall the hoi polloi and give the members of the fourth estate who covered me, including Gail, their shot at a Pulitzer. But I'm not resentful. I fully intended to record my story in a longer form than these musings. I'll start in prison. I'll have all the time in the world. The Son of Sam law be damned—I won't be telling my story for the money. I want to give the people what they want. My goal, in fact, has always been to satisfy.

Judge Bloomfeld called a recess, but because it would be

for only five minutes, I was to keep my seat. I was lonely at the defendant's table. No lawyers at my side. No friends—you could call Gail a friend—nearby. Just my thoughts and memories for company. My erection had subsided. Porky had been escorted from the courtroom. I felt safer. I thought about my last night with Mattie. The night she pulled into the Jalm parking lot early to announce that she was going to leave her husband and move in with me. She couldn't keep silent about our affair a moment longer. She just had to tell everyone, and if she was drummed out of town for it, then we'd just have to find another place to live.

The sound of her words nearly paralyzed me. I was making good money at Jalm. I was sleeping with a couple of other women by then—including Mattie's best friend, Stacy. I was happy with the status quo, and on my way to being wealthy. Mattie was my favorite lady of Short Hills, but her announcement could mean only one thing for me: the end of life as I wanted it.

I kissed Mattie passionately on the lips to silence her crazy scheming. The air inside the Infiniti was suffocating that night, but I forged on. My lips traded down the familiar passage beyond her belly button. I gave her a screaming orgasm, performing my usual routine with new vigor. Instead of reciprocating, she promised to wait until I could talk to my boss at Jalm. I made the case that it was only fair to give him a warning of the scandal. Mattie never got to make her big announcement. By the next morning, she was dead. An embolism of the brain killed her body. Her soul, now beyond reach, was free to do whatever the fuck it wanted.

Recess over. The prosecutor called Stacy's husband to the witness stand. She was my number two. I killed her within a week of sending Mattie to the great unknown. Stacy loved to talk. Talk, talk, talk. I found her silver-blond straight hair beautiful and her small-breasted body exciting. If she didn't talk so much, I might have fallen completely in love with her. Her husband was a tall, broad-shouldered tennis-player type. Stacy told me she loved him like a brother. Their sex life had dwindled to nothing after their kids went to college. Stacy assumed Thomas had affairs. But whenever she tried to raise his interest, he'd kiss her on the forehead, turn the other way, and go to sleep.

Thomas Muldoon was stone-faced when he read a pre-pared statement from a piece of paper, "Isolation. Anger. Depression. Sleeplessness. Nervous sweats. Fits of incon-solable tears. Humiliation. Fatigue. Loss of appetite. Loss of ambition. Distraction. Paranoia." The man paused. He folded his notes and put them in his suit pocket. "I think my list of symptoms speaks for all the surviving victims of Mr. Styvestant. There's another one that deserves special men-tion: guilt. The idea that I drove my wife into the arms of this sadistic monster has caused me to contemplate suicide. If only I'd been a better husband, maybe she wouldn't have had to seek . . . comfort from Mr. Styvestant. That mur-derer"—he pointed at me—"took advantage of my wife in a way I couldn't have anticipated, nor had a chance to defend against. I'm so humiliated."

In other words, Thomas was impotent, and he might as well cut off his useless penis and die. I found it interesting that he drove Stacy to me and that I was this "sadistic mon-ster." But that he holds Stacy completely unaccountable for her actions? It takes two to have an affair. I know I wasn't alone in the backseat of her Lincoln Town Car during all those lunch hours. Stacy and I used to drive up to the Millburn Township nature reservation. We'd take her car as far along the trail as we could and then park. Stacy liked it best when we kept our clothes on. We'd unbutton and unzip, but she got off on the illicitness of pants around the ankles and shirts pushed up around the neck. I found the whole thing convenient, and I'd often mock-gag Stacy by stuffing the end of her scarf into her mouth. It shut her up, which I liked, and gave her a hostage fantasy, which she liked. Her husband, Thomas, was the last thing on her mind when I performed my magic on her. She was never tortured by her own infidelity the way Mattie had been at first. Stacy told me I wasn't her first, but I was her best (naturally). Like me, she was just in it for fun.

And it *was* all fun and games until she found out I was sleeping with her arch-rival, Mrs. Brenda Klensh. The suburban details bored me to death, but the story went something like this: Brenda's kid beat out Stacy's for some national scholarship and then ended up choosing not to accept after it was too late for the runner-up to claim it. Where parents send their kids to college was a source of fierce competition in Short Hills. By the time I met both ladies, their kids had been out of college for years. But a feud can feed on itself. A missed dinner invitation here, a bit of muddy gossip flung there. And before you know it, the women are hurling cantaloupes at each other's head at King's, the local supermarket.

The fact is, the feud between these two women was what got both of them killed. According to Brenda—a far quieter but acidly sophisticated woman—Stacy was bragging about her newest lover to a friend while in line at King's. Brenda was several places back in line. Some detail of Stacy's made Brenda think of me. You can imagine what happened next. Many confrontations ensued, and the truth came out.

Sharing a lover with a rival wasn't possible for either woman. Each tried to convince me to drop the other. I explained to both of them that my love was free and I would place no limitations on it. If I were to limit myself to one woman, then I might as well put fences around my capacity to love. I believe this philosophy, though I understand why it sounded like crap to them. Brenda and Stacy accused me of bullshitting my way into both of their pants. I shrugged through several conversations about this and made no choice between them.

I thought I'd heard the end of it. Then, in a surprise turn of events, these two old rivals teamed up against me. Shortly after work, Brenda and Stacy cornered me in the Jalm parking lot. They were holding hands when they announced that I had to choose one, or they'd both tell their husbands they'd been taken advantage of by a slick gigolo who was after their money. I couldn't quite comprehend the bounds of female competition until I heard this speech: Both women were willing to sacrifice their reputations and marriages just so a winner and a loser could be appointed. I asked for a night to think it over, but first I needed one more session with each lady to help me make my decision. Stacy waited in her Lincoln while Brenda and I romped in her Mercedes. Once I'd satisfied each woman, I promised a hasty decision. We all went our separate ways.

Of course, I never intended to choose between them. Instead, I decided to spare them both the pain of losing and silence their battle cries forever. I used the same method as with Mattie. Brenda collapsed behind the wheel of her car on the drive home, only minutes after leaving Jalm. She veered into a street sign, her head hitting the horn *Chinatown*-style. The paramedics pronounced her dead on the scene. Stacy died an hour later. She complained to her housekeeper of a weakness in the arms and legs and went to lie down. She never got up. Both died of massive embolisms in the brain.

Thomas Muldoon stepped down and took his seat alongside the man I knew to be Brenda's husband. He wasn't going to speak today. I wasn't sure why. Perhaps he was too humiliated to get up in front of a roomful of spectators, reporters, and TV cameras to discuss his wife's infidelity. Another husband, must be Casey's, was sworn in. I kept wondering, where are the kids? Do the children of Short Hills run so far and so fast from their parents that none were present to point an angry finger at their mother's killer? Just goes to show, women go through hell to bring them into the world, and then they spit all over their graves.

Husband number three was bereft. Unlike Porky who fumed or Thomas who postulated, Casey's husband, Craig, merely sobbed. I wished I had a tissue for him. He wiped at his nose and cheeks on the back of his suit sleeve. Aside from that display of uncleanliness, he was an attractive older man. Gray hair, weathered face. His back was long and straight. He looked like he'd driven at least five thousand golf balls. After a moment to collect his emotions, he spoke directly to the judge. "Your Honor, this is very hard for me. Casey was my life. Now I have nothing but shame, pity, and aching loneliness. I want this man to suffer even a tenth of what I'm going through. It seems only fair that he get a taste of my pain. I can't bear to look at him because I can see by the expression on his face that he doesn't understand what he's done."

A wave of pity passed up my chest, over my shoulders, and down my back. This man was so unhappy. The kind of unhappiness that a six-figure book deal won't fix. He looked broken from the inside out. Like his soul had been wadded up into a tight ball and chucked in the can. His obvious and genuine pain, however, couldn't be my fault. Two facts will always remain: (1) his wife made her decision all by herself, and (2) no matter how blissful he thought she'd been, Casey was happier now.

I could feel her presence in the courtroom. Unlike all the others, Casey's soul stuck around for a few weeks after I freed it. I stopped sleeping with other women until I knew she'd gone. It wasn't that I felt guilt. I remained celibate out of respect. Casey Roberts was a breathtaking woman with long black hair and lean arms. She had splashes of freckles—not liver spots—all over her cheeks. She was fifty-two going on thirteen. Always tan. Always a new scrape on her elbow or knee. She wore white cotton underwear and tiny A-cup cotton bras with no underwire. I adored her. She made me feel young. Of course, I was twenty years her junior, but she had that eternal-kid air about her. After an hour or two in her old Chevy, I always had a hankering for ice cream on a stick. She said our affair was her secret. She loved having secrets, just like all little girls. She felt some guilt about cheating, but she said she needed some excitement in her life, or she might as well die.

Her husband, Craig, the man currently sobbing freely with his head in his hands in the witness stand, was the reason I killed Casey. He found a note she was writing to me in her pocketbook as he was looking for money to tip the gardener. Casey never had any intention of revealing our affair—ironically. Craig was the only husband to find out about it before I was arrested. With tears coating the freckles on her cheeks, she pulled up at Jalm one afternoon and told me she was going to have to quit our friendship. I asked, "Don't I make you happy?"

She said, "I wouldn't be crying if you didn't make me happy."

"Then I completely understand why you want to stop seeing me," I quipped ironically. I'd never been dumped before in my life.

She sighed. I could almost see her mind working. She said finally, "I can't hurt my husband of thirty years like this just so I can get off in the backseat of my car a few times a week."

No woman had ever been so blatantly honest with me. I have to admit that my feelings were hurt. "I thought I was pouring my life's energy into satisfying you," I said. "I think of our time together as a moving art form. I suppose creating higher levels of consciousness pales in comparison to your tired, worn-out marriage to a man whose greatest passion is mulching the lawn." I had no idea why I was fighting to keep her. Sure, I loved Casey as I loved all the women in my life, but I never wanted commitment from her. In hindsight, I can understand how my speech might have forced her to say what she said next.

"I don't love you, Reggie." She wiped her nose cutely. "But if you feel that strongly about me, we can do it one more time to say good-bye." For a good half hour into it, I debated whether I should bump Casey into the astral plane. I wanted to be sure I did it out of love and not revenge. She had hurt me—and I feel more profoundly than ordinary people. In the end, I went ahead with it. She suffered her embolism while making love to her husband. According to what I read in the papers, he described her final moments to the coroner: her facial muscles clinched tightly on one side of her face; her left arm and leg were limp; a sudden spasm rocked her entire body, and she died in his arms with his penis still inside her.

A sudden feeling of remorse pinched my mind. I shook it off and searched for Gail's face in the crowd of spectators. She was frowning and tapping her fingers on her steno book. Craig was sobbing uncontrollably on the witness stand. The prosecutor was trying to help him down. Gail looked toward me. When we made eye contact, I winked. She blushed immediately and managed a smile. We'd have fun in prison while she helped me with my official biography.

I pictured us in my cell together. Talking. The vision was nice and cozy. I was about to let my mind create a fantasy about the two of us—I even felt the stirrings of another erection—only to be rudely interrupted by Craig. He'd pulled himself together enough to shake off the prosecutor. He turned toward Judge Bloomfeld and said, "I thought long and hard and came to the conclusion that I have nothing else to live for than making sure this man feels my pain." He reached down into his sock and straightened up with a pistol in his hand. It appeared to be ceramic—the only way he could have gotten past the courtroom's metal detectors. He didn't stand up. He merely aimed his gun and fired. The bullet hit me inches above the heart. It felt like Wiley Coyote had dropped an anvil on my chest. I never lost consciousness, but my vision blurred from pain. The picture of Craig Roberts putting the pistol, to his temple and blasting the better part of his brains onto Judge Bloomfeld's lap was pretty comic. And I would have laughed if blood wasn't seeping sloppily out of my mouth.

I was on the floor Gail was leaning over me. Something about the fall of her silky brown hair reminded me of Abby, the woman who was responsible for my arrest. Abby was my last lady of Short Hills. She was younger—maybe forty. We'd been seeing each other for only a few weeks when she picked me up in her Range Rover and said she was pregnant. She didn't know if the baby was mine or her husband's. She was upset about it, but excited. This was her first pregnancy, and her last chance at having a child. She refused to have sex that day. Had she not, I'd have tried to transform both her energy and the baby's then and there. I had no intention of being a father. I'd had enough of child-birth as a kid. The whole enterprise was a giant mess. I wanted nothing to do with it.

She told me she was going to the doctor the next day. She'd call me with news of "our" baby. But instead of a phone call, the police showed up at Jalm and arrested me. Abby, apparently, was greatly concerned that she wouldn't be able to enjoy cunnilingus during her pregnancy. She had an active sex life, and this was her favorite part. The doctor assured her it was fine, as long as her partner didn't blow air directly into the vagina. If the force is great enough, an air bubble could find its way into the woman's bloodstream and cause a fatal brain embolism. The doctor explained that any woman was at risk of this, not necessarily pregnant ones. Abby knew about me and Stacy (like I said, Stacy loved to talk). Abby, a smart lady, put two and two together. I admitted to performing oral sex on Mattie, Brenda, Stacy, and Casey. But I denied knowledge of the grave effects of my personal style of blowing puffs of air into their vaginas. The dogged prosecutors somehow learned of my mother's profession, however. They contacted her, and she told them that her Reggie used to stay up nights, masturbating to medical texts. In one of those texts, there was a description of how a tiny air bubble can travel from the vagina into the bloodstream, through the heart, into the brain, and then explode. On my own mother's testimony, I was convicted.

Gail was screaming my name. I felt and heard nothing but the whoosh of blood from my wound. I tried to smile at the woman who would chronicle my glory. I said, "Write about me. And don't forget to mention that I never cried at the end." I was definitely dying. In the certainty of my energy transforming, I never felt more free. I closed my eyes and saw images of my ladies of Short Hills floating near the ceiling of the courtroom. They held out their arms to me. Devilish Stacy even parted her legs slightly. I tried to open my eyes to say good-bye to Gail but couldn't muster the strength. I let myself float upward, toward my lovers. My last words were: "Finally, ladies, here I come."

Turning the Witness

JEREMIAH HEALY

ONE

Riding the elevator alone to Steve Rothenberg's floor, I finished reading an article in the *Boston Globe* about the lame-duck governor of New York and the dead-duck mayor of its largest city, the latter committing political suicide by crossing party lines to endorse the former. We don't have those kinds of problems in Massachusetts. No, our electorate votes overwhelmingly in favor of term limits on the Commonwealth's pols, then on the same ballot returns Teddy Kennedy to continue his fourth decade in the Senate. You figure it out.

When the elevator stopped, I tucked the paper under my arm and walked down the corridor to Rothenberg's door. He shared space with six or seven other attorneys, the individual names on wooden cross-bars, each done by a different artisan. The overall effect would remind you of a primitive, vertical xylophone.

Inside the door was a cluttered, shabby waiting area, but I didn't need the receptionist. Rothenberg already stood by her desk.

"Steve."

"John, I'm glad you're here."

"Client getting a little nervous?" I said.

Rothenberg just ran a hand through his thinning, graying hair. The beard was a shade darker, his tie already tugged down from an unbuttoned collar, even though my watch read only nine-thirty A.M.

"Come on back," he said, shrugging out of his suit jacket.

As we entered the office, a man in his thirties rose from one of Steve's client chairs. About six feet tall and sturdy, he had curly black hair and blue eyes that might have gained some sparkle from contact lenses. His complexion was ruddy above the collar of an oxford shirt and repp tie, the herringbone suit looking custom-tailored.

Hanging his own jacket on a battered clothes tree by the desk chair, Rothenberg said, "Rick Blassingale, John Cuddy."

Solid handshake, but he also placed his left hand over our joined right ones. "Mr. Cuddy, I really appreciate your coming down on such short notice."

The voice was gravelly, and I placed him from the media coverage of his wife's killing. "Mr. Blassingale—"

He released my hand. "Rick, please."

Rothenberg said, "Why don't we all sit down?"

Settling back into his chair, Blassingale said, "I guess the first issue here would be confidentiality."

I remembered the newspaper describing him as an investment adviser. "You have any law school, Rick?"

A modest smile. "Graduated but never practiced. You?"

"One year, nights. Steve didn't tell you there's a confidentiality provision in the licensing statute on private investigators?"

"He did. I just wanted to be sure we were all aware of it."

I was beginning not to like Blassingale very much, and I wondered why an apparent high-roller would be represented by a hand-to-mouth criminal lawyer like Steve

Rothenberg.

Blassingale let out a breath. "As you've probably heard, the police think I killed my wife. We were separated, and the probate and family court was in the process of cleaning me out, but good. The police say that's plenty of motive, since Libby had no other living relatives, which means everything comes back to me."

"If you're acquitted."

A very steady "Yes" with a glance toward his attorney. "And the bail bond just about tapped me out of what I did have left."

Meaning he had to go with a low-rent lawyer and keep his fingers crossed. I looked to Steve. "Where do I fit in?"

Rothenberg twiddled a pencil on the desktop. "The evidence against Rick is completely circumstantial. Libby Blassingale was still living in their marital home, a condo on upper Marlborough Street. Nothing missing from the apartment, and she was bludgeoned to death, weapon not found."

"Suggesting premeditation," I said.

Rothenberg nodded. "No sign of forced entry, either, and time of death is a wide bracket, six P.M. to sometime around midnight on Tuesday, November fifteenth. The body wasn't discovered till the next morning when the decedent didn't meet a neighbor for coffee as scheduled."

Blassingale said, "Libby was a platinum blonde, John, very flashy. She could have picked somebody up or just let them in."

"What makes you think that?"

"It's how we met." He let that sink in some. "I've learned my lesson, though. Strictly brunettes for me now."

A poor joke, and I couldn't remember the last time I'd

heard somebody actually use the word *brunette* in a spoken sentence.

Blassingale mistook my silence and grinned, man-to-man. "You married, John?"

I thought of Beth, lying in her hillside overlooking the harbor in South Boston. "Used to be."

"Then you understand what I mean."

I looked at Rothenberg, who in turn looked out his window at the Boston Common across Boylston Street.

I said, "My wife died, Rick."

"Oh." He shifted in his chair. "Jesus, I'm sorry, huh? What I meant was, Libby was crazy enough to try anything, anybody, even in these times."

I turned back to Rothenberg. "What else does the prosecution have?"

"Rick's fingerprints all over the apartment."

"Hey, it used to be my place, too."

I said, "Any other forensics?"

"Fibers from her carpet on a pair of Rick's shoes." A glance to his client. "Her new carpet, laid down after Rick moved out. And some blood of hers on the top of those shoes."

I looked at Blassingale, who said, "I was over there after I moved out. September, two months before Libby was killed. We were talking about trying to work something out on the settlement—the divorce stuff—and she got nervous, pulled a hangnail. It must have dripped blood on my shoes when we said good-bye at the door."

A hangnail. "How hard did you hit her, Rick?"

Blassingale opened and closed his mouth. Then, "She never reported it, but that coffee friend of hers saw the mark

212

and told the cops about it when they questioned her."

From the tone of his voice, Blassingale thought that awfully unfair of the friend. I said, "Didn't the papers say something about an eyewitness?"

Blassingale just looked at me, but Rothenberg said, "Two, actually, the night of the killing. One was a woman walking her dog, says she saw a man wearing a Celtics warmup jacket on the right block about eight P.M. that night."

Within the bracket. "She identify Rick as the man?"

Blassingale said, "Couldn't pick me out of the lineup, but the guy she described was close enough to me."

I turned to him. "You have that kind of jacket?"

"Had."

"What happened to it?"

"I don't know. It was old, and I must have left it somewhere."

I didn't say anything. Blassingale grew more earnest. "You know, all the warm weather we had back in October? I must have taken it with me someplace and just left it. I don't remember where, but give me a break, huh? Everybody and his brother has one of those."

To Rothenberg, I said, "Sounds like enough for the DA to get to the jury."

"It is, but the second witness is what you're here for."

"Go ahead."

"This second witness is named Claire Kinsour, K-I-N-S-O-U-R. She lives on the next block of Marlborough intown from Mrs. Blassingale." Rothenberg drew in a deep breath. "Ms. Kinsour came forward a few weeks ago, just after the prosecution said it was going to trial against Rick. She says she saw the man in the Celtics warmup jacket that night of the fifteenth, too, only it was about eight-thirty. And she saw him running east down the block away from the decedent's building."

I said, "Where do you live, Rick?"

Blassingale shifted again in his chair. "Waterfront." A grunt. "Like I'd walk two miles to Libby's place in my own jacket to kill her."

"Where on the waterfront?"

"Where I live, you mean?"

"Yes."

He gave me the name, one of the chi-chi wharf buildings that stick out into the harbor. "Only about a mile and a half, Rick."

"That's not the problem."

Rothenberg said, "The problem is, Ms. Kinsour definitely identifies Rick as the man she saw that night."

"How can she be so sure?"

Blassingale said, "Claire and I used to work together."

Great. "Go on."

"She was a trainee at Goff Searle, this brokerage house I worked for until I went out on my own three years ago. Claire had the hots for me then, and I wasn't interested."

"And Ms. Kinsour just happens to live down the street from your wife?"

Rothenberg said, "Moved in a month before Mrs. Blassingale was killed."

"Did they know each other?"

Blassingale said, "I don't know. I sure never took Libby to any Goff Searle events when Claire was there."

"You have an alibi for the night in question?"

"No. I was home, reading. I even pulled the phone out of

the wall jack."

I shook my head.

"Hey, I do that sometimes, get some peace and quiet. Claire's lying. She's going to commit perjury to get even with me, and Steve here says there's nothing he can do about it."

I couldn't remember a perjury indictment for the past ten years. "What kind of plea bargain did the prosecution offer?"

Blassingale's face got ruddier, the color high at the cheekbones. "That seems pretty damned defeatist, don't you think?"

Rothenberg made a calming gesture with his hand. "Before Ms. Kinsour came forward, twenty and change. Afterward, *nada*."

I thought about it. "And Ms. Kinsour comes forward only after the news hits about Rick going to trial."

"Yes."

"Why?"

Rothenberg smiled. "One of the many questions we'd like you to ask her." Then the smile died. "We have to impeach her, John. The other stuff I can deal with on cross of the Commonwealth's witnesses. The blood on the shoes through the coffee friend and the abuse incident—"

"I didn't abuse her, for Chrissake! I slapped her, once."

Another calming gesture. "But Ms. Kinsour sinks us, John. We have to turn her as a witness, or the jury sees this thing only one way."

I looked to Blassingale. "Any other help you can give me on that?"

A shrug, "I don't know. Claire had a girlfriend at Goff

Searle, another trainee. Gina Ferro—that's F-E-R-R-O—was her name, but we checked the phone books, and she's not listed anywhere."

"Might the brokerage know?"

"Might." Blassingale brightened. "Yeah, they might. I should have thought of that."

Yes, he should. "Anybody still there I could contact?"

"Try Mike Oldham. Ferro worked with him the most."

I watched Blassingale. "One more thing?"

"Shoot."

"You seeing anybody now?"

"Seeing . . . ?" Blassingale looked down at his shoes. "Yes."

"She with you that night?"

Blassingale looked up. "No."

"You sure?"

"I said no. Besides, she's married."

"And brunette?"

The flesh around the cheekbones got ruddier again.

TWO

Marlborough Street stretches east to west for nine blocks from the Public Garden through Boston's Back Bay neighborhood. The buildings are three- and four-story townhouses in brownstone and brick, some still single-family. Most are divided into condos and apartments, though that doesn't diminish the imitation gas lamps and residential parking restrictions or the red-bricked sidewalks, frost-heaved into stumble-humps. The trees whose roots helped with the heaving were bare of leaves and stark against the sun on the north side of the block where Claire Kinsour lived.

At the front entrance, I walked up the stoop and pushed her buzzer. Getting a tinny "Who is it?" from the speaker, I asked if Ms. Kinsour could speak with me about a court case. Two minutes later, the massive formal door opened, and an ash blonde in her late twenties looked out coyly at me. Kinsour was slim but big through the chest under a cotton cowl sweater, and she cocked her hip, straining some bleached jeans.

"And who might you be?"

I showed her my identification.

Kinsour took the folder, holding it up to the light. "John Francis Cuddy." She looked from it to me, using her free hand to tap the index fingernail against her lower front teeth. "Irish, right?"

"At some point."

Kinsour handed back the ID. "What's this about?"

"I'm working for the lawyer representing Rick Blassingale."

"And you'd like to ask me some questions, help to trap me later on in court."

"Something like that."

A coy smile joined the look. "Well, at least you're honest, which is more than I can say for Rick." She canted her head. "The prosecutor said I didn't have to talk to anybody if I didn't want to."

"And you don't."

"But you're cute enough to spend some time with." One tap of the nail. "And I don't have anything else to do, so come on up."

As Kinsour climbed the central stairs ahead of me, I said,

"It's good luck to find you home."

"Not really. I'm unemployed. Those of us out of work spend a lot of time at home." She half turned. "Or hadn't you heard?"

"Heard what?"

"About the latest decline in the securities industry. First there was Black Monday in 'eighty-seven, and then came just the slow torture of the last year or so."

We reached the second floor, and a door stood open around the corner of the landing. Kinsour beckoned me over the threshold into a front unit with nice sunlight streaming from the bay window onto an Oriental rug. The furniture was tasteful and fairly new; an elaborate stereo system was arrayed under the window.

"Nice place for being unemployed."

She laid a hand on the back of an easy chair, then made for the one opposite it. "I wasn't out of work when I landed here."

We sat. "Which I understand was just early October?"

Kinsour became a little defensive. "That's right."

"Did you know Libby Blassingale?"

"Before she died, no."

"But you're sure you saw Rick Blassingale the night of the killing."

"That's right."

"From this room?"

"It was only about eight-thirty, but I wanted to turn in early, so I was in the bedroom." The coy smile. "Alone. Then I came out here to be sure the CD player was off, and I saw Rick across the street."

I got up and walked over to the bay window. "From

here, then?"

"Right where you're standing."

I looked through the panes of angled glass. Squeaky clean, and a nice view for one block east and another west. "And where exactly was Mr. Blassingale?"

"Rick was on the other side of the street—his wife's side, it turns out. Running toward the Public Garden."

Meaning eastward. "Wearing?"

"One of those shiny Celtics jackets. You know, that kind of off-green you see everywhere on St. Patty's Day?" A pause. "No offense meant."

"None taken." There were two gas lamps across the way, and the trees would have been bare by then, even with the warmer weather we'd had. "Was he carrying anything?"

"Some kind of bag, like for gym stuff."

Which could have held the weapon. "Hat?"

"Wearing one, you mean?"

"Yes."

"No. I got a good, clear look with the streetlights, and I recognized him."

"Because you two once worked together."

"That's how I'd describe it. Rick, though, he wanted it to be more than that."

I turned to her, came back to the chair. "How so?" Kinsour rotated her neck on the shoulders a little, then tapped again with her index nail against the teeth. "Sex so."

"Anything come of it?"

"I was a trainee at Goff Searle. I wasn't about to cut my own throat, so I didn't make any sort of complaint."

Which wasn't exactly what I'd asked her. "Were you and Blassingale ever intimate?"

Kinsour puffed out a breath. "Only in his dreams."

"Why were you so late in coming forward to the authorities?"

"Identifying him, you mean?"

"Simple. All I saw was Rick running down the street that night. No big deal, right? Then the next morning, I had a dawn flight to Seattle. That's why I was going to bed so early."

"Seattle."

"Yes. Job interview, and I stayed with a friend of mine from college for a few days. So I guess I left before the wife's body was found, and all the TV stuff about Rick had died down by the time I got back."

"Then what led you to contact the police?"

"There was this thing on the news about Rick going to trial soon, and I just kind of freaked. Then I said, 'Oh my God, I bet they could use me,' so I called them."

"To get even with Rick."

"That's why I called them." Tap, tap. "But that's not what I saw or why I saw it that night."

"And you remember it was that night—"

"November fifteenth, because my flight was the sixteenth. I didn't get the job, but check it out with the airline, you want to."

"Thanks, I will." I rose, and she did, too, slowly, even languidly.

"One other thing," I said. "Have you heard from Gina Ferro recently?"

"Gina . . . ?" Tap, tap. "What does she have to do with this?"

"Maybe nothing. I'd just like to speak with her."

"Well, I don't know how'd you'd reach her."

"No idea at all?"

A theatrical shrug. "She got married, I heard. Don't know about the name."

"Her husband's name?"

A patient look. "No, her name. If she changed it, I mean. A lot of women still do, you know?"

THREE

"Law offices."

"Steve Rothenberg, please. John Cuddy calling."

"One moment, please."

A click and a burr, then, "Steven Rothenberg."

"Steve, John Cuddy."

"How does it look?"

"Bleak, if Claire Kinsour is on the level."

He paused. "Well, that's the question, isn't it?"

"I know, Steve. But Kinsour says your client's the one who made the move at the place they worked."

"You believe her?"

"I'm not sure I want to believe either of them, but a jury would like her more than Blassingale, I'd say."

"Oh, that's just ducky." Again a pause. "On the other hand, whether he rejected her or she rejected him, I can show Kinsour's biased." A third pause. "You going to the brokerage house next?"

"Unless you have a better idea."

"If I did, I wouldn't have hired you, right?"

The receptionist at Goff Searle & Associates led me deftly

221

to a rear corner office. Plaques recounting good deeds and photos displaying hearty handshakes occupied every available square foot of wall space. The desktop was covered by two different computer systems and God knows what else to support them. Michael Oldham seemed nearly buried behind the equipment. Even when he stood to greet me.

About five-three and slightly bow-legged, Oldham reminded me of a miniature Dick Van Dyke from the old TV show as he dimmed the screens he'd been studying. Half-glasses on the end of his nose over a bow tie and suspenders, Oldham was very old-school and pushing fifty but not showing an ounce of fat doing it. "Have a seat, Mr. Cuddy."

"Thanks."

Oldham signaled to the receptionist, who withdrew and closed the door behind her. Taking off the glasses, he said, "Now, just what can I do for you?"

I told him.

The stockbroker's face looked as though the market had just hit the 'dive' button. "Distasteful business."

"I agree. But that doesn't get it done."

His expression returned to normal. "No, you're certainly right there. Very well. What do you want to know?"

"What was the relationship between Rick Blassingale and Claire Kinsour while they worked here?"

"Relationship?"

"How did they get along?"

Oldham knew that wasn't what I meant. "Claire was a trainee. I matched her up with Rick. My fault, really."

"What was?"

"There was some kind of tension between them. Friction.

You could almost see it jumping off their bodies whenever they were together."

"Sexual tension?"

"As I said, distasteful business." A snort. "I'd guess possibly, but I never saw or heard anything that would confirm such a thing. Rick was married at the time, but I take it you already know that."

I nodded. "Any sense that one of them was being jilted?"

"No."

Oldham's reply brooked no further discussion. "How about Gina Ferro?"

"Ah, Gina. Wholly different person."

"From, Kinsour?"

"From both of them." Oldham seemed to warm up a little. "Rick was always a bit too . . . positive for his own good. Arrogant, even. I don't mean just ego, either. Ego you need in this business, along with nerve and judgment, Rick had all those, but his arrogance kept him from reconsidering his own decisions over time, and over time that failure can pummel a portfolio, simply pummel it."

"And Claire Kinsour?"

"Awfully aware of her good looks. And more than a bit too deferential. Waited for others to move before she would. Insufficient initiative, I'd have said. But Claire didn't stay long enough to gauge that for certain."

"Blassingale have anything to do with her leaving?"

"No. At least, I don't believe so. Claire simply moved on to another house. I couldn't say if she's still there or not."

"And Gina Ferro?"

"Would have made a fine broker, but she didn't really enjoy it. The thrill of the game just wasn't there for her.

223

Pity, too. Fine mind, excellent at analysis, projections—ah, but you hate to lose the best of the younger ones."

"You have any idea where Ms. Ferro is now?"

She left the industry entirely. Married, settled down. A pity, but . . ." Oldham shrugged.

"Would you happen to have an address on her?"

"Home address, you mean?"

"Or any way I could get in touch with her."

The frown. "Don't know that I would have her married name, but . . . wait a minute." Oldham brought up one of the screens, clacked away a minute, then traced his middle finger down the screen. "Yes Yes, Gina sent me an announcement when she had her baby, and I made a note of the address, Day Boulevard. All the way over in Southie, I'm afraid."

It had been a while since my last visit. "Not a problem."

I wouldn't have thought they'd still have tulips, this time of year.

I looked down at her headstone, Elizabeth Mary Devlin Cuddy. "Mrs. Feeney said they weren't from Holland, but that was all she knew."

"Well, they're beautiful, John. Special occasion?"

"I've never needed one before."

I just stood there for a while, watching a boat from the Boston Police harbor unit rise and slap against the chop as it patrolled the water below her hillside.

What's bothering you?

"A case. Husband accused of killing his wife, maybe abusing her, too. Some possible hanky-panky at the office when both sides weren't willing. And I don't know who to

224

believe out of it."

Would the case be any easier if you did?

I smiled. "Not necessarily."

Maybe you just haven't found the right person yet.

"The right person?"

The one you can believe.

We talked about other things for a while after that. Old friends and older times, back when we were together and the world seemed easy. Then I noticed the police boat's running lights were on, and I figured it was time to say good-bye.

FOUR

The address Michael Oldham gave me turned out to be an expansive two-decker just west of the L Street Bath-house on Day Boulevard. The woman who answered the bell was holding a little boy between the ages of one and two. Her eyes were chocolate brown, as was her hair, in a pageboy flip, like she took care of it. About the same height as Claire Kinsour, she was a little bigger all around, as though she might not yet have shed the extra pounds childbearing had imposed on her.

"Yes."

"Gina Ferro?"

A smile. "Not anymore." Then a cautious look. "Wait a minute. How did you get this address?"

"I'm helping Rick Blassingale's lawyer, and I was able to track you down."

Still cautious. "You have some identification?"

I showed her my ID. After reading it, she pointed to the

name laminated under the buzzer I'd pushed. "I'm Gina Shukas now. My husband's folks are from Lithuania."

"It would be a help if I could have a few minutes of your time."

"Sure, I guess. Come on up."

The second floor was sun-filled, even on a December afternoon. Spacious living room, modestly furnished but beautifully kept, despite the time burdens the child must have created. Gina Shukas took the couch, allowing the little boy to crawl off her lap onto the cushion. I sat across from her in a rocking chair.

Mother patted son's rear end, causing him to giggle. "Arthur Junior."

"Fine-looking boy."

"He has his daddy's eyes but his mommy's hair." A different tone. "Now, what do you need to know?"

"Whatever you can tell me about Rick Blassingale and Claire Kinsour."

"If you're helping Rick's lawyer, why do you need to know about Claire?"

Neutrally, I said, "She might be a witness at the trial."

"Oh. Well, I haven't really followed the case, so I don't know what to tell you. When we all worked together at Goff Searle, I know Claire thought he was kind of cute."

"She did."

"Yeah, but I don't know if it went anywhere. I mean . . . you know what I mean. When I saw in the paper that he was accused of killing his wife, I thought about calling her back—Claire, I mean—but I just never got around to it."

"Calling her back?"

"About his wife getting killed that same night. Like I said,

I haven't really followed the case and all, but how many people do you know have ever been charged with murder?"

When I didn't say anything, Shukas said, "Oh, right. For a minute there, I forgot who you . . . well, never mind. I didn't get a chance to call her after we had dinner."

I was still confused. "Dinner?"

"Yes. Claire called me in early November, said she was going out of town for a while, and did I want to get together with her. I thought it was kind of funny, but I said sure, why not. I mean, the baby's kept me kind of home-tied for over a year now—they say you can watch TV and all? Don't believe it, especially when Art—my husband, I mean—is out of town."

"Ms. Kinsour called, and you thought it was 'kind of funny'?"

"Well, yeah. I mean, Claire and I weren't exactly close at Goff Searle, and she left before I did. But you know, once you leave a place, you lose touch with the people, especially if you aren't working somewhere else. Claire said she wasn't working, either, and was flying to Seattle, maybe to move there, and 'Why don't we get together around seven,' you know? So I said sure."

"And so you did?"

"Yes." She ruffled her son's hair, and he giggled again, kicking his leg sideways. "I got Art's mom to baby-sit— she isn't too keen on me going out when he's gone, tell you the truth, but that's just her way. So I met Claire for a drink, and we talked about her new job possibility and Arthur Junior here. One drink turned into two, and two turned into dinner. Just pasta and salad, but it was nice. Kind of reminded me what I liked about working downtown."

"And when was this?"

"When we went out? The night before her flight."

"Wait a minute. The night Libby Blassingale was killed?"

"Like I said. Of course, I didn't hear about it right away—Arthur Junior keeps me pretty occupied, don't you?" More ruffling, and the boy plodded around, like a cat coming back to be scratched. "But I remember saying to Claire at dinner, 'Girl, you're gonna be dead on your feet tomorrow, you don't get to bed early,' and thinking later how weird it was that Rick's wife got killed, probably around the time I was saying that. But Claire wouldn't hear of cutting the evening short. Said how often would we ever see each other, and she had a good point there."

Very slowly, I said, "What time did you and Ms. Kinsour finally part company?"

"Oh, ten, ten-fifteen? I know it was ten-thirty before I got home, because Art's mother was in a funk over how late I was out with my 'girlfriend.' "

Two hours after Claire Kinsour supposedly stood in her apartment, seeing Rick Blassingale running down Marlborough Street. "Where did you eat?"

"This little place on Beacon Hill. It wasn't very expensive, but even so Claire insisted on treating me."

"She did."

"Yes. Said, 'So long as I have plastic, I can't be broke, right?' I felt kind of bad, her being out of work and all, but she gave the check and her credit card to the waiter before I knew what was happening."

Which meant a receipt and maybe even . . . "Ms. Ferro, do you remember the name of the restaurant?"

228

FIVE

The weather had finally turned to winter by the time of Rick Blassingale's trial in a ninth-floor session of Suffolk Superior Court. At Steve Rothenberg's request, the female, fiftyish judge allowed me to sit inside the bar enclosure at counsel table with him and his client. What a treat.

The courtroom itself was old-fashioned. High, almost church windows over mahogany wainscoting and scarred oak furniture. Fifteen years ago, the jury would have been three housewives, three retired people, three welfare recipients, and three postal workers. Now, with the "one day, one trial" system, almost everyone was subject to jury duty, even lawyers and judges, and the men and women staring back at us seemed as close to a cross-section of society as one could draw.

The prosecutor was a guy about Blassingale's age, and the case for the Commonwealth went in smoothly, a tide building from the jury box against the defendant. On cross-examination, Rothenberg chipped away at each witness where he could: getting the dog walker to admit she couldn't pick the defendant out of a lineup, the coffee friend to venture that the mark on Libby Blassingale's face might have bled a little, the forensic expert to concede that the bloodstain on Rick's shoe might have been left there months before the killing.

The prosecutor saved Claire Kinsour till last. Her ash blond hair was pulled back into a conservative bun, her suit a dark blue that complemented her coloring. Kinsour was composed, even compelling. I could feel the tide from the jury rising to a wave against Blassingale.

When the prosecutor passed the witness to Rothenberg, Steve rose and requested permission to approach the bench. When he got there, he asked the judge if "this item" in his hand could be marked as Defendant's Exhibit No. 5 for identification. After the court reporter scribbled on it, Rothenberg showed it to the prosecutor, who did a good job of not fainting. Then Steve requested and received permission to approach the witness.

At the stand, Rothenberg said, "Ms. Kinsour, it was your testimony a few minutes ago that you saw Rick Blassingale running eastward on Marlborough Street about eight-thirty on the night of his wife's death, is that correct?"

Kinsour didn't have to think. "Yes."

Nodding to the jury, Rothenberg handed her the "item" and said, "I show you now Defendant's Exhibit Number Five for Identification and ask you if that's your signature at the bottom."

Kinsour said, "Yes," and then her eyes bugged as they moved up the restaurant receipt to the top.

Rothenberg lowered his voice. "And what is that exhibit, Ms. Kinsour?"

"It's . . . it's a charge card . . ."

"The exhibit is a charge card receipt you signed at a restaurant half a mile away from your apartment on the night in question, is it not?"

"Yes."

"Please note the computer time-stamp under the name of the restaurant, and tell the jury what it says."

"It . . . it . . ." Claire Kinsour rubbed a hand over her face. "I can't . . . oh, God, I can't believe this." She turned to the jury. "I lied. I was attracted to Rick when we worked together—"

The jurors all came forward in their seats, some with mouths open.

"Objection, Your Honor!" cried the prosecutor.

The judge started to say something, but Kinsour's voice caromed around the courtroom. "I didn't see Rick that night at all. At ten-thirty, I did see a man running down the block, carrying a bag and wearing a green Celtics jacket like I knew Rick had."

"The witness will please—"

"When I heard Rick was going to trial, I went to the police and lied. The man I saw, and saw clearly that night, was not Rick Blassingale."

Steve Rothenberg moved back to the defense table. The judge told Claire Kinsour that her next unresponsive sentence would leave her open to contempt of court, but you could tell the judge's heart was barely in it.

In disgust, the prosecutor said, "No questions. That's the Commonwealth's case, Your Honor."

The judge looked over toward us. "Mr. Rothenberg?"

"I don't see the need for any defense witnesses, Your Honor."

"Yes, well, why don't you keep your editorial comments to yourself? Ms. Kinsour, you are excused."

As the witness left the stand, eyes down and almost trotting out of the courtroom, the judge turned to the jury. "After I hear some motions by counsel, we may have closing arguments tomorrow morning." Then she told them when and where to report and excused them for the day.

After the last juror had filed out and the court officer closed the door, Rick Blassingale threw his arms around Rothenberg, then extended his hand to shake mine, again closing his left over our two hands, saying warmly, "All I could ask for, John. Thank you, thank you, thank you."

For some reason, I felt sick.

Usually, cases are hard. Occasionally, they're easy. Virtually never is one served up on a silver platter, and so dramatically.

Leaving the courthouse, I went back to my office and sat with my eyes closed, going over in my head what I'd learned and how I'd learned it. Blassingale giving me Claire Kinsour, Michael Oldham, and Gina Ferro. Kinsour telling me Rick was after her, not the other way around, but also mentioning that Gina might have changed her name after getting married. Oldham not knowing that new name but having a new address in his computer. Ferro remembering the date and time of her dinner with Kinsour, who paid for it in a way that produced a time-stamped receipt. Almost like I was following directions.

At the cemetery, I'd told Beth that I didn't know who was telling the truth. If what Claire Kinsour said from the stand after seeing the receipt was reality, then Rick Blassingale had been honest with me in Rothenberg's office. Ferro might have mentioned over dinner that she wasn't keeping up on the news, given the baby and all. But if Kinsour wanted to nail Rick as vengeance, why not just say she saw him running down the street at ten-thirty, not eight-thirty, which was still within the time-of-death bracketing? Especially when Kinsour had to know that

Ferro, if found and interviewed, could destroy the eight-thirty version?

There was only one complete explanation, and I just hoped Michael Oldham's take on the players was right enough to help me prove it.

Dressed in dingy work pants, a sweater torn at the neck, and an old parka with the stuffing peeking out, I put a liter bottle of Sprite in a brown paper bag and crimped the paper at the top. Then I drove down to the waterfront, parking three blocks from Rick Blassingale's building on the wharf. I walked to the building, a little unsteadily, and slumped down against a wall across from the main entrance, taking a slug now and then from the Sprite as though it were something stronger.

Nobody was on duty inside the door, which didn't surprise me. People came and went, several on entering having some trouble getting their keys to turn in the lock. Then a brunette appeared, her back toward me, walking toward the front door. Her hair was done in a pageboy flip, the long winter coat bulky around her body, making it hard to estimate weight.

She had trouble with the key, too. Then she held it up to the light, tapped with her index fingernail on her lower teeth, and tried the key again, this time getting it to work.

The woman disappeared inside, and I watched an upper floor light come on, then go off. Shortly afterward, what might have been a living-room light dropped to a romantic level.

Oldham was right. Arrogance on the one hand and deference on the other.

Leaning over, I poured out the rest of the Sprite and went home.

. . .

Steve Rothenberg said, "John, thanks for coming, but we really don't need you for the closings."

I looked at both of them, people bustling around us in the corridor outside the courtroom. "The judge denied your motions?"

Rothenberg glanced confidently at Rick Blassingale beside him. "Yes, but I expected that. Without the Kinsour woman's testimony, there was still barely enough for the prosecutor to carry his burden of production, so the judge is letting the case go to the jury. But after what happened yesterday on the stand, I'm not worried about this one."

"You should be."

Rothenberg darkened as the color ripened in his client's face. "What does that mean?"

I pinched Blassingale's arm gently at the elbow. "Why don't we go over here, where it's a little more private."

In the dead-end alcove, they stood while I sat on the stiff bench and crossed my arms, leaning back. "I'm going to give you my own closing here, guys. Tell me what you think of it."

Neither of them said anything.

"Rick Blassingale is going through a bad divorce but has a new—or not so new—girlfriend. It'd be great to be a widower, he thinks. Unfortunately, though, he'd be the prime suspect, a role he'd rather not play. Then he sees a way to get what he wants without having to duck the role."

Blassingale said, "You don't know what you're talking about."

"It gets better. Rick has his girlfriend move into an apartment almost across the street from his wife's place. Using that as a base of operations, he ventures forth on the night of November fifteenth around eight P.M. in a fairly common jacket that was expendable. Unfortunately, a woman walking her dog spots him, but that alone isn't fatal. He uses his old key to get in his wife's building, then gets her to open up the apartment door on some pretext, maybe more talk or 'I have a let's-make-up present in the bag, Libby.' "

"You're nuts," said Blassingale.

Rothenberg said quietly, "Let him talk, Rick."

I nodded toward the client. "You get back to Claire's place pretty quickly, leaving her the weapon, the Celtics jacket, and probably everything else you were wearing that night in the bag, to take to Seattle with her and dump safely. You're home free, except you forget to throw away the shoes you wore in September, the night you hit Libby, the shoes that had her blood on them as a result. Bad luck, but then, you can't be expected to think of everything, right, Rick?"

No response.

Rothenberg said, "But then why have Kinsour come forward at all?"

"She doesn't, Steve, not until after the lab tests on the shoes, together with the other evidence, give the DA enough to go to trial. That's when Rick's reserve plan has to kick in. Not a great plan to a practicing lawyer, but it must have seemed awfully clever to somebody who only graduated law school. Have the witness, with an apparent motive to get even with the defendant, testify against him, then be turned by an incontrovertible piece of evidence, like the restaurant receipt or Gina Ferro's testimony on timing that night."

Rothenberg shook his head. "So that Kinsour first implicates, then exonerates, Rick as the killer?"

"Exactly. Otherwise, she just testifies that she saw the definite Ricker here at ten-thirty, leading to no impeachment of her testimony by receipt or Ferro."

I fixed Blassingale, who was breathing badly and looking worse. "And you used me to set it up for you, Rick. Knowing that the system wouldn't bother prosecuting Claire for perjury, you led me by the hand to Kinsour, Oldham, and eventually Ferro and the restaurant. Neat, but a little too neat."

Blassingale managed to say, "I told you, I swore off blondes."

"Not based on what I saw last night, at your building's front door, with her own key. A brunette to the outside world, an ash blonde inside your apartment?"

Blassingale clenched his hands into fists and took a step toward me on the bench.

I said, "Keep coming, Rick. You'd look great to the jury with a broken nose."

Rothenberg turned to Blassingale. "Calm down. I need to know whether John's just blowing smoke here."

The ruddy face pushed toward the lawyer's. "You don't need to know anything. You just need to go back in that courtroom and argue to the jury what they heard from the stand."

I shook my head this time. "Sorry, Rick. No go. I seem to remember the DA offering you a plea bargain of twenty and change before Claire Kinsour came forward. I have a feeling the prosecutor would jump at that if you were to tell

236

im through Steve here that the offer looked good, that you
didn't want to risk what the jury might still do."

Blassingale stared. "You're asking me to send myself to
prison?"

"Rick, it's plead out, or I go to the prosecutor myself with
what I know and hang you in front of this jury or the next
one."

Blassingale's face looked like it was about to explode.
"No way! That's double jeopardy."

I looked to Rothenberg, who said, "Not until the verdict
comes back, and we haven't even closed yet. With what
Cuddy has, the judge could declare a mistrial and start you
in front of a whole new jury."

His face back to me, Blassingale started to dissolve. "But
you promised me confidentiality. I'll go . . . I'll file a complaint . . ."

"That's just a license, Rick. This is murder. I lose my
ticket, I lose it. But one way or the other, you're going to
pay for killing your wife. And I have a feeling that after I
talk with the other side, the twenty and change won't make
it back onto the bargaining table."

Tears actually started from Blassingale's eyes, rolling
down his ruddy cheeks, spotting his collar and tie. "What
are you doing to me?"

I stood up. "Just turning the witness, Rick. That's the
problem with the technique, though. Sometimes they turn
back on you."

Steve Rothenberg and I walked away from Rick Blassingale, to give him time to make up his mind.

That Day at Eagles Point

ED GORMAN

The day was dark suddenly, even though it was my four in the afternoon, and lightning like silver spider's legs began to walk across the landscape of farm fields and county highways. It was summer, and kids would be playing near creeks and forests and old deserted barns, and their mothers would see the roiling sky and begin calling frantically for them, tying to be heard above the chill damp sudden wind.

The rains came, then, hard slanting Midwestern rains that made me feel snug inside my new Plymouth sedan, rains making noises on the hood and roof like the music of tin drums.

That was the funny thing, I told Marcie I was buying the Plymouth for her, and she even went down and picked out the model and the color all by herself, but even so, a couple of weeks later, she left. Got home one day and saw two suitcases sitting at the front door, and then came Marcie walking out of the bedroom, prettier than I'd seen her in years. "I'm going to do it, Earle," was all she said. And then there was a cab there, and he was honking, and then she was gone.

I didn't handle it so well at first. I just read and reread the letter she left, trying to divine things implied, or things written between the lines, sort of like those Dead Sea scholars spending their whole lives poring over only a few pages.

Her big hang-up was Susan Finlay, and how I'd never

really gotten over her, and how there was something sick about how I couldn't let go of that gal, and how she, Marcie, wanted somebody to really love her completely, the way I never could because of my lifelong "obsession" with Susan Finlay.

That was a year ago. She only called once, from a bar somewhere with a loud country-western jukebox, said she was drunk and missed me terribly but knew that for me there'd never be anybody but Susan, and she was sorry for both of us that I'd never been able to love her in the good and proper way she'd wanted.

Another thing she hadn't liked was my occupation. Over in Nam, I was with a medical unit, so when I got back to New Hope, the town where I was raised, I just naturally looked for work at the hospital. But the hospital per se wasn't hiring, so they put me in touch with the two fellows who ran the ambulance service. I became their night driver, four to midnight, six nights a week. The benefits were good, and I got to learn a lot about medicine. In the beginning, Marcie was proud of me, I think. At parties and family reunions, people always came up to me and wanted to know if I had any new ambulance stories. Old ladies seemed to have a particular fascination with the really grim ones. Marcie liked me being the one people sought out.

But then my novelty faded, and there I was just this Nam vet with the long hair and Mexican bandit mustache, and a little pot belly, and glasses as thick as Palomars, bad eyesight being a family curse. Forty-three years old, I was, time to get a real job, everybody said. But this was my real job, and it was likely to be my real job the rest of my life . . .

I'd hoped to catch a good glimpse of the hills on the drive up this late afternoon. The hills were where David and Susan and I liked to play. This was Carstairs, the town I grew up in and lived in till the year before they shipped me off to New Hope. Dad got the lung disease, and Mom felt it was safer to live in New Hope where they had better hospital facilities.

But in my heart, Carstairs would always be my hometown, the town square with the bandstand and the pigeons sitting atop the Civil War monuments, and the old men playing checkers while the little kids splashed in the hot summer wading pool. If I tried hard enough, I could even smell the creosote on the railroad ties as Susan and David and I ran along the tracks looking for something to do.

The three of us grew up in the same apartment house, an old stucco thing with a gnarled and rusty TV antenna on the roof and a brown faded front lawn mined with dog turds. We were six years old the first time we ever played with each other.

We had identical lives. Our fathers were laborers, our mothers took whatever kinds of jobs they could find—dime store clerking, mostly—and we had too many brothers and too many sisters, and sometimes between the liquor and the poverty, our fathers would beat on our mothers for a time, and the "rich" kids at school—anybody who lived in an actual house was rich—the rich kids shunned us. Or shunned David and me, anyway. By the time Susan was ten, she started working her way through all the rich boys, breaking their hearts one at a time with that sad but fetching little face of hers.

But Susan had no interest in those boys, not really. Her

only interest was in David and me. And David and I were interested only in Susan. I was jealous of David. He had all the things I did not, looks, poise, mischievous charm, and curly black hair that Susan always seemed to find an excuse to touch.

I guess I started thinking about that when I was eleven or so. You always saw the older kids start pairing off about the time they reached fourteen. But who was going to pair off with Susan when we got to be fifteen—David or me? Sometimes she seemed to like David a little more than me; other times she seemed to like me a little more than David.

Then one day, when we were thirteen, I came late up to Eagle's Point, and when I got there, I saw them kissing. It looked kind of comic, actually, they didn't kiss the way movie stars did, they just kind of groped each other awkwardly. But it was enough to make me run over and tear him from her and push him back to the edge of the cliff. The fall would have killed him, and right then that was what I wanted to do, take his life. I pushed him out over the cliff, so he could get a good look at the asphalt below. All that kept him from falling was the grip I had on the sleeve of his shirt.

But then Susan was there, crying and screaming and pounding on me to pull him back before it was too late.

I'd never seen her that upset. She looked crazed. I pulled him back.

I didn't speak to either of them for a few months. I mostly stayed home and read science fiction novels. I'd discovered Ray Bradbury that spring.

School started again, and David could be seen in the halls with this cute new girl. I started hanging around Susan again. If she was sad about David, she never let on. She even asked me to go to the movies with her a couple of times. David kept hanging around the cute new girl.

In October, the jack-o'-lanterns on the porches already, I went to Susan's house one day. I kind of wanted to surprise her, have her go overtown with me. Nobody answered my knock. Both the truck and the car her folks drove were gone. I tried the kitchen door. It was open. I figured I'd go in and call out her name. She slept in some Saturday mornings.

That's when I heard the noise. I guess I knew what it was, I mean it's pretty unmistakable, but I didn't want to admit it to myself.

I didn't want to sneak up the stairs, but I knew I had to. I had to know for absolutely sure.

And that's what happened. I found out. For absolutely sure.

They were making love. I tried not to think of it as "fucking" because I didn't want to think of Susan that way. I loved her too much.

"Oh, David, I love you so much," Susan said.

Susan's bedroom was very near the top of the stairs. Their words and gasps echoed down the stairs to me and stayed in my ears all the time I ran across the road and into the woods. No matter how fast I ran, their voices stayed with me. I smelled creek water and deep damp forest shadow and the sweetness of pine cone. And then I came to a clearing, the sunlight suddenly blinding me, to the edge of Eagle's Point. I watched the big hawks wheel down the sky. I wanted them to carry me away to the world Edgar Rice Burroughs described in his books, where beautiful princesses and fabled cities and fabulous caches of gold awaited me, and people like me were never brokenhearted.

What I'd always suspected, and had always feared, was true: she loved David, not me.

I stayed till dark, smoking one Pall Mall after another, feeling the chill of the dying day seep into my bones, and watching the birds sail down the tumbling vermilion clouds and the silver slice of moon just now coming clear.

In the coming days, I avoided them and of course they were full of questions and hurt looks when I said I didn't have time for them anymore.

Dad died the autumn I was sixteen, the concrete truck he was driving sliding off the road because of a flash flood and plunging a few hundred feet straight down into a ravine. Mom had to worry about the two younger ones, which meant getting a job as a checkout lady at Slocum's Market and leaving me to worry about myself. I didn't mind. Mom was only forty-six but looked sixty. Hers had not been an easy life, and she looked so worn and faded these days that I just kept hugging her so she wouldn't collapse on the floor.

I saw Susan and David at school, of course, but they'd months ago given up trying to woo me back. Besides, a strange thing had happened. Even though they lived on the wrong side of town and had the wrong sort of parents, the wealthy kids in the class had sort of adopted them. I suppose they saw in Susan and David the sort of potential they'd soon enough realize, first at the state university, where they both graduated with honors, and then at law school, where honors were theirs once again.

I stayed around the house after college, working the part-time jobs I could get, hoping to work full-time eventually at the General Mills plant eighteen miles to the north. I dropped by the personnel department there a couple of times a month, just so they'd know how enthusiastic I was about working for them.

But by the time they were ready to hire me, Uncle Sam he was downright insistent about having me. So they gave me an M-16 and a whole bunch of information about how to save your ass in case of emergency and then shipped me off with a few hundred other reluctant warriors and set us down in a place called Dau Tieng, from where we would be dispatched to our bunkers.

I've always wished I had some good war stories for the beer nights at the VFW and the Legion. But the truth is, I never did see anybody around me get killed, though I saw more than a few men being loaded into field hospitals and choppers; and so far as I know, I never killed anybody, either, though there was a guy from Kentucky I thought about fragging sometimes. I did not become an alcoholic, my respiratory system was not tainted by Agent Orange, I was not angry with those who elected not to go (I would not have gone, either, if I'd known how easy it was to slip through the net), and I never had any psychotic episodes, not even when I was drinking the Everclear that sometimes got passed around camp.

While I was there, Susan wrote me three times, each time telling me how heroic she thought I was, and how she and David both missed the old days when we'd all been good friends, and how she was recovering from a broken arm she got from falling down on the tennis court. Tennis, she said, had become a big thing in their lives. They'd both been accepted by a very prestigious old-line law firm and were both given privileges at the city's finest country club.

I wrote her back near the end of my tour in Nam, telling her that I'd decided to try golden California, the way so many Midwestern rubes do, and that I was planning on becoming a matinee idol and the husband of a rich and beautiful actress, ha ha. Her response, which I got a day before I left Nam, was that they were going to Jamaica for their vacation this year, where it would be nothing but "swimming swimming swimming." She also noted that they'd gotten married in a "teeny-tiny" civil ceremony a few weeks earlier. And that she'd been married in a "white dress and a black eye—clumsy me, I tripped against a door frame."

Well, I went to California, Long Beach, Laguna, San Pedro, Sherman Oaks . . . in three years, I lived five different places and held just about double that number of jobs. I tried real estate, stereo sales, management trainee at a seven-eleven, and limo driver at a funeral home, the latter lasting only three weeks. I'd had to help bury a four-year-old girl dead of brain cancer. I didn't have it in me ever to do that again.

By the time I got back to New Hope, Mom was in a nursing home equidistant between New Hope and stairs. I saw her three times a week. Back then, they weren't so certain about their Alzheimer's diagnoses. But that's what she had. Some days she knew me, some not. I only broke down once, pulling her to me and letting myself cry. But she had no idea of our history, no idea of our bond, so it was like holding a stranger from the street, all stiff and formal and empty.

I met and married Marcie, I got my job at the ambulance company, I joined the VFW and the Legion, I became an auxiliary deputy because my Uncle Clement was the assistant county sheriff and he told me it was a good thing to do, and I made the mistake of running into a cousin of Susan's one day and getting Susan's address from her.

The funny thing is, I was never unfaithful to Marcie, not physically anyway. I had a few chances, too, but even though I knew I didn't love my wife, I felt that I owed her my honor. Bad enough that she had to hold me knowing that I wanted to be holding Susan; I didn't have to humiliate her publicly as well.

I never did write Susan, but I did call her. And then she called me a couple of times. And over the next six, seven years, we must have talked a couple of dozen times. Marcie didn't know, and neither did David. She told me about her life, and I told her how crazy she was and where it would all lead, but she didn't listen. She loved David too much to be reasonable. I made all kinds of proposals, of course, how I'd just sit down with Marcie and tell her the truth, that Susan and I were finally going to get together, and how I'd give Marcie the house and the newer of the cars and every cent in the savings account. One time, Susan laughed gently, as if she was embarrassed for me, and said, "Earle, you don't understand how successful a trial lawyer David is. He makes more in a month than you do in a year." Then her laugh got bitter: "You couldn't afford me, sweetheart. You really couldn't."

There were a few more conversations. She saw a shrink, she saw a priest, she saw this real good friend of hers who'd gone through the same thing. She was going to leave, she had the strength and courage and determination to leave now, or so she claimed, but she never did leave. She never did.

The prison was a WPA project back in the Depression. Stone was earned from a nearby quarry for the walls. The prison sits on a hill, as if it is being shown to local boys and girls as a warning.

You pass through three different electronically controlled gates before you come to the visitors' parking lot.

You pass the manufacturing building where the cool blue of welding torches can be seen, and the prison laundry where harsh detergent can be smelled, and the cafeteria that is noisy with preparations for the night's meal. I walked quickly past all these areas. The rain was still coming down hard.

You pass through two more electronic gates before you reach the administrative offices.

The inmates all knew who I was. I wouldn't say that there was hostility in their eyes when they saw me, but there was a kind of hard curiosity, as if I were a riddle to be solved.

The warden's office had been designed to look like any other office. But it didn't quite make it. The metal office furniture was not only out of date, it was a little bit grim in its gray way. And the receptionist was a sure disappointment for males visiting the warden: he was a bald older guy with his prison-blue shirt sleeves rolled up to reveal several faded and vaguely obscene tattoos. He knew who I was.

"The warden's on the phone."

"I'll just sit here."

He nodded and went back to his typing on a word

processor. He worked with two fingers, and he worked fast.

I looked through a law enforcement magazine while I sat there.

The receptionist said, "You do anything special to get ready?"

I shrugged. "Not really."

He went back to typing. I went back to reading.

After a time, he said, "It ever bother you?"

I sighed. "I suppose. Sometimes." I got into this five years ago when the state passed the capital punishment bill. MDs couldn't execute a man because of the Hippocratic oath. The state advertised for medical personnel. You had to take a lot of tests. I wondered if I could actually go through with it. The first couple times were rough. I just keep thinking of what the men had done. Most of them were animals. That helped a lot.

"It'd bother me." He went back to his typing again. Then: "I mean, if you want my honest opinion, I think it'd bother most people."

I didn't respond, just watched him a moment, then went back to my magazine.

George Stabenow is a decent man always in a hurry. Pure unadulterated Type A.

He burst through his office door and said, "C'mon in. I'm running so late I can't believe it."

He was short, stout, and swathed in a brown three-piece suit. This was probably the kind of suit the press expected a proper warden to wear on a day like this.

He pointed to a chair, and I sat down.

"The frigging doctor had some sort of emergency," Stabenow said. "Can you believe it?"

"You getting another doctor?"

"No, no. But he won't be here for the run-through, which pisses me off. I mean, the run-through's critical for all of us."

I nodded. He was right.

He walked over to his window and looked out on the grounds surrounding the prison.

"You see them on your way in?"

"Uh-huh."

"More than usual."

"Uh-huh."

"Maybe a hundred of them. If it's not this, it's some other goddamned thing. The environment or something."

"Uh-huh."

"That priest—that monsignor—you should've heard him this afternoon." He grinned. "He was wailing and flailing like some goddamned TV minister. Man, what a jackoff that guy is."

He came back to his desk. To his right was one of those plastic cubes you put photos of your family in. He had a nice-looking wife and a nice-looking daughter. "You eat?"

"I had a sandwich before I left New Hope," I said.

"I'm going to grab something in the cafeteria."

I smiled. "The food's not as bad as the inmates say, huh?"

"Bad? Shit, it's a hell of a lot better than you and I ever got in the goddamned Army, I'll tell you that." He shook his head in disgust. "Food's the easiest target of all for these jerkoffs—to get the public upset about, I mean. The public sees all these bullshit prison movies and think, they're for real. You know, cockroaches and everything crawling around in the chili? Hell, the state inspector checks out our kitchens and our food just the way he does all the other institutions. Even if we *wanted* cockroaches in the chili—" He smiled. "They wouldn't let us."

I said, "I need a badge."

"Oh, right."

He dug in his drawer and found me one and pushed it across his desk. I pinned it to my chambray shirt. The badge was "Highest Priority." All members of the team wear them.

"The rest of them here?"

"The team, you mean?"

"Uh-huh," I said.

"Everybody except the goddamned doc."

Before he could work up a lather again, I said, "Why don't I just walk over there, then, and say hi?"

"You've got twenty minutes yet. You sure you don't want a cup of coffee at least?"

"No, thanks."

He looked at me. "You know, I was kind of surprised that he requested you."

"Yeah."

"You sure you'll be all right?"

"I'll be all right."

"Some of the team, well, they had some doubts, too, said maybe it wasn't right. You knowing him and everything."

"I know. A couple of them called me."

"But I said, 'Hell, it's his decision. If he thinks he can handle it, let him.' Anyway, this is what the inmate wanted."

"I appreciate that."

"You're a pro, and pros do what they have to."

"Right."

He smiled. "I'm just glad Glen Wright has to handle the media. If it was up to me, I'd just tell them to go to hell."

He was going to upset himself again, and I wanted to get out of there before it happened. I stood up.

"You fellas used to carry little black bags," he said.

"Yeah."

"Just like doctors. Guess you don't need them anymore, huh? Now we provide everything."

"Right."

We shook hands, and I left.

There are six members on the team.

Five of us stood in the chamber and went through it all. You wouldn't think there'd be much to rehearse, but there is.

One of the men makes certain that the room is set up properly. We want to make sure that the curtains work, that's the first thing. When the press and the visitors come into the room outside the chamber, the curtains are drawn. Only when were about to begin for real are the curtains drawn back.

Then the needles have to be checked. Sometimes you got a piston that doesn't work right, and that can play hell for everybody. They get three injections—the first to totally relax them, the second to paralyze them so they won't squirm around, and the third to kill them. In my training courses, I learned that only two things matter in this kind of work: to kill brain and heart function almost immediately. This way, the inmate doesn't suffer, and the witnesses don't get upset by how inhumane it might look otherwise.

After the needles are checked, the gurney is fixed into place. If it isn't anchored properly, a struggling guy might tear it free and make things even worse for himself.

Then we check the IV line and the EKG the doctor will use to determine heart death. Then we check the blade the doctor will use for the IV cutdown. We expose the inmate's vein so there no chance of missing with the needle. That happened in Oregon. Took the man with the needle more than twenty minutes to find a vein. That wasn't pleasant for anybody.

Then I went through my little spiel to the man about to be executed. I'm always very polite. I tell him what he can expect and how it won't hurt in any way, especially if he cooperates. He generally has a few questions, and I always try to answer them. During all this, everybody else is rechecking the equipment, and Assistant Warden Wright is out there patiently taking questions from the press. The press is always looking for some way to discredit what we do. That's not paranoia, that's simple fact.

We didn't time the first run-through, which was kind of ragged. But the second run-through, Wright used his stop-watch.

We came in a little longer than we should have.

In the courses I took, the professor suggested that fifty-one minutes is the desired time for most executions by lethal injection. This is from walking into the chamber to the prisoner being declared legally dead by the presiding doctor.

We came in at fifty-nine minutes, and Wright, properly, said that we needed to pick things up a little. The longer you're in the chamber, he said, the more likely you are to

252

nake mistakes. And the more mistakes you make, the more
he press gets on your back. Speed and efficiency were
everything, Wright said. That's what my instructors always
said, too.

Finally, I checked out my own needles, went through the
motions of injecting fluids. My timing was off till the third
run-through. I picked up the pace then, and everything went
pretty well. We hit fifty-three minutes. We needed to shave
two more minutes. We'd take a break and then come back
for one more run-through.

When we wrapped up, Wright said we could all have
coffee and rolls if we wanted. There was a small room off
the chamber that was used only by prison personnel. The
rest of the team went there. I walked down the hall to
another electronic gate and told him that I was the man the
warden called him about. Even though visiting hours were
over, I was to be admitted to see the prisoner.

The guard opened the gate for me, then another guard led
me down the hall, stopping at a door at the far shadowy
end.

He opened the door, and I went inside.

The man was an impostor.

David Sawyer had gotten somebody to stand in for him at
the execution. Last time I'd seen him was at the trial, years
ago.

The sleek and handsome David Sawyer I remembered,
the one with all the black curly hair that Susan had loved to
run her fingers through, was gone. Had probably fled the
country.

In his place was a balding, somewhat stoop-shouldered

man with thick eyeglasses and a badly twitching left hand. He was dressed in gray prisoner clothing that only made his skin seem paler.

I must have struck him the same way, as an impostor because at first he didn't seem to recognize me at all.

On the drive up, I tried to figure out how long it had been since I'd seen David Sawyer. Eighteen years, near as I could figure.

"Son of a bitch," he said. "You changed your mind. The warden didn't tell me that."

I guess what I'd expected was a frightened, depressed man eager to receive his first sedative so he wouldn't be aware of the next three hours. You saw guys like that.

But the old merry David was in the stride, in the quick embrace, in the standing-back and taking-a-look-at-you.

"You're a goddamned porker," he said. "How much weight have you put on?"

"Forty pounds," I said. "Or thereabouts."

He sensed that he might have hurt my feelings, so he slid right into his own shortcomings. "Now you're supposed to say, 'What happened to your hair, asshole? And how come you're wearing trifocals? And how come you're all bent over like an old man?' C'mon, give me some shit. I can take it."

For a brief time there, he had me believing that his incongruous mood was for real. But as soon as he stopped talking, the fear was in his eyes. He glanced up at the wall clock three times in less than a minute.

And when he spoke, his voice was suddenly much quieter. "You pissed that I asked for you to do this?"

"More surprised than anything, David."

"You want some coffee? There's some over there."

"I'd appreciate that."

"You go sit down. I'll bring it over to you." Then the eyes went dreamy and faraway. "I was always like that at the parties we gave, Susan and I, I mean, and believe me, we gave some pissers. One night, we found the governor of this very state balling this stewardess in our walk-in closet. And I was always schlepping drinks back and forth, trying to make sure everybody was happy. I guess that's one problem with growing up the way we did—you never feel real secure about yourself. You always overdo the social bullshit so they'll like you more."

"You were pretty important. Full partner."

"That's what it said on the door," said the bald and stooped impostor. "But that's not what it said in here." He humped his chest and looked almost intolerably sad for a moment, then went and got our coffee.

The first cup of coffee we spent catching up. I told him about Nam, and he told me about state capital politics and how one got ahead as a big-fee lawyer. Then we talked about New Hope, and I caught him up on some of the lives that interested him there.

We didn't get around to Susan for at least twenty minutes, and when we did, he jumped up and said, "I'll get us refills. But keep talking. I can hear you."

I'd just mentioned her name, and he was on his feet, going the opposite direction.

I suppose I didn't blame him. The courts had made him face what he'd done, now I was going to make him face it all over again.

"Did you know she used to write me sometimes?"

255

"You're kidding? When we were married?"

"Uh-huh."

He brought the coffee over, set down our cups. "You two weren't—"

I shook my head. "Strictly platonic. The way it'd always been with us. From her point of view, anyway. She was crazy about you, and she never got over it."

We didn't say anything for a time, just sat there with our respective memories, faded images without words, like a silent screen flickering with moments of our days.

"I always knew you never got over her," he said.

"No, I never did. That's why my wife left." I explained about that a little bit.

Then I said, "But I was pretty stupid. I didn't catch on for a long time."

"Catch on to what?" he said, peering at me from the glasses that made his eyes flit about like blue goldfish.

"All the 'accidents' she had. I didn't realize for a long time that it was you beating her up."

He sighed, stared off. "You can believe this or not," he said, "but I actually tried to get her to leave. Because I knew I couldn't stop myself."

"She loved you."

He put his head down. "The things I did to her—" He shook his head, then looked up. "You remember that day back on Eagle's Point when you almost pushed me off?"

"Yeah."

"You should've pushed me. You really should've. Then none of this would've happened." He put his head down again.

"You ever get help for your problem?" I said.

"No. Guess I was afraid it would leak out if I did. You know, some of those fucking shrinks tell their friends everything."

"I blame you for that, David."

His head was still down. He nodded. Then he looked up: "I had a lot of chicks on the side."

"That's what the DA said at the trial."

"She had a couple of men, too. I mean, don't sit there and think she was this saint."

"She wasn't a saint, David. She never claimed to be. And she probably wouldn't have slept with other men if you hadn't run around on her—and hadn't kept beating the shit out of her a couple of times a month."

He looked angry. "It was never that often," he said.

"Still."

"Yeah. Still." He got up and walked over to the window and looked out on the yard. The rain had brought a chill and early night. He said, "I've read where this doesn't always go so smooth."

"It'll go smooth tonight, David." He stared out the window some more. He said, "You believe in any kind of afterlife?"

"I try to; I want to."

"That doesn't sound real convincing."

"It's not the kind of thing you can be real sure about, David."

"What if you had to bet, percentage-wise, I mean?"

"Sixty-forty, I guess."

"That there *is* an afterlife?"

"Yeah. That there is an afterlife."

Thunder rumbled. Rain hissed.

He turned around and looked at me. "I loved her."

"You killed her, David."

"She could have walked out that door any time she wanted to."

I just stared at him a long time then and said, "She loved you, David. She always believed you'd stop beating her someday. She thought you'd change."

He started sobbing then.

You see that sometimes.

No warning, I mean. The guy just breaks.

He just stood there, this bald squinty impostor, and cried.

I went over and took his coffee cup from him so it wouldn't smash on the floor, and then I slid my arm around his shoulder and led him over to the chair.

I had to get back. The team had one more run-through scheduled before the actual execution.

I got him in the chair, and he looked up and me and said, "I'm scared, man. I'm so scared, I don't even have the strength to walk." He cried some more and put his hand out.

I didn't want to touch his hand because that would feel as if I were betraying Susan.

But he was crying pretty bad, and I thought Susan, being Susan, would have taken his hand at such a moment. Susan forgave people for things I never could.

I took his hand for maybe thirty seconds, and that seemed to calm him down a little.

He looked at me, his face tear-streaked, his eyes sad and scared at the same time, and he said, "You really should've pushed me off that day at Eagle's Point."

"I've got to get back now," I said.

"If you'd pushed me off, none of this would've happened, Earle."

I walked over to the door.

"I loved her," he said. "I want you to know that. I loved her."

I nodded and then left the room and walked down the hall and went back out into the night and the rain.

The next run-through went perfectly. We hit the fifty-one-minute mark right on the button. Just the way the textbook says we should.

Celebrity and Justice for All

JOHN JAKES

There was this dream. His mother, whom he couldn't stand because all her life she transmitted silent signals: she didn't like him. As he was coming up through law school, or taking crap with two hundred fifty other hungry associates in Wasserman Sheinberg, he'd try to tell her about some accomplishment, some shining nugget of logic in a brief he'd contributed to, and the old lady would smile her phony smile and study his earlobe while he talked, and when he was through she'd say, "All right, Mickey, but remember what's important. Publicity. Did anyone take notice? Was your name in the paper?"

She was gone now, thank Christ; she'd hung on till she was ninety-seven, driving him nuts; she was *still* hanging on in the dream, which he suffered through many times each year.

He woke up in a sweat with his heart pounding. His first thought was, *Got to win. Today's the day. Got to win.*

He couldn't precisely remember it, but he felt he'd had the dream again last night. He hated his mother most because of one thing. The old bag was *right.*

His chauffeur was waiting outside the mansion half an hour later. Because of the day's foul fog, yellow and slimy, he could barely see the man, let alone the deep-green Jaguar superstretch with the special solid gold justice-and-scales upright on the hood. "Arm the defenses," he said as he jumped in; day like this, greaseballs from the underclass might dart out of the fog at an intersection and try to cut away the hood ornament with a pocket torch.

The chauffeur, a big ugly Peruvian Indian recently arrived on an illegal immigrant sub, knew enough Spanglish to grunt and throw the switches. Soon they were rolling, out the armored gates, away from the forty room mansion where he lived in his lonely splendor. He'd just gone through a fifth divorce. He couldn't keep a wife, or maintain a family. His hours were too long, he was too dedicated to the law.

By eight, he was in his office on the hundred and seventeenth floor of Heston City North, a complex of guaranteed earthquake-proof cylindrical towers named in honor of the old-time actor who'd starred in some picture about "the big one." Heston City was opened two years ago; so far, so good.

The office of Miguelito Chang, Esq., occupied half a floor, a whole one-hundred-eighty-degree arc of the building. Beyond the armorglass, you absolutely couldn't see a sign of life, let alone any other illumination, because of the yellow shit that passed for the LAX atmosphere. Never mind, he knew the important building was out there; the building on which his dreams were centered this day of all days, this day when he might, oh God yes, just might achieve the acme of professional recognition because of the case whose verdict he and the entire worldwide media community were certain would come in before five o'clock.

To confirm that, he voice-activated the sixteen monitors spread on the inner wall in rows of four. "Up six." The volume of six slowly escalated, bringing in the modulated tones of the silver-haired, pseudo-humanistic king of

261

morning talk Philo Downey. What a phony. Okay, but he was seen in a hundred and four countries, last count.

". . . guest this morning is Billy Esperanza, parking lot superintendent at Criminal Courts out in LAX. Señor Esperanza has seen and heard it all during these seventy-six weeks of the trial of the half century, right, Señor? Seventy-six weeks in which an all-star team led by one of the country's top defense lawyers, Mickey Chang, has been fighting to keep the Trailer Court Terrorist, Sheela Mane Kooperman, from getting the big-needle verdict."

The parking lot superintendent, for Christ's sake. Stupid. Really reaching.

On the other hand, who was left after nearly three and a half years since Sheela Marie's arrest? Everybody had been interviewed, you couldn't blame Philo. "Remember what's important . . ."

He slipped his thousand-dollar no-lapel cutaway into the wardrobe and patted down his pleated shirt. Had to stop sweating so much. Had to stop the fast lubbing of his heart. He'd gone through so much fucking stress during pretrial hearings, case preparation, then the actual trial, witness coaching, opening statements, direct and redirect, closing arguments, facing the glare of media lights outside Criminal Courts every day, dozens of mikes shoved in his face by dipshit recent graduates who thought Blackstone was some old-timer who did tricks with floating light bulbs, it was a wonder he wasn't dead of stroke or myfarc. But this, by stupid coincidence, was finally *it,* the big day, make or break . . .

"Now tell us in one word, Señor Esperanza, will the twenty-six good citizens and true bring in their verdict this afternoon as we've heard for days? In one word, now . . ."

"Absolutely definitely," said the Señor, flashing a big mess of gold front teeth.

Mickey went, "Hah," and clapped his hands. He took a shot of Caff from the bottle in his desk and rang for Miss Prynne.

Miss Prynne came in sinuously with her hidden petticoats swishing under her tight charc-gray pseudo-Vic outfit that was supposed to minimize her build, but you couldn't minimize tits and ass like Miss Prynne's with a block of cement. Miss Prynne was up for her third centerfold in the *Legal Review*, but Mickey hadn't heard from the rag's lawyer in two days; made a quick note to jab him.

"Good morning, sir," Miss Prynne said demurely, as though he hadn't been sampling those goodies intimately for five months.

"Hiya, hon. Want to give me the layout?"

"Slim Gross at ten. He's to have his rough outline and sample chapter—"

"Slim, I remember. Fucking hack." But the ghostwriter knew how to turn out a celeb best-seller. He was doing *My Plea to You,* the third authorized memoir of Mickey's client, Sheela Marie Kooperman, a sixteen-year-old blond beauty who'd been knocked around and abused by two stepfathers in Sandy Lakes Modular Estates, a two-bit Florida trailer park, and had been so traumatized that she'd persuaded a boyfriend to steal a weapon for her, a rapid-fire NRA Special, with which she'd invaded a private golf community in Boca Raton and gone from house to house, putting a lead period after the lives of thirty-eight householders. Mickey had led the defense team, winning a coastal change of venue and a seventy-five-percent cut of all major and subsidiary rights; he'd been on the telly almost every day with his all-star team of colleagues from seven countries, and he'd run a hell of a defense, if he did say so. *Ladies and gentlemen of the jury, you heard my client weeping as she told you of her deranged state. She lost control She was not responsible Firstly, she was a victim of abuse, parental and societal. Secondly, she was a victim of impossible expectations inflamed by constant media merchandising overkill. A consumer with no wherewithal to consume the electronic banquet pitilessly shoved at her by four hundred channels of sell—sell—SELL. But she saw a lot of fat cats who did gorge at the banquet, and she snapped. "They all got so much more than me, I been deprived, that's why I did it—there, ladies and gentlemen, there is the plaintive cry of a hurt, wounded victim who has been physically and spiritually raped again and again, by lust-crazed white Euromales, and by a society that rewards and favors our rich brethren while it throws our starving underclass on the ash heap.*

Mickey counted seven jurors openly crying at the end of that little number—three of them men, for Christ's sake! He'd won, and today would validate it—the proof, the payoff, began at half after five . . .

He visualized the Jaguar superstretch pulling up, himself in white tails and modest black boutonniere, pressing through thousands of fans, law buffs, fans who'd been hanging behind the barricades since before daylight. There'd be cameras, scores of paparazzi—and Miguelito "Mickey" Chang would walk away with the big one. He'd hired a chippy from the swank Puss-to-Go agency, some bim who'd be appropriately clingy when the camera panned around just seconds before the announcement. He had to hire someone, he didn't know any girls who'd go out with him after his five divorces and his reputation for ferocious pursuit of excellence in his profession. Miss Prynne screwed on the QT, in-house only, for bonuses and perks.

But the tension—God, it was terrible. Mickey hated to sweat, it was undignified and, sometimes, had a repulsive smell. But he just couldn't help it, today was make-or-break. *Remember what's important* . . .

"Three o'clock, here in the office, you have a wash, trim, and touch-up from Mr. Phyllis."

"Right. Noted. Did we get the jury report from our mole?"

"Yes, chief, confirming what everyone's been hearing for the past three days." Miss Prynne seated herself and crossed her legs provocatively so that the outline of a garter showed beneath her skirt. "He says that unless the sky falls, the jury will come in between four and five this afternoon."

"Philo Downey said so, too. I set up the schedule based on that. Rotten coincidence, the ceremony at practically the same time. But the ceremony was calendared a year ago. So okay. Randy's ready for the defense?"

"Mr. Greenstone is calendared, yes, sir."

"Tell him to come in sometime before lunch. I want personal confirmation."

"Of course, sir," Miss Prynne said, rising and leaning over his desk so he could smell her passion fruit perfume. She gave him her hand. "I want to wish you all the luck in the world." They shook, and Miss Prynne lightly tickled his palm with her index finger

"Be there whenever I can get there," he promised. "I'll

show you my prize."

"I'm counting on it, sir."

She wiggled out of the sanctum; but even the sight of her marvelous ass, which he would enjoy again that evening *sans* pseudo-Victorian getup, didn't, couldn't occupy his mind for long. Today was *the* day. Biggest day of his life . . .

Mickey spent the morning on various phases of client. He yelled and screamed for a half hour with the business affairs veep at Dreampix, who wanted rights for a second MOW on Sheela Mane. Finally, Mickey lost his temper. "Seven and a half percent adjusted gross or nothing, you fucking putz!" He was so exercised, he tore the speak box out of the desktop jack and flung it. Two minutes later, Miss Prynne entered with a new box, jacked it in, and whispered, "Mr. Spielman calling back."

The business affairs veep rolled over and said yes. Mickey called him a visionary Christian gentleman and promised to do brunchy-lunchy soon.

Slim Gross was fifteen minutes late. He was one of those sorry writer types, of which there were a zillion out here. Slim belonged to the subgenus *erzatz hick,* alternately bragged about his West Texas upbringing and yapped about his Yale lit degree. He had a studied sappy country-boy smile on his pale bearded face, a carefully sprayed forelock hanging over his forehead, antique stone-washed jeans, and Texas boots complemented by a collarless shirt with rhinestone studs and a formal jacket.

"I've got a new angle for the lead chapter I'd like to pitch, Mickey," the writer began, proffering his document which Mickey could see was prepped on the cheapest of computer

266

paper, this guy was strictly Grub Street West. But he could be brow-beaten, which made him a bargain.

"Leave it," Mickey said with an imperious wave; his eyes were elsewhere.

Slim picked at his forelock. "I was hoping—wondering—could we discuss it today? Maybe get an okay or—" Slim gulped. "Possibly an advance on the advance? My life's companion just vamoosed, and she's suing me for everything. I'd even be willing to cut the royalty to five and a quarter in exchange for a little consultation with the fir—"

Mickey laughed. "*This* firm? Forget it, kid. You couldn't afford the associate toilet cleaner in this firm. I'll read this and get back to you next week."

"Mickey, I'm really desper—"

Mickey jumped up in majestic wrath. "Do you know what day this is? Do you know what's happening this afternoon?"

Shamed, Slim hung his head. "Yes, sir. The verdict in the trial of the half century."

"Asshole. The awards. The *awards*. Get out. And take this shit with you. I already know I don't like it."

He threw the copy at Slim, who caught it like a drunken wide receiver; fortunately, Slim wasn't so cheap that he couldn't afford brass brads; at least the pages didn't fly all over.

Slim slunk out. Mickey sat down, mopping his face. "That was tacky," he said. "Jesus, that was so tacky." He excused himself: he was excited. He laid his hand over his thumping heart to feel just how excited. From another drawer, he rooted out a 400 mg pop of Tranx to take the edge off the Caff.

267

Everything seemed to calm down then, proceed less stressfully for the next hour. At half past twelve, Miss Prynne announced his colleague, Randy, over the box. Mickey's brows quirked up. Odd, her using the box instead of announcing another member of the firm personally.

"Randy," he said, racing from behind the desk to shake his colleagues hand. "Great suit." Randy Greenstone was wearing a handsome deep purple number that could have come from nowhere but the atelier of Mr. Rodeo, "Suiter to the Stars."

"Just great, you'll look super this afternoon—eyes of the whole world on you, all that shit. Sit down, pal."

Something was drastically wrong, Mickey could see that in his colleagues demeanor. Randy Greenstone, a wholesome blond South African ten years Mickey's junior, was a sharp defense attorney but less oriented to the limelight than Mickey. Randy had had but one wife, with whom he shared six children. He did fool around some, but not so flagrantly anyone would make print or pix about it, with one exception.

"Mickey," Randy said, "you know my daughter Bunny—"

"Yeah, swell girt, lot of pluck, that girl."

"Well, she's the star of her team, and—Mickey, I don't know how to say this."

Mickey felt a chill. Decidedly less friendly, he said, "Just spit it out."

"There was a last-minute schedule change for the Wheelchair Soccer League. It's the state championship, you know."

"I don't know from shit about kids doing headers in

wheelchairs," Mickey said with outright menace. His heart was doing a real speed number again, but not for the right and proper reason. "Quit jerking me around. What—?"

"Bunny's match was scheduled under the lights at eight o'clock, but they shifted it back to four, don't ask me why. I told Felicity and Bunny I'd be there, promised . . ."

"At four, you will be at Criminal Courts. You will be at Criminal Courts because I can't be there to front the team, I will be home getting ready for the big one, do you understand me?"

Mickey was practically screaming, while Randy seemed to be practically weeping as he said, "I can't do it, Mick, I can't disappoint my daughter."

"You think I'm going to miss the ceremony because of that, is that what you think, you putz?"

"Maybe we can hire an attorney from ABA Central. I know one, fairly imposing, older guy, done a lot of whiskey adverts. His practice has dried up, and he's starved for cash. He looks a little like me, he could front—"

"Bring in a ringer just for image, are you out of your fucking mind? They'd be on to us yesterday. *You* are the second lead of the team, and *you* are going to be there to hear our client get the big n.g. from the jury."

Randy agonized, hung his head, but ultimately said: "I can't. I can't disappoint Felicity and Bunny."

The floor was sinking. The room was reeling. His arteries were closing off. He was going insane. This putz was ruining *everything* . . .

But Mickey was nothing if not a masterful performer. He threw his head back and uttered a jolly "Hah-hah!"— admittedly insincere-sounding—and then he got in the

269

groove, waving as he reached for the phone.

"Oh, well, okay, that's how you feel, family first, sure. You go to your fucking soccer game for cripples while I make a little phone call to Lew Monarch." Lew Monarch was the king of night talk, a brassy-voiced interrogator who could be nice as cappuccino yogurt if he liked you, dangerous as a cobra if you had a secret and he wanted it.

Finger poised over the fifty-button autodial, Mickey said softly, "Maybe I'll just tell him I know a certain criminal practice attorney who prepped the Tupper twins—you remember the Tupper twins, don't you? *We Had to Do It* was on the *Times* list for nineteen weeks, the MOW had a thirty-six share—and maybe I'll suggest to my pal Lew that you not only prepped them both as witnesses, you prepped one of them in a different way by peeling off her clothes in a hotbed motel, what was she, sixteen? Make it fourteen."

Randy whispered, "You dirty headline-chasing son of a bitch."

"Yeah? Sorry. That's the game, kid. This is the big day. You aren't going to blow it for me." His fingertip hovered ever closer to the Lew Monarch button. "You enjoy your soccer game, and then Felicity and Bunny can enjoy hearing about the Tupper twins on Lew Monarch next week."

A mantle of defeat dropped over Randy. "I'll be in court at four."

Mickey lifted his hand, grinned. " 'Course you will. Your family'll understand. Now go wash your face and prepare to be a celebrity big-time, counselor. Sheela Marie's going to get off. N.g.—no needle. Your family wouldn't want you to miss that moment of triumph for our team."

Randy about-faced and left.

. . .

Mickey's moment came later, just before the closing of the three-hour awards program. The femcee stepped to the glass podium and said with stentorian seriousness. "Ladies and gentlemen of the bar, we've come to the big one. The award for the best performance by an attorney in defense of a client accused of a capital crime."

A busty accountant showing a lot of cleavage minced out on stiletto heels and handed over the envelope. Mickey was half blind with sweat and excitement. His hired date squeezed his arm, whispering, "Oh, wow, oh, wow, Mickey," but she could have been an orangutan for all he cared. Two hundred and seventy million pairs of eyes were watching the worldwide 'cast of this star-studded event. Ever since the epochal O.J. days, trial lawyers had been superstars.

The pounding of blood in his ears was so loud, he hardly heard the recitation of nominees, cases, and verdicts, presented together with flashing audiovisual displays on the huge stage of the Music Pavilion. He was fixed, focused, attuned only to the fateful amplified sound of the envelope ripping . . .

The femcee, Supreme Court Justice Clara Thomas-Hill, peeped into the envelope.

Smiled . . .

Come on, come on, for Christ's sake!

"And the winner of this year's Clarence Darrow award is—the man who led his dream team to this afternoon's stunning exoneration of his client—the winner is *Miguelito 'Mickey' Chang!*"

"Oh, WOW!" his companion screamed orgasmically as

he rocketed from his aisle seat and raced forward amid the glaring, flaring follow spots that hit him, lit him up, while the ninety-piece symphony orchestra in the pit played the love theme from Sheela Marie's first MOW.

And then he was onstage, at the podium, the femcee handing him the beautiful statuette, the pot-bellied Great Defender grittily rendered in bronze, shirt sleeves, suspenders, and all. "Oh, gosh, it's heavy," he gasped in his best little-boy voice, nearly bringing down the house with laughter.

The Supreme Court justice kissed him on the mouth and whispered congratulations. Mickey was dizzy with visions of what the moment would mean. Book deals, film deals, merchandise deals; limitless possibilities . . .

He was so overwhelmed, he forgot to reach inside his jacket for the acceptance remarks he'd worked on for a week. All he could do was improvise, standing there in the lights, the music, the glory—*Jesus Christ, they're on their feet in the orchestra! Also the balcony! A couple thousand of the best and brightest of the profession—a standing ovation!*

Finally, they settled down, but he was still so overwhelmed, he wasn't quite coherent. He raised the glittering Clarence over his head and wiped his eyes with his other hand.

"What a system. It's a great system, our system of justice. The greatest."

He was crying.

"I didn't win this by myself. I have so many people to thank."

He was crying, bawling; couldn't stop.

"First of all, there's my mother . . ."

272

For the Good of the Firm

MAYNARD F. THOMSON

You asked for the truth, and you'll get it, starting with the most basic truth: I'm not sorry Clark Roy is dead. I'm not even sorry I killed him.

Oh, I know, I know—that doesn't sound like a Barton, Allard lawyer, does it? I might be forgiven the failure to feign remorse—after all, we routinely boast of the brutality with which we claim we dispatch our adversaries, and who among us is ready to admit that it's all metaphor, no deed— but an unequivocal statement, one allowing no wriggle room? No chance to turn that seeming admission into a denial, no evasions, circumlocutions, reservation of rights? Contrary to every tenet of good practice, no doubt, and a terrible example for the kids coming up through the ranks. Once clients start getting the idea that lawyers can express ideas in simple, declarative sentences without losing the law's *juju,* there's no telling *where* it might end: secretaries drafting contracts, messengers arguing motions, and lawyers . . . well, better hang on to your notary seal, eh?

Tough. One compensation for the position in which I find myself is that for once I don't have to write like a lawyer: I'm going to give it to you straight, and you can make of it what you will. Nothing will be conditional, no rights will be reserved. No hypothetical questions, no "assuming arguendo," no "I didn't do it, but if I did I was provoked," none of the weasel words by which lawyers avoid sounding as though they actually *believed* anything.

273

You will know what I believe. With what I'm giving you, you can destroy me, if you choose to; I am, by this declaration, committing my future one hundred percent to your discretion. I know of no other way to demonstrate that if I cannot practice law as a Barton, Allard partner, I don't care to practice law at all.

Hence I say, no ifs, ands, or buts: I'm not sorry Clark Roy is dead. I'm not even sorry I killed him.

I will lay out every squalid little detail, ending with the most squalid detail of all: his death. However, I first intend to explain *why* I deliberately, consciously, and, yes, *joyfully* destroyed Clark Roy. You may decide I'm unfit to practice law—much less law at Barton, Allard—but at least you'll know that I didn't act capriciously. Indeed, by the time I finish, I think you'll agree that I didn't even act with "malice": "the intentional doing of a wrongful act *without just cause or excuse. . . .*"[1] Hear my case, then decide if my cause was just. Finally, understand this: at all times, I acted for the good of the Firm. You may decide I was intemperate, foolish, or rash, but *no one* can challenge my devotion to Barton, Allard. At all times, I acted only for the good of the Firm.

To begin: Clark Roy was a first-class turd. The stain he left at the bottom of the stairwell can't compare to the one his very existence imposed on the Firm. He was bad for morale, bad for business, and bad for our prospects for the future, and were all better off that he's dead.

I anticipate the response: yes, perhaps Roy had become an embarrassment to the Firm, but surely it would have been enough merely to sever ties, winnow him from the

[1]*Hanley v. Dixon*, 48 S.W. 2d 867, 871 (Mo. 1957, emph. added).

274

partnership, wasn't your conduct a bit . . . *extreme?* Isn't moderation in all things the hallmark of a Barton, Allard partner?

To which there are two replies. First, with what Roy had hanging over him by the end, he might have left us physically, but he wouldn't have removed himself from Barton, Allard; we would never have shed the stigma of his former association. It would have been the subject of endless comment in the trade press, endless gossip, and our competition's endless glee. Roy's death won't stop that, but the "tragedy" of it ensures that considerations of taste should keep the comments and speculation muted.

Second, you will appreciate as this report unfolds that, while I accept full responsibility for everything *I* did, I can hardly be charged with culpability for *Roy's* conduct. I was at all times ready to call a halt to my campaign; it was Roy who heedlessly pressed on to the final, fatal moment. He could have withdrawn from the partnership at any time; had he possessed a shred of decency, he would have. Yes, I killed him, but he left me no choice.

Another thing: I'm hardly alone in delighting in the prospect of a Roy-free world—I'm just honest enough to admit it. I don't think *anybody* will pretend he *liked* the bastard—that level of hypocrisy died with Roy, thank God. It's just that a lot of the lawyers around here don't have the intestinal fortitude, if you will, to admit that they would have stood in line to push him down that stairwell. I've already heard Rawlings, for example, mumbling about "the tragedy," yet no more than a month ago, I sat at lunch with him while he declared to anyone who'd listen that Roy was "a disgrace to the Firm," which, of course, is—was, I should say—absolutely true.

I wonder why so many people can't understand that death doesn't retroactively upgrade one's moral worth; Roy's sudden departure didn't effect some *nunc pro tunc* revision of his Martindale entry. The text following his name is still, and always will be: self-aggrandizing, deceitful, malicious, sycophantic little turd.

The evidence is overwhelming. All I ask is that you hear me out before reaching your verdict; I will accept it with good grace, whatever it should be.

Start with the relatively trivial: Clark Roy was a monumental toady. You could calibrate with inerrant accuracy one's place within the Firm's hierarchy merely by noting the effusiveness of Roy's salutation.

As managing partner, Dick McSorley received something resembling idolatry, more appropriate to a banana republic dictator than to the leader of one of the nation's great law firms. "Dick—how *are* you?" "*Loved* your speech to the Chamber, Dick." "Heard you got a *great* result in the Wilson case, Dick."

It can't have escaped your attention that as soon as Dick took over as managing partner, Roy began dressing like Dick's clone: the same black tassel loafers; identical navy pinstripe suits with the too-neat pocket hankie; blue shirts with white collar—even the same gold collar pin (on Dick, it's just a little precious, on Roy, binding the collar under that round, Pillsbury Doughboy face, it was grotesque).

It is a tribute to Dick's modesty that he never seemed remotely impressed by, or even aware of, Roy's feverish fawning. I'm sure that if he had had any idea how Roy's groveling looked to others, he would have felt demeaned by it. God knows, I was not alone in cringing when clients witnessed it.

My reactions, of course, were of no interest to Roy. As a younger partner (and thus, as he saw it, at best an irrelevancy, at worst a rival), I was the recipient of patronizing waves of the hand—Queen Elizabeth moving down the Mall—or innuendo designed to impress others, even as it belittled me: "*Hel*-lo, John. Oh—let me know if you need any more help with those foreclosures; they're a little tricky until you've done a few" was a typical, completely fabricated sally, delivered as I was standing in the reception area with some new clients.

In a way, associates and other low-lifes were better off— all they got was a baleful glare, until and unless *they* first kowtowed sufficiently to Roy. Then perhaps they would be deemed worthy of a dismissive nod or, if the associate had been sufficiently self-abnegating long enough, a fat, palsy forearm thrown over the shoulders or, in the case of women associates, a little neck and back rub (my flesh crawled at the sight; I can only imagine the suffering of the victim).

Secretaries and other forms of *Untermensch* were beneath notice and had no one to blame but themselves if they failed to get out of the way in time—many's the docket clerk sent sprawling by Clark Roy, so lost in Olympian revery that he could hardly be expected to take heed of mere mortals.

Too petty, just a set of unfortunate idiosyncrasies, hardly creditable but scarcely worthy of capital punishment? I quite agree. If Clark Roy had been no more than a toady, he would not be the subject of this report; he would not even be the subject of much remark around Barton, Allard, or

277

most other great enterprises, for that matter. Toadying is the emollient of the hierarchical organization, the tribute paid to the organizing principle. "Our Father," and all that.

No, Roy's sycophancy was not the characteristic that set him apart, rendered him uniquely odious, brazen and obvious as it was. What was most intolerable in Roy—what eventually led me to the actions I took—was his complete lack of collegiality, of loyalty to the collective well-being of his partners. While the Lew Whites and David Poutasses spare no effort to ingratiate themselves with the power structure, I have never doubted their ultimate devotion to the Firm; Roy's ultimate devotion was, always, to Clark Roy, and only Clark Roy.

Example: A few years ago, I read in the new business reports that Roy was proposing to represent a new client, City Mills, in a suit involving a company called Hydex. I told Roy we couldn't appear for City Mills in this matter, since Hydex was about to be acquired by our good client Jenco, and Jenco wouldn't understand why we couldn't represent *them* in the suit, once they acquired Hydex. He said sure, he understood, he'd tell City Mills we would have a conflict and couldn't take the business.

A couple weeks later, I happened to find out that he had Wendy Schultz—a young litigation associate, who didn't know about the issue—appearing in court on behalf of City Mills, exactly as though our conversation had never occurred. Fortunately, Jenco didn't call us on it, but that isn't the point. City Mills paid us roughly one hundred thousand for the representation, and it was a one-off—it's not a local company, they have regular counsel in Chicago, and we'll probably never see any more business from them.

Jenco pays us ten times that *every year,* but in Roy's mind it was no contest: City Mills would count as money *he* brought in, Jenco was my responsibility, end of analysis. What was relevant to him was what was good for him; what was in the best interests of the Firm was irrelevant.

Tame stuff—too much about turf, too parochial? Okay, then think about the man's malice, the corrosive poison he liked to spread as he clawed ahead.

Consider the time he took over Bill Stetz's billing responsibility for FoSoCo. Bill had that bout with cancer, and Roy had been assigned to "cover" for him until he returned. Which he did, raring to go, only, of course, Roy had no intention of passing the billing folder back. So he put it out to key FoSoCo personnel that, while it was all hush-hush, the Betty Ford Clinic had "done wonders" for Bill. Bill never knew why FoSoCo insisted on staying with Roy; I only found out long after, when the general counsel let something slip during a meeting.

Or remember Roy's letter, the one he leaked when Warren Hanford stepped down as administrative partner? I kept a copy, as an exemplar of malicious sycophancy at its worst. Here, after carrying on a *savage* whispering campaign against poor old Hanford for years, is what Roy wrote Dick McSorley when Dick finally had to give Warren the chop. Just see if it doesn't make your gorge rise:

Personal & Confidential

Dear Dick:

I thought that, on the occasion of Warren Hanford's well-earned retirement, it would be appropriate for me to indicate to you, in your capacity as Managing Partner of

Barton, Allard, just how deeply I have appreciated Warren's many kindnesses over the years, and how much I will miss him.

All of us at Barton, Allard owe Warren our deepest gratitude for his unstinting patience, professionalism, and attention to the details that enable us to practice law with mercifully few distractions. Certainly it is no exaggeration for me to say that I doubt I would have enjoyed even the modest successes that have come my way over the years without Warren's tireless support as Administrative Partner.

It is hardly a wonder that the load eventually overwhelmed even so stalwart a practitioner as Warren; I know from our discussions how painful you found the step you were forced to take (and never have I admired your leadership more than in those hours when you accepted that the cup, however bitter, could not be passed). I know I speak for every man and woman in the Firm when I bid Warren a speedy recovery and a long and happy retirement.

/s/Clark Roy

"Personal & Confidential"—that's a laugh! Roy just *happened* to leave a copy of the letter in a Xerox machine, where he knew it would be found. "I bid Warren a speedy recovery!" Right—after he'd done everything in his power to undercut Warren's authority, belittled him at every turn, and, I eventually learned, was the source of that disgusting and totally fraudulent story about Ruth Hanford that, more than anything else, shattered Warren and, I am convinced, was the major contributing factor in Warren's breakdown. Dick McSorley did what had to be done, under the circumstances, but the circumstances didn't *have* to happen—that

280

was Clark Roy's doing.

The letter was vintage Roy: note the feigned sympathy for Hanford, the shameless flattery of Dick McSorley, the intimation that Dick only acted after long "discussions" with Roy, all the while making sure that even the mailroom personnel understood that Hanford's supposed "retirement" was a graceful cover for his forced withdrawal from the partnership. In its way, a masterpiece of malicious toadying: suck and stab, suck and stab. It made me sick.

I think it was when someone showed me this oleaginous piece of tripe that the idea that the world would be a far better place if Clark Roy were removed from it first came into focus, although the events that finally drove me to the measures that accomplished the objective[2] were still some way down the road. The Hanford letter definitely "put me in touch with my feelings," as the younger associates might put it, subsequent events simply took an idea that might have remained nothing more than an idle fantasy and gave it a substance that ultimately could not be denied. When the moment arrived, I was ready.

You want to know what I did. All right—you shall.

It started, I suppose, as a prank, a little practical joke with a twist, intended to embarrass Roy—see what an optimist I was—and let him know some of us were on to him and ready to retaliate. Things just escalated, you might say.

Late last year, Linda Browne, my secretary, came into my office, sporting an ear-to-ear. "Guess what I've got," she said.

"A sexually transmitted disease?" (We have a nice, TV sitcom relationship; more of our partners should loosen up with the support staff.)

[2]See below.

281

"Ha, ha—the Firm loge!" From behind her back, she produced a fistful of tickets. "I put in, and nobody had it reserved for the Cardinals game."

You may not know it, but the skybox is coin of the realm to the support staff; we lawyers may think being dragged along with a bunch of dud clients to see two last-place team sleepwalk through a meaningless ball game is living death, but it's a perk of almost incalculable glamour to people acculturated to bleacher life.

"My parents are coming in from Pittsburgh, Bob thinks I'm wonderful, and the kids are delirious. I *love* Barton, Allard." She almost skipped out of my office, and it did my heart good; she's a nice lady.

I was still envying Linda a life so easily lightened when I passed her workstation that afternoon and noted tears. Upon inquiry, she told me that the loge was gone: "Mr. Roy took it for clients." Brave, acquiescent sniffles acknowledged the bum deal that fate had cast.

The Firm policy that client entertainment preempts all other calls on the loge is unassailable; it is a significant expense, and we all understand that personal use must defer to business interests. So when I happened to encounter Roy in the hall a little later, I was only being civil when I said that I hoped he'd enjoy the game.

"I really shouldn't be going," he replied. "I've so much to do here. But Marcus [his spawn] is having friends over, and we thought they'd like it."

I was staggered. "I thought you were having clients in."

"Oh." He smirked, his thick lips twisting into that curl that begged for smashing. "If your own *children* aren't your clients, then who is? You'll understand, if you and your

282

wife are ever able to have any."

As I watched his fat butt waddle away, I gave serious thought to dispatching him there and then: a stealthy rush from behind, the pen thrust into a vulnerable place on the bloated neck—*voilà*.

But I am, after all, a lawyer—and a Barton, Allard lawyer at that—which is to say, let's face it, somewhat gelded. Direct action is alien to our nature, more's the pity.

The compensation is that we can calculate—and I did. The man coveted the sporting life—very well, I would introduce him to a world of sport beyond his wildest dreams.

I doubt you've spent any time rummaging through the back pages of certain periodicals, but they've crossed my path from time to time, and they're a treasure trove. I picked up a copy of the raunchiest over lunch, and that afternoon I ordered Mr. Roy all *sorts* of "sporting" media. Periodicals, mailing lists, and videotapes specializing in athletic activity of a most refined sort: animal husbandry, *exotic* wrestling poses, *strange* uses of the bathroom, and the kind of discipline I was sure Roy needed but too rarely received. And since he professed a fondness for children, a selection devoted exclusively to that particular passion.

I *love* Sam Davis, our unflappable Master of the Mailroom. When those magazines started arriving for "Mr. Roy," he never skipped a beat. I'd see him pull them out of the mail cart, shuffle into Roy's office, and drop them on his desk exactly as though *all* "his boys" were regular readers of *Golden Showers* and *Kiddie Korner*. And if he thought those videotapes were anything other than CLE courses on inter vivos trusts, he certainly never said.

283

Granted, the postal inspectors were less sanguine. They seemed *quite* excited when they appeared in the office with their search warrant.

Please understand: I truly hadn't meant to bring outsiders into this. I didn't know until after Roy's arrest that most of those ads are placed by the government, precisely to trap the kind of pervert he appeared to be. If Roy had taken the sudden arrival of those unsought gifts as the subtle rebuke I'd intended and had curbed his inclinations accordingly, there would have been no further evidence of debauchery, his protestations of innocence would have eventually availed, and the charges of interstate transportation pending against him at his death would have long since abated. But the man was uninstructable, as the next development demonstrated.

You may remember David Norquist—the corporate associate who went to Dawkins, Heller last year? A good guy and a terrific young lawyer. David was muscle, not fat, on the Barton, Allard body—a thoroughly competent, hardworking, and decent fellow who loved the Finn, had the respect of the corporate partners with whom he worked, and was, in my opinion, a lock for partnership.

He was working on a deal for Roy, that Sintex spin-off? David was the senior associate, doing all the heavy lifting. As I'm sure you realize, Roy didn't like getting down in the trenches and actually slugging it out with the other side, much less wielding the red pen and marking up the papers until all hours—that was too much like work, and besides, that way his incompetence was too easily exposed. Roy fancied himself the rainmaker, bringing in the deals, although if you take a hard look, I think you'll agree that almost all his "rain" really came from clients he inherited, Sintex being an example.

Anyway, David was putting in sixteen-hour days, doing all the paperwork and basically honchoing the deal—and very well, too, I don't doubt. So Roy decided that he and JoAnne could take off for the Bahamas, do a little R&R after the rigors of their cocktail party circuit. Only Roy had some stupid article he wanted published in *Corporate Counsel* magazine, something he had David ghosting for him, and after a few days in Nassau, he called David and told him to fax him the revisions—because, of course, Roy wouldn't dream of going anywhere without a fax machine.[3]

David said he hadn't been able to get to it, that he was all tied up on the Sintex thing, and besides, he hadn't realized there was any hurry, since it was just an article on director liability that no sane person was going to read anyway. As David tells it—and I believe him—Roy promptly went nuclear, reamed him out over his pool-side telephone, and *ordered* him to go in the next day to finish the article. Which David did, even though it was a Sunday, he basically hadn't been home in two weeks, his wife was eight months pregnant, and going in meant he had to miss his grandmother's funeral!

I was close to David, sort of a mentor, and as you can imagine, he was plenty steamed. I cooled him off, commiserated, but when he left my office, I had an overwhelming desire to do something, *something* to let Roy know there were limits. It was beyond me how anyone could wallow

---

[3] I checked with Roy's secretary; she had standing orders to fax or call him every few hours—it didn't matter if there was anything important, only that he be seen receiving an endless stream of faxes and calls. He also made sure he was paged periodically at the partners' meetings, although in that I suspect he was hardly alone.

by the ocean while ordering David to give up his one day off to ghost a pointless bit of self-promotion. I was musing on this when it came to me that what Roy needed was an absolutely symmetrical punishment, complying with strict, eye-for-eye sentencing guidelines: Roy had to lose his vacation, as the result of some arbitrary, heartless directive from someone Roy would be powerless to resist.

Once the issue was framed, it wasn't hard to execute sentence. Roy, of course, would *leap* to any request that came in from Dick McSorley, and I knew he was dying for plum, high-profile overseas assignments that offered lots of preening, two-hour lunches, and little work. Since Dick was traveling in the Far East, I also knew Roy wouldn't find it easy to reach him on short notice, so I, shall we say, *borrowed* Dick's authority. I admit it—I composed a memo over Dick's name, slipped it into the In tray in the fax room, and let events run their course.

The memo that duly arrived in the Bahamas read:

Urgent you attend meeting Polish Trade Bd. as my designee tomorrow, 10 A.M., Krakow. Regret short notice; no other BA partner qualified. Briefing upon arrival Hotel Metropole. Contact Stanislaus Woczek. Strictest confidentiality *essential*.
Regards,

/s/Richard J. McSorley
Managing Partner

I had first satisfied myself that it was possible—just—to get from Nassau to Krakow in the eighteen hours between the arrival of the memo and the time for the "meeting," but only if my boy didn't waste a minute trying to run down Dick to find out what was going on. I hadn't bothered to see if there was, in fact, a Hotel Metropole in Krakow; I preferred the thought of an increasingly desperate Clark Roy, braving the savage winds howling across the Vistula in aloha shirt and shorts, exhorting cabbies to find him a nonexistent hotel so he could be briefed by a nonexistent Pole about a nonexistent meeting. I went home happier than I'd been in weeks.

I admit I awoke a bit anxious: it wasn't going to take Roy long to figure out a little joke had been played on him, and I didn't think he was going to laugh it off. I knew Dick wouldn't be happy about me appropriating his name, and, indeed, I wasn't at all sure Dick had an inkling what a deserving victim Roy was. Dick's always been above the fray. I began to fear an investigation, fantasizing all sorts of things—lie detector tests, the police, God knows what.

Yet as the days passed, it became clear that I had pulled off a triumph. I now assume that Roy was too humiliated to have said anything to anybody; my guess is Dick McSorley never knew to what good use his signature had been put in his absence. And best of all, it was a somewhat subdued, even sullen Roy who could be seen during his forays through the halls. Gone was the supercilious nod, the patronizing "Good morning" offered as though bestowing a blessing. Did I imagine it, or was he in fact darting paranoid glances at those he passed? I hoped so, and if his little holiday in hell had taught him to hunker down in his office and stay out of other people's way, I wouldn't be writing this now.

But, of course, Roy hadn't been issued a new personality,

and soon enough he reverted to form. Once again, an associate was the victim.

Roy had a deal for Hastings Corp., some asset sale any moron could have handled. A normal lawyer would have turned it over to an experienced associate and kept out of it, beyond vetting the end product, but, of course, Roy wasn't normal in any sense. He *had* to stay involved, at least in the client hand-holding, because otherwise the associate would be dealing directly with the client, a relationship might flower, and next thing you know . . . who needs Roy, right?

One day, the Hastings general counsel tells Roy he needs a legal opinion for the deal, a simple "duly incorporated" piece of boilerplate. Roy tells Henry Worrel, the associate, and Henry, a capable kid, has it out and back to Roy in an hour.

Only Roy forgets to pass it along to the general counsel. Which we know, because almost three weeks later, what does Henry find on his desk but a letter "he'd" just signed and faxed to the general counsel, apologizing profusely for *failing to send the opinion the general counsel had requested,* due to an "inexcusable oversight"! Attached to this letter was the opinion Henry had given Roy three weeks before. The signature on the mea culpa letter *said* "Henry Worrel," only Henry knew damn well he hadn't signed it. But he knew who had.

Right—Roy, having dropped the ball, foists the responsibility off on a young associate, forges his name to a confession of error, and faxes the thing off, figuring no one would ever be the wiser, since he never let the associate talk to the client. Only Roy forgot that once a fax is sent, the telecommunications office returns a copy to the "sender," confirming delivery.[4] Seeing Worrel's name on the fax, the office duly sent the confirmation copy to Worrel.

When I got wind of this—I've always tried to keep open lines of communication with the associates, and I think most of them trust me—I was outraged. My first reaction was to take it to Dick McSorley and demand that Roy be cut loose. On reflection, though, I decided not to. I've never been sure of the basis for Roy's seemingly inexplicable cachet in the Firm, but clearly he was a vicious in-fighter, with God knows what chits he could call in. I wasn't too worried about myself, but I knew that if I took this tale to Dick and Roy survived, a vengeful Roy would make Henry Worrel's future at Barton, Allard highly problematic. Anyway, I quickly saw a better approach, one hewing to my policy of countervailing vengeance: Roy had shifted the responsibility for his malpractice onto an innocent party; now an innocent Roy was going to take responsibility for a whole heap of someone else's malpractice.

Roy's office was next to mine, the only consolation being that he was frequently away from it, either creeping around prying into other people's business, truckling to the powerful, or attending endless conferences at Firm expense. Hence it was no trick to nip in from time to time over the next few weeks and remove various items of unopened mail that had come in for Roy in his absence: doing-business renewal notices, the odd pleading or two, a couple of letters from clients, some UCC filings.

I deep-sixed them after first, in a few instances, returning enclosures, improperly filled out and lacking registration

---

[4]Something *I* had been careful *not* to forget; I had nipped into Dick McSorley's office and recovered "his" fax to Roy.

effectiveness.[5] Then I waited. It took a few months, but the day we got the notice from our insurer that a claim had been asserted against Roy for "neglect of a client's affairs," I knew my first Scud had landed.

After that, things started moving with increasing speed, most markedly the deterioration in Roy himself. For one thing, he became reluctant to leave his office, so much so that one night I saw him slipping out clutching a bottle, the contents of which *appeared* to suggest that he was attending to his bathroom needs in a somewhat unconventional manner. When he *did* emerge, he would shut the door behind him, then scurry along, never more than a few inches from a wall, darting backward glances every few feet. I also thought his eyes took on a feral quality, although that may have been wishful thinking.

Of course, he *was* under a lot of pressure, what with outraged clients demanding to know why they'd lost their right to do business in Oklahoma, or why the security interest they thought they held in someone's inventory turned out to be illusory. The best part of it was that it was like the unexploded mines left behind in Kuwait: Roy had no way of knowing what he *hadn't* gotten, so he never knew when another limb was going to be blown away. No doubt, even now there are a few default judgments yet to come, although Roy's beyond any more of the malpractice actions that started then.

I *do* want to make it clear that I *deeply* regret that my

---

[5] I gather that the Bar Association's counsel produced one of these half-completed forms to devastating effect on Roy's "But I never got it" defense during the disbarment proceedings. While Roy's death presumably moots that action, I have it on good information that down in the Secretary of State's office, "But I never got it" is now known as "copping a Roy"; it pleases me to think that I purchased him a little immortality, however unintentionally.

action led to the loss of a few clients. Where I knew the client, I pulled out Roy's Bill Stetz ploy, doing my best to intimate that the foul-up was attributable to Roy's drinking problem, of which Barton, Allard had been completely unaware (not surprisingly, since drinking was, as far as I know, one of the few problems Roy *didn't* have, at least at that juncture). I was able to salvage several client relationships, in some cases taking over the billing responsibility myself. In a particularly happy reversal, I persuaded FoSoCo to reestablish its relationship with Bill Stetz.

When I say that things speeded up after "Roy's" malpractice began to surface, I mean not only that his manner became increasingly bizarre but that, paradoxically, the rate at which he did things demanding retribution accelerated. So far from learning his lesson, Roy now entered into a downward spiral of offensive behavior that quickly brought us to the endgame.

The next thing that happened was the reason David Norquist left—you remember, the fellow who had to give up his day off and miss his grandmother's funeral at Roy's behest? I thought I'd salvaged *that* situation, but that was before Roy struck again.

You don't always get the real story, you know—people like David don't kick over the coffee table their last trip out the door. They expect to be practicing around town for a long time, and they can't afford to burn bridges. So they say, "I really hate leaving, but I've got a chance to work. with someone who's a perfect fit, and I'll always respect Barton, Allard, and I was really torn," and all that.

I'll tell you why David left, and it made Roy's previous dealings with David seem like a model of sensitive interpersonal relationships.

David's daughter was in an accident, a rather serious one. She required surgery, and afterward she was in a lot of pain. So David was down at the hospital with his wife, when he gets a call—it's Clark Roy, and guess what he wants? Right—drafts of some deal papers, and no delay: "If you're not ready to put your clients ahead of your family, you don't belong at Barton, Allard" was the way Roy put it—this from the man who'd stolen Linda Browne's loge because "his kids were his best clients," remember?

So David leaves the hospital, goes back to the office, delivers the drafts, and puts his resignation on Dick's desk on the way out. David, you know, was editor of the *Harvard Law Review*, a Supreme Court clerk, and a budding superstar. Three days later, he's at Dawkins, Heller, and they're happy as hell to have him. Incidentally, guess who's handling their recruiting, seeing everybody who's also talking to us? Somehow I don't think we'll be landing a lot of *Harvard Law Review* types if they talk to David first—it would be easier to sign them up for the Marines. That's Roy's legacy in that quarter.

When I heard this, I realized Roy hadn't taken my previous points at all. *Well,* I thought, *apparently Mr. Roy needs a little instruction in family values.*

That was easy. A few days later, I happened to overhear him talking on the phone to his wife, JoAnne, about a birthday party she was taking their daughter to that afternoon. It came right through the wall, since he was screaming. Roy was apparently concerned that "they"—whoever "they" were—were a "threat" to his family, and he was counseling extreme caution (actually, I believe he was telling her not to leave the house, but it was hard to tell, because he seemed to be using some sort of code).

That precipitated a call to his office a few hours later, a mumbled message: "Doctor Forbes here; we've got your wife and daughter down at Metro in intensive care," and a hang-up. He looked positively ill as he raced out. It was nice to learn there was *someone* he cared about besides himself.

I only meant to throw a scare into him, I swear it. I never dreamed he'd pull out of the garage without looking, and certainly the police estimate that he was going almost fifty when he slammed into the truck can't be right. After all, the truck driver suffered relatively minor contusions (I'm sure the amount claimed in the lawsuit is unrealistic, even if Roy's estate could satisfy that large a judgment). As for Roy, I hope I've demonstrated that his aberrant behavior long antedated the accident. Those who are now saying that Roy's activities in the weeks between the accident and his death can be traced to his head injuries are being too charitable; when he left the intensive care unit at Metro (ironic, that), he had a clean bill of health.

Certainly he came back *physically* strong enough to take up where he had left off, as far as truly repugnant behavior was concerned. The Gilkins episode is illustrative, and it was what put me over the top.

Laura Gilkins—another topflight young associate—had had the misfortune to find herself assigned to one of Roy's projects, back when he still had some. All the associates hated working for him, for obvious reasons, but the women associates most of all, because when he wasn't demeaning them, he was trying to peer down the front of their dresses. This didn't keep him from chairing United Appeal, from

293

being a deacon at First Presbyterian, or from playing the devoted husband whenever he thought it would got him some brownie points, but it sure kept him from being a favorite of the women, since the idea of commingling DNA with Clark Roy must be one of the world's great anaphrodisiacs.

Anyway, Laura found herself stuck with him, and, sure enough, no more than a week after he got back, I'm hearing from another associate that Laura had been overheard crying in her office. I had a premonition what it might mean, so I dropped in on her, and, after a lot of resistance, she opened up: Roy had been coming on harder and harder, the hints about her partnership chances and the reports he'd be putting in were coming fast and furious, and she was desperate. Should she go to see Dick McSorley?

I took it upon myself to say no. I had no doubt Dick would intervene, but I also thought he'd rather not have to get dragged into a "he said/she said" from which there wasn't likely to emerge a clear winner. Besides, Roy was such an evil little pustulence, there was no telling what he might do to retaliate, even in his debilitated condition; the wounded beast is most likely to bite, that sort of thing. I didn't want us to lose another talented, embittered associate. This seemed to me to be the occasion for yet another lesson, this one even swifter and more terrible than those that had gone before, with too little notice paid.

I had to let Laura into my scheme. I did so reluctantly, since I'd been a solo operative up to then, but I needed her cooperation. It wasn't hard to persuade her, once I explained the concept, although understandably she found the prospect of physical contact with him distasteful in the extreme.

One disclaimer: Laura Gilkins acted *solely* at my direction; no opprobrium should attach to her for anything that happened. She would have been well within her rights had she brought a sexual harassment claim against Roy *and* Barton, Allard; she loyally agreed not to after I pointed out the harm that would do the Firm—which she reveres as much as I do—and in light of the alternative I offered. Ms. Gilkins's conduct should be taken as evidence of her commitment to the Firm, and not in any way as grounds for censure.

It was a simple matter to arrange for the speaker phone to be on in the conference room where Laura had the deal papers spread out when Roy slithered in in response to Laura's urgent call. It wasn't much harder for me to tape the conversation that ensued, all per the script Laura and I had worked out. The "Oh, Clark—I don't *know*" told me we had liftoff; her "God, I *do* want to—but wouldn't it be better if we waited until you get your divorce?" proved, ironically, the line that did the most to *get* Roy the divorce he had, of course, never dreamed of—something about it must have really rubbed his wife the wrong way, since I gather the settlement she was demanding when Roy mooted it by his sudden appearance on the basement floor struck seasoned observers of the domestic relations bar as more than a little vindictive.

Laura's "Oh, Clark—not here" was my cue to set off the fire alarm and break up the tryst; after that, it was a simple matter to drop the tape in the mail to JoAnne Roy, with a little note from "a friend."

After that, the deterioration in Roy's condition became palpable. Within days after I sent the tape, I noticed Roy was unshaven, and his clothes looked like he'd slept in them. He had! It seems that after JoAnne threw him out, he moved into his office, sleeping on his settee and cleaning up as best he could in the men's room. I loved it, and sent him a bottle of whiskey to help him sleep.

There isn't much more. The bottle I sent *did* help him sleep, so he started getting lots of bottles in. His office became increasingly fetid, but that was all right, since fewer and fewer people had any reason to drop in, as business turned to lawyers whose breath wasn't quite so rank and whose advice didn't come in largely incoherent sentences that sounded more and more like glossolalia.

Frankly, by the time Roy made his exit, there wasn't a lot left; if he hadn't drawn upon some last remaining reservoir of malice and targeted *me,* no less, I'm sure I would have been quite content to wait for the inevitable day when building management came along to hose out his office. But the last thing was really intolerable, I'm sure you'll agree.

It started a couple of nights after Roy moved into his office full-time. I was proofing a brief that had to be filed the next day, and it must have been close to midnight when I glanced out my door and spotted Roy tiptoeing across the hall toward the staff lunchroom. A minute later, back he came, clutching a white cardboard cake box. He ducked into his office, and I thought no more of it.

Until the next day, when Helen Trosch, a *wonderful* secretary, comes out of the lunchroom, breathing fire: "Who the hell took the cake I bought for the staff party?"

Well, I knew the answer, but I don't think anyone can accuse me of being a mere snitch, and I held my tongue. When, all of a sudden, Roy's door springs open, and he's standing in it, saying, *"He took it, I saw him,"* while pointing at *me!*

I wasn't about to lower myself to answering an accusation from Roy, that was for sure, so when Helen turned a questioning eye on me—we've always gotten along well—I just nodded and mumbled an apology. In fifteen minutes, I was back with a new cake and cookies as well, and all was harmonious again on that front, with playful chiding about my "sweet tooth" now a regular part of Helen's repertoire.

Yet, as you may well imagine, a false accusation of theft, even petty theft, is not to be condoned in a profession whose practitioners have nothing if not their reputation for probity in all things large and small. As far as I was concerned, Roy's malicious fabrication forfeited his right to exist.

You know the rest. It was child's play to remove the petty cash from the business office late that night; during one of Roy's furtive forays through the, halls, I slipped into his office and planted the evidence. The trail of change made it easy for building security to find the cash box in the back of his file drawer. I never really understood the concept of *res ipsa loquitur*—the thing speaks for itself—until I listened to Roy trying to explain that. To be honest, I don't think that by that point *he* was sure of his innocence; God knows, he didn't sound like it.

Why did he come back after making bail? Who knows. Why did he wander into the construction area and take that leap off the new stairwell—that's easier, don't you think?

As I said—I'm not sorry Clark Roy is dead. I'm not even sorry I killed him. You'll do what you have to do; I know I did.

/s/ John Ferris

"Yes, that'll do nicely, Jack." The neat, green-eyed man in the navy pinstripe looked up from the statement and shook his head. "Cynical little bastard, isn't he?"

The old man chuckled, or maybe his emphysema was acting up again. "Reminds me of another one, not too long ago."

The younger man thought about it, nodded. "Maybe. Don't think much of that crack about my 'too neat' hand-kerchiefs and 'precious' collar pins, though." His lips drew into a thin line.

"Thought that'd get to you. Told you you dress like a nou-veau mick, now maybe you'll believe me."

The flicker in the green eyes might have been amuse-ment, might have been something else: I *am* a nouveau mick; that's why you picked me as managing partner, you could have picked Prescott, and we could have gone the way of the other white-shoe firms."

"True enough, true enough." The old man smiled, serenely. "And Ferris is the same kind of scrapper you were at his age; took balls to do those things." A bony finger pointed at the report the green-eyed man had just finished reading. "Lot of balls."

"I wasn't sure he was up to it." The green-eyed folded the papers and stuck them in his inner breast pocket.

The old man took a bird-sip of his bourbon, neat. "Never doubted it for a moment, Dick. Watched him for years.

Haven't lost my eye. Most other parts, but not my eye."

"How'd you get him to produce this?"

"Told him I'd seen him with the cash box. He understood t was give us the report or he might as well follow Roy lown that stairwell. Not a hard choice, when you put it like hat, and he's a quick study." The old man wheezed again.

"Lucky you spotted him coming out of the business office."

"Luck had nothing to do with it, and you know it. I've peen creeping around the corridors at all hours for weeks now, ever since Roy told me he was sure Ferris was behind his troubles. Haven't had so much fun since my last safari. Back's hurting like hell, though."

"I miss Roy, in a way."

"The hell you will—you were the one who said he was through."

"I know, I know—and he was." The man with the little emerald eyes looked at his glass as though a fly were floating in it. "People were starting to say he reflected on me—that I *needed* him kissing my ass all the time, that he was 'my boy' and all that. Ferris got that right, and once that happens, a fellow's no more use than yesterday's *Journal*. Still, Roy had his moments—that's all I meant."

"Better than Prescott was, any day." The old man's voice held a baiting note. "Tougher."

"Prescott wasn't any pushover, Jack. Things had gone a little differently, he'd be sitting here with you now—and you'd be just as happy."

The old man didn't rise to it. "Things have a way of sorting out. I think you'll be happy with Ferris."

The younger man broke off his stare. "I hope so—I don't

feel like going through this again for a while."

"If there's a next time, it'll be when you're senior partner, Dick."

The green-eyed man started to protest, but the old man waved his thin hand dismissively. "Clinic says six months, a year at most. Doesn't matter—I'm ready."

"Sorry to hear that, Jack. The Firm will miss you. So will I."

"I'm sure my memory will be revered. You'll see to that, Dick."

The green-eyed man smiled, a little, tight crease, no more. "But then who will see to it that people who don't know when it's time to quit get a little encouragement, hmm?"

"That'll be your job, Dick as senior partner. You'll know what to say when and if the time comes."

" 'Saw your light was on, thought you might want to talk? Let's see how the new construction's going while we're at it, something like that?' "

"Something like that." The old man wheezed "Yep— you'll know what to say. What to do." He shook his head, the wisps of white hair floating over the cadaverous scalp. "You know, I don't think he was even all that sorry. Didn't utter a peep on the way down."

"I suppose. Well, if Ferris works out, he'll be taking over as managing partner by and by."

"By and by."

A white-jacketed waiter appeared from out of the gloom. "Your guest is here, gentlemen—a Mr. Ferris."

The old man smiled. "Excellent, excellent. Show him in, Hawkins, show him in."

The young man stepped hesitantly through the gloom,

took the proffered seat, accepted a glass from the green-eyed man The old man poured from the nearly full bottle, his hand steady.

"Good of you to drop by, Ferris. No point in beating about the bush: I've . . . we've, Jack and I, been watching you. We like the way you handle yourself. I can use a man like you in management. What do you think, hmm?" The green eyes bore in, the famous twinkle working.

The young man met the look until his eyes dropped, fractionally, focusing on the green-eyed man's neck. He started to form a phrase, paused, and then a slow smile spread across his face. "I think I'd like to know where I could get one of those collar pins, Dick." He raised his glass, slowly, dipped it in the direction of the older men. "Yes—I've always wanted one just like yours." Then the quiet click of ice cubes was the only sound in the small, warm room.

Dead Drunk

Lia Matera

My secretary, Jan, asked if I'd seen the newspaper: another homeless man had frozen to death. I frowned up at her from my desk. Her tone said, *And you think you've got problems?*

My secretary is a paragon. I would not have a law practice without her. I would have something resembling my apartment, which looks like a college crash pad. But I have to cut Jan a lot of slack. She's got a big personality.

Not that she actually says anything. She doesn't have to, any more than earthquakes bother saying "shake shake."

"Froze?" I murmured. I shoved documents around the desk, knowing she wouldn't take the hint.

"Froze to death. This is the fourth one. They find them in the parks, frozen."

"It has been cold," I agreed.

"You really haven't been reading the papers!" Her eyes went on high-beam. "They're wet, that's why they freeze."

She sounded mad at me. Line forms on the right, behind my creditors.

"Must be the tule fog?" I guessed. I've never been sure what tule fog is. I didn't know if actual tules were required.

"You have been in your own little world lately. They've all been passed out drunk. Someone pours water over them while they lie there. It's been so cold, they end up frozen. To death."

I wondered if I could get away with, *How terrible.* Not

302

that I didn't think it was terrible. But Jan picks at what I say, looking for hidden sarcasm.

She leaned closer, as titillated as I'd ever seen her. "And here's the kicker. They went and analyzed the water on the clothes. It's got no chlorine in it—it's not tap water. It's bottled water! Imagine that. Perrier or Evian or something. Can you imagine? Somebody going out with expensive bottled water on purpose to pour it over passed-out homeless men." Her long hair fell over her shoulders. With her big glasses and serious expression, she looked like the bread-baking, natural foods mom that she was. "You know, it probably takes three or four bottles."

"What a murder weapon."

"It is murder." She sounded defensive. "Being wet drops the body temperature so low it kills them. In this cold, within hours."

"That's what I said."

"But you were . . . anyway, it is murder."

"I wonder if it has to do with the ordinance."

Our town had passed a no-camping ordinance that was supposed to chase the homeless out of town. If they couldn't sleep here, the theory went, they couldn't live here. But the city had too many parks to enforce the ban. What were cops supposed to do? Wake up everyone they encountered? Take them to jail and give them a warmer place to sleep?

"Of course it has to do with the ordinance! This is some asshole's way of saying, if you sleep here, you die here."

"Maybe it's a temperance thing. You know, don't drink."

"I know what temperance means." Jan could be touchy. She could be a lot of things, including a fast typist willing to work cheap. "I just don't believe the heartlessness of it, do you?"

I had to be careful; I did believe the heartlessness of it. "It's uncondonable," I agreed.

Still she stooped over my desk. There was something else.

"The guy last night," Jan said bitterly, "was laid off by Hinder. Yew ago, but even so."

Hinder was the corporation Jan had been fired from before I hired her.

She straightened. "I'm going to go give money to the guys outside."

"Who's outsider! Not my creditors?"

"You are so oblivious, Linda! Homeless people, right downstairs. Regulars."

She was looking at me like I should know their names. I tried to look apologetic.

Ten minutes later, she buzzed me to say there was someone in the reception area. "He wants to know if you can fit him in."

That was our code for, *He looks legit*. We were not in the best neighborhood. We got our share of walk-ins with generalized grievances and a desire to vent at length and for free. For them, our code was, "I've told him you're busy."

"Okay."

A moment later, a kid—well, maybe young man, maybe even twenty-five or so—walked in. He was good-looking, well dressed, but too trendy, which is why he'd looked so young. He had the latest hairstyle, razored in places and long in others. He had running shoes that looked like inflatable pools.

He said, "I think I need a good lawyer."

My glance strayed to my walls, where my diploma announced I'd gone to a night school. I had two years' experience, some of it with no caseload. I resisted the urge to say, *Let me refer you to one.*

Instead, I asked, "What's the nature of your problem?"

He sat on my client chair, checking it first. I guess it was clean enough.

"I think I'm going to be arrested." He glanced at me a little sheepishly, a little boastfully. "I said something kind of stupid last night."

If that were grounds, they'd arrest me, too.

"I was at the Club," a fancy bar downtown. "I got a little tanked. A little loose." He waggled his shoulders.

I waited. He sat forward. "Okay, I've got issues." His face said, *Who wouldn't?* "I work my butt off."

I waited some more.

"Well, it burns me. I have to work for my money, I don't get welfare, I don't get free meals and free medicine and a free place to live." He shifted on the chair. "I'm not saying kill them. But it's unfair I have to pay for them."

"For who?"

"The trolls, the bums."

I was beginning to get it. "What did you say in the bar?"

"That I bought out Costco's Perrier." He flushed to the roots of his chi-chi hair. "That I wish I'd thought of using it."

"On the four men?"

"I was high, okay?" he continued in a rush. "But then this morning, the cops come over." Tears sprang to his eyes. "They scared my mom. She took them out to see the water in the garage."

"You really did buy a lot of Perrier?"

"Just to drink! The police said they got a tip on their hot line. Someone at the bar told them about me. That's got to be it."

I nodded like I knew about the hot line.

"Now"—his voice quavered—"they've started talking to people where I work. Watch me get fired!"

Gee, buddy, then you'll qualify for free medical. "What would you like me to do for you, Mr. . . . ?"

"Kyle Kelly." He didn't stick out his hand. "Are they going to arrest me or what? I think I need a lawyer."

My private investigator was pissed off at me. My last two clients hadn't paid me enough to cover his fees. It was my fault; I hadn't asked for enough in advance. Afterward, they'd stiffed me.

Now the PI was taking a hard line: he wouldn't work on this case until he got paid for the last two.

So I made a deal. I'd get his retainer from Kelly up front. I'd pay him for the investigation, but I'd do most of it myself. For every hour I investigated and he got paid, he'd knock an hour off what I owed him.

I wouldn't want the state bar to hear about the arrangement. But the parts that were on paper would look okay.

It meant I had a lot of legwork to do.

I started by driving to a park where two of the dead men were found. It was a chilly afternoon, with the wind whipping off the plains, blowing dead leaves over footpaths and lawns.

I wandered, looking for the spots described in police

reports. The trouble was, every half bare bush near lawn and benches looked the same. And many were decorated with detritus: paper bags, liquor bottles, discarded clothing.

As I was leaving the park, I spotted two paramedics squatting beside an addled-looking man. His clothes were stiff with dirt, his face covered in thick gray stubble. He didn't look wet. If anything, I was shivering more than him.

I watched the younger of the two paramedics shake his head, scowling, while the older talked at some length to the man. The man nodded, kept on nodding. The older medic showed him a piece of paper. The man nodded some more. The younger one strode to an ambulance parked on a nearby fire trail. It was red on white with "4-12" stenciled on the side.

I knew from police reports that paramedics had been called to pick up the frozen homeless men. Were they conducting an investigation of their own?

A minute later, the older medic joined his partner in the ambulance. It drove off.

The homeless man lay down, curling into a fetal position on the lawn, collar turned up against the wind.

I approached him cautiously. "Hi," I said. "Are you sick?"

"No!" He sat up again. "What's every damn body want to know if I'm sick for? 'Man down.' So what? What's a man got to be up about?"

He looked bleary-eyed. He reeked of alcohol and urine and musk. He was so potent, I almost lost my breakfast.

"I saw medics here talking to you. I thought you might be sick."

"Hassle hassle." He waved me away. When I didn't

leave, he rose. "Wake us up, make us sign papers."

"What kind of papers?"

"Don't want to go to the hospital." His teeth were in terrible condition. I tried not to smell his breath. "Like I want yelling from the nurses, too."

"What do they yell at you about?"

"Cost them money; I'm costing everybody money. Yeah, well, maybe they should have thought of that before they put my-Johnny-self in the helicopter. Maybe they should have left me with the rest of the platoon."

He lurched away from me. I could see that one leg was shorter than the other.

I went back to my car. I was driving past a nearby sandwich shop when I saw ambulance 4-12 parked there. I pulled into the space behind it. I went into the shop.

The medics were sitting at a small table, looking bored. They were hard to miss in their cop-blue uniforms and utility belts hung with flashlights, scissors, tape, stethoscopes.

I walked up to them. "Hi," I said. "Do you mind if I talk to you for a minute?"

The younger one looked through me; no one's ever accused me of being pretty. The older one said, "What about?"

"I'm representing a suspect in the . . ." I hated to call it what the papers were now calling it, but it was the best shorthand. "The Perrier murders. Of homeless men."

That got the younger man's attention. "We knew those guys," he said.

"My client didn't do it. But he could get arrested. Do you mind helping me out? Telling me a little about them?"

They glanced at each other. The younger man shrugged.

"We saw them all the time. Every time, someone spotted them passed out and phoned in a 'man down' call, we'd code-three it out to the park or the tracks or wherever."

The older paramedic gestured for me to sit. "Hard times out there. We've got a lot more regulars than we used to."

I sat down. The men, I noticed, were lingering over coffee. "I just saw you in the park."

"Lucky for everybody, my-Johnny-self was sober enough to AMA." The younger man looked irritated. "Against medical advice." We get these calls all the time. Here we are a city's got gang wars going on, knifings, drive-bys, especially late at night; and we're diddling around with passed-out drunks who want to be left alone anyway."

The older man observed, "Ben's new, still a hot dog, wants every call to be the real deal."

"Yeah, well, what a waste of effort, Dirk," the younger man, Ben, shot back. "We get what? Two, three, four man-down calls a day. We have to respond to every one. It could be some poor diabetic, right, or a guy's had a heart attack. But you get out there, and it's some alcoholic. If he's too out of it to tell us he's just drunk, we have to transport and work him up. Which he doesn't want—he wakes up pissed off at having to hoof it back to the park. Or worse, with the new ordinance, he gets arrested.

"Ridiculous ordinance," the older medic interjected.

"And it's what, maybe five or six hundred dollars the company's out of pocket?" his partner continued. "Not to mention that everybody's time gets totally wasted, and maybe somebody with a real emergency's out there waiting for us. Your grandmother could be dying of a heart attack while we play taxi. It's bullshit."

"It's all in a night's work, Ben." Dirk looked at me. "You start this job, you want every call to be for real. But you do it a few years, you get to know your regulars. Clusters of them near the liquor stores; you could draw concentric circles around each store and chart the man-down calls, truly. But what are you going to do? Somebody sees a man lying in the street or in the park, they've got to call, right? And if the poor bastard's too drunk to tell us he's fine, we can't just leave him. It's our license if we're wrong."

"They should change the protocols," Ben insisted. "If we know who they are, if we've run them in three, four, even ten times, we should be able to leave them to sleep it off."

Dirk said, "You'd get lawsuits."

"So these guys either stiff the company or welfare picks up the tab, meaning you and me pay the five hundred bucks. It offends logic."

"So you knew the men who froze." I tried to get back on track. "Did you pick them up when they died?"

"I went on one of the calls," Ben said defensively. "Worked him up."

"Sometimes with hypothermia," Dirk added, "body functions slow down so you can't really tell if they're dead till they warm up. So we'll spend, oh God, an hour or more doing CPR. Till they're warm and dead."

"While people wait for an ambulance somewhere else," Ben repeated.

"You'll mellow out," Dirk promised. "For one thing, you see them year in, year out, you stop being such a hard-ass. Another thing, you get older, you feel more sympathy for how hard the street's got to be on the poor bones."

310

Ben's beeper went off. He immediately lifted it out of his utility belt, pressing a button and filling the air with static. A voice cut through: "Unit four-twelve, we have a possible shooting at Kins and Booten streets."

The paramedics jumped up, saying " 'Bye" and "Gotta go," as they strode past me and out the door. Ben, I noticed, was smiling.

My next stop was just a few blocks away. It was a rundown stucco building that had recently been a garage, a factory, a cult church, a rehab center, a magic shop. Now it was one of the few homeless shelters in town. I thought the workers there might have known some of the dead men.

I was ushered in to see the director, a big woman with a bad complexion. When I handed her my card and told her my business, she looked annoyed.

"Pardon me, but your client sounds like a real shit."

"I don't know him well enough to judge," I admitted. "But he denies doing it, and I believe him. And if he didn't do it, he shouldn't get blamed. You'd agree with that?"

"Some days," she conceded. She motioned me to sit in a scarred chair opposite a folding-table desk. "Other days, tell the truth, I'd round up all the holier-than-thou jerks bitching about the cost of a place like this, and I'd shoot 'em. Christ, they act like we're running a luxury hotel here. Did you get a look around?"

I'd seen women and children and a few old men on folding chairs or duck-cloth cots. I hadn't seen any food.

"It's enough to get your goat," the director continued. "The smugness, the condemnation. And ironically, how many paychecks away from the street do you think most people are? One? Two?"

"Is that mostly who you see here? People who got laid off?"

She shrugged. "Maybe half. We get a lot of people who are frankly just too tweaked-out to work. What can you do? You can't take a screwdriver and fix them. No use blaming them for it."

"Did you know any of the men who got killed?"

She shook her head. "No, no. We don't take drinkers, we don't take anybody under the influence. We can't. Nobody would get any sleep, nobody would feel safe. Alcohol's a nasty drug, lowers inhibitions; you get too much attitude, too much noise. We can't deal with it here. We don't let in anybody we think's had a drink, and if we find alcohol, we kick the person out. It's that simple."

"What recourse do they have? Drinkers, I mean."

"Sleep outside. They want to sleep inside, they have to stay sober, no ifs, ands, or buts."

"The camping ban makes that illegal."

"Well," she said tartly, "it's not illegal to stay sober."

"You don't view it as an addiction?"

"There's AA meetings five times a night at three locations." She ran a hand through her already-disheveled hair. "I'm sorry, but it's a struggle scraping together money to take care of displaced families in this town. Then you've got to contend with people thinking you're running some kind of flophouse for drunks. Nobody's going to donate money for that."

I felt a twinge of pity. No room at the inn for alcoholics, and not much sympathy from paramedics. Now, someone—please God, not my client—was dousing them so they'd freeze to death.

With the director's permission, I wandered through the shelter.

A young woman lay on a cot with a blanket over her legs. She was reading a paperback.

"Hi," I said. "I'm a lawyer. I'm working on the case of the homeless men who died in the parks recently. Do you know about it?"

She sat up. She looked like she could use a shower and a makeover, but she looked more together than most of the folks in there. She wasn't mumbling to herself, and she didn't took upset or afraid.

"Yup—big news here. And major topic on the street."

"Did you know any of the men?"

"I'll tell you what I've heard." She leaned forward. "It's a turf war."

"A turf war?"

"Who gets to sleep where, that kind of thing. A lot of crazies on the street, they get paranoid. They gang up on each other. Alumni from the closed-down mental hospitals. You'd be surprised." She pushed up her sleeve and showed me a scar. "One of them cut me."

"Do you know who's fighting whom?"

"Yes." Her eyes glittered. "Us women are killing off the men. They say we're out on the street for their pleasure, and we say, death to you, bozo."

I took a backward step, alarmed by the look on her face.

She showed me her scar again. "I carve a line for every one I kill." She pulled a tin St. Christopher out from under her shirt. "I used to be a Catholic. But Clint Eastwood is my god now."

. . .

I pulled into a parking lot with four ambulances parked in a row. A sign on a two-story brick building read "Central Ambulance." I hoped they'd give me their records regarding the four men.

I smiled warmly at the front-office secretary. When I explained what I wanted, she handed me a records-request form. "We'll contact you within five business days regarding the status of your request."

If my client got booked, I could subpoena the records. So I might, unfortunately, have them before anyone even read this form.

As I sat there filling it out, a thin boy in a paramedic uniform strolled in. He wore his medic's bill cap backward. His utility belt was hung with twice the gadgets of the two men I'd talked to earlier. Something resembling a big rubber band dangled from his back pocket. I supposed it was a tourniquet, but on him it gave the impression of a slingshot.

He glanced at me curiously. He said, "Howdy, Mary," to the secretary.

She didn't look glad to see him. "What now?"

"Is Karl in?"

"No. What's so important?"

"I was thinking instead of just using the HEPA filters, if we—"

"Save it. I'm busy."

I shot him a sympathetic look. I know how it feels to be bullied by a secretary.

I handed her my request and walked out behind the spurned paramedic.

314

I was surprised to see him climb into a cheap Geo car. He was in uniform. I'd assumed he was working.

All four men had been discovered in the morning. It had probably taken them most of the night to freeze to death; they'd been picked up by ambulance in the wee hours. Maybe this kid could tell me who'd worked those shifts.

I tapped at his passenger window. He didn't hesitate to lean across and open the door. He looked alert and happy, like a curious puppy.

"Hi," I said. "I was wondering if you could tell me about your shifts? I was going to ask the secretary, but she's not very . . . friendly."

He nodded as if her unfriendliness were a fact of life, nothing to take personally. "Come on in. What do you want to know?" Then, more suspiciously, "You're not a lawyer?"

I climbed in quickly. "Well, yes, but—"

"Oh, man. You know, we do the very best we can." He whipped off his cap, rubbing his crewcut in apparent annoyance. "We give a hundred and ten percent."

I suddenly placed his concern. "No, no, it's not about medical malpractice, I swear."

He continued scowling at me. "I represent a young man who's been falsely accused of—"

"You're not here about malpractice?"

"No, I'm not."

"Because that's such a crock." He flushed. "We work our butts off. Twelve-hour shifts, noon to midnight, and a lot of times we get force-manned onto a second shift. If someone calls in sick or has to go out of service because they got bled all over or punched out, someone's got to hold over. When hell's a-poppin' with the gangs, we've got guys working forty-eights or even seventy-twos." He shook his head. "It's just plain unfair to blame us for everything that goes wrong. Field medicine's like combat conditions. We don't have everything all clean and handy like they do at the hospital."

"I can imagine. So you work—"

"And it's not like we're doing it for the money! Starting pay's eight-fifty an hour; it takes years to work up to twelve. Your garbage collector earns more than we do."

I was a little off balance. "Your shifts—"

"Because half our calls, nobody pays the bill—Central Ambulance is probably the biggest pro bono business in town. So we get stuck at eight-fifty an hour. For risking AIDS, hepatitis, TB."

I didn't want to get pulled into his grievances. "You work twelve-hour shifts? Set shifts?"

"Rotating. Sometimes you work the day half, sometimes the night half."

Rotating; I'd need schedules and rosters. "The guys who work midnight to noon, do they get most of the drunks?"

He shrugged. "Not necessarily. We've got 'em passing out all day long. It's never too early for an alcoholic to drink." He looked bitter. "I had one in the family," he complained. "I should know."

"Do you know who picked up the four men who froze to death?"

His eyes grew steely. "I'm not going to talk about the other guys. You'll have to ask the company." He started the car.

I contemplated trying another question, but he was already shifting into gear. I thanked him, and got out. As I

316

closed the door, I noticed a bag in back with a Garry's Liquors logo. Maybe the medic had something in common with the four dead men.

But it wasn't just drinking that got those men into trouble. It was not having a home to pass out in.

I stood at the spot where police had found the fourth body. It was a small neighborhood park.

Just after sunrise, an early jogger had phoned 911 from his cell phone. A man had been lying under a hedge. He'd looked dead. He'd looked wet.

The police had arrived first, then firemen, who'd taken a stab at resuscitating him. Then paramedics had arrived to work him up and transport him to the hospital, where he was pronounced dead. I knew that much from today's newspaper.

I found a squashed area of grass where I supposed the dead man had lain yesterday. I could see pocks and scuffs where work boots had tramped. I snooped around. Hanging from a bush was a rubber tourniquet. A paramedic must have squatted with his back against the shrubbery.

Flung deeper into the brush was a bottle of whiskey. Had the police missed it? Not considered it evidence? Or had it been discarded since?

I stared at it, wondering. If victim number four hadn't already been pass-out drunk, maybe someone helped him along.

I stopped by Parsifal MiniMart, the liquor store nearest the park. if anyone knew the dead man, it would be the proprietor.

He nodded. "Yup. I knew every one of those four. What

kills me is the papers act like they were nobodies, like that's what 'alcoholic' means." He was a tall, red-faced man, given to karate-chop gestures. "Well, they were pretty good guys. Not mean, not full of shit, just regular guys. Buddy was a little"—he wiggled his hand—"not right in the head; heard voices and all that, but not violent that I ever saw. Mitch was a good guy. One of those jocks who's a hero as a kid but then gets hooked on the booze. I'll tell ya, I wish I could have made every kid comes in here for beer spend the day with Mitch. Donnie and Bill were . . . how can I put this without sounding like a racist? You know, a lot of older black guys are hooked on something. Check out the neighborhood. You'll see groups of them talking jive and keeping the curbs warm."

Something had been troubling me. Perhaps this was the person to ask. "Why didn't they wake up when the cold water hit them?"

The proprietor laughed. "Those guys? If I had to guess, I'd say their blood alcohol was one-point-oh even when they weren't drinking, just naturally from living the life. Get enough Thunderbird in them, and you're talking practically a coma." He shook his head. "They were just drunks; I know we're not talking about killing Mozart here. But the attitude behind what happened—man, it's cold. Perrier, too. That really tells you something."

"I heard there was no chlorine in the water. I don't think they've confirmed a particular brand of water."

"I just saw on the news they arrested some kid looks like a fruit, one of those hairstyles." The proprietor shrugged. "He had a bunch of Perrier. Cases of it from a discount place—I guess he didn't want to pay full price. Guess it wasn't even worth a buck a bottle to him to freeze a drunk."

Damn, they'd arrested Kyle Kelly. Already.

"You don't know anything about a turf war, do you?" It was worth a shot. "Among the homeless?"

"Sure." He grinned. "The drunk sharks and the rummy jets." He whistled the opening notes of *West Side Story*.

I got tied up in traffic. It was an hour later by the time I walked into the police station. My client was in an interrogation room by himself. When I walked in, he was crying.

"I told them I didn't do it." He wiped tears as if they were an embarrassing surprise. "But I was getting so tongue-tied. I told them I wanted to wait for you."

"I didn't think they'd arrest you, especially not so fast," I said. "You did exactly right, asking for me. I just wish I'd gotten here sooner. I wish I'd been in my office when you called."

He looked like he wished I had, too.

"All this over a bunch of bums," he marveled. "All the crime in this town, and they get hard-ons over winos!"

I didn't remind him that his own drunken bragging had landed him here. But I hope it occurred to him later.

I was surrounded by reporters when I left the police station. They looked at me like my client had taken bites out of their children.

"Mr. Kelly is a very young person who regrets what alcohol made him say one evening. He bears no one any in will, least of all the dead men, whom he never even met." I repeated some variation of this over and over as I battled my way to my car.

Meanwhile, their questions shed harsh light on my client's bragfest at the Club.

"Is it true he boasted about kicking homeless men and women?" "Is it true he said if homeless women didn't smell so bad, at least they'd be usable?" "Did he say three bottles of Perrier is enough, but four's more certain?" "Does he admit saying he was going to keep doing it till he ran out of Perrier?" "Is it true he once set a homeless man on fire?"

Some of the questions were just questions: "Why Perrier? Is it a statement?" "Why did he buy it in bulk?" "Is this his first arrest? Does he have a sealed juvenile record?"

I could understand why police had jumped at the chance to make an arrest. Reporters must have been driving them crazy.

After flustering me and making me feel like a laryngitic parrot, they finally let me through. I locked myself into my car and drove gratefully away. Traffic was good. It only took me half an hour to get back to the office.

I found the paramedic with the Geo parked in front. He jumped out of his car. "I just saw you on TV."

"What brings you here?"

"Well, I semi-volunteered, for the company newsletter. I mean, we picked up those guys a few times. It'd be good to put something into an article." He looked like one of those black-and-white sitcom kids. Opie or Timmy or someone. "I didn't quite believe you, before, about the malpractice. I'm sorry I was rude."

"You weren't rude."

"I just wasn't sure you weren't after us. Everybody's always checking up on everything we do. The nurses, the docs, our supervisors, other medics. Every patient care report gets looked at by four people. Our radio calls get monitored. Everybody jumps in our shit for every little thing.

"I didn't have time to be Studs Terkel. "I'm sorry, I can't discuss my case with you."

"But I heard you say on TV your guy's innocent. You're going to get him off, right?" He gazed at me with a confidence I couldn't understand.

"Is that what you came here to ask?"

"It's just we knew those guys. I thought for the newsletter, if I wrote something . . ." He flushed. "Do you need information? You know, general stuff from a medical point of view?"

I couldn't figure him out. Why this need to keep talking to me about it? It was his day off; didn't he have a life?

But I *had* been wondering: "Why exactly do you carry those tourniquets? What do you do with them?"

He looked surprised. "We tie them around the arm to make a vein pop up. So we can start an intravenous line."

I glanced up at my office window, checking whether Jan had left. It was late; there were no more workers spilling out of buildings. A few derelicts lounged in doorways. I wondered if they felt safer tonight because someone had been arrested. With so many dangers on the street, I doubted it.

"Why would a tourniquet be in the bushes where the last man was picked up?" I hugged my briefcase. "I assumed, a medic had dropped it, but you wouldn't start an intravenous line on a dead person, would you?"

"We don't do field pronouncements—pronounce them dead, I mean—in hypothermia cases. We leave that to the

321

doc." He looked proud of himself, like he'd passed the pop quiz. "They're not dead till they're warm and dead."

"But why start an IV in this situation?"

"Get meds into them. If the protocols say to, we'll run a line even if we think they're deader than Elvis." He shrugged. "They warm up faster, too."

"What warms them up? What do you drip into them?"

"Epinephrine, atropine, normal saline. We put the saline bag on the dash to heat it as we drive—if we know we have a hypothermic patient."

"You have water in the units?"

"Of course."

"Special water?"

"Saline and distilled."

"Do you know a medic named Ben?"

He hesitated before nodding.

"Do you think he has a bad attitude about the homeless?"

"No more than you would," he protested. "We're the ones who have to smell them, have to handle them when they've been marinating in feces and urine and vomit. Plus they get combative at a certain stage. You do this disgusting waltz with them where they're trying to beat on you. And the smell is like, whoa. Plus if they scratch you, you can't help but be paranoid what they might infect you with."

"Ben said they cost your company money."

"They cost you and me money."

The look on his face scared me. Money's a big deal when you don't make enough of it.

I started past him.

He grabbed my arm. "Everything's breaking down." His tone was plaintive. "You realize that? Our whole society' breaking down. Everybody sees it—the homeless, the gangs, the diseases—but they don't have to deal with the physical results. They don't have to put their hands right on it, go all bloody and dirty with it, get infected by it."

"Let go!" I imagined being helpless and disoriented, a drunk at the mercy of a fed-up medic.

"And we don't get any credit"—he sounded angry now— "we just get checked up on." He gripped my arm tighter.

Again I searched my office window, hoping Jan was still working, that I wasn't alone. But the office was dark.

A voice behind me said, "What you doin' to the lady, man?"

I turned to see a stubble-chinned black man in layers of rancid clothes. He'd stepped out of a recessed doorway. Even from here, I could smell alcohol.

"You let that lady go. You hear me?" He moved closer.

The medic's grip loosened.

The man might be drunk, but he was big. And he didn't look like he was kidding.

I jerked my arm free, backing toward him.

He said, "You're Jan's boss, aren't ya?"

"Yes." For the thousandth time, I thanked God for Jan. This must be one of the men she'd mother-henned this morning. "Thank you."

To the medic, I said, "The police won't be able to hold my client long. They've got to show motive and opportunity and no alibi on four different nights. I don't think they'll be able to do it. They were just feeling pressured to arrest someone. Just placating the media."

The paramedic stared behind me. I could smell the other man. I never thought I'd find the reek of liquor reassuring.

"Isn't that what your buddies sent you to find out? Whether they could rest easy, or if they'd screwed over an innocent person?"

The medic pulled his bill cap off, buffing his head with his wrist.

"Or maybe you decided on your own to come here. Your coworkers probably have sense enough to keep quiet and keep out of it. But you don't." He was young and enthusiastic; too much so, perhaps. "Well, you can tell Ben and the others not to worry about Kyle Kelly. His reputation's ruined for as long as people remember the name—which probably isn't long enough to teach him a lesson. But there's not enough evidence against him. He won't end up in jail because of you."

"Are you accusing *us* . . . ?" He looked more thrilled than shocked.

"Of dousing the men so you didn't have to keep picking them up? So you could respond to more important calls? Yes, I am."

"But who are you going to—? What are you going to do?"

"I don't have a shred of proof to offer the police," I realized. "And I'm sure you guys will close ranks, won't give each other away. I'm sure the others will make you stop 'helping,' make you keep your mouth shut."

I thought about the dead men, "pretty good guys," according to the MiniMart proprietor. I thought about my-Johnny-self, the war veteran I'd spoken to this morning.

I wanted to slap this kid. Just to do *something*. "You know what? You need to be confronted with your arrogance, just like Kyle Kelly was. You need to see what other people think of you. You need to see some of your older, wiser coworkers look at you with disgust on their faces. You need your boss to rake you over the coals. You need to read what the papers have to say about you."

I could imagine headlines that sounded like movie billboards: "Dr. Death." "Central Hearse."

He winced. Held done the profession no favor.

"So you can bet I'll tell the police what I think," I promised. You can bet I'll try to get you fired, you and Ben and whoever else was involved. Even if there isn't enough evidence to arrest you."

He took a cautious step toward his car. "I didn't admit anything." He pointed to the other man. "Did you hear me admit anything?"

"And I'm sure your lawyer will tell you not to." If he could find a halfway decent one on his salary. "Now, if you'll excuse me, I have a lot of work to do."

I turned to the man behind me. "Would you mind walking me in to my office?" I had some cash inside. He needed it more than I did.

"Lead the way, little lady." His eyes were jaundiced yellow, but they were bright. I was glad he didn't look sick.

I prayed he wouldn't need an ambulance anytime soon.

The Court of Celestial Appeals

SUSAN DUNLAP

Death is not all it's cracked up to be.

Heaven or hell, or the forty days and nights traveling through the Bardo to the next incarnation? Limbo, purgatory, or a return to the elements from which the body came? I wouldn't have bet my life on the location of my eternal domicile, but I assumed at least I would recognize the place when I got there.

But this? It's like waking up in another beige hotel room in another overcast city; you can't remember where you are or why you're there. For a moment, you don't know who you are. I remember that feeling in . . . but the city's gone. Of course.

I'm gone.

I don't know who I am, or was. Or where I am. Or why I'm here. I just know I'm dead. And I've been summoned back to the Court of Final Appeals, for the third time. There's a lot I don't know about this place, but I do know that in this court, the third time is not a charm.

The halls are all off-white here. They glow a little, but not as gaudily as the near-death books suggest—no blinding white light at the end of every corridor and—thank God—no powerful suction toward it. Moving down a corridor is hard enough as it is when you've got wings.

Actually, the wings were the first disappointment. To fly! I loved it. I raced down the hall, veering left, scraping the wall, correcting, overcorrecting, ignoring the rasping pain on my wing edge, caught up in anticipation of that wonderful moment of takeoff. But the snack machine room at the end of the corridor came first. I turned, banging a wing into the ambrosia machine, and raced full-out down the hall. No luck. Maybe flying was like water-skiing, a sport more difficult for the pear-shaped.

It wasn't till I saw the Sub-Authority that I accepted the humbling truth. In this place, we only fly in the sense that penguins fly. Sort of a scurry and bounce. It's most appealing to those deceased meditationists who see it as levitating and take their newfound ability as a sign of enlightenment.

They're not in danger of arriving unprepared for a third hearing in the Court of Final Appeals.

I should be spending my time researching my case, but . . . I play a little game. It involves twisting one of the Celestial Rules till there is a hole to peek through. The rules aren't shouted out over a loudspeaker like specials in the supermarket: "Attention, dead shoppers! Ultra Gold Halo Cleaner on aisle six! Snap it up while the supply lasts!" There are no proclamations, no notices posted. Here, things are just known. One of those "things" is that you are forbidden to open the doors along the corridor. No reason for the off-limits. The Boss doesn't need to give out his rationale. And it seems superfluous to ask the punishment.

But few things are so seductive as a closed door. A closed *unlocked* door. There's a reason temptation has maintained its appeal all these centuries.

So I try a handle now and then. It's how I learned there are worse places to spend eternity than the white corridor.

In my first peek, I just about killed myself (or I would have if I weren't already dead) checking up and down the corridor for spies. No footsteps broke the silence, no telltale swish of wings or whispered orders, not even a waft of air from the sudden raising of a hand.

Finally, not so much reassured as impatient, I inched open the door and found myself in a room that contained another world. Outdoors. San Francisco. And I, standing on the railing of the flyover that merges into the Bay Bridge. Traffic was backed up as far as the eye could see (and one thing you get up here is twenty-twenty). Rain bombarded the idling cars; the sky was five o'clock dark. A broken-down semi blocked the inner lane, and traffic was down to one lane. Half a mile back, cars from the on ramp to the right had merged in, too. The surviving line of vehicles jerked forward and stopped, jerked and stopped, in reaction to the cars ahead poking into the unyielding bridge traffic. A yellow Volkswagen Bug puttered along in the lane, the driver's face tight from the half hour of stop-and-go. A big blue Chevy pickup raced up the ramp lane. As he neared the point where his lane merged into nonexistence, half a mile beyond the point he should have merged, the pickup slowed, veered closer to inching cars, eyeing each one predatorily until he spotted the little VW Bug, pounced left, barely missing the fragile bumper as the Bug's brakes squealed. *It's Volkswagen hell!* I thought, my hand tightening on the doorknob. But just then, the Volkswagen driver hit his horn, an air horn loud enough to wake the . . . well . . . dead. And to jolt the pickup driver into a sudden pull right. The big blue pickup smashed into the guard rail. Ah. *Volkswagen heaven!*

The pickup driver leaped from his wrinkled vehicle and glared back at . . . at *me*. Panicked, I jumped behind the door and was just pulling it shut when I spotted the real focus of his anger; a highway patrol motorcycle screeching to a halt right behind him. Not just Volkswagen heaven but *pickup hell!*

The pickup driver could have pocketed his ticket and exited his hell. He could have walked right out through the door with me. Instead, he leaped angrily into the driver's seat, screeched back, shifted into first, gunned the engine, and found himself a mile back on the entry ramp, desperate to try to cut the line again, eternally.

I shut the door and spun around with a second to spare before the Sub-Authority glided down the corridor. Had he spotted me? He didn't let on. But coincidences rarely occur up here.

The Sub-Authority is as well beloved as any successful bureaucrat. His office does not have framed Cover Thy Ass, or Brown Thy Nose." There is no picture of himself with the Boss's arm around him or, more realistically, of him smiling uncharitably at a list of postmortem transgressions—like mine. He doesn't like to be reminded that his glide resembles a flightless fowl.

I should have clutched my close call to my breast that day and never turned another doorknob. A wise person would have.

A wise person would be in heaven.

Doors became my life, so to speak. I "lived" to lurk, to sidle, to snoop. Held breath, panicked gasps became my norm of respiration. I tried every door on the corridor, every corridor that crowd mine. I turned right and left, checking

329

for spies till my wings were rubbed bare. The Sub-Authority never returned. I don't know when it struck me that the coast was always clear. I was the only real person on the corridor. It was then that I had the worse thought someone else might be sneaking open a door on a more rar-efied corridor, looking down and spotting me peering into forbidden rooms, eternally.

But now the call has come; they have pounced. The Boss frowns on dawdling when He's called you to court. If I thought there was any chance of escaping it, I would dawdle eternally. The Court of Final Appeals.

Like all the dead, I had had my day—*days*—in court when I arrived. The time of endless appeals is long gone up here. Once the Boss decides, who's to appeal to? That's one thing you know when you arrive. Not that it makes your initiation any easier.

Some of the newly dead—we call them Cools—have solid expectations of what this place should look like and how the Boss should handle things. Many expect to see their own face or similar ones all around. They all expect the Boss to resemble them. At least to be of their own race. And sex!

If they had survived long enough to outlive friends and relatives, they expect the dear departed to be assembled and waiting anxiously. Not just rounded up, but on their best behavior, in many cases better behavior than they ever exhibited on earth. In the mind of the Cool, the cousin he cheated, left destitute, pushed into suicide, will not merely have forgiven him. That cousin will not have forgotten the event, but instead will see the Cool's motivation in a new light. He will, in fact, be eager to admit that he was wrong and it was the Cool who was the true victim. He'll be pushing in front of the dear departed to beat his breast and open his arms.

No other evidence need be shown to prove how quickly Cools forget life below. They expect the rest of those waiting relatives to be holding out hands toward them, comforting them after their traumatic experience, waiting anxiously for their first words. They never picture cousins bored, uncles scarfing beers and dozing off in armchairs, and aunts too busy quarreling to be bothered with them.

But explicit as their expectations are, almost invariably the Cools' ideas of the final hearing are vague. They mutter about sheep and goats as if the hearing—the only real thing among their fairy-tale expectations—is all Brothers Grimm.

I don't know what I expected from my own final hearing, but what I found was certainly not it.

My first misapprehension was architectural. No way would I have guessed that the design of the Celestial Hearing Chamber would be based on the municipal court in Contra Costa County in California. Not even Superior Court! But there it was, a room paneled in middling wood, a judge's bench, and on the wall above and behind it a muted gold disk about four feet across. The Great Seal of the State of Finality. In a world-class show of insensitivity, Contra Costa County's seal boasts a conquistador, an invader who marched north from Mexico subjugating the native population with weaponry or decimating them with disease. Our seal, up here, has that kind of luminescent quality they have on credit cards. As if when you held it up to the light, it would change form—from Eden to Inferno.

331

There is a bailiff—not in the ill-fitting tans of below but in an off-white robe (straight out of the movies). "All rise," he calls. "The honorable Sub-Authority presiding." It's a bit of show, since no one but the Cool is in the room, and he's much too nervous to sit, even if there were a place to sit, which there isn't.

The bailiff reads the charges. He lists every trespass in deed, in word (and in words Cools assumed were whispered in confidence, not recorded for the ears of the heavenly host), and worst of all the bailiff delineates, rather too lovingly, every transgression in thought. I mean, who would have thought . . .

The list goes on . . . and on . . . and on. It's the first time the Cool realizes what's meant by eternity. There may in the fullness of time be worse moments, and longer ones. I doubt it. Hours, days, eons pass; his knees quiver like earthquakes, floods of sweat deluge his body, his eyes glaze over, and the synapses in his brain fire off in a war of their own. And when the list finally ends, and the Cool is reduced to a little formless blob of fear, the Sub-Authority looks him straight in the eye, pauses, and pronounces: "All is forgiven."

All is forgiven!

You would think the Cool would be ecstatic, right? Some are. Some inhale that forgiveness like oxygen into the lungs of the suffocating; they smile sheepishly, humbly, amazedly, clutch their clean slates to their breasts, and then, as if wary the Sub-Authority might realize his mistake, they race through the great double doors that lead to— But that *I* don't—cannot—know.

Some Cools accept the gift with grace. But not most.

Most are, well, suspicious. To accept forgiveness is one thing, to sign on to clemency for "all" is another matter entirely. Just how all-encompassing was that divine pardon, they want to know. *I* wanted to know. Then their court-appointed lawyer asks for a continuance to the next day. The Sub-Authority granted *my* continuance, and my lawyer took me out in the hall, gave me a videotape of my transgressions, and said, "You know what a section seventeen is?"

I didn't.

"The judge lowers your crimes from felonies to misdemeanors. Know what then?"

I shook my head.

"Then he dismisses those misdemeanors. Not even a blot on your record. Like you never once broke the law. Go over that tape, and think about how lucky you are."

I did.

The next day, I arrived back in court. The procedure was repeated. I knew I should have taken the offer—most people do by this stage, con men and crooks faster than the rest, they're used to playing the odds, and they know when those odds are not likely to improve. But I couldn't accept it. I don't know why. I wish I did. I would give a lot to know why. But here I have nothing to give.

My lawyer glared down the length of his nose at me and asked for another continuance. The Sub-Authority's face pulled into a similarly less than angelic expression. But in the end, he shrugged and granted the delay.

This time, when my lawyer took me out into the hallway, the very air was colder, thicker against my ribs. Each panicked breath smacked my ribs against the air, every beat of my heart hurt—phantom pain of phantom heart, but all too real panic. My lawyer's voice rasped my ears as he said, "You know what three strikes means?"

I hardened my face, as if no one up here had ever seen a quivering "tough guy." "When am I out?"

"Tomorrow, if you don't wise up and take the offer."

"And if I can't?"

He shook his head, smacked his wings tight against his scapulae, and glided away.

So I pace, up one corridor, down the next, hoping as I come to the intersections that I'll turn the corner on my own problem and be whisked back to the final, triumphant hearing, and then on to . . . well, on to something so superbly wonderful it defies description. Or so the theory goes. I'm not sure I believe that, trust enough to step off the familiar into the unknown no matter how good its PR. Maybe I can just wait a bit, dangle my toe in the unseen waters of the unknown a while, see if the Evermore is warm enough to step in.

I've opened a lot of closed doors, seen many things that shocked me, but none more than the scene inside the room marked "Please Do Not Enter."

I inched the door open and stood peering in on the Sub-Authority himself in his ostentatiously simple robe, thin lips pulled back in a scowl, glaring down his chiseled Puritan nose at a memo.

And facing him was the one Personage powerful enough to tell him no. All-powerful. All-knowing. All-seeing.

Quickly, I slid behind the door.

It was then that I heard the Sub-Authority saying, "Can't stay here, Your Selfness."

It was *me* he was talking about.

"The corridor is for temporary stays, the occasional *one*-night lodging for extremely indecisive and extremely *rare* souls."

I stuck my head beyond the door frame in time to see him shaking that memo impatiently.

I stood holding my breath. Surely the Great Personage would come to my support. If this wasn't the time to demonstrate all-lovingness, what was?

But it was the Sub-Authority who spoke. "They all choose by the third hearing, The third hearing is *always* within a day of the second. This one"—I cringed—"has been staffing for longer than that already. This one is no closer to decision now than upon entry." His fingers tightened around the memo.

I strained to hear the reply. The Sub-Authority's jaw tightened; his fingers clenched into a fist. Dammit, if I could just get closer and *hear* . . . it was then I realized it wouldn't have mattered how close I was. I could have been standing between them. The voice of the Boss is never *heard*—He doesn't communicate in words.

"That one," the Sub-Authority countered, "has been spotted breaking the rules. What we've got here is a troublemaker. A troublemaker who cannot decide to go on and cannot keep the nose out of other penitents' business while here. Take that into account, Your Selfness. Make the judgment. Send that one down."

My whole soul went cold. I wanted to rush into the room, throw myself at the Authority's feet—if He had feet—and scream, I'll take the forgiveness! Please don't send me down. I'll forgive anyone—*all*."

But even with the smell of brimstone rank in my nostrils, I couldn't. I just couldn't bring myself to. I folded my wings tight against my back and prepared for descent.

The Sub-Authority inhaled sharply and leaned forward, both hands shaking angrily. "But, Sire, we can't justify making an exception so unprecedented, not for this one."

My wings relaxed a scintilla.

"I know it's an important job," he admitted. "Admittedly, this one has shown abnormal aptitude for the work. I suppose we *could* suspend the rules if the job is performed to satisfaction. But one failure, and it's—" He glanced abruptly down, the hint of a smile on his face. In a moment, the smile broadened.

And the door slammed shut.

I stood in the icy corridor, suddenly aware that this was the best things might ever be for me. Damn, why couldn't I have accepted the forgiveness? Why? What could have been so terrible that I couldn't forgive it, even at the cost of my own eternal damnation? I strained, but not one image came to mind. Even under such extreme pressure, I couldn't recall who I was, much less what had happened to me.

If I didn't figure out how to remember, I was going to be in deep brimstone. But I had no idea how to go about it.

After that, the one thing you'd have expected of me was good behavior. You would assume I'd never have peered through another door. But somehow the tenuousness of my position made me dart around more rashly than before. I felt like a gourmand sworn to start a diet in the morning, an alcoholic drinking his last bottle of scotch. It was that same day I came upon the pickup driver on the Bay Bridge.

So, you see, I know how the Cools feel. Most of them go over and over that tape the first night, reliving some of the transgressing deeds they enjoyed entirely too much, shuddering at the antisocial thoughts that had sailed through their minds as if sent by a sociopath. By that second day, they jump at the hearing offer and nearly trip themselves running through the great double doors.

But the man at this trial . . .

I realized now I wasn't just *remembering* but was actually *at* a new trial. Time is funny here.

The defendant at today's trial was shaking his head, when his lawyer asked not for a continuance—under the rules, he couldn't do that at that point—but for a short recess.

Then he turned to me and said, "He can't make up his mind. He doesn't have a clue. He knows *how* he died, but he can't move on till he finds out *why* he died. You're the detective, you hunt that down."

"How am I going to—"

"My client doesn't have time for chatter. Were only recessed till after lunch." (The lawyer almost smiled. Up here, we hardly "do lunch." There is no Food for the Soul Café, no Veal Valhalla, no fresh greens from the Garden of the Hesperides.) "He's waiting for you in the hall."

What does a detective do? There had to be some job qualifications besides nosiness. Had I been a detective in life? I sure didn't picture myself as a premortem, gumshoe. How do you start an investigation, particularly when the subject is up here and the facts are down there? If I were such a natural detective, I'd have been able to find out why I died myself, instead of wandering around baffled up here.

A flash of anger shot through me. They expected me to

337

find out how he died when *I* had died and no one had been assigned to do it for *me!* The hell to them! I'd refuse. A celestial sit-down strike. If they didn't like it, they could.

An acrid whiff of brimstone cut through the bland air.

Then it occurred to me that I had a chance here. There was time on the off-white hallway to peek into rooms, I could make time in this investigation for my own search. Hundreds of thousands of people died every day; hundreds of thousands of trails went on simultaneously. As I headed out to this job, the Sub-Authority would have plenty more to consider than my time card. I would just need to keep an eye out for my chance.

I walked slowly out the door and glanced at the defendant on the bench, sitting there within moments of the possibility of eternal damnation. He was a tidy, lightly tamed Caucasian male of middle age, wearing an expensive blue pinstriped suit with lines so subtle I almost missed them, and a maroon silk handkerchief in his pocket. His hair was still dark, and, despite his age, no looseness of skin marred the firm, square line of his jaw. And his expression—had I considered the possibilities beforehand, I might have expected fear or remorse—was one of outrage.

"You people have made a mistake!" he said by way of introduction.

"Wha—" I let out before I caught myself. *You people,* indeed. He considered me one of the whip-snappers, the guard dogs, the heel nippers, one of *them!* What did I look like, a sub-Sub-Authority? I was offended. And shocked at how offended I was. And at how quickly I realized there was cover in this new role of mine.

I settled next to him on the wooden bench. This hallway,

too, was à la Contra Costa County, California: sound muted by carpeting, light muted by lack of windows. But we could have been screaming now; there was no one to hear us.

I restrained the urge to say, *A mistake? Ah, they all say that, Mr. Girard.* Humor is so unappreciated in this place. There are times I think the real reason people are kept here at all is they are insufficiently venal to be sent below and too dull to be tolerated above. The Boss, after all, has to live up there. It's probably why he keeps the Sub-Authority down here.

I glanced over at Charles Girard, noting with some surprise how well he suited the name I hadn't known till a moment ago. "Mr. Girard, up here all things are possible. We can make whatever He wants. Mistakes is not one of those things."

He opened his mouth to protest. The words seemed to hover at the outlet of his lips. "How could this happen to me?"

"How could *what* happen to you?"

"The bit—woman killed me!"

"Well, something had to." The moment the words left my lips, I knew they were a mistake. Again, I wondered why I had been chosen to be a celestial detective—obviously not for my tact. "Start at the beginning"—I resisted the impulse to say: *Just who are you?* I may not be naturally tactful, but I can learn—"with your name."

"Stone Girard," he said, as if it were a household word.

"Stone?"

"Nickname. Had it for years."

"Because you did drugs?"

God, why did I keep poking at the man? He was hardly

339

the type I could picture sprawled with a hookah or hypo-dermic. Nor, I gathered from the raise of his eyebrows and the angry clamp of his jaw, could he. "Never! I never broke the law!"

"Let me remind you where you are, Stone. Up here, you are always under oath."

It was a moment before he regained enough composure to insist, "Never once did I knowingly break the law."

"Knowingly? Aha!" Having to tell the truth, that's a shock for a lot of them. In some cases, it leaves them nothing to say. Stone was being honest, if not helpful. And I could hardly ask him what law it was that he didn't know he'd broken.

"*I* would hardly have broken the law," he insisted, as if he'd read my mind. "Before I ran for office I was a judge."

In a great show of control, I said nothing.

"And I was running for the United States Senate!"

I couldn't help it; I laughed. "Senator from—?"

"California."

Another laugh escaped. California, the bastion of political frivolity. That state whose citizens viewed sending politi-cians to Washington as civic comic relief. They prided, themselves on delivering to statehouse and D.C. the flashy, the weird, the nascent politicians with more dollars than sense, victors who became known as Teflon or Moonbeam, losers who refused to admit defeat till a third of a year after the vote. Californians tended toward high comedy, spiritual eccentricity, or facade. They had never raised political cor-ruption to the art form of states like New Jersey, where city councils could have had quorums, behind bars. But dishon-esty was not unknown in the Golden State. I considered whether Stone's protest was indicative of remarkable naïveté, and decided that he merely meant a senatorial candidate was wise to be circumspect.

Stone clutched a bunch of newspapers and shook them at me. The rustling of the pages grated oddly on my ears. The breeze chilled my bald head. It's so warm up here, I'd almost forgotten why the stiff-living have hair. "I'm not— I *wasn't*," Stone said, "one of those political idiots who can't keep it zipped."

Before I could ask to just which of the telltale openings he was referring, he smacked the papers into my hand.

That he still had the papers didn't surprise me. Death is such a loss. To lose a loved one can be hard. But when that loved one is the one you hold most dear—yourself—it gives *hard* a new definition. Cools come across kicking and screaming and clinging on for dear life. Literally. To calm them, the Sub-Authority offers them a last look below. An invisible box seat at the event of their choice. Some of the Cools who join us in January choose to see the football playoff games. Artists up for awards and scientists in the running for grants often choose to see the ceremonies and whether they have, albeit posthumously, won. Parents opt for views of children's graduations. The occasional charismatic leader needs to see who his followers chose to succeed him.

But far and away the most popular event for a Cool is his funeral—the one time he is the true and deserving center of attention. A Cool may hate the idea of being up here, but the offer to swap good behavior for a birds-eye view of his wake is more than most can pass up. Cools love the sobbers and the bawlers wailing as if their old hearts would break.

They cherish the priestly eulogies long on their noble natures, their wit embellished, their most minor generosity extolled. They clutch to their now formless breasts their friends' sincere emotions unspoken in life. Equally do they treasure their enemies' counterfeit grief, the "loving memories," the panoplies of insincere praise those enemies have no choice but to choke out. Richard Nixon just about fell off his chair in the viewing room. I hadn't realized the man had such a sense of humor.

The Sub-Authority allows that. He doesn't object to the Cool clinging, to a newspaper account of the event. In the line for the initial hearing, Cools with obituaries therein clutch copies of the *Times* or the *Post* with unseemly pride.

But three papers—that was a bit much.

I looked down at the top one so summarily smacked in my hand. Stone Girard was a well-known man. His death was not an addendum in the obit column. It was front-page news.

"Girard Dead at Lovers Leap!" the *Los Angeles Times* screamed in a banner headline.

"Girard Found Dead with Mystery Woman," the *San Francisco Chronicle* proclaimed.

"Political Fall: Same Old Story." The *Bay Guardian* shook its printed head. "If Stone Girard had taken stock of himself before he threw his hat in the ring, he wouldn't have felt obligated to toss the rest of himself onto the Great Highway. If Girard couldn't wait till after the election to take up with Olivia Cummings, what his choice tells us is California is left with the better man."

Marc Bellingham, by default the senator-elect presumptive, clearly understood the better part of valor. From the length of the headline article, Bellingham was the only one within the Golden State or the United States Senate who did not have a comment on Girard's passing.

I read the coverage in all three papers and every one of the comments. And while the word *stupid* was never employed, and no one recalled Gary Hart and his sailboat per se, I doubted there was a euphemism in the English language that had gone unused or any two lines that could not be read between. The closest reporters came to censuring the defunct candidate was denigrating his choice of leap, from an outcropping of rock above the Great Highway. If Girard hadn't died in the fall, he'd have been crushed by a tourist bus. Stone Girard may have been, as he had insisted to me a minute earlier, "not one of those political idiots who can't keep it zipped." But his way of departure was unlikely to garner him the epitaph of political visionary

"Mr. Girard—"

"Stone."

"Stone, you and Olivia Cummings were found dead, *together,* at the bottom of Sutro Heights promontory."

Girard pulled his tidy form up to his full, if not impressive, height. "Don't even suggest that I was philandering. I am a man of principle. I did not entertain assignations. I wasn't called Stone for nothing."

A variety of reasons jumped to mind. Repressing a smile, I asked, "Why were you called Stone, Stone?"

"Because, young . . ." Stone assessed my, hairless pate, swept his eyes discreetly down the front of my robe, apparently unaware that the soul is without sexual indicators. "My detractors called me Stone because I was sufficiently upright to cast the first one. They aimed to castigate me, to

343

make me a laughing stock, but I wasn't laughing—"

That I believed. I'd yet to see any indication that Stone Girard had a sense of humor. He had the makings of the Sub-Authority's right-hand man.

"—I took that name and made it my slogan. Voters want a man they can trust. They want to vote for a man who could cast the first stone. Bellingham may scoff at purity, but I'll tell you, little . . . person . . . these days purity is a plus—"

"But, Stone, your body was found with this woman. How do you explain that?"

His jaw quivered. "I don't know."

"You don't know?"

"No, dammit, I have no idea."

I started to retort, then backed off. Maybe he was being truthful. His chiseled face was hewn into an expression of bewilderment. If so, it was no wonder he couldn't come to a decision at his hearing.

Newly arrived Cools have no memory of the day of their death. Death can be traumatic, and judgment is no piece of cake, either. The Cools have plenty to contemplate without recalling their dying days. Memory blackout is a good rule, but it was going to make my job harder. "Okay, Stone, for now we'll skip the reason for your presence on Sutro Heights. Tell me about the woman. Who was Olivia Cummings?"

"Nobody."

"Hardly nobody, Stone. An contraire, not just a body but a corpus delicti. Was she an old flame?"

"No, no, no. I barely knew the woman. She was married to someone else."

"Are you sure?"

"Of course I am. I married her myself."

A grin pulled at my lips.

"When I was a judge, I performed the ceremony. My one and only marriage—"

"How come no more?"

He shot glances in both directions of the hallway, then, lowering his voice, said, "I wouldn't want this to become public—"

"Don't worry. The old adage that the cemeteries vote Democrat isn't true. There are no absentee ballots from here."

He flushed, then his eyes widened in horror. I had the feeling that for the first time, he was really taking in the fact that he didn't have to worry about the election.

"You gave up performing marriages because—" I prompted.

"They take a lot of time, and a judge can't accept payment for them. California Penal Code, section ninety-four point five."

"Why not, so the judge can't be bribed?"

"It doesn't matter whether the payment was intended as a bribe or not. No money, no thing of value. Not before the wedding, not after."

"A judge can't be paid ever?"

"Not unless the wedding is performed on a Saturday, Sunday, or holiday."

"California, Land of Loopholes!" I threw my head back and laughed so hard my wings flapped. I nearly flung myself into the wall.

Stone cleared his throat, magistratively.

"Okay," I said, shifting my wings back in place. "But you did perform this one marriage, Olivia Cummings's wedding. Why?"

"It was a spur-of-the-moment thing. They just called me because I was handy."

"Can you clarify that?" That sounded bland and legal enough for Stone.

"Olivia's father called me because I was spending the weekend in the other half of their cottage in Tahoe."

Cottage in this case could be a euphemism worthy of Stone's wake. "How big a cottage?"

"I don't know, three, four bedrooms."

"Who was Olivia's father?"

"Avery Cummings."

"Avery Cummings, the shipping magnate?"

"I don't know."

"Stone, remember where you are. The truth?"

"Cummings owned some ships."

"How many?"

"I don't—the Pan Asia Line."

I smiled to myself. Maybe I *was* cut out for this job. If the cases were all this easy, it'd be a snap. At this rate, I would have plenty of time to check up on my own demise. "And so, Stone, afterward Avery Cummings supported your political campaign, right?"

"Wrong."

"The truth, remember?"

Girard jutted out his chin. "Cummings never gave me a dime. Never promised a loan or twisted an arm."

"He supported your opponent?"

"Him neither. Took no sides in politics. Said it didn't

matter who won, nothing changed. Sounded like a god-damned radical. Said the best political investment for him was keeping his money in his pocket. And that's just what he did."

Surely not. I tried again. "But he let you use his vacation house."

"Let me *rent* it, at the going rate."

Okay, so the banker didn't go out of his way. But his daughter's wedding—half the money in California could have been invited. A couple of well-placed introductions, and Stone could have been set for his whole campaign, particularly in those early days when he wasn't running for Senate but merely hoping to leave the bench for a congressional seat. "At the wedding, he did introduce you to his influential friends, right?"

"He introduced me to his scatter-brained daughter, his cotton-headed son-in-law-to-be, and the maid and gardener he called in to be witnesses."

"And—?"

"That's all. No one else was there. They had to drag the maid out of bed. And the gardener. The guy didn't live on the grounds—we're just talking a house here, sizable but not an estate. The gardener lived in a cabin ten miles into the woods. Cummings called the guy's brother in town, got him up, convinced him to drive out to the guy's cabin and bring him back."

"Convinced him how?" I said, perking up.

"Financially," Stone said in the tone he'd have used with a particularly dim-witted lawyer he'd called to the bench for the fourth time in an hour.

But I wasn't about to be deterred, not when I knew the

consequences of his being recompensed. "Did you hear him offer the gardener cash?"

"It was understood."

"Aha!"

"What does that mean?" he demanded icily.

"That you, too, could expect him to make it worth your while."

"I didn't! *He* didn't. Expect it or receive a cent from him. He didn't give me the benefit of his influence. He never once contributed to a campaign of mine. I don't think the man voted at all. And his damned daughter gave a couple thou to Bellingham. In fact, the whole affair ended up costing me."

"Costing you?"

"Right. I slept though a nine A.M. meeting I'd scheduled with Donald Davis, the financier. Davis was a potential contributor. With all the shenanigans connected with the wedding, the miserable affair took half the night. The groom was so drunk, Cummings had to throw him in the shower to sober him up. Then Olivia decided she'd made the right decision when she called off the formal wedding—it was scheduled for a couple of weeks later—and flounced off to bed. If I'd been smart, I'd have hightailed it out of there, out of Cummings's cabin and to a hotel."

"But you didn't?"

"No. Big mistake. Cummings asked me to have a brandy with him, to settle us both down after the fiasco of an evening. So he pours the brandy, and we're sitting there, and out comes the son-in-law-to-be. By now, he's alert enough to realize he's been jilted for a second time, and he's prowling the house, moaning like a dog with a churning stomach he discovers anew each time he moves. I wanted to force some bicarb down his jaw and tie him to a stake in the yard."

I glanced at Stone's face to see if he intended to be amusing. Nothing suggested so.

"I just sat with Cummings, sipping the brandy. Sat silent. Just calming down. Should have kept watch on the son-in-law. Boy must have groaned his way down the hall to the girl's room. Must have made her sorry enough or horny enough to reconsider. Whatever. I was just about out the door when the two of them came racing in, grins ear to ear, announcing they'd changed their minds."

"What about the gardener?" The question had nothing to do with the answers I needed, but I was too caught up in the story not to wonder about the groggy gardener and his groggy brother and the cabin ten miles into the woods.

"He was still at his brother's. It had started to rain about midnight, and he'd decided not to make the trip back to his own cabin. So Cummings called a cab for him. When he got there, I lined 'em up, performed the ceremony—the actual legal necessities don't take long—and was back in my half of the cottage before the groom had kissed the bride." He shook his head. "Got myself so soaked I had to take a hot bath. Probably the reason I overslept, snubbed Davis, teed him off, basically kicked him into the other camp. Almost lost the election because of it. Davis has big bucks." He hesitated, glanced around furtively, then said, "Or at least he did. Dead now. Is he . . . here?"

"They all come through here, Stone. Where they go after, I can't say."

"Not in the loop, eh?"

"Can't say," I managed to get out in a neutral tone. Of course, I didn't know what had become of money man Davis. The Sub-Authority doesn't report to me on the disposal of souls. But I wasn't about to admit that to Stone. Much less was I willing to show my pique. Up here, they frown on pique.

The smell of brimstone wafted past my nose. I shot a glance behind me, but, of course, there was no fire, not yet. Whatever the source of that evil smell, it did snap my attention back to the vital task at hand. Fail to solve Stones dilemma, and I would have eternity to contemplate the fate of Davis. Maybe he'd be right down there next to me, fanning the flames.

"What became of Olivia and her groom?"

If Stone said they had a storybook marriage, topped by three charming children, all Rhodes scholars, I would have been surprised.

I wasn't.

"Divorced. Marriage lasted fifteen years. I would've put money on less than one. I'm not often wrong."

"But you were this time." I grinned.

"True. Figure it took Oren that long to run through Olivia's money. No prenuptial agreement. Doesn't surprise me. They didn't plan anything else, why would they all of a sudden get responsibility and think about that?"

"Surely old man Cummings, a banker, would have pressed for it."

"You didn't know Olivia. Stubborn as she was spoiled and self-centered. Thought the world owed her a living. Figured as long as there was a world, she'd go on living high. As for old man Cummings, he must have decided it wasn't worth the fight to buck Olivia on this. He was only in his fifties at the time. He must have figured he'd long outlive the marriage."

"Didn't he?"

"Nope. Heart attack the next year. That's why Oren and Olivia stayed married as long as they did. If they hadn't had her inheritance to go through, they would have seen each other in the cold light of dawn a lot sooner. But money and illegal substances can rose-color the worst of situations."

"So they divorced?"

"Three years ago. Oren's a viper, but he's got a certain reptilian charm. Married more money within the year. Lives on an estate in Hillsborough."

"And Olivia?"

"Not so fortunate. High living took its toll. She was one of those chipmunk-faced girls kept from being plain by youth and money. Without either, she resembled a sharpei."

I shivered for Olivia; rolls of skin are more appealing on the face of an exotic dog than a matron. So what did she do for money?"

"Hit up everyone she knew. It was embarrassing. I mean, how sorry can you be for a whiny woman who's run through a couple mil? Oh, some friends of the family helped out. An aunt gave her a studio in the city. A cousin took her by the scruff of the neck and explained the facts of life."

"Like?"

"Work! Said he'd pay for her to take classes. Paralegal, it turned out. Olivia made it through a semester, maybe two. But when you expect the world to support you, work isn't part of the plan. Dropped out."

"And then?"

He shook his head. "Heard not a thing about her till she called. Yesterday." Girard paled. "God, just yesterday I was . . . alive."

"Don't think about that! You don't have time. Not now. *Olivia!* What happened after she called?"

She had arranged to meet him at Sutro Heights. Because all that happened the day of his death, he wouldn't remember it. He wouldn't know why he went, or what happened. Maybe she was so enraged he'd gotten her married to Oren in the first place that she pushed him over the cliff. Or perhaps he saw her in a new and seductive light, reached passionately for her, and together they slipped into oblivion.

I didn't picture Stone rushing to an amorous tryst with a whiny vindictive woman who looked like a Chinese fighting dog. Certainly not the week before the election. At that time, a candidate risks no chance encounters. He doesn't open the front door to bring in the paper without having his advance man check first. No way would Stone Girard set up a clandestine meeting at a lover's leap with a woman of questionable reputation.

Still, he did.

I started to ask him, more pointedly, what possessed him. But before I could speak, he faded into the off-white wall.

"Get back here!" I yelled.

No response.

I banged my fist in fury, but it's a waste of time in a room where there's nothing solid to hit.

"Hey!" I yelled into the atmosphere where the Sub-Authority was probably lurking. "This is really unfair. If you expect me to investigate, you've got to give me access to my client!"

No reaction at all.

"You know what kind of deal this is? Huh? A diabolical one!" That's a big insult, but not big enough to draw the Sub-Authority out. Clearly, I'd gotten all I was going to get from Stone Girard. I hoped it was all I needed.

Once again, fetors of brimstone rasped against my nose. No time for anger. I had to think. I coasted back and forth in front of the courtroom door. Why do people kill? Love. None of that lost here. Hate. Stone and Olivia were too inconsequential to each other. Envy, jealousy, revenge, greed—ah, greed. Blackmail. One of the few ways of income acquisition left for Olivia. The conclusion quite pleased me.

Until her lack struck me. What had she blackmailed him with? The man had merely done her a kindness. Still, blackmail was all Olivia Cummings had left. But facts I didn't have.

What I did have, I realized, was one chance to peruse the evidence in person. I could choose my scene and go below, back to the time, and be there as it occurred. One scene, but only one. I'd take the minute before he died.

No, I wouldn't. The time he'd blocked out was blacked out for me, too. I had to travel through *his* memory. Somehow, from all the minutes and hours in his life, I had to pick out the key moment. If I didn't . . . but I was already sick of brimstone.

Rain dripped down my neck, soft as if the drops broke their falls just before they landed on my skin, caressingly cool against the warm, humid late-summer air. The fresh and pure scent of an incense cedar cut the smell of wet grass. In the distance, cars accelerated on the dark, empty stretch of road behind Cummings's Tahoe duplex, roaring in quickening passion, gasping for breath, for gear change, speeding faster to a climax out of my hearing. Whiffs of gasoline came and were gone. In the shock of silence that followed, the gentle lapping of the lake seemed to pound like a chorus line of tsunamis.

Cummings's house was everything I might have imagined: large, shingled, living space secluded from roadside eyes. Standing ten feet off the path by the front door, I watched as the portal opened. Stone stalked out. Face pinched, breath heaving angrily, his ire focused on a foot-high glass jade plant in his hands. He stalked across the wet lawn toward the other door, *his* door, soft leather shoes squishing in the mud, pant legs transferring the wet of the grass to his socks. He barely noticed that, so intent was he on stripping off the small glass leaves of the jade plant, one after another, and pitching them into the bushes. "A leaf for every damned minute!" he grumbled as he tossed the last one against the shingles and fingered his pocket for the door key. "Some 'thank you.' "

He stepped inside.

I could feel myself fading. I couldn't be pulled back yet! I hadn't solved Girard's death, and hadn't even thought about my own demise! I couldn't go back up there with nothing! I curled my toes, trying to clutch the earth, to wrap myself around the smell of the cedar, the sound of the icy lake water splatting on the shore. Of earth. I hadn't had any clue how much I missed it. Greedily, I moved my gaze back and forth over the sky, the clouds, the trees, the lawn, imprinting them all on my memory. The pull grew stronger, a budding tornado in reverse. My job was to step, float up.

Feeling the lovely damp grass on my ankles, I walked toward it.

On the road, a horn blew.

I slipped behind a redwood, raced to the bushes, stooping low behind them. Sweat coated my neck. I inched toward Girard's front door, hoping he'd been too distracted to lock it. The wind, the *pull,* sucked the fallen leaves off the grass, twisted the fronds of the redwoods. I reached for the door-knob and was inside.

In a vestibule with a closet, mirror, narrow table, and a book, *The Perfect Crime* by Leigh Ward. I grabbed it and slid into the safety of the closet.

The hallway outside the courtroom was empty, no Cools, no staff, no smells, not even a familiar soundless word. Footsteps came down the hall toward me, slowly, from a distance. Stones steps. When he reached me, we would go into the courtroom, he would turn to me, then he'd have to give his answer.

Stone paused next to me, reached for the double door, and we walked in. The great seal gleamed down at us. From under it, the Sub-Authority exhaled slowly. "Charles Stone Girard, all is forgiven. Do you accept forgiveness for all?"

Stone turned to me.

I pictured the pickup driver in the room on the corridor, trying to cut the line, smashing into the railing, getting the ticket, and starting over again, endlessly, blocking out reality with his insistence. Stone had been a judge. He should have known what was in the penal code. Laws can be foolish, but only a fool ignores them, particularly if he's running for Senate. Only a fool drives into the same railing again and again. Only a fool assumes a jade plant is so insufficient a "thank you" as to be of no value at all.

I said, "California Penal Code, section ninety-four point five." The code appeared in his hand:

Acceptance of fee by judicial officer for performance of marriage. Every judge, justice, commissioner, or assistant commissioner of a court of this state who accepts any money or other thing of value for performing any marriage, including any money or thing of value voluntarily tendered by the persons about to be married or who have been married by such judge etc. Whether the acceptance occurs before or after performance of the marriage and whether or not performance of the marriage is conditioned on the giving of such money or the thing of value by the persons being married is guilty of a misdemeanor.

It is not a necessary element of the offense described by this section that the acceptance of the money or other thing of value be committed with intent to commit extortion or with other criminal intent.

This section does not apply to an acceptance of a fee for performing a marriage on Saturday, Sunday, or a legal holiday.

"And section ninety-eight":

Officers to forfeit and be disqualified from holding office. Every officer convicted of any crime defined in this chapter, in addition to the punishment described, forfeits his office and is forever disqualified from holding any office in this state.

It was a moment before Stone groaned. "You mean the fucking jade plant? I could lose the Senate seat because of that jade plant?"

I nodded.

His shoulders slumped, he started to sag toward the floor. Then, abruptly, he pulled himself up. "No, wait. That's what she thought, the greedy bitch. But she was wrong. Look back at ninety-four point five: *does not apply to legal holiday*. The wedding was on Labor Day!"

I shook my head, "No, Stone. The wedding would have been on Labor Day if Olivia and Oren hadn't squabbled and put it off. By the time they got around to marrying, it was well after midnight. Late enough to be Tuesday. Late enough to bar you from the Senate. She blackmailed you, then, regardless of who pushed whom, she killed you."

"All is forgiven, Mr. Girard. Do you accept that?" the Sub-Authority repeated.

Stone hesitated, his face tightening as I'd seen it tighten over the jade plant. Then he surprised me; he nodded.

As he walked through the double doors at the far side of the courtroom, I realized how much he had given up losing his Senate seat. The man was meant to be a politician; he knew how to accommodate himself. Now he had accommodated himself into heaven.

I walked back into the hall. The vague scent of brimstone had returned. I had succeeded at this job. The SubAuthority wouldn't be able to commit me to brimstone. Not yet. But he'd never trust me down below again, either.

I had merely extended my stay on the corridor. If I succeeded case after case, I could stay here forever, endlessly ignorant of who I was and why I kept myself here.

What had been so horrendous, appalling, galling about my own death to make me less willing to forgive than Stone Girard?

I, the celestial detective, had not a clue.

My left wing felt stiff, tense, tired. I pulled out the book I'd hidden under it. *The Perfect Crime.* Stone Girard's death had hardly been a perfect crime.

I looked at the book and smiled.

The perfect crime had to be mine. So perfect I couldn't part with it. But what crime? Victim or killer? How had I— I peered down toward the book, but it was gone.

A new Cool shuffled out of the hearing room, head down, face pinched in confusion. Up here, the authorities have to be fair. They can't offer one Cool benefits and deny them to the next. I moved beside him. "Need a detective?"

Boobytrap

BILL PRONZINI

tick . . .

He finished making the third bomb just before nine Sunday night.

Except, of course, that it wasn't a bomb. No. It was a "destructive device." That was the official legal definition in the California Penal Code. Chapter 2.5: Destructive Devices. Section 12303.3: Explosion of Destructive Device. He knew the section's wording by heart. It had been drummed into his head at the trial; he'd read it over and over again in the prison library.

"Every person who possesses, explodes, ignites, or attempts to explode or ignite any destructive device or any explosive with intent to injure, intimidate, or terrify any person, or with intent to wrongfully injure or destroy any property, is guilty of a felony, and shall be punished by imprisonment in the state prison for a period of three, five, or seven years."

Point of law, Mr. Sago.

Ah, but that hadn't been enough for them. The destructive devices he'd made six years ago, the three destructive devices he'd manufactured here, were *more* than just destructive devices. They were also Chapter 3.2: Boobytraps. Specifically, Section 12355: Boobytraps—Felony.

"Any person who assembles, maintains, places, or causes to be placed a boobytrap device as described in subdivision

(c) is guilty of a felony punishable by imprisonment in the state prison for two, three, or five years." Subdivision (c) stating, in part: "For purposes of this section, 'boobytrap' means any concealed or camouflaged device designed to cam great bodily injury when triggered by an action of any unsuspecting person coming across the device."

Point of law, Mr. Sago.

Guilty as charged, Mr. Sago.

Five years of hell in San Quentin, Mr. Sago.

The rase was in his blood again, rising. He tamped it down by focusing on the bomb, destructive device, boobytrap on the table in front of him. And by thinking about Douglas Cotter lying dead on his lawn with his self-righteous, "You need psychiatric help, Mr. Sago," four-eyed head blown off. Beautiful image, that, provided by this morning s newscast. Device number one mission accomplished. But Cotter was the one he hated least of the trio, a minor collaborator in the legal conspiracy. Much more satisfaction when device number two made a pincushion of Judge Norris Turnbull. And when this pretty little baby here, pretty little surprise package number three right here tore the life out of Patrick Dixon . . . why, then he would really have cause for rejoicing.

Vengeance is mine, saith Mr. Sago.

Carefully, he rearranged his tools in the kit he'd bought in San Francisco. Put the rest of his materials away in their various containers and then wiped his hands on a rag. When he stood and felt the creak of his stiffened muscles, he realized for the first time how tired he was. And how hungry. He hadn't eaten since noon. Better put something in his stomach before he went to bed, he'd sleep better 3:00

A.M. was only a few hours off, and there wouldn't be time for even a quick breakfast. Drop the judge's present off first, then drive all the way to mountain Lake—two and a half hours, at least—and find a proper place to leave Dixon's package. Very tight schedule.

He went into the cramped kitchen. The pilot light on the stove had gone out; he relit it, opened a can of Dinty Moore beef stew, and emptied it into a saucepan, put the pan on to heat. Miserable place, this. "Charming one-bedroom seaside cottage, completely furnished," the ad in the paper had read. Drafty Half Moon Bay shack with bargain-basement furnishings, no central heating, a propane stove that didn't work right, and a toilet that wouldn't stop running no matter what you did to the handle or the float arm or the flush valve. Four hundred dollars rent, in advance, even though he would be here less than two weeks. Criminal. Even so, it was better than the studio apartment near the beach in San Francisco—and palatial compared to his prison cell. Away from that hellhole two months now, and still the nightmares kept coming—the worst one again last night, the one where he was still trapped in the cell, crouching in a corner, the giant rats in guards' and cons' uniforms slavering all around him.

Cottage did have plenty of privacy, at least. Nearest neighbor was three hundred yards up the beach. And most important, it was even closer to the Pacific than the city apartment; the sound of the surf was with him every minute he spent here. He'd needed so badly to be close to the ocean when they let him out. Still did. Freedom. All that bright blue freedom after five years of torment.

The stew was ready. He poured it into a bowl, opened a

packet of saltine crackers, and sat down to appease his hunger.

He thought about Kathryn while he ate. Did she feel warm and secure tonight, snuggled up to that bastard Culligan? Did she think he wouldn't find out she'd married Lover Boy and moved to his old hometown in Indiana and had the brat she'd always wanted? Or was she afraid, huddled sleepless in the dark, knowing he'd come for her sooner or later? He hoped she was afraid. Aware that he was out on parole, knowing he'd come, and terrified.

All her fault, the bitch. Ruined everything, the good life they'd had together—blew it all up as surely as if she'd set off a destructive device of her own. "Intent to wrongfully injure." *She* was the one who was guilty of that, not him. *She* was the one who should have suffered. *J'accuse, Mrs. Sago. Guilty as charged, Mrs. Sago.*

The sentence is death, Mrs. Sago.

The fourth boobytrap, the one he would begin making tomorrow afternoon, the biggest and best and sweetest of them all, was for Kathryn—and Lover Boy and the brat, too—back there in Lawler Bluffs, Indiana.

tick . . . tick . . .

Mountain Lake lay nestled in a deep hollow among pine and fir-crowded Sierra foothills, glittering like a strip of polished silver under the late-morning sun. It made Patrick Dixon smile as it always did when he first glimpsed it from, the crest of Deer Hill. And, as always, memories flooded his mind. The day his father had let him take the outboard's tiller for the first time. The day he'd swum the length of the ake and back on a dare from one of the other summer kids ınd nearly drowned from exhaustion. The night he'd lost ıis virginity with Alice Fenner in the woods along the east .hore. Sixteen, then . . . no, still fifteen, three weeks shy of ıis sixteenth birthday. Lord, what a young stud he'd been hat night. Four times, one right after the other—bam, bam,)am, bam. Twenty-five years ago already. Didn't seem half hat long. Now, though, the tired old stallion was lucky if he :ould go the distance once a week . . .

". . . looks like their car down there."

"What?" He glanced over at Marian beside him. "Sorry, I vas woolgathering."

"I said I think the Andersons are here. Car down there ooks like theirs."

"Good." He liked the Andersons. Half of the ten cottages hat ringed the lake were now owned by newcomers who'd)ought within the past five years, and of all of them the \ndersons were the friendliest and most compatible.

"I'll go over after we're settled and invite them for dinner ınd bridge one night."

"Dinner, anyway." He didn't like bridge.

In the backseat, Chuck had been leaning out the window or a better view. He drew his head back in and said, "Bet here's some big babies in those reeds at Rocky Point this /ear. Bass, not crummy channel cats."

"We'll find out soon enough."

"When? Tonight?"

"Or first thing in the morning."

"Bass bite better at dusk, Dad, you know that."

Twelve years old and a fishing junkie. It was all Chuck alked about. Didn't seem to be a passing fad, either; his room had been cluttered with angling books and parapher-nalia for two years now. Hemingway in training; he was already making plans to go down to Florida when he turned eighteen, to troll for sailfish and marlin.

Dixon thought again, as he often did, how lucky he and Marian were. Their son could have turned out like so many other kids these days, even ones from good homes—that other kind of junkie he saw nearly every day at the Hall of Justice and City Hall, the ones the DA's office sometimes had to prosecute as adults . . .

Uh-uh, he told himself, *none of that. You're on vacation.* Fourteen days of sorely needed R&R, thanks to Nils Oster-gaard's insistence that he take his first two-week block a month early. No work, no phone at the cabin to yank him back into the urban jungle he occupied for forty-some weeks a year. Felons and felonies—and tragedies like the bomb killing of poor Doug Cotter yesterday morning—were part of his life in San Francisco. Up here, they were *verboten.*

At the bottom of the hill, he turned onto the narrow blacktop that skirted the lake's rim. The road dipped up and down, cutting sharp around trees and outcrops. Most of the cottages were set below it, down near the water's edge. Theirs was the third to the north of the intersection, half hidden among moss-hung lodge-pole pine and Douglas fir. He smiled again when he saw the wooden arrow marker with the name "Dixon" burned into the wood. His father had nailed that sign to the tree nearly forty years ago, the day he'd finished building the cabin, and it had remained there ever since—a symbol of security and stability. If he had his way, it would continue to be nailed there at least hroughout Chuck's lifetime. Father to son, father to son.

He swung the station wagon onto the two-car parking
)latform opposite the marker. The cabin and its lakeside
leck were mostly visible from the platform: old redwood
)oards, shingles, and shakes and dark green shutters. Built
o last with simple materials. Below the deck, the ground
;loped to the boathouse and stubby dock. Trees and other
vegetation grew densely on both sides, almost to the water-
ine, to provide additional privacy.

Chuck bounced out of the car and began to unload his
iishing gear from among the clutter in back. Tucked away
n the storage shed behind the cabin were poles and reels
ind tackle that had belonged to Dixon's father, more than
:nough equipment for all three of them. But Chuck preferred his own new Daiwa rod and reel. He'd even learned
o tie flies and had brought a case of his creations along to
ry out on the bass population. He was tired of yanking in
)ullheads and catfish, he said; he'd designed *his* flies to
ittract only bass. Mr. Optimism.

Marian said, "I wish I had half his energy."

"Me, too. We'll build up fresh reserves after a few days."

"Sure, but then you'll want to work them right off."

He waggled an eyebrow at her. "Good old mountain air
loes wonders for the libido."

"Doesn't it, though."

Dixon went down and unlocked the cabin and took a turn
through each of its five rooms, as he always did first thing
to make sure everything was in order. Okay. No one had
1ad any real problems with break-ins or vandalism up
1ere—one of the cottages was owned by Bert Unger, a
etired Sacramento sheriff's deputy, and his wife who lived

365

at the lake year-round and kept a sharp eye on things—bu
nowadays you were wise not to take anything for granted.

The day was hot, and several trips up and down the plat
form stairs had them all sweating when they were done. In
the kitchen, Chuck said, "I'm for a swim. How about you
Mom?"

She sneezed. "Not right now. This place needs airing ou
before I do anything else."

"Dad?"

"Pretty soon. You go ahead." Marian sneezed again
Dixon said to her, "Must be bad this year, whatever you're
allergic to. Usually you don't start sneezing and snuffling
until we've been here a few hours."

"I wish I knew what it was. I'd rip every bit of it out of
the ground with my bare hands."

"Better settle for taking an allergy pill."

"Thank you for your advice and sympathy, Doctor
Dixon."

He grinned and helped himself to a cold beer from the ice
chest they'd brought. He carried it out onto the deck, stood
admiring the lake's silver-blue placidity. It was a mile and
a half long, a third of a mile wide toward the middle, and
much narrower at the ends, tightly hemmed by trees and by
bare-rock scarps along the south shore. All of the land was
privately owned, and so far the newcomers had kept the
faith and brought in none of the trappings of modern
society to spoil its natural beauty. Peace and privacy were
what the people who came here were after—people like
Marian and him, who had stressful city jobs. Mountain
Lake offered plenty of both qualities. And you really did
need to love bucolic isolation, because it was nearly ten

miles by switchbacked mountain road to the village of Two Corners and the nearest dispenser of beer, bread, and toothpaste.

Lean and wiry in his trunks, long hair flying, Chuck came racing out of the cabin and down to the boathouse. He had Marian's symmetrical features, her intense blue eyes, her ash-blond hair—and a good thing, too, that her genes had dominated. Nobody had ever accused Pat Dixon of being a handsome hunk, "craggy" was about the most complimentary word that had been used to describe his looks—

"Dad! Hey, Dad!"

Dixon shaded his eyes. Chuck was at the side door to the boathouse, excitedly waving an arm.

"What's the matter, sport?"

"Somebody's been in the boathouse."

Under his breath, Dixon said, "Damn!" and went to join his son. Sure enough, the padlock was gone from the hasp, and the boathouse door stood open a crack. Chuck had hold of the handle and was tugging on it, but the bottom edge seemed to be stuck.

"Crap," he said disgustedly. "Who do you figure it was? Homeless people?"

"Way up here? Not likely."

"I'm gonna be pissed if they stole our boat."

Dixon took the handle, gave a hard yank. The second time he did it, the bottom popped free, and the door wobbled open. He leaned inside. There were chunks between warped wallboards; in-streaming sunlight let him, see the aluminum skiff upside down on the sawhorses, where they'd laid it at the end of last summer. Its oars were on the deck beside it. The Evinrude outboard had been locked

367

away in the storage shed.

"Whew, still there," Chuck said. "Looks like everything else is, too. So how come they busted in?"

"Place to sleep, maybe." But it didn't look as though anyone had been sleeping inside. Or had used the boathouse for any other purpose.

"You think they got into the storeroom, too?"

"We'll soon find out."

The shed was attached to the back wall of the cabin, and much more solidly constructed than the boathouse. The padlock was missing from the hasp there, too. Tight-mouthed, Dixon opened the door. He had put fuses in the switchbox just after their arrival; he pulled the cord to light the overhead bulb.

"Hey," Chuck said, "this is weird."

Weird was the word for it. Nothing seemed to be missing from the shed, either. The Evinrude outboard, their fishing equipment, shovels, rakes, an extra oar for the skiff, miscellaneous items and cleaning supplies—all in place on shelves and the rough wood floor. No sign of disturbance. No sign that anyone had even been inside.

"Maybe it's the padlocks," Chuck said.

"What?"

"What they were after. You know, a gang of padlock thieves."

Dixon didn't smile. Both locks had been the heavy-duty variety, with thick staples—the kind that were advertised on TV as impregnable. They couldn't be picked or shot open, maybe, but the staples were certainly vulnerable to hack-sawing. You'd need the right kind of blade, though, and it would take some time even then. Why go through all the trouble, if you weren't going to steal anything? There didn't seem to be any sense in it.

Gang of padlock thieves. It was as good an explanation as any.

Dixon turned off the light, shut the door, and walked around to the front, Chuck at his heels. Marian was doing cleanup work in the kitchen. She turned to glance at him with allergy-reddened eyes and then said immediately, "What's the matter? You look odd."

He told her, with embellishments from Chuck. "But that's crazy," she said. "Kids, you think, playing some kind of game?"

"I don't know what to think. I'm going to have another look around in here."

He found nothing amiss this time, either. No objects gone, no indication that anyone but the three of them had been inside.

"Weird," Chuck said again. "Weird, man."

Marian said, "Well, it's not anything we should worry about. I don't see how it could be."

"Neither do I," Dixon said.

But it did worry him, a little. City-bred paranoia, maybe; but he thought he'd talk to the Andersons and the Ungers about it, just to be on the safe side.

tick . . . tick . . . tick . . .

Two down, four to go.

The news bulletin came over the car radio as he was driving back from Mountain Lake. Explosion in the garage of Judge Norris Turnbull's Sea Cliff home at seven-forty this

369

morning. Turnbull dead on arrival at Mt. Zion Hospital. San Francisco police refuse to speculate on a possible motive or link between this bombing incident and the one yesterday morning that claimed the life of attorney Douglas Cotter.

He laughed when he heard the last part. And when he pictured Turnbull lying broken and bloody with his wrinkled old face full of metal barbs like porcupine quills, he laughed even harder. Always hunching forward at the trial—a big vulture in his black robes. Always peering down through his glasses, too, stem-faced, eyes like hot stones, as if he thought he was God on the judgment seat. Hunched and peered once too often, didn't you, judge? Passed judgment once too often, didn't you?

I sentence you to five years in the state prison on each count, Mr. Sago.

I sentence you straight to hell, Judge Turnbull.

He laughed so hard, tears rolled down his cheeks.

tick ... tick ... tick ... tick ...

"The Andersons haven't had any trouble on their property," Dixon said. "No break-ins or missing items, no acts of vandalism. Tom hasn't seen anyone around who doesn't belong at the lake. But then, they've only been up from Stockton four days."

Marian sneezed, said, "Damn allergies," irritably, and blew her nose. Then she said, "Are you sure you're not worried about those missing padlocks?"

"It's the inexplicability that bothers me."

"Well, there has to be some logical explanation. Why

don't you go see what Bert Unger has to say about it?"

"I will, after lunch. But I doubt he knows anything. Tom went fishing with him yesterday, and Bert didn't say a word about any trouble."

Marian blew her nose again and then went to the sink to wash her hands. Through the kitchen window, Dixon could see Chuck with his snorkeling mask on, swimming back and forth beyond the end of the dock.

"Pat, do you know where we put the bread board?"

"Bread board? Not where it always it?"

"No. I can't find it anywhere."

"Did you look in the pantry?"

"What would it be doing in the pantry?"

"I don't know—having sex with the toaster, maybe?"

"Ha ha. Why don't you take a look? My eyes are so teary, I might've missed it."

The pantry was a tiny alcove about as large as the storage shed. Dixon put on the light and wedged himself inside. And found the bread board in thirty seconds—on a top shelf, half hidden in the shadow of a slanted ceiling beam. Now what had possessed one of them to put it way up there? He caught hold of the paddle-shaped handle, started to pull it down.

Something that had been on top of the board came flying down at him.

His reflexes were good; he twisted and managed to jerk his head out of the path of the failing object, though in the process he cracked his elbow against the wall. The object clattered against another shelf, dropped at his feet. Muttering, he bent to pick it up with his free hand.

"Pat? What was that noise?"

"Damn can of pork and beans. It nearly brained me."

"Be more careful, will you?"

"Wasn't my fault." He set the can down so he could rub his elbow. "Somebody put the board on the top shelf and the can on top of the board."

"Well, I don't think it was me, and Chuck's not tall enough. Guess who that leaves?"

"Okay, so maybe it was my fault. In a hurry or distracted at the time."

"At least you found it," Marian said when he brought the bread board out to her. Then she sneezed again, explosively, and almost dropped it. *"Damn* these allergies!"

"That medicine of yours ought to be working by now. Maybe you'd better take another pill."

"I would, except that I don't have any more."

"I thought you packed an entire bottle."

"So did I. But I had two, one full and one almost empty. I put the wrong one in my case."

"Uh-huh. The old in-a-hurry-or-distracted excuse."

"I'll need to take a couple tonight, or I won't sleep."

"I know. And then I won't, either. I'll drive down to Two Corners after lunch, before I see Bert Unger."

"Do you mind? I'd go myself, but the way I keep snuffling and sneezing . . ."

He kissed her neck. "I don't mind," he said.

tick . . . tick . . . tick . . . tick . . . tick . . .

Sago's good humor lasted most of the way back to Half Moon Bay. Would have lasted the entire distance if it hadn't been for the car overheating as he rode up through Altamont Pass. He had to swing off the freeway in Livermore and find a service station and wait around until a mechanic fixed the problem with the cooling system.

Fifteen-year-old piece of crap, that car. But it was all he'd been able to afford when he was released from San Quentin. A wonder he'd had any money left after his lawyer and Kathryn and her lawyer and all the creditors got done slicing up his assets. A few thousand dollars, that was all they'd left him—and at that he'd had to hide it away in cash in a safety deposit box. On top of the world one day, successful business, financial security, nice home, good clothes, a Porsche to drive, what he'd thought was a rock-solid marriage—and then Kathryn had brought it a crashing down around his ears. Bitch! Having an affair with that bastard Culligan, a lousy big-eared pharmacist, and then telling him it was all *his* fault because she was starved for genuine love and affection. Calling the cops and filing an assault charge when he smacked her. Finally walking out on him, straight into Lover Boy's scrawny arms. He'd had a right to do what he'd done in retaliation. He'd had a *right*.

Not according to Cotter and Turnbull and Dixon, though. They'd picked up where Kathryn left off, persecuting him, all but destroying what little of him was left. Well, now they were the ones who were being destroyed. And with perfect justice, too. As ye sow, so shall ye reap, and they'd sown the seeds of their own destruction.

Maybe he'd make a few others pay, too, when he was done with Kathryn. Maybe he'd come back here and send a present to that lawyer of hers, what was his name? Benedict? Snotty, self-righteous prick. And the tough cop, Michaels, who'd arrested him after the destructive device

373

blew the ass end off of Lover Boy's house; treated him like dirt. And Arthur Whittington, his old buddy the banker, who wouldn't give him even a small loan so he could pry himself out of debt; he'd made the son of a bitch thousands in mutual funds investments, and that was the thanks he got. *They* deserved to suffer, too, by God. So did a couple of other business associates and fair-weather friends who'd deserted him before and after the trial, left him to endure five years of torment alone. Make little presents for all of them.

He kept hoping there'd be another news bulletin before he reached the charming furnished seaside shack in Half Moon Bay, but there wasn't. Not yet, but soon. Inside the cottage, with the door locked, he switched on the portable radio on his worktable and tuned it to an all-news station. He didn't want to miss the announcement when it finally came.

Surprise, Mr. Dixon.
Surprise!

tick . . . tick . . . tick . . . tick . . . tick . . . tick . . .

The owner of Two Corners Grocery, a talkative old man named Finley, was watching television behind the counter. Another victim of the satellite dish, Dixon thought wryly. He paid no attention to the flickering images and droning voices as he was fetching Marian's allergy medicine; but when he gave it to Finley to ring up, a familiar name registered and turned his head toward the screen. And he found himself staring at an enlarged photograph of Judge Norris Turnbull.

"Terrible thing, isn't it?" Finley said.

"What is? What happened?"

"Mean you don't know? Special news reports all day."

He shook his head. It was a family rule that they left the car radio off on long drives, and even Chuck's boom box had been silent so far.

"Well, that judge was killed this morning," Finley said. "Somebody blew him up with a bomb."

Dixon grimaced. Blew him up . . . Douglas Cotter yesterday, and now Judge Turnbull . . . good God! After a few seconds, shock gave way to an impotent anger. He hadn't seen much of Cotter since Doug left the DA's office four years ago to open his own practice, but they'd worked together for two years and had been friendly enough; and Turnbull was a man he'd respected and admired. It seemed unthinkable that either of them, of all the attorneys and jurists in the city, would become the target of some crazy bomber. Unthinkable and outrageous.

The news report was ending, what few details he was able to pick up from the newscaster's closing remarks were sketchy. Finley tried to tell him about it, but he had no interest in a third-hand rehash. He cut the old man short and hurried out to where a public phone box was affixed to the grocery's front wall. He used his long-distance credit card to put in a call to Nils Ostergaard's private line. The DA was in; he answered immediately.

Nils, I just heard about Judge Turnbull. Two in two days—what the hell's going on?"

"No idea yet, Pat." Ostergaard sounded tense and harried. "There has to be a connection; nobody buys coincidence. But aside from the fact that both men were in the legal profession, the link isn't there yet."

"No notes or calls from the bomber?"

"Not a word."

"Same kind of device in both cases?"

"No. Both were set as boobytraps, but the one that killed Cotter was a simple type—black powder and metal frag packed into a lawn sprinkler and initiated by a tripwire hidden in the grass. The one that killed Norris . . . nasty. I hope I never hear of a nastier one."

"Nasty how?"

"As near as the bomb techs could tell, the device was a small box of some kind left on the front seat of the judge's car. Inside his garage; bomber gained access through a side window. When Norris opened the box to look inside, it blew fifty or sixty thin, sharpened steel rods straight up into his face."

"Jesus," Dixon said.

"Yeah. It's obvious we're dealing with the worst kind of psycho here—intelligent enough to construct a more or less sophisticated explosive device, crazy enough to believe he's got a good reason for ripping a man's head apart with sharpened steel rods."

"Who's in charge of the investigation? Dave Maccerone?"

"Dave, and Charley Seltzer of the bomb squad. Ed Bozeman's working with them from our end. A-priority, down the line."

"If Ed's working with the PD, that cuts you thin. Maybe I'd better come in."

"No, no," Ostergaard said. "We're okay. For now, anyway. You've earned your vacation, Pat. I'll yell if I need you. Where're you calling from?"

"Grocery in Two Corners, a village about ten miles from Mountain Lake. But there's a closer phone. Neighbors of ours, the Ungers, have one."

"Give me the number. I'll call if I—" Ostergaard broke off, and Dixon could hear the mutter of voices in the background. Then, "Pat, hold on a minute, will you? Dave Maccerone just came in."

"Right."

Ostergaard put him on hold. The phone box was in a slant of direct sunlight, and Dixon was sweating; he wiped his face with his handkerchief, dried his hands. Thinking: why the two different types of bombs? The simple explanation was that the perp had hated Judge Turnbull even more than Doug Cotter, but that still didn't explain the use of sharpened steel rods. Some significance in those rods? He couldn't imagine what it might be, if so—

Click on the line, and Ostergaard said, "Pat?"

"Still here."

"The lieutenant wants to talk to you." There was a different inflection in the DA's voice, a new tension that made Dixon grip the receiver more tightly. "Just a second . . . here he is."

"Yo, Pat," Maccerone's heavy voice said. "Good thing you called in; timing's right all around, for a change. Listen, I think we've got a handle on the bombings."

"You know who's responsible?"

"Pretty sure we've ID'd him. You know how each of these serial bombers has his own signature—the way he puts his device together, the kinds of connections he makes, the types of powder, cord, solder, circuitry he uses. Each signature's different, and it seldom varies. Well, the lab techs finished going over the post-blast evidence from this morning, and the signature's not only the same as on the Cotter case but as on one other about six years ago. Computer match probability is ninety-five percent."

"Whose signature?"

"Man named Leonard Sago. Name ring any bells?"

"Sago, Sago . . . vaguely familiar. Should I know him?"

"Financial consultant here in the city," Maccerone said. "Ex-Marine with explosives training. Went over the edge when he found out his wife was having an affair. Put a boobytrap bomb in the trunk of the boyfriend's car, hooked to the inside trunk release; that one didn't go off because of a bad solder joint. A second bomb under the back porch of the guy's house did go off—cut him up some with flying glass and debris. Sago claimed he didn't intend bodily harm, the bombs were just messages to leave his wife alone. Insufficient evidence to nail him on attempted homicide, but enough to convict on two other felony counts: explosion of a destructive device and setting boobytraps. Five years on each count. Coming back to you now?"

Dixon had gone rigid. "Yes."

"Well, Sago served a total of five years and was paroled two months ago. I just talked to his PO. Sago seemed okay at first, rehabilitated, but then he started to show signs of continued hostility toward his ex-wife and the people who put him in prison. He disappeared last week. The PO violated him right away, but he still hasn't turned up."

Dixon said thinly, "Doug Cotter was the assistant prosecutor on the case. Norris Turnbull was on the bench."

"Afraid so, Pat."

"And I was the chief prosecutor. Sago struck me as arrogant and unrepentant, and still dangerous, and I went after him hard. Now he's after me, right? Cotter, Turnbull, and now me."

"Looks that way," Maccerone said. "But it's not as bad as it could be, believe me. If he did set a trap for you, it's probably at your house here. I've already sent the bomb squad out; they'll spot it if it's there."

"Suppose it isn't. Suppose he found out I was going on vacation. He could have—I didn't make any secret of the fact. He could've found out about my summer place, too—"

"Take it easy, counselor. You're not in any immediate danger, if Sago was that smart, you wouldn't be talking to me right now. You're in a place called Two Corners, Nils says. Okay. Go back to your cabin, collect your family, drive to the nearest motel. If the bomb squad strikes out at your house here, I'll call the Sacramento PD and have them send up a crew to sweep the cabin—"

The padlocks! Sweet Jesus, the missing padlocks!

Dixon threw the phone down and ran for the station wagon.

tick ... tick ... tick ... tick ... tick ... tick ... tick ...

Kathryn's surprise was really going to be something.

As tired as he was from all the driving, he was ready and eager to start assembling it. The carton he'd gotten from the supermarket dumpster, a little larger than the one he'd used for the judges package, was on the floor next to the table, along with the bag of bubble wrap for packing. And on the table, all neatly arranged, were the tools and other materials he would need. Pliers, screwdrivers, cold chisel. Soldering gun and spool of wire solder. Aluminum canister Microswitch. Six-volt battery. Fresh tin of smokeless black powder, the last of the three he'd bought at the gun shop in Pacifica (said he was a duck hunter and loaded his own shotgun shells). C-4 plastic explosive, the kind they used in Nam, would have been better, more pucker power and a hotter blast, just right for sending Kathryn on her way to hell. But you needed connections to get C-4, and his military ties were a thing of the past. Along with just about everything else that had mattered in his life.

The other item on the table was one of two *pièces de résistance*—a glass jar, full to the brim. The second was spoiling on a shelf on the rear porch, where he didn't have to smell it. He'd put that one in the package after he got to Lawler Bluffs, Indiana, just before he was ready to spring the surprise.

He'd given a lot of thought to what to add to Kathryn's present. Something just for her, the pharmacist and their brat were incidental. The devices for Cotter and Turnbull and Dixon had been easy to arrange, but Kathryn was a different story. Had to be just right. He'd discarded half a hundred possibilities before he made his selections, and as soon as he thought of each, he knew it was perfect.

She'd taken everything from him; she'd gotten all the marbles. Okay, then, he'd give her two hundred more than she bargained for—two hundred cheap glass marbles from a toy store in Half Moon Bay, the kind that would fly apart in a million fragments from the force of the blast.

What else do you give an unfaithful bitch for her final sendoff? Why, a bagful of rancid bones, of course. Soup bones that would splinter and gouge and tear the same as the marbles.

Too bad he couldn't tell her beforehand what she was getting. Too bad she'd never know. Always accusing him of not having a sense of humor. Well, this proved different, didn't it? He had a terrific sense of humor, much better than hers.

Kathryn would go a bang out of her present, all right.

And then he'd have the last laugh.

tick. . . tick . . . tick . . . tick . . . tick . . . tick . . .
tick . . . tick . . .

Dixon drove too fast, twenty and twenty-five miles an hour faster than was safe on the twisty mountain road; braking hard on the curves, recklessly passing the two other cars he rushed up behind. And he had to fight the urge to increase his speed even more. Any faster, and he was liable to wrap the station wagon around a tree, send it hurtling off the road into one of the canyons, and what good would he be to Marian and Chuck then?

What if he was already too late?

No. Don't think it, it isn't so.

Where in God's name had Sago hidden the bomb? Boathouse or storage shed, one or the other—had to be. Both padlocks missing, he must've been looking for something in one that wasn't there, and so he'd gone to the other. But what? Some kind of container for the boobytrap? And what would initiate it? Tripwire, triggering mechanism attached to a box lid, something else entirely? The can of pork and beans that had come flying off the shelf when he'd pulled on the bread board . . . a bomb could be initiated that

381

way, too. Usually bomb type and packaging and initiating mechanisms followed a pattern, part of the bomber's signature, but Sago had varied the first two, and that made the third problematical.

Marian, Chuck stay away from the boathouse, the storage shed.

Don't be hurt—please don't be hurt.

Four more miles to go. He felt cold and feverish at the same time, a prickling on his skin as though it had sprouted stubble, his insides so knotted up that even his bones seemed tight. A gritty sweat kept stinging his eyes, he blinked and rubbed constantly to clear his vision.

Leonard Sago. He remembered him now, all too well. Classic profile of a bomber: intelligent but skewed and illogical in his thought processes sociopathic tendencies; and a paramilitary attitude toward life. Owned guns, including a couple of semi-automatic weapons; even had a subscription to *Soldier of Fortune*. Workaholic, too, to the point of exhaustion. Add all of that together, and you had a ticking bomb in human form. His wife's infidelity had been the first trigger. But the boobytraps aimed at her lover were only a partial release, Sago had been capable of more and greater violence, a fact made evident by his attitude and behavior. They could have plea-bargained if he'd been willing to accept psychiatric help, but Sago refused to admit he had a problem wouldn't even let his attorney plead temporary insanity. No choice but to go after him hard, put him away where he couldn't harm his wife or her boyfriend or an innocent bystander. Except that the prison time had been counterproductive, had made him worse instead of better. True psychopath now. Sharpened steel rods . . . good

God! His hatred must be an inferno, all-consuming, for him to contrive a horror like that.

What horror did he contrive for me?

No, don't even . . .

Wait, those other bombs . . .

Tripwire, sharpened rods. Glimmer of a connection, and of a connection to something else, but I can't quite . . .

Think, think!

Gone.

Dammit, how much farther? Two miles.

Please don't be hurt.

Please.

tick . . . tick . . . tick . . . tick . . . tick . . . tick . . . tick . . . tick . . . tick . . .

Still no report on the radio about Dixon.

Didn't mean anything; he just hadn't opened his present yet. Or if he had, way up there in the Sierra foothills, the media hadn't had time to get wind of it. Pretty soon now, either way. Pretty soon. Nothing to worry about.

The chief prosecutor wouldn't get off the hook.

Ha! No, he sure wouldn't. Chuckling, Sago paused in his work on Kathryn's package to visualize what Dixon would look like after the blast. So much quieter, so much more bloody fetching than he had been in the courtroom. Strutting around during the trial like a rooster in a barnyard. Demanding that the jury convict Mr. Sago, demanding that Mr. Sago be given the maximum penalties as prescribed by law.

Well, Mr. Dixon, now I'm the one doing the demanding.

I demand that you receive the maximum penalty for your crimes, as prescribed by Leonard Sago.

I demand that you be blown up, torn up, and spend eternity strutting your stuff in the Pit.

tick . . . tick . . . tick . . . tick . . . tick . . . tick . . . tick . . . tick . . . tick . . . tick . . .

They were all right, still all right.

No explosion, no fire everything lakeside normal and quiet in the heat-drowsy afternoon.

He saw that much from the top of Deer Hill, with a thrust of relief so acute it blew his breath out in a grunting sigh. But the relief lasted for only a few seconds. He still had to get down there, round up Marian and Chuck . . . they were still in harm's way.

He barreled the station wagon through the hill's snake turns, skidded onto the lake road. Their parking platform appeared ahead; he could just make out the cabin's roof through the trees. He braked hard as he came up on the platform, cut the wheel too sharply, and almost lost control as the wagon bumped off the road onto the pine-needled boards; the front bumper cracked against the low back wall. He shut down the engine, tried to run as soon as he was out. But he'd been driving under such tension that the muscles in his legs and upper body were constricted. His right knee cramped as he came around behind the wagon toward the stairs. He would have fallen if the railing hadn't been there to catch his outthrust hands.

He saw Chuck in his first quick scan below. The boy was standing in the open door to the boathouse, looking up at him held there by the unexpected tire and engine noise and the bumper hitting the wall. When he recognized his father, he waved and turned to go inside.

"Chuck! No!"

Another wave, and he vanished. Dixon flung himself down the stairs, hobbling until he reached solid ground, then running with speed as the cramped leg muscle unknotted. Chuck was doing something, inside the boathouse: shifting sounds of metal on wood. The skiff—moving the skiff. The door seemed to rush at Dixon as if it and not he were being propelled; he caught its edge, levered his body around it and inside, squinting to see in the dim light.

"Chuck, leave it alone!" The boy swung toward him, startled. The sudden movement caused him to jerk the painter rope trailing from his hand to the skiff's bowring; and that caused the skiff, already half off the sawhorses, to tilt and slide the rest of the way. Dixon lunged for it, but Chuck was in the way; he couldn't reach it in time. He cringed, twisting to shield his son, as the skiff hit the decking with a booming metallic clatter—

That was all, just the clatter. And the after-sounds of the skiff bouncing off the deck boards, splashing upright into the narrow channel that bisected the enclosure.

"Jeez, Dad, you scared the crap out of me. What—?"

"Where's your mother?"

"Mom? Why? Dad, you look—"

"Answer me, Chuck, where is she?"

"She said she was gonna go get the fishing stuff, yours and hers. We were gonna go out early to Rocky Point—"

The storage shed.

"Stay here, you hear me? Stay here!" He ran out into the blazing sunlight. At first, after the gloom of the boathouse, the glare half blinded him; he faltered, swiping at his eyes. The cabin swam into focus, but from this angle he couldn't see the shed. And there was no sign of Marian.

Running again, he shouted her name.

And she appeared, walking around the lower corner of the cabin. He slowed, another faltering step. Surge of relief . . . but in the next second, when he realized what she was carrying, it died under a new slice of panic. Two bamboo fishing rods in her left hand, his father's battered old tackle box in her right. That tackle box . . . sinkers and flies and hooks—

Hooks.

He yelled at her, "Stop! Wait there! Don't move!" and plunged ahead.

She froze in surprise, the tackle box hanging so heavy from her hand that she listed slightly to that side.

"Don't let go of the box!"

It was as if he ran the last few steps in slow-motion, the mired, slogging slow-motion of a dream. The sensation was the opposite when he reached her, reached out to clutch at the box: everything then seemed to happen at an accelerated speed. He worked the box free of her grasp, warning himself not to wrench it, it was liable to explode if it were shaken or jarred or dropped. Marian didn't struggle, but he heard her say in a thin, frightened voice, "What's gotten into you? Have you gone crazy?" Then he was backing away, lowering the box gently to the ground. His hands tingled when he let go of it, as if its lethal contents had imparted a subtle radioactivity to his flesh.

He straightened, staring down at it. Ordinary-looking tackle box. But inside . . . God, inside . . .

He turned as Chuck, disobedient, came racing up. Dixon caught hold of his arm, of Marian's arm, and herded both away from there, pulling and prodding until they were all the way up onto the parking platform. Only then did he release them. And when he did, the act seemed to release the tension in him as well, leaving him weak-kneed and sagging against the station wagon's fender.

"Pat, for heaven's sake, what—?"

"The tackle box." He had to draw several deep breaths before he could go on. "It's boobytrapped. There's a bomb inside."

Chuck said, "A bomb!" Marian blanched, staring at him goggle-eyed.

"And hooks," he said. "Fish hooks, probably, I don't know, but a lot of them. Attached to lines or wires or both."

"What're you *talking* about?"

Penal Code, he thought. Chapter 3.2, Section 12355, sub-division (c): "Boobytraps may include, but are not limited to, explosive devices attached to tripwires or other triggering mechanisms, sharpened stakes, and lines or wire with hooks attached."

Stakes, not rods. Tripwire, sharpened stakes, and lines or wire with hooks attached.

We convicted Sago on that statute. He twisted it to suit his own perverted brand of justice, condemned us with the letter of the law.

Dixon pushed himself off the fender. "It's a hell of a story," he said to Marian. "Literally. I'll explain on the way to the Ungers'." And explain by phone to Dave Maccerone and Nils Ostergaard once they got there.

tick ... tick ... tick ... tick ... tick ... tick ...
tick ... tick ... tick ... tick ... tick ...

He finished making the bomb, destructive device, booby-trap, big-bang present for Kathryn a few minutes past eight.
Nice job, Mr. Sago.
Why, thank you very much, Mr. Sago.
He sat back, smiling, pleased. Even the lack of news on the radio about Dixon failed to dampen his spirits; still nothing to worry about there. If the chief prosecutor hadn't opened his present today, he'd open it tomorrow. Verification of that, on top of a good night's sleep, and he'd be ready to leave for Indiana. Once in good old Lawler Bluffs, all he had to do was arrange the rancid bones inside the package, connect the leads to the microswitch, and then find a spot to leave it for Kathryn and Lover Boy and their brat. Just where depended on her living arrangements these days. A fining and proper spot, wherever. Maybe even one where he could linger nearby and watch it happen. Wouldn't that be sweet!

His stomach growled. He'd been so intent on his work that he'd forgotten to eat again. He started to put his tools away, then changed his mind. Cleanup tonight could wait. Good work deserved a reward; it was time for his reward right now.

He stood, stretched, and padded into the kitchen. And, of course, the damn pilot light on the stove had gone out again. Annoyed, feeling martyred, he reached for the box of kitchen matches.

tick!

The vacation had been temporarily postponed. Even if he and Marian and Chuck had wanted to spend the night at Mountain Lake after bomb techs from Sacramento removed the tackle box, which they hadn't, it wouldn't have been a wise decision with Leonard Sago still at large. So they'd slept at a motel in Jackson and driven to San Francisco that morning. For the time being, they were better off in the urban jungle.

Dixon felt that way even after Dave Maccerone's telephone call, not long after they got home.

"I've got some good news, counselor," Maccerone said.

"You can quit worrying about Leonard Sago. We found him."

He sank into a chair. "Where?"

"Half Moon Bay. Just enough of him for a positive ID."

"You mean he's dead?"

"They don't get any deader. He blew himself up."

"Christ. How? Making another bomb?"

"No," Maccerone said. "Well, he was making another one, but that wasn't what finished him. Pretty ironic, actually."

"Ironic?"

"He was living in this cheap rented place, not much more than a shack on the beach. It had a faulty propane stove, one of those old ones that the landlord should've replaced a long time ago. Connection worked loose or corroded through, and gas leaked out. You know how volatile propane is when it builds up. Sago lit a match or caused some other kind of spark—*boom.*

One of the investigators down there called the stove an explosion just waiting to happen. Fire marshal had a better term for it."

"I'll bet he did."

"Yeah. He said it was a regular damn boobytrap."

Center Point Publishing
600 Brooks Road • PO Box 1
Thorndike ME 04986-0001 USA

(207) 568-3717

US & Canada:
1 800 929-9108

LARGE PRINT   25.95
Turow, Scott
Guilty as charged

D

WITHDRAWN
UPPER MERION TOWNSHIP LIBRARY

/

UPPER MERION TOWNSHIP LIBRARY
175 WEST VALLEY FORGE ROAD
KING OF PRUSSIA, PA 19406

ADULT DEPT. - (610) 265-4805
CHILDREN'S DEPT. - (610) 265-4806

5-01

GAYLORD M

Plate 1 Ashamed of his activities, King Indra fell down to touch the lotus feet of Pṛthu Mahārāja. (*p. 787*)

His Divine Grace A.C. Bhaktivedanta Swami Prabhupāda
Founder-Ācārya of the International Society for Krishna Consciousness

Plate 3 "Just see how this chaste lady, Arci, is still following her husband upwards, as far as we ca
see." (*p. 1007*)

Plate 2 The King took the water which had washed the lotus feet of the Kumāras and sprinkled it over his hair. (*p. 891*)

Plate 4 Lord Śiva addressed the Supreme Personality of Godhead with his prayer. (*p. 1063*)

Plate 5 The cowherd boys of Vṛndāvana treat Kṛṣṇa as their equal. (*p. 1082*)

Plate 6 The Lord is superexcellently beautiful on account of His open and merciful smile and His sidelong glance upon His devotees. (*p. 1085*)

Plate 7 "My dear Lord, those who desire to purify their existence must always engage in the meditation of Your lotus feet." (*p. 1091*)

ALL GLORY TO ŚRĪ GURU AND GAURĀṄGA

Śrīmad-Bhāgavatam

of

KṚṢṆA-DVAIPĀYANA VYĀSA

पदा   शरत्पद्मपलाशरोचिषा
नखद्युभिर्नोऽन्तरघं   विधुन्वता ।
प्रदर्शय   स्वीयमपास्तसाध्वसं
पदं गुरो मार्गगुरूस्तमोजुषाम् ॥५२॥

padā śarat-padma-palāśa-rociṣā
nakha-dyubhir no 'ntar-aghaṁ vidhunvatā
pradarśaya svīyam apāsta-sādhvasaṁ
padaṁ guro mārga-gurus tamo-juṣām (p. 1,088)

OTHER BOOKS by
His Divine Grace A.C. Bhaktivedanta Swami Prabhupāda

Bhagavad-gītā As It Is
Śrīmad-Bhāgavatam, Cantos 1-4 (11 Vols.)
Śrī Caitanya-caritāmṛta (2 Vols.)
Teachings of Lord Caitanya
The Nectar of Devotion
Śrī Īśopaniṣad
Easy Journey to Other Planets
Kṛṣṇa Consciousness: The Topmost Yoga System
Kṛṣṇa, The Supreme Personality of Godhead (2 Vols.)
Transcendental Teachings of Prahlād Mahārāja
Transcendental Teachings of Caitanya Mahāprabhu
Kṛṣṇa, the Reservoir of Pleasure
The Perfection of Yoga
Beyond Birth and Death
On the Way to Kṛṣṇa
Rāja-vidyā: The King of Knowledge
Elevation to Kṛṣṇa Consciousness
Lord Caitanya in Five Features
Back to Godhead Magazine (Founder)

A complete catalogue is available upon request.

International Society for Krishna Consciousness
3959 Landmark Street
Culver City, California 90230